Light Vision

Simultaneous Dimension Series

Book One

Coco Tralla

Tralla Productions

www.sevenbooks.com

Coco Tralla

Tralla Productions

Tralla Productions is a division of Coco Tralla, LLC.
Copyright © 2004 by Coco Tralla, LLC.

ISBN: 0-9752659-0-3

Library of Congress Control Number: 2004090997

This is a work of fiction; however, it is called reality fiction because some events, places and situations actually do occur or exist in real life. Names, characters, places and any incidents of the storyline are products of the author's imagination or used fictitiously and are not to be construed as real. Although extensive research has been done to portray reality, any resemblance in the storyline of this work that depicts actual events, locales, organizations or persons, living or dead, is entirely coincidental.

Special thanks for the original cover design by George Romvari at PlanetGrafix (www.planetgrafix.com) and for Teri Rider's invaluable help as Assistant Graphics Designer. Thank you Chris Nurse for the cover image © Digital Vision (www.digitalvision.com). Special acknowledgement to Giuseppe Ametrano of the *Roma Sotterranea* (www.underome.com) for his assistance in touring and researching underground Rome.

Coco Tralla, LLC
Tralla Productions
5082 E. Hampden Avenue, Suite 219
Denver, Colorado 80237

Printed in the USA.

Cover and text printed on recycled paper.

This book is dedicated to the nonfiction authors who continue to document and record a ubiquitous subject matter. By accessing this knowledge, I was able to create a book based on the reality of near-death experiences, past life regressions, the ways of the *Strega*, the Life Force or Zero Point Field and many other realities. With gratitude, I thank these authors for their continued writing and research:

Braden, Gregg. *The Isaiah Effect.*
    New York: Harmony Books, 2000.
Grimassi, Raven. *Italian Witchcraft.*
    Minnesota: Llewellyn Publications, 2000.
Grimassi, Raven. *Encyclopedia of Wicca & Witchcraft.*
    Minnesota: Llewellyn Publications, 2000.
Guiley, Rosemary Ellen. *The Encyclopedia of Witches & Witchcraft.*
    New York: Checkmark Books, 1999.
Kraig, Donald Michael. *Modern Sex Magick: Secrets of Erotic Spirituality.*
    Minnesota: Llewellyn Publications, 1999.
McTaggart, Lynne. *The Field: The Quest of the Secret Force of the Universe.*
    London: Element, 2001.
Moody, Raymond. *Life After Life: The Investigation of a Phenomenon—Survival of Bodily Death.*
    New York: HarperSanFrancisio, 2001.
Pavia, Carlo. *Guide to Underground Rome/Guida di Roma Sotterranea.*
    Rome: Gangemi Editore, 2001.
Sergiev Gilly. *A Witch's Box of Magick.*
    New York: Barron's Educational Series, 2002.
Weiss Brian. *Only Love Is Real: A Story of Soulmates Reunited.*
    New York: Warner Books, 1996.

This book is dedicated to the nonfiction authors who continue to document and record a ubiquitous subject matter. By accessing this knowledge, I was able to create a book based on the reality of near-death experiences, past life regressions, the ways of the *Strega*, the Life Force or Zero Point Field and many other realities. With gratitude, I thank these authors for their continued writing and research:

Braden, Gregg. *The Isaiah Effect.*
    New York: Harmony Books, 2000.
Grimassi, Raven. *Italian Witchcraft.*
    Minnesota: Llewellyn Publications, 2000.
Grimassi, Raven. *Encyclopedia of Wicca & Witchcraft.*
    Minnesota: Llewellyn Publications, 2000.
Guiley, Rosemary Ellen. *The Encyclopedia of Witches & Witchcraft.*
    New York: Checkmark Books, 1999.
Kraig, Donald Michael. *Modern Sex Magick: Secrets of Erotic*
    Spirituality.
    Minnesota: Llewellyn Publications, 1999.
McTaggart, Lynne. *The Field: The Quest of the Secret Force of*
    the Universe.
    London: Element, 2001.
Moody, Raymond. *Life After Life: The Investigation of a*
    Phenomenon—Survival of Bodily Death.
    New York: HarperSanFrancisio, 2001.
Pavia, Carlo. *Guide to Underground Rome/Guida di Roma*
    Sotterranea.
    Rome: Gangemi Editore, 2001.
Sergiev Gilly. *A Witch's Box of Magick.*
    New York: Barron's Educational Series, 2002.
Weiss Brian. *Only Love Is Real: A Story of Soulmates Reunited.*
    New York: Warner Books, 1996.

Author's Message

Long ago, many diverse ancient cultures around the world intentionally hid messages for humanity to find thousands of years later. Several of these classic cultures have been entirely destroyed, but the messages of the ancient visionaries remain intact. The visionaries hid their messages so the missives would not be destroyed by those who had already tried to eliminate what was to be intentionally left behind. Some of these messages, which were hidden in pyramids, temples, caves and other ancient sites in various places around the world, have been discovered recently by archeologists and researchers. The messages come through in many forms: some were written as manuscripts on papyrus, copper or animal hide; others were carved in stone as glyphs or hieroglyphics; and many were painted in caves as signs and symbols so the message would not weather and disappear over time.

Regardless of how it was left, ancient visionaries throughout the world essentially left the same message—we would need this wisdom during our time of need. And according to the ancient timekeepers, our time has come. The *Simultaneous Dimension Series* delves into the messages hidden by the ancient visionaries thousands of years ago, and what they perceived as a necessary "shift" in human thought and experience—necessary because an awakening or a perceptive awareness would be needed in order to survive this time period.

Coco Tralla

PART ONE

THE CALL

Over the years I have become concerned with the preservation of ancient traditions and ancient beliefs. While it is important to be open to new and unique ways, I feel it is equally important to bear in mind that the Old Ways are the foundation upon which the New Age rests. The New Age represents knowledge and the Old Ways represent wisdom; one might say that the Old Ways are the "DNA" within the body of the New Age.

Raven Grimassi
Italian Witchcraft

CHAPTER ONE

DIANA

Aspen, Colorado

September 10, 2003
Full Moon

"*Il mio amore.*" Antonio DeMarco's lapse into Italian still made Diana melt, but this time the resonating quality of his voice was different—not so seductive. "There's something I need to tell you," he said.

Concerned by her husband's tone, Diana tried to make eye contact but couldn't because she needed all her concentration to drive Antonio's favorite car, the Ferrari, down the Atwoods' steep driveway in Starwood Estates. "Are you okay?" she asked.

"I've been meaning to tell you this, but everything happened so fast." Antonio touched her hand on the wheel. Once Diana let him hold her hand, Antonio positioned it on the console, then interlaced his fingertips with hers and slowly inched his way up between her fingers toward her palm. *How can fingers be so erotic?* she wondered.

"It's been a whirlwind since we met, no?" Antonio's deep voice had an indescribable Italian American accent that quickened Diana's pulse.

Diana nodded and wisps of her long, blonde hair fell into her eyes. Since they met, it had been more like a hurricane than a whirlwind. In the past six months, she had gotten married, changed her name and now carried a baby. After she and Antonio were introduced by Tess, they went out every evening for an entire week. Then on the seventh night, she finally gave in to his passion.

3

It was difficult to say no, and since Diana didn't adhere to every confining rule of the Roman Catholic Church, she succumbed. In her late teens, she had decided it was archaic Catholicism to wait until marriage to have sex, and now that she was twenty-eight, she had already made love to numerous men. Thankful she didn't abide by every rule of the church anymore, Diana now knew she would be miserable with any of those American males she had slept with because they were clueless about how to make love to a woman.

Antonio was different because he knew what a woman wanted. It wasn't just about *him;* it was about *them* being erotic together. At thirty-five, Antonio didn't *do it* like he was ten years older; he *did it* better than any American male of any age. Most, if not all, American men thought having sex was all about the body, but sex with the mind, or this invisible realm Antonio understood, was by far the greatest sex of all. Now Diana knew why so many women hated sex with American men—they were one dimensional. They were inept at seducing a woman with just a glance, gesture or touch; whereas, Italian men not only knew how to express emotion with their hands, they knew how to make love to a woman with their eyes.

After their tumultuous love fest on that fateful seventh night, she agonized about not having used any birth control. Even though they used protection from then on, she still worried. And to make matters worse, ever since those seven exclusive nights together, Antonio had left town four days out of every week because of his "top secret" position in some confidential company. When she was two weeks late for her period that month, she bought a take-home pregnancy test, only to discover she was with child. Once Diana told him about her pregnancy, he immediately proposed.

With Diana's Catholic roots, she could never get an abortion, so she was thankful Antonio wanted them to get married. And now that she didn't have to use birth control, she would try to be a good Catholic girl once again even if it was just for the sake of her late parents.

But that was just the beginning of the whirlwind. In the first week of March, they decided to marry as soon as possible, then disagreed on the details. Antonio insisted the ceremony take place in the grove near his mansion on the outskirts of Aspen with a justice of the peace presiding, but she wanted to marry in a nondenominational church with a traditional minister. Because she knew Antonio didn't like the Roman Catholic Church, Diana suggested Unitarian. But after many heated discussions, she discovered Antonio believed in the Old Ways of Italy, which was a lifestyle that he said would take years for her to understand. Antonio vehemently opposed getting married in a church, and after Diana realized how important location and ceremony were to Antonio, she finally agreed to let him arrange everything. In the end, she was glad they had kept it private, especially since there were so many surprises that day.

It all started with the wandering eyes of the handsome, black-robed justice of the peace. His enticing smile and tactile hands unsettled her, and when he kept admiring her low-cut, full-length wedding dress, Diana didn't know what to do. Feeling guilty that she would even notice another man during her own marriage ceremony, Diana tried not to look into his penetrating eyes, but when the justice kept touching her arm, she couldn't ignore his advances. And although she didn't understand a word he said during the ceremony, she never even asked Antonio to translate. When Antonio introduced The Honorable Benandanti as an old friend of the family from *Roma*, Diana could only blush while the justice grinned seductively. Although Antonio laughed and fervently spoke in Italian whenever the justice flirted, Diana still felt intimidated by The Honorable Benandanti's blatant advances. Her best friend Tess was there, but she just laughed when Diana expressed her concerns, because Tess couldn't translate his heavy dialect either.

The other big surprise was that the ceremony took place inside a circle of strange flowers scattered on the ground. At one point, she almost fainted from the exotic scent; although, the wedding cake soon revived her. But even the cake was a surprise, because they began the ceremony by eating a piece of it. Even though her wedding wasn't anything like she originally envisioned, Diana wanted to etch that day, March 18, 2003, in her memory, like the melodic sound of Italian verse resonating with the bubbling water from the hidden well because it created their magickal setting.

When Tess left immediately after the wedding as if something was planned, it wasn't long before Diana was surprised again. She never wanted to forget that surprise because after the wedding Antonio took her to an ancient well hidden in the grove, then kissed her until everything spun out of control. By the light of the full moon, in a clearing encircled by the forest for privacy, he unfastened all the buttons of her wedding dress, slid off every piece of her ivory lingerie and made love to her on a bed of rose petals. Since Antonio masterminded all the flowers that day, the aroma from the red roses strewn about in the circular clearing of the forest made his touch even more erotic. At the time, she feared the justice was watching, but her concerns made Antonio laugh. He told her The Honorable Benandanti also upheld the Old Ways and would never dishonor her "perfect hourglass" body. Wanting to remember their special day forever, Diana smiled as she navigated the Ferrari down Trentaz Drive. She felt good about sharing the silence as well as words with Antonio. And now that she was five months pregnant, their relationship had mushroomed into total commitment and anticipation of their first baby.

Antonio massaged the palm of her hand with his thumb. "There's something I haven't told you," he said. "And it changes everything, because it's a part of me that I want to experience together."

"It changes us?"

"I'm a witch. An Italian witch—a *Stregone*. As I told you before, I was raised in the Old Ways and have kept the faith ever since. Being pagan connects me with nature and the universe. I honor the physical body as well as—"

"You never said anything about being a witch." At first Diana wanted to laugh, but Antonio's silence snapped her back to reality. She thought the baby kicked, so she slipped her hand out of Antonio's to feel the life inside her.

"It's not something to be afraid of." Antonio paused, then continued. "It's a part of me that our child must know, especially after I'm gone. When I die, someone else must carry on the Ways."

"The Old Ways are witchcraft?" Diana tried not to sound shocked. "You're demanding we raise our child to be a witch?"

"I'm not demanding, I'm telling you how important this is to me. It's a way of life that adheres to a new sense of time based on the moon that brings people on earth together. This way of life is connected to the universe, the phases of the moon and certain times of the year that act as portals. Through these portals, we align ourselves with our destiny, this planet and the universe. The problem is many people misunderstand *Stregheria* and our ways. That's why I want our child to carry on the legacy—because it's nothing harmful or evil. It's something that could save our planet from dying."

Diana felt like she was ready to die. Her stomach churned as if she could vomit any second. Even though she wasn't used to the winding turns on this road, she had wanted to drive tonight because driving normally stopped her from getting motion sickness. But this time it wasn't working. Or maybe it was the subject that made her sick. She couldn't be sure. Nothing was certain anymore.

"I don't believe it." Diana gripped the wheel harder and tried to concentrate on the road. "You can't be serious. Why didn't you tell me this before we were intimate, or better yet before we got married?"

"Fear. I didn't know if you would accept me." Antonio shook his head, then brushed his fingertips over hers, but Diana kept her hand on the wheel.

"It's a religion?"

"More like a way of life." Antonio paused before he whispered, "I love you. I want to share my beliefs with you so we can be together in spirit too."

"What's that supposed to mean? You said you honor the physical body—whose body?" Diana bit her lip knowing she was jumping to conclusions, but she wondered if he'd been honoring the bodies of female witches since he'd been gone four days out of every week ever since their first fateful week together.

From the beginning, Diana had questioned one thing about their relationship—his absence from her because of work—but he told her that would change once the baby came. To make things worse, when he was gone he couldn't call her because the location and even the company he worked for were at the highest level of security—so high, he couldn't even talk with her about it. Every time she mentioned it, he either changed the subject or reminded her about some oath he took. not once had she questioned his fidelity until now.

Antonio cleared his throat as if he were choosing his words carefully. "I am a solitary, meaning I practice alone. I learned the Old Ways from *la mia nonna*, my grandmama. My brother and I were taught the teachings of Aradia long ago in *Roma*, but my brother distorted the words of the *Gospel*, then became obsessed with Leland's interpretation and documentation of the teachings, some of which were evil and untrue. no matter what happens, you must never—"

"Brother, what brother?" Diana felt an overwhelming sense of dread, as if she were losing her grip on reality. She tried to see the road ahead, but it disappeared in a whirling cloud of glittering powder.

Antonio touched her arm. "He's not someone you can—"

"Oh my God, look."

"Be careful. Slow down."

The road vanished as white clumps feathered up the hood. "no way, I can't drive in this. It was clear just a second ago." Panicked, Diana leaned forward, desperately trying to see the road. "I've never seen a whiteout come on so fast."

"It's the wind."

"An autumn squall." Diana's nausea returned, and she wanted to stop the car to vomit. "It was in the sixties today, there wasn't supposed to be any wind or snow."

"Pull over as soon as you can. I'll drive."

Clutching the steering wheel, Diana squinted, then slowed the car down to a crawl as she tried to find a place to pull over. With the mountainside on her left, and the ravine on her right, fear gripped every muscle in her body when she realized there were no turnout lanes on this twisted road. She couldn't just stop in the middle of a narrow, two-lane road because someone might hit her from behind. There was absolutely no visibility.

"Why did we take the Ferrari anyway?" Diana moaned, knowing sudden weather changes frequently occur in the mountains, but since the Atwoods' party was black-tie and today's weather had been summer-like, they decided to drive Antonio's favorite vehicle.

"We should have taken the four-wheel drive," Antonio whispered.

Diana flipped the windshield wipers on high and strained to see marks on either side of the road, but there was nothing to guide her. She checked the rearview mirror for cars, but her taillights only illuminated a thick veil of snow. If someone did come from behind, they'd never be able to stop in time.

"This is a nightmare."

"Pull over as soon as you can." Antonio ransacked the glove compartment as he spoke. "Here's the flashlight in case we get stranded," he added, tossing it on the console.

When the road vaguely came into focus, Diana patted her queasy stomach and sighed with relief. The white veil dissipated as quickly as it appeared. Still unsure of the winding road, she hunted for a place to pull over, but there was none. "It's okay, baby," she said, talking as if her unborn child could hear.

She tensed when a white spectral haze appeared just ahead. Diana drove toward the squall and her stomach knotted. Snowy globs licked up the hood until it consumed the entire car with a thick fog of silver dust once again.

"I can't see," she said.

"Neither can I. Just slow down and stay calm. We'll get through this."

Once she entered the whiteout, crimson taillights flashed inches away from her front bumper.

"Oh, no," she cried, tapping her foot on the brake as the back end of the Ferrari swerved on the icy road.

"Keep it steady. Here, let me help."

Antonio reached over and steered the car as the rear tires veered to the left. He slowly turned the wheel until they gained control inches away from hitting the car ahead. *Thank God for my husband,* she thought, letting Antonio take control of the wheel as she crossed herself and said a prayer. The burgundy glow from the car ahead slipped into the shroud of snow and disappeared. As soon as she placed her hands on the wheel, Antonio let go.

"Isn't there a turnout lane soon?" Diana asked, trying to control her shaky voice.

Antonio tensed, then yelled, "Up ahead, watch out—"

Surprised by Antonio's sharp tone, Diana tried to focus, but she couldn't see anything except the white, powdery veil. Unprepared for the hairpin turn, Diana yanked the steering wheel to the left to try to make the sharp turn, but the car went into a swerve that never stopped. She lost control just as the back end hit a patch of ice. The Ferrari skidded sideways toward the edge of the drop-off on the side of the road. Antonio spun into action as he tried to help her steer out of the skid, but the wheels had no traction on black ice. As if the car had a mind of its own, it kept sliding toward the edge. Once the tires slipped off the road, the car catapulted sideways down the ravine for what seemed like an eternity.

Everything went into slow motion when they flew off the cliff. The Ferrari, turned on its side, dropped straight down into the ravine, then hit rock bottom. On impact, Antonio smashed against the car door, his head hitting the glass window as it slammed into the rock and shattered into a million pieces. The car caved in on Antonio's side, and its impact made his massive body move toward Diana. The eerie sound of the Ferrari squishing like an accordion made her scream. Once the metallic wail stopped, Antonio hunched over the console with a moan. Horrified, Diana struggled with her seat belt to be near him. Because the car landed on Antonio's side, Diana remained strapped in place on the upward side. Looking down at him, Diana moved, and it felt like the Ferrari teetered on whatever it had landed upon.

"Antonio." She reached out for him, but he didn't move. "Antonio?"

Then she noticed the air bags hadn't worked. *His seat belt wasn't fastened,* Diana realized. *Please God, let him still be alive.* Frantic, Diana pulled at her seat belt, then groped at her side to find the buckle. The belt cinched her stomach like a noose tightening on its victim.

An enormous flood of warm liquid oozed between her legs and kept coming in oceans onto the seat, then seeped toward Antonio's side of the car. Diana's eyes welled with tears when she realized her water had broken.

Desperate for help, she reached for the cell phone, but it wasn't in the cradle. Feeling trapped, Diana hunted for a way to get out. Fluffy puffs of snow whipped through the wind as she scanned the moonlit terrain where they crashed. It struck her as strange how the storm was silent down in the ravine, while it had raged on the road high above. She gasped when she discovered they hadn't slammed into a boulder; they were on a slippery ledge—a sheered edge pointing down into the dark void of the seemingly endless ravine. Struggling to help Antonio, she reached for his crumpled body, but the car moved as she moved until she feared it would slide down the ravine.

Diana touched his black, wavy hair and yearned to hear his deep, Italian voice once again. She blinked back the tears and turned his face up toward hers. Illuminated by the bluish cast of the full moon, Antonio's face had an enormous gash that extended from his jaw line to the side of his brow. Gliding her fingertips across his strong jaw and thick, motionless lips, she waited for him to stir, but he didn't move. Placing her fingers against his neck to feel a pulse, she willed Antonio to still be alive. But there was no pulse.

"Antonio, my one and only love," she whispered.

Bathed in purple-blue moonlight, his pronounced Italian features looked as though they were chiseled out of stone. From the beginning, Diana called him a Roman God, and now he bore the resemblance more than ever.

Diana struggled to kiss his rugged brow, and the car slipped again. It slid, screeching as it descended. Scraping over icy rock, the Ferrari tilted on the ledge and slid down the flat surface, picking up speed from the sharp incline. Diana tried to scream as the car slipped off the edge, then rolled over onto its side, but Antonio's body fell into her arms and stifled the scream. She held him tight, but everything happened too fast after that. The car, set in motion from the tumble, rolled over again on the steep incline. Diana held onto Antonio as long as she could, but, succumbing to the perpetual motion, his body flew out the window on the downward roll as the car continued down the treacherous ravine.

As the life inside her kicked vigorously, Diana felt the pain of labor and closed her eyes to pray for a miracle. When the car skidded over an outcropping of rocks, she screamed the words *God help us.* But there was no answer when the Ferrari rocketed down the mountainside. It gained momentum from the perpetual roll, then started bouncing from boulder to boulder. And then Diana's consciousness snapped into a void.

"Is she dead?" the man asked. Dressed in scrubs, he looked agitated.

"We need help over here," the woman cried, trying to revive whoever it was on the gurney.

Hovering above the scene, Diana became confused. *Who's dead?* she wondered. The eerie view intrigued her as she watched everyone in the emergency room rush over to help resuscitate the woman. Diana tried calling out—she even made an attempt to wave at the technicians below—but her voice wouldn't work, and her body felt like thin air. She was floating as if in a dream. And when she tried to move or look down at herself suspended in midair, a mist blurred her vision.

Mesmerized by the frenetic activity below, she realized she was the one that the doctors were concerned about. With her tousled, long blonde hair matted with blood and her cadaverous white skin, her body looked like it belonged in a morgue. She appeared to be dead on the table, yet still alive as she floated in midair high above the scene. Seeing herself this way gave her an overwhelming sense of sadness. *This must be what it feels like to die,* Diana thought. A female doctor yelled orders as they prepared to use the defibrillator. But just as Diana began to panic from the surreal sight, a spectral white light appeared to her immediate right.

The sphere of light emitted rays of shining alabaster hues highlighted with threads of golden light beams weaving in and out of the ball. Its incandescent light warmed Diana and gave her an overall sense of well-being, then it vibrated as if responding to that thought. Its form kept changing as Diana watched; misty vapors transformed into threads of gold changing yet again into shimmering waves of opalescent colors illuminated from within the ball of light. It moved faster as if it pulsed with energy. Immediately, all Diana's fears melted away, and her hopelessness transformed into a sense of awe.

Diana instinctively knew it was telling her, if she melded with the light, she'd be taken care of.

"I understand," she replied, realizing that only the light heard her words, while the people in the room didn't even look up.

Diana became fascinated with the way the light communicated because it actually transferred thought. When it did this, its vapors moved like gold dust floating in the air. At that moment, she understood the ball of light was there because of her. Diana stared at the golden rays as they beckoned her to enter yet another part of the universe by following one of the luminous threads.

She heard the soft-spoken words, *Are you ready?*

"No," she quickly answered. But the light's warmth made her waver. On second thought, maybe she should go. *But my husband and our unborn baby,* Diana thought. *Our baby.*

Instead, she looked down at her dead body on the gurney, and a profound sadness consumed her again. Then her vision blurred and her mind faded back into the void.

When she opened her eyes, no pulsating ball of light or radiating presence beckoned her, only sterile, fluorescent light bulbs. She stared at the ceiling, but it wasn't the same one she had seen in her dream. It had to have been a dream, yet it seemed so real.

Diana moved her hand across her abdomen and rubbed the bandages of gauze. Her abdomen seemed different now—empty, flatter. She wanted to scream, but couldn't move her lips. Dark shadows on the ceiling became clouded through the tears in her eyes, and the walls in the dimly lit room looked distorted. Tears streamed down her face as she desperately prayed for the life that was once inside her.

She pulled at the bandages and was certain her stomach didn't bulge like before. Raw pain gripped her body and forced her to cry out. She moved her head from side to side on the pillow, agonizing over what had happened. Maybe they were able to save her unborn baby. Five months wasn't that premature, was it? She blinked through the tears and glared at the red button to call the nurse. Images of the taillights and Antonio helping her steer the car flashed through her mind, but the rest of the night was a blur. Diana jabbed the button with her fingertip, then used the bed sheet to brush away the tears. But her eyes clouded over just as soon as she wiped them off. Seconds lapsed into a minute until she pushed the button again, harder this time, and the woman from the dream entered—the one who had tried resuscitating Diana's lifeless body on the gurney in the emergency room, as Diana had watched the frantic scene from high above.

"What happened?" Diana cried, realizing that her words were caught between a wail and a moan. "Where's Antonio?"

"You scared us. We thought we lost you. I'm Dr. Kurns," the woman said, as she leaned over the bed and took Diana's hand. "You are going to be all right, if you can get some rest and let your body heal."

"Please tell me," she begged.

The doctor squeezed her hand, then pushed the hair away from Diana's face. The doctor's sad eyes spoke volumes. "First, let's make sure you get some rest. How about we give you something to help you relax so you can sleep?"

Diana nodded, dreading what the woman was about to tell her.

As the doctor motioned for the nurse to add the sedative, her eyes moistened.

"Is he gone? And my baby too?" Diana had barely said the words when the doctor slowly nodded and moved in closer to squeeze her shoulder.

Diana pulled away and slid down under the covers to stifle a scream. Images of the crash and the blow to Antonio's head flooded into her mind as she felt the pain of losing him forever. Curling into a fetal position, she writhed beneath the sheets and cried out as the doctor uttered words of comfort. The doctor's words became muffled as the intravenous drugs numbed Diana's body until she surrendered to the darkness. This time, she welcomed it.

CHAPTER TWO

LUCA

Rome, Italy

Time Warp
September 11, 2003
DUSK

"Shall I ignore the edict and bury you in the *Pincio* Gardens?" Luca DeMarco asked his dying father, Janus, the renowned *Sacerdote* of the *Roma Sotterranea*. Since burying the dead was illegal in *Roma*, Luca knew he could find a way to bury his father on what had once been their property. Long ago, Janus donated the grounds that were called *Pincio* Gardens to ensure their privacy in the underground just below the well-known public gardens donated by the DeMarco family.

The old man struggled to breathe, and Luca squeezed his father's hand to comfort him. Luca nodded at his beloved *Sacerdote* trying to answer for him, but his father still struggled to speak.

"Cremate me in the *Sotterranea*," Janus whispered, his raspy voice dwindling to almost inaudible over the past hour. "Then, scatter my remains in the *Cripta* and perform the Rite of Passage for my soul."

The Rite of Passage was a *Stregherian* rite of community, which traditionally involved cremation, yet Luca had never cremated anyone in the *Sotterranea* because no one in their *boschetto* had died and gone to Luna before. Luna, the place where the physical body died, could be reached after passing through the veil between this world and the others.

Luca's eyes moistened as he realized his father's spirit was diminishing along with the light of the setting sun. Although he had disagreed with the *Sacerdote* or High Priest's policies, Luca would still mourn his father's passing.

"How can I burn flesh in the middle of *Roma?*" Luca asked, curious that his father would want his ashes scattered in the *Sotterranea.*

"The columbarium in the *Cripta dei Morti* vents to the surface," Janus said, speaking fluent English, yet the heavy Italian accent remained. "*Malocchio,* be careful with ashes of the dead, because ashes used for talisman and charged are lethal."

Luca frowned when he heard his father call him *malocchio* rather than *Malandanti. Malocchio* meant "the evil eye;" whereas, *Malandanti* was the name for Luca's coven, who followed him to *Roma* after leaving New York. Luca, secretly known for leading the *Malandanti,* had not shared this aspect of himself with his father because it involved sex magick rites to fight wars. Long ago, when someone blurted out in front of his father that Luca was a *Malandanti,* his father must have heard *malocchio,* because he had used that nickname for Luca ever since. It bothered Luca that his father called him *malocchio* because Luca wasn't evil—Luca was the leader of the *Malandanti,* or the ones who would save their people. Shaking his head, Luca decided to let it go this time and not fight over the *Sacerdote's* choice of words. More importantly, Luca needed to present his plan and convince his father that they must protect the *Stregheria* from being annihilated in the near future. If their accusers were eliminated, then they could thwart the Vatican's plan for the Second Inquisition.

"Charge ashes?" Luca asked, leaning forward.

Luca methodically "charged" his tools for ritual, but never anything like ashes of the human body. Much like filling an empty battery with energy, charging actually infused the thing being charged with power. Charging worked by using thought with a purpose on the thing being charged. Common people had forgotten this simple magick used by the ancients long ago, because magick won't manifest without understanding invocation. Charging required intent, focus and emotion—responses that were evoked in most common people through watching television or movies, which meant the producers and writers had the potential to elicit a "charge" by evoking emotion and intent in whomever watched their program. But common folk, much less producers and screenwriters, didn't understand invocations that brought an idea or a thought into form. Luca called it wasted brain waves because people didn't realize the power of the mind.

Janus struggled to breathe before he continued. "That particular columbarium has vents from the diggers—nobody will notice the stench at midnight."

"Diggers?" Luca asked. "You mean archeologists, Father."

Luca wondered about the feasibility of burning human flesh in the columbarium of the *Cripta dei Morti*. In ancient *Roma*, catacombs were devised to stack the dead and maximize burial space, making it an ingenious way to accommodate a large number of bodies in a small area by using dovecote niches poked into the earth. In the fourth century, an edict by the Senate did not allow Romans to bury their dead inside the city for obvious health-related reasons, which forced the wealthy to cremate their dead to keep treasured ashes nearby in elaborate tombs. Since the columbarium or tomb was the only way for the wealthy to eulogize the dead inside the city, the elaborate tomb and sarcophagus became the norm. But in the *Cripta dei Morti*, the sarcophagus Janus referred to looked like an oven—an oven with a casket instead of a grill.

"Over the years, I've used English because you and your brother were raised with the language in the states after your mother died. I am sorry that you speak so little of our beautiful language, but *la mia nonna* didn't school you properly."

Luca turned away from his father and hoped he wouldn't talk about his mother dying while giving birth. It was Luca's birth that made his mother die, and he couldn't listen to his father talk about it anymore, because there was nothing Luca could do to bring her back.

"I should have raised you and your brother," Janus continued. "But instead, I returned to *Roma* to my sacred *boschetto* with its new insurgence of youth that joined us. I am sorry I wasn't there for you. But now I have been for the past seven years. The *boschetto* has changed since you arrived. It's gotten stronger, more independent, don't you agree?"

Luca looked down, knowing that he had purposefully changed his father's *boschetto* by weeding out, then recruiting the kind of people who eventually would serve his purpose—his mission in life. Thankful that Janus talked with such a strong, clear voice but still saddened by it, Luca nodded. His father had gotten a second wind, but Luca knew the *Sacerdote* would die soon. Usually right before dying, the body and mind have a resurgence of spirit.

"My Donata did not want to have young children around during the rites," Janus continued. "Had I not left America, I never would have met my new *Sacerdotessa*, even though she's gone now too. I'm glad that you found it in your heart to forgive me for leaving you with your grandmama, but she was a far better parent than I. Seems Antonio could never forgive me, could he?" The feeble grip of his father's hand made Luca's eyes mist. "Antonio never liked Donata. But then, he didn't like your passion for leadership either, my *malocchio,* did he?"

"Antonio calls me *malocchio* too, but I'm not. I'm only doing what I must do to save our people from further torture and persecution. Tell me Papa, what should I do with your ashes?" Luca pleaded.

"Use my remains as a talisman to bless and consecrate our *Roma Sotterranea.*"

"Ashes as a talisman?" Luca lifted his brow. "Just how powerful is this talisman?" Luca hadn't considered cremating humans before. But then he had never thought of turning ash into a talisman either. Luca rubbed his jaw as he realized the columbarium would be perfect for burning human flesh, especially if it were vented.

"Protect my remains as if your life depended on it." Janus choked on the words. "Because if the ashes become charged with evil intent, mere contact on the third eye causes a slow, severe illness. It can even kill if the talisman is potent enough. And if it's ingested, you're doomed."

"Tell me how to make it potent." Luca leaned forward in his chair, elbows on his knees.

"Draw down the power of the universe for a higher good, then scatter my ashes in the tunnels, especially the *Cripta dei Morti.* Do this with pure intent to create peace and bring clear vision for the *boschetto.*" Janus paused, frowning at Luca. "Why make it potent? Potency depends on the source. The more powerful people are during their lifetime, especially previous lifetimes or incarnations, the more potent the ash."

Luca froze when he realized the meaning of his father's words. "Past lives make the ashes more powerful?"

The last conversation Luca had with his brother, when he used to be on speaking terms with him that is, was about incarnations—the incarnation of Antonio's new wife. From the beginning, Antonio was convinced his beloved was Diana, the Goddess of All Witches incarnate, and Luca knew better than to argue with his psychic brother. When it came to sizing people up, Antonio had the gift. He had an ability to see right through people, straight into the places where their soul had journeyed. His last words were, *I can prove it too.* Luca still didn't know what his brother meant, but if there was ever a powerful talisman, the Goddess of All Witches would be the one.

Luca sat up straight, sensing the voice from within. His ears always burned when the voice came, and this time they throbbed as if on fire. Many times the voice came to instruct him, and this time was no exception. *If the talisman is potent enough, then the entire Roman Catholic Church could be destroyed,* the voice said.

He nodded at the darkness to indicate he understood, then spoke to his father, who clearly had not heard the omnipresent voice that had spoken to Luca. "This is our answer." Luca turned and gazed at his reflection in the glass door of the *terrazzo* and tried to absorb the implications of his father's words.

Slicking back his obsidian hair with both hands, he could see his widow's peak even in the reflection of the glass. He looked like Count Dracula instead of a *Stregone.* Turning his head from side to side, he stroked his angular jaw, searching for answers from his mirrored reflection. His pronounced lips and pasty face made him look Transylvanian. Luca turned away from his image in the glass as the sound of his father's shallow breathing brought him back into reality.

"Actually, it's exactly what we need to survive," Luca whispered, then moved close as his father struggled to talk. "Donata treated you good, didn't she? I've tried to take care of you here at the *Castello,* but I am nothing like your *Sacerdotessa.*"

"I regret not having a legacy of a *Sacerdotessa,* but it could never be possible to replace my Donata with another woman. You will be the next *Sacerdote,* no?"

Luca nodded and agreed once more to his father's daily request. "I will take care of our *boschetto,* Father, and you must hear me when I tell you what I am about to do. I will address the crisis with the church, and the *boschetto* will help me. As *Sacerdote,* it is time to heed the warning and reverse the prophecies."

Unable to use his normal voice, Janus whispered. "What do you mean by this word, *reverse?*"

Luca stood and marched through the faded dusk, eyes riveted on the silvery haze of the one tome he coveted, the *Gospel.* No one owned this rare book except him, and he knew the ramifications of its wisdom. He grabbed the crumbling volume from the shelf, opened it to the place where his bookmark rested, then read the words. "They will openly hunt us down and slay us. In their prisons they shall torture us and create all manners of lies, forcing us to bear witness to all that they say."

Janus, shaking his head, waved his wiry hands in the air. "You're talking about the Inquisition. That's over, my son."

"They did it before, and this says they will do it again."

"The church does not harm those who practice *Stregheria* in this day and age. Look at our people who attend church, yet still follow the Old Ways."

"I have made sure that our *boschetto* avoids the Vatican, unless there is work to be done there. News of child molestations by Catholic priests forced those few with the strange custom of *Stregheria* and Catholicism to stop." Luca placed his finger on the worn pages of the volume before reading more. "Life must not be taken without necessity."

"How long have you thought this?" Janus shook his head. "We cannot harm others—it's against our creed."

Multicolored rays of silver hues shapeshifted into a stream of ruby-red light that transformed Janus's ashen skin into a fiery pyre. When his father's eyes rolled back into his sockets, Luca knew death was near. Trying to be strong, Janus made an effort to straighten himself and be more lucid, but his body crumpled over in pain.

Janus grimaced, then touched his throat as if that would help him speak. "You know as well as I, our creed is to harm no one," he whispered, motioning for Luca to hand him the oxygen mask. "Air, give me—"

Luca rushed over to the oxygen tank, then untangled the tubes around the mask. Quickly returning to his father's bed, Luca tried to place the mask over his father's face, but he pushed it away. "You must take care of the *boschetto*," he said, clutching at his chest. "The church must not torture our people again."

It appeared to Luca that Janus shuddered when he explained his interpretation of the words from the *Gospel,* and as he handed his father the oxygen mask, he heard him sigh. After seven years of research, Luca finally had the proof he needed to back up his claim of a Second Inquisition, and as he shared his findings with his father, Luca became even more passionate about his mission. Although Janus had disagreed when Luca told him the *Holy Strega* predicted a Second Inquisition, he couldn't argue after Luca presented the discoveries made by his spies at the Vatican. Through his various contacts undercover there, Luca knew the Second Inquisition was now becoming a reality. Once he had shown his father the confidential memos and presented the records of secretive meetings and clandestine phone calls in the Vatican that confirmed the church was planning a Second Inquisition, Janus surrendered and gave Luca his blessing.

Luca did all he could to help his father, but in the end it wasn't air Janus needed; it was a new heart. Luca tried to ring the authorities, but his father insisted Luca be near. Janus had always wanted to die at home rather than be kept alive in some sterile medical facility. Finally, when the slate-colored moonbeams snuffed out the light in the room, his father passed. In a tragic stupor, Luca performed the Rite of Passage for his father's soul. Trying to absorb the loss, Luca knelt by the bed in total darkness, still holding his father's hand. The thought that he would never see his father again on the physical plane made Luca cry out in pain. He tried to gather the strength to go on without his *Sacerdote,* but he couldn't move.

Finally, he reminded himself of the mission they talked about just before his father's death, and Luca realized it was critical for him to continue. He had to stop the terrorists at the church and their diabolical plan. Slowly, he moved into the light of the hallway sconces of the second floor and descended into the shadow slithering before him down the stairs into the great hall. His inky silhouette blended into darkness on the main floor as he opened the small wooden door, flicked on the light, then took the cement steps down into the murky depths of the cellar.

The dank coolness invigorated Luca as he made his way toward the portal, which was an oval-shaped mirror bolted onto a trapdoor. Fingering the lever behind the mirror, he released the metal latch. When he opened the portal, an eerie light automatically illuminated a narrow opening with tiny, carved-out steps that led straight down into the bowels of the earth. To steady himself, he pressed the palms of his hands against both sides of the narrow passageway. Carefully, he stepped down onto the tiny carved-out ledge, then began his descent down into the earth, and when he reached the base of the stairs, Luca entered the *Roma Sotterranea*.

Stepping into the darkness, Luca reached out his hand and blindly searched for the lamp in the recessed ledge. In the meager light of the tunnels, he needed the lantern because the holes that had been drilled long ago during the excavation just weren't enough. He raked his hand through the moldy dirt in the niche, and spiders flitted over his fingertips. Knocking the tip of the oil lamp on the chiseled-out ledge, he finally grabbed it, then used the small flame of his lighter to see the wick inside. Golden lamplight slid through the darkness to illuminate a slender tunnel shaped like a teardrop with the point overhead. These carved-out passageways were not like the catacombs that had been used for the dead outside the city. This part of the underground was different than all the rest because this tunnel led to Luca's sacred site in the underground for sex magick ritual—the *Villa de Marco*. A *Villa* that was entirely underground.

He forged his way through the narrow corridor, ignoring the black water as it dripped from the tapered brickwork overhead. Since he was only ten feet below ground, the muffled sound of the traffic above on *Trinità dei Monti* was the only sign of life among these earthen walls. But hidden inside these silent layers beneath the city Luca understood the life as the earth's energy, and that was what mattered: the invisible, the darkness and the void.

Romans feared this subterranean realm because it was rumored that ghosts of the dead lurked in the *Roma Sotterranea*, but Luca knew better. He had seen many an apparition down here, and none dared come close enough to harm him. With the invisible forces beside him, ghosts wouldn't dare haunt him. But after a sharp turn in the dank tunnel, Luca saw a light gathering at the end of the tunnel—a light where there should be no light at all. Stepping back, Luca grimaced from the ethereal sight.

"*Laissez-moi,*" he said. "Stay away."

Luca froze as he watched the translucent cloud gather itself at the top of the tapered tunnel. *Must be a tortured soul or lost spirit from the Cripta dei Morti just beyond,* Luca thought. The apparition moved closer, inching its way toward him. In a misty haze, the misshapen outline of a body formed at the end of the tunnel—an outline that looked like the light of the living dead.

"*Laissez,*" Luca repeated, watching the apparition become more defined until it shapeshifted into a form much like that of his brother Antonio.

Beads of sweat formed on Luca's brow as he started to turn back. But his legs wouldn't work, and the oil lamp became far too heavy for him to hold anymore. The lamp slid out of his fingers and clamored onto the stony ground, transferring the only light to that of the apparition.

An icy chill seeped through the darkness engulfing Luca and the area around him. He shivered from the swirling mist. Watching in horror, Luca stared at the wispy image of Antonio moving closer with inhuman slowness. When the apparition came close enough to touch, the spirit raised his translucent arms, palms up, as if the vaporous form could express surrender. Transfixed by the image of his brother, Luca stepped back, confused because his brother was in spirit. Surely Antonio was alive, not dead.

"Speak to me, Antonio," he said. "What's happened to you? Is something wrong?"

Wanting to make amends with his estranged brother, Luca placed his hand on his brother's shoulder, but it passed through the misty form and the spirit dissipated, vanishing as quickly as it had appeared. It took Luca a moment before he regained his senses and rummaged through his pockets for the lighter. His hands trembled when he picked up the lamp and lit it again.

After slipping through the vaporous remains of his brother's spirit, he reached another stairway with hollowed-out steps, then descended to the deepest part of the *Sotterranea*. The entire distance from his house to the *Grotto* was about seven hundred meters; even though it wasn't far, Luca still gasped for breath. The thin air, laden with the musty smell of raw earth at its deepest level, made it hard to breathe.

Luca stopped for a moment to steady his breath, then cautiously made his way through the narrow tunnel that led to the sacred *Grotto*. Usually, pagan temples in the *Roma Sotterranea* were beneath cathedrals or holy places aboveground, and this *Grotto* was no exception. Frowning, Luca thought of the church overhead with its devoted parishioners. Directly above the *Grotto*, Catholics traditionally gathered in the *Trinità dei Monti* for mass. Most sacred sites were built directly atop each other and were separated not only by layers of earth, but also by layers of different beliefs.

Sacred sites overlaid the pagan ones because the ground absorbed the power of human thought, and that force accumulated over time. When Luca visited sacred sites aboveground around the world, he watched common people sense this force, yet not one of them had any clue of its origin. But the *Stregheria* knew the force of sacred sites came from an "imprint," or an emotional memory embedded in the earth. Momentous imprints, whether tragic or inspiring, were passed down through time and stored in the earth as energy. Just like the atrocity that occurred in New York City only two years ago, that spot of land would never be the same again after thousands of people died there. Because the intensity of emotion determined the strength of the current or energy field within the layers of the earth, recognizing the force that had accumulated was important not only to honor the imprint upon the earth, but also to honor the dead who gave it the charge.

Imprints caused people to feel the energy of ancient sites because there was power behind the thought, power behind the action that had occurred on the land. In the *Roma Sotterranea*, Luca immediately sensed imprints in the earth because he not only felt the current, he also saw the invisible charge as a mist that protected the site with its vapors. Luca understood imprints because he spent most of his time in the underground. *As above, so below.* Frowning at the thought of the layer above the *Grotto*, it saddened him that the present-day imprint didn't honor its origin.

He stepped into the *Grotto*, then acknowledged the sacred waters in the center pool that seeped over the rim of the well onto the layered rock. Behind the well, water rhythmically trickled from a fissure in the rock, then oozed down into the pools. Dipping his hand into the sparkling water, Luca closed his eyes to concentrate on the flow. Evoking his power and accessing the source, Luca kept his hand in the flowing water until he felt the earth's energy meld with his. Feeling refreshed, Luca scanned the cavern, then began his daily ritual of lighting the candelabrum and burning the frankincense and myrrh. The *Grotto* comforted him with its heated pools, low lights and hot-water heat his father installed long ago. Because of those luxuries in this part of the underground, the *Grotto* felt more like home to Luca than the *Castello del Pincio*. Luca's eyes blurred as he felt his father's spirit nearby.

"I'll avenge the Roman Catholic Church in the name of our ancestors, Father," he shouted. Luca watched the shadows move through the iridescent light of the venerable cavern. After he finished lighting the candles, Luca watched the silver mist form over the pools and veil the bubbling well with a shroud.

Long ago, Christians covered the wells and built their churches over the blessed springs of the Druids, Celts and *Strega*, because Christians wanted to stop the various clans from gathering at the sacred well. But the churches built atop those sacred wells couldn't destroy the imprint that was already there from the energy stored inside the earth. And since the ancients and the pagans had blessed these sites in the past, the charge remained. Layers of the earth accumulated energy through focused thought, so once a site was blessed, it remained sacred because of the charge bestowed upon it. But if the ground was polluted, then the charge became garbled and confused like scrambled radio waves. Sites that had been destroyed still had a charge, it just wasn't amplified through human thought like the historical and officially recognized ones. Sites that weren't appreciated or declared as ancient around the world still had a charge, but only people with a heightened sense of perception could recognize the force and therefore channel it.

Luca walked around the center pool and stepped into the opening in the rock that jutted out behind the fissure. In the hidden passageway, Luca cleared his mind to ready himself for the highest level of energy in the underground. Luca knew the strength of the energy currents or ley lines because he used his copper rods to dowse the lines. Through dowsing, he could feel the energy force and could therefore pinpoint where his rituals would be the most effective for channeling this current into his rites. The *Grotto* held intense energy, but the *Cripta dei Morti* contained a far greater charge amplified by the pain and torture that occurred on this sacred ground in the past. The *Cripta* contained a massive charge because it held the intense energy of human thought and emotion from his ancestors. It could be any thought, any emotion, but the collective energy from pain and torture made it a powerful force to use for other purposes. Because the *Cripta dei Morti* was the strongest center for the currents that snaked deep into the earth's core, the *Cripta* had been made into a memorial long ago. The *Cripta* served as a living legacy of the tragedy his ancestors experienced after being tortured and put to death simply because their way of life was one that not only honored nature and the body, but also the earth's energy.

He stepped into the most hallowed realm of the underground and bowed his head. "In the names of Tana and Tanus, I bless this sacred place," Luca whispered.

Used as a prison for the accused during the Inquisition, the remains of the dead had been preserved in the *Cripta* by means of saving their bones. Skulls, stacked one on top of another, covered the walls, and layers of femur and pelvic bones served as a reminder of the chamber's namesake—*Cripta dei Morti* or Crypt of the Dead. Luca kneeled at the altar, then prostrated himself on the ground to honor the skeletons towering over him. In this sanctuary of bones, three skeletons of three separate beliefs stood before him, dressed as if they were still performing the rites of an Alchemist, Druid and *Strega*. Luca stood, then stepped forward to commune with the skeletons. These bones were what remained of his ancestors, who had been tortured and put to death during the Inquisition. Luca felt the skeletons respond when he acknowledged their pain, and the penetrating glares in the empty sockets of their skulls made it clear that they supported his mission to destroy the church.

Once Luca finished conversing with his ancestors at the altar, he turned toward the side chamber, then faced the columbarium his father spoke of before he died. Luca eyed a funerary urn in a dovecote niche, picked it up and opened the lid. He slid his fingers over the cold, rough stone inside to make sure it was empty. Nodding, he decided to store his father's ashes here until he was ready to use them against the church.

Luca would never forget the hatred Catholics harbored toward his faith, and because the Roman Catholic Church created its own laws, he had to protect his people. This past year, grown men who were abused in their childhood by church officials came forward and testified. And after these heinous acts surfaced, the media revealed a sordid past whereby church officials simply moved the accused to other parishes, which in turn helped them evade prosecution. Because the Vatican had a track record of shielding sex offenders from the law, Luca felt it was his duty to weed those criminals out. Destroying the power base in Vatican City would thwart the Second Inquisition, as well as protect the children. Certain he was justified, Luca would not allow the Catholics to rule anymore. Annihilating the Catholics would be the karmic result of the acts of torture committed during the Inquisition and the injustices of disregarding the law as it is written today. Once the Roman Catholic Church was eliminated, there couldn't be another Inquisition.

Luca stepped inside the crematorium and stood under the arched enclosure of travertine blocks. Inlaid within that arch was a second arch, and even further inside that one was the carved-out niche in the shape of a casket where a body could be laid out and cremated.

Vents had been dug through the walls surrounding the crematorium—vents large enough to handle the smoke that would ensue from burning human flesh. He had never noticed those hidden vents before. The vents made it possible to cremate, even though the crematorium was entirely concealed underground. Luca examined the space and realized how efficient it would be to burn a body. After all these years, he never knew the *Cripta dei Morti* had a built-in crematorium.

Tears formed in his eyes as Luca envisioned the funeral pyre for his father's body in the ancient columbarium. Luca turned to go, determined to cremate his father, because it would give him the ashes he needed for the talisman. Finally, he could do what he considered to be his life's work—save his people from extinction. Through cremating his father, the remains would become the talisman. And once he had the ash, he could amplify the charge until the talisman was strong enough to annihilate the terrorists in Vatican City.

CHAPTER THREE

VINCENT

Rome, Italy

September 11, 2003
DUSK

To prepare himself for his next appointment, Vincent Bellisimo listened to the message again. An Italian American who called herself Raven Slade rang at midnight to tell him Antonio DeMarco was dead, then left the cryptic question, *What did you find after you uncovered the layers of Antonio's soul?*

The voice on the phone demanded to know what happened in his hypnotherapy with DeMarco. Her question surprised Vincent, because it sounded as if she knew about his groundbreaking research, which wasn't common knowledge because his book wasn't even published yet. How did she know about the layers of the soul in hypnotherapy? Vincent wasn't sure how Raven fit into the picture either, but her question suggested that she knew more about the soul than most people did. And the thought of DeMarco dead troubled him. Vincent had delved deep into DeMarco's mind, yet they needed more time together. DeMarco had just decided to commit, had just gotten married and now he was dead?

Shaking his head, Vincent walked over to his usual place by the window overlooking the *Piazza di Spagna*. Violent winds swirled debris at the top of the steps as if an invisible presence lurked in the distance while teenage revelers partied on the steps, unaware of the impending tempest. Overlooking the scene, the double domes of the *Trinità dei Monti* poked at the festering vapors above. Black, restless clouds signaled the urgency of September

29

rain. Thankful to be in *Roma* with its warm climate, he wondered if Raven was caught in the storm and delayed, or maybe she decided not to come after all. After starting his practice years ago, from the beginning, Vincent tried to establish the right mix of patients who were willing to be part of his research. Although he had yet to wait more than ten minutes for a client, this time he had already waited fifteen. Vincent frowned at his watch, wondering if she would even come at all.

Caught up in his thoughts, Vincent turned away from the window to sort the jumbled papers on his desk. Still wondering why Raven mentioned the layers of the soul, Vincent reminded himself to be careful. No one knew about the mysteries he had unraveled, and he wanted to keep it that way until his book was published. He was thankful that he only had a select group of clients, because he preferred working on his manuscript, *The Evolution of the Soul,* rather than people's problems. Lately though, his practice had grown because his father, a famous Hollywood director, had been telling people about his son's "bizarre" work in *Roma.* Since Vincent was an only child, his dad was always trying to help. Help was something Vincent didn't need though, because he was financially independent already, and his doctor network kept him far too busy to need any more clients.

After graduating from college and starting a wellness business, Vincent established a network of doctors in Italy who distributed health products and therefore provided him and his network with residual income. Even though Vincent hadn't gone to medical school, he had relentlessly pursued getting his credentials in hypnotherapy so that he could build a business in health, wellness and the mind. Now that his skills in hypnotherapy were proven and his products were known for solving a wide range of problems, he had the freedom to pick and choose his clients.

Vincent understood the effectiveness of natural alternatives when combined with the power of the mind to heal. But American doctors didn't; in fact, they didn't seem interested in learning anything new or "alternative." After a long, arduous fight with the American Medical Association, Vincent finally gave up on doctors in the United States and enlisted a group of MDs in Italy who agreed to offer natural alternatives to patients rather than routinely prescribe drugs. Now Vincent got referrals from those doctors, because they wanted their patients to undergo hypnotherapy too.

Doctors in America shunned his approach because the AMA frowned upon it and therefore pressured any doctors who offered wellness products to patients to stop. The Association was more interested in pleasing big businesses and the drug companies than they were in providing a new level of wellness to patients. According to Vincent, the Association was more like a cult than a guiding light for wellness in America. Because doctors were in good standing as members of the Association, the entire medical community adhered to the Association's standards. Because Vincent's approach profited the small business or private practice and allowed doctors to offer a greater level of wellness to patients, his entrepreneurial thinking was ostracized and debunked by the Association from the beginning. Vincent's approach didn't fit into the MD mentality of being "ethical," even though he thought it more unethical to only prescribe drugs to patients rather than to provide an alternative. The American Medical Association's adverse reaction to his approach indicated that the drug industry had some sort of power over the Association and its membership. Because most medical schools and the association did not promote courses in nutrition or alternative therapy, doctors weren't even trained in wellness.

After all his efforts with the American doctors, Vincent discovered they were stuck in their limited view of the mind and wellness because they ignored the human experience. They obstinately required double-blind, placebo-controlled studies provided by the drug companies, rather than accepting wellness products that had more than a decade of proven success with consumers. Most American doctors were blinded by the "scientific" evidence that "proved" the results of drugs; the Italian doctors, on the other hand, valued the feedback from thousands of people who had become healthy by consuming supplements and natural alternatives, as well as those who had made positive changes through hypnotherapy. In the end, Vincent decided doctors in America had no freedom because traditional MDs weren't allowed to offer anything "alternative" to their patients without being ridiculed by the medical community.

At age twenty-eight, he didn't need the American doctors sabotaging his ideas with erroneous perceptions and bad press about his dream of providing a new level of wellness for humanity. People had a tendency to fear the unknown, and thus misunderstand his research and his approach to alternative therapy. Vincent knew the power of combining hypnosis with health and wellness though. His style of therapy was successful in that it focused on unraveling the mysteries of the unconscious mind through hypnotic trance.

Pompous attitudes and erroneous perceptions were why Vincent left America. Now, due to his successful Italian network, a group of traditional MDs, Vincent was well-known for his alternative therapies in Italy. His Italian network knew the benefits of his approach because they kept experiencing successful results with their patients. Obesity, libido issues, sleeplessness and lethargy were just some of the problems that became non-issues when patients underwent his therapy. His doctor network consistently referred patients to him because they knew the effectiveness of hypnotherapy, and those select patients being treated by Vincent overcame their problems through their unconscious mind as he helped them develop self-mastery and personal power.

Vincent yanked open the desk drawer to search through the file folders for DeMarco. He wanted specifics. DeMarco was troubled as a child, and what happened to him still affected his ability to function in a long-term relationship. Vincent found the file, then pulled out the record along with the release form. Scribbled on the form under the section for family, DeMarco had written *none.* But in therapy, Vincent learned about Luca and later on, when Diana came into DeMarco's life, he heard about her. During their therapy together, DeMarco had met Diana, gotten married and was headed toward fatherhood. He never mentioned anyone named Raven in their sessions.

Vincent left the file folder open on his desk and walked over to the half bath to splash water on his face. In the faded mirror, he watched himself rake his hands through his disheveled brown hair. His blue eyes showed no expression as he wondered what Raven really wanted.

Thoughtfully, Vincent rubbed his scruffy, unshaven jaw and hoped he could help her deal with the pain of DeMarco's death. As he recalled the tone of her voice on the phone, he could sense her deep sorrow. She sounded so desperate, so forlorn with that deep, raspy voice, as if she could jump through the phone and collapse in his arms because DeMarco was gone. Usually Vincent was good with women, but this time he hadn't been able to get a read on Raven like he normally did with a voice or the sound of a person's walk.

She'd caught him off guard with her Italian American voice, and when he wouldn't give her any details about the case, she demanded to meet him in his office. Usually he wasn't so easily swayed to meet someone immediately, but this time he couldn't say no. Maybe it was the tone of her voice or the silence between her words, but he had to take time to help her. Not only that, he had to find out how she knew about the layers of the soul.

Although Vincent's practice was thriving, he didn't really need any more patients, or any more money for that matter. Vincent and his doctor network could live comfortably off the residual income from the products the network sold, and he had already become independently wealthy because of his entrepreneurial approach. Not only was Vincent the first hypnotherapist in this country, but he was also one of a handful of therapists who even practiced in Italy. He could never retire from hypnotherapy because of its many rewards with his patients, especially when his sessions continued to shed light on the journey of their soul.

Staring at his reflection, Vincent realized how esoteric he must look compared to his doctor network of MDs in Italy. Many of those doctors called him a mystic, and he had reveled in that description. His olive complexion marked by a goatee and small mustache gave him that exotic, other-world look that usually worked in his favor when pushing people to their limits. At least that was what his friends told him. And he had to admit, with his straight hair cut just below his ears, he looked different from most Americans in Italy. His father was from L.A. and his mother was from Sicily, so he had enough Italian ancestry to give him some sort of magnetism; maybe it would help him with Raven. At the

end of their conversation, when she sounded like she was about to
cry, he told her to come later on that very same day. Vincent
shrugged, knowing that a passionate woman would always have
her way with him.

Shaking his head at his image in the mirror, Vincent recalled
DeMarco being traumatized by childhood memories that affected
his life, as well as his brother's. Because DeMarco had been
raised as a *Strega,* Vincent wanted more time with his patient to
process and understand what happened in his childhood, but now
it was too late.

From the beginning, DeMarco had always insisted on being
regressed in his sessions, and Vincent agreed to his patient's request. Vincent's technique of regressing patients to their first life
didn't serve him well in this case though, because he should have
focused on the present life with DeMarco. Regressions provided
Vincent with a more comprehensive background about his patients
and helped him determine treatment, as well as provide information for his research. But once he knew there was a problem in De-
Marco's childhood, Vincent regretted not examining the current life
in more detail a year ago because what happened to DeMarco as
a child deeply affected his state of mind once it surfaced. Vincent
knew the regressions had uncovered that hidden part of DeMarco's
life, which regressions often did, because last week was the first
time his patient mentioned it.

That day, DeMarco hesitated at the start of the session, then,
in a break from tradition, he requested there be no regression. Trying to remember more, Vincent walked back to his desk, then
stared at the chair as if DeMarco were still there. In an instant,
the memory of the session flooded into his mind.

DeMarco leaned back in his chair and hesitated before speaking. "I have something to tell you," he said. "It all came back to
me in a dream last night, because over the years I had to forget
the past to protect myself."

Always ready to listen to his patients, Vincent was quick to
urge him to talk. "Please, go ahead."

"My grandmama, *la mia nonna*, had to teach her two grandsons about our heritage, our past—teachings that changed us forever because they affected our mind, our soul."

Vincent nodded, encouraging him to continue.

"She told us stories at the well in the groves by our house, stories that I had forgotten until our regressions. You see, the regressions uncovered memories that had been buried in my mind for some twenty years. It was this past experience that drove a wedge between my brother and me, because Luca became obsessed with the heinous acts of the past."

"Heinous acts?" Vincent asked, wondering if there had been child abuse or emotional trauma of some sort.

"My grandmama taught us the Old Ways, and told us stories about her ancestry and the legacy that lived on even though those ancestors lived in the mid-fourteenth to seventeenth centuries. That's a legacy that isn't easily forgotten. She meant well, *la mia nonna*, but her recollections of the stories passed down from ages ago were so vivid that it changed us forever. That was when we lived in our Aspen estate where we kept ransacking the hidden crypt of volumes that document this past—volumes with rough sketches of the cruelty in the prisons and journals with pleas for help moments before death. When we were barely old enough to read, we would sneak into the library and look at the pictures, then show each other the atrocities we found in the multitude of volumes in the hidden crypt. Luca internalized his anger and would not speak of it to me as we grew older. But those stories twisted his mind until his rage for the Roman Catholic Church became an obsession. They were stories of torture and hideous acts instigated by the church."

"How old were you?"

"We had just learned to read—small children without a care in the world, until we discovered the horrid evil that changed us forever. And now Luca won't stop for anyone or anything. He's possessed by the horrors inflicted upon his people."

"Where was your mother?"

"Deceased," DeMarco said. "She died giving birth to my brother, Luca."

"And your father?"

"He left after she died because he couldn't go on. He felt incompetent as a father. He deserted us, yet made us both financially independent, then he came back into our lives whenever we traveled to *Roma*. That's why Luca moved here, and I keep coming back in hopes we'll someday reconcile, but it's futile. Father banished me from his *boschetto*."

"Banished? Have you communicated with him since we last spoke of him?"

"The *Strega* use banishing rituals to protect against unwanted spirits. I've told you, we've parted ways because Father thinks he must protect Luca from the demons in his head, but Luca's ways should not be protected nor followed."

"You never contact your father in *Roma?*"

DeMarco shook his head. "I tried, but I cannot be a part of the *Malandanti*, because Luca continues to deceive our father. Luca hides his magick from the *Sacerdote*, while Father denies his youngest does anything deviant. I've tried to tell Father, but he won't listen to anything about his youngest child being evil."

"*Malandanti? Sacerdote?*"

"Luca's coven is called the *Malandanti*, because he uses magick to fight his war. The *Sacerdote* is our father, the High Priest."

"Those deviant things—what do they have to do with the tales your grandmama told you?"

"She did not tell us tales. These things really happened. It's all written down in the *Malleus Maleficarum*. Grandmama tried to comfort us, but the journals my brother and I found in the crypt made the images and scenes too vivid to forget. She told us the stories because she didn't want that part of history forgotten, but her words made us want to know more. Grandmama raised my mom in the ways of the *Strega*, and we were meant to carry on those ways. But the heinous acts of torture made practicing the rites against the law."

"You're talking about the Inquisition, aren't you?"

DeMarco nodded. "I was just as terrified as Luca because we thought they would arrest us for our beliefs, our customs."

Vincent raised his hand, motioning for DeMarco to slow down. "What do you mean, arrest you?"

"We were raised in the Old Ways, and our training started at birth. My benevolent grandmama taught us the ways until she died. We both loved her for what she passed down, but in the end, it was a burden to carry. We didn't know there had been an Inquisition until Grandmama told us, and quite frankly it shattered our world."

Vincent nodded, wanting him to continue.

DeMarco waved his hands in the air to illustrate his point. "The way Grandmama told the stories made them come to life. She was doing it to protect our faith, our way of life from those who tried to destroy us in the past. But it was hard on my brother because, as he got older, his fear and anger escalated into hatred against the Roman Catholic Church."

Vincent watched the troubled man hesitate, as if it were hard to discuss his private life. There was something he couldn't put his finger on with DeMarco's concern about Luca. It was plain to see that he loved his brother, yet didn't know how to express it.

"I remember one time," DeMarco said, "when Luca read the journal that described the torture our people endured. I thought he might take his own life. He was so afraid the church would take him away because the victims in the story were just like us."

"What did you do?"

"Once our reading ability matured, I listened to him read those journals and relive the torture. What else could I do? I was too young to do anything about it. I didn't know how to help Luca, but after that, something happened to my little brother. Something snapped because after he read the horrors inflicted upon our people during that time, all he wanted was revenge."

"What made your brother snap?"

"You must understand that by the time the Inquisition added witchcraft to its list of heresies, torture was an ancient institution. Under Roman law, it was legal, and for centuries it had been used with criminals and innocent people to *make them talk*. At least twenty-eight treatises on the evil of witchcraft were written by demonologists and clerics. And with the Pope Innocent VIII's declaration of papal decree against witches in 1484, the persecution of witches accelerated into mass genocide. The worst tortures and exterminations occurred on the continent with Germany, France and Italy as they fell victim to both Catholic and Protestant inquisitors. They never will have a count on how many died, but it was in the millions. It wasn't just the *Strega* who were tortured and killed; it was the Druids, Celts or anyone who thought differently from the church."

Vincent watched DeMarco's eyes moisten as he stopped for a moment, unable to continue. His massive size along with his wavy, coal-black hair and dark complexion made DeMarco a formidable man. Witnessing emotion in such a man humbled Vincent. He nodded, not wanting to deter his patient from talking.

Finally, DeMarco continued. "We don't have the numbers on how many innocent victims were tortured and executed, but the inquisitors followed procedures outlined in the *Malleus Maleficarum,* which was written by the Dominican inquisitors to Pope Innocent VIII. First, they urged the accused to confess, then they stripped them naked and shaved their body to prick for insensitive spots and examine for blemishes they called Devil's Mark. The *Malleus* warns that most witches wouldn't confess at this point, so they would have to endure the *engines of torture.*"

Vincent watched as DeMarco composed himself and stood. His large frame, shadowed by the gloomy light of the window behind him, remained a silhouette as he spoke. "While they were tortured, the inquisitor repeated questions and the clerk recorded what was said. The margin for error was great because of the lack of education, dialect or terror of the accused. So the torture continued until the victim confessed. Many times they made the victims confess to things they didn't even do, and even if they did confess, they were killed. But if they didn't confess or tell the torturer what he wanted to hear, then the torturer had to be careful not to kill his victim and had to know when to stop after the victim collapsed yet hadn't died. Then, the victim was taken back to the dungeon to rest and gain strength for the next round of torture in a few hours or the next day. The torturers were paid from the victim's belongings, and if the victim had no money, the relatives were forced to pay the costs. In the end, the victims paid for the food, lodging, travel and entertainment of their torturers. Even the entertainment was gruesome, because they used the women to satisfy their sexual desires."

Vincent frowned as DeMarco groaned and walked over to the half bath, poured himself some water in a paper cup, and offered it to Vincent, who shook his head. DeMarco swallowed the entire contents of the cup, then smashed it in his massive hand and tossed it into the trash.

"So tell me," Vincent said, wanting DeMarco to calm down. "What did this experience do to two young men?"

"It turned us into zealots, defiantly hating the Roman Catholic Church, yet relentless in passing on the Old Ways. Now I know this is one of the reasons why I sought therapy—because I still need to forgive the church for what they did to my people. But one thing is certain, my brother hasn't forgiven them. He'll get revenge."

The ringer, signaling that Raven had arrived, snapped Vincent out of his reverie. Trying to shake off DeMarco's haunting words, he buzzed her in, vowing to keep his session with DeMarco confidential. But Vincent froze when he heard Raven ascend the marble steps. When her heels clicked on each step with a distinct gait, he knew Raven had another story to tell.

His instincts told him that her entire body moved with that walk. As if she had been a dancer or had heard a different drummer all her life, her step said it all. One thing was certain; most people didn't walk up the stairs that way. With a light yet decisive step, she paused at each turn in the stairway, making a distinct stop as if accompanied by someone, but there was no one else there because there were no other footfalls.

Nonetheless, when she stopped, she turned and spoke as if there was someone else there, but he couldn't decipher the words. She stood there before opening the door, and he watched the outline of her body through the celadon-colored glass insert of the door. She paused for a moment, and her shapely figure made him raise his brow.

With a vengeance, she opened the door, looked him up and down, then put her hands on her hips. Vincent stood to acknowledge her stark beauty and self-assured pose. Raven hair, emerald eyes, crimson lips. Admiring her shapely figure, Vincent stepped forward to take her hand. Normally, he wouldn't take the hand of a client and guide her to the couch; usually, he'd shake the hand of a client, then let the client decide where to sit. But this woman commanded attention. He steered her to the couch and helped her sit down, then took his place in his chair.

Her crescent-shaped earrings dangled against her neck as she shook her head from side to side until the wild curls of her long hair moved out of her eyes. "I must know what happened between you and Antonio."

"It's confidential."

"How can it be confidential when he's dead?"

"I don't know any such thing," Vincent said, repositioning himself in his chair so that he could look directly at her. He cleared his throat, then added, "Last time I saw DeMarco, he was very much alive."

"That's because he wouldn't want anyone to know."

Vincent frowned. "I must keep my patient confidentiality—"

"I know your rules. Italians generally don't see any kind of therapist, let alone a past life regression therapist, so I cannot fathom how you make it here in *Roma*." She rummaged through her bag, pulled out a rumpled piece of paper, and handed it to him. "Here, read this."

Vincent examined the picture of DeMarco and his wife in the news clip from the internet. "That's tragic. He was an incredible man." Vincent paused to examine the article, then looked up. "Are you from Aspen too?" he asked.

"No."

Vincent stared at the star-like charm dangling from the fastener at her neck—a charm attached to the zipper that started at the hem of her skirt and continued up to her neck. "But you're Italian American, no?"

"Spent most of my life living in various places around the world," Raven said, fingering what Vincent now recognized as a pentacle charm on the zipper. "*Roma* is my home now."

"This says he's survived by his wife, Diana," Vincent said, noticing the flush in Raven's cheeks. "You're not family, are you?"

"Please, I need your help. He spoke to me after the accident."

"What did he say?"

"He came to me in spirit just after midnight. He came to me right after he died," Raven said, pausing for a moment. "Antonio said you uncovered his past and his heightened awareness of it returned. Before he dissipated, he insisted you take care of Diana."

"Dissipated? You saw him in spirit?" Vincent raised his brow. "Look, hypnotherapy can make people understand more about themselves, even facilitate self-mastery, but it is not magick, negative or evil. What do you know about the spirit and its layering in the soul?"

"You study these things. According to Antonio, there will come a time when you will need to help Diana. Are you willing to do that?"

Vincent stared in disbelief at Raven. "How can I help someone I don't even know? And what do you know of Diana anyway? She never came here because DeMarco wanted to tell her about his past in his own time. We had many discussions about his relationship with her, but he never mentioned you."

Raven straightened herself, arching her back so that her posture brought out the best in her figure. "Be that as it may, something happened to Antonio in your last session, because he visited Luca after that," she said. "And Antonio never has anything to do with Luca's magick."

Vincent frowned, frustrated that she was ignoring his questions. "DeMarco was concerned about his brother, but he never said anything about magick. What kind of magick?"

"Why don't you start by telling me what Antonio told you. What do you do in your sessions anyway?"

Apparently, this was the type of woman who couldn't answer questions yet would expect him to answer hers. Vincent shook his head, then stood and walked over to his usual place by the window. Black umbrellas popped up and huddled figures rushed for cover on the *Piazza di Spagna* as raindrops splattered on the weathered cobblestone streets. Vincent watched the frenzied scene below as Giuseppe's fresh flower stand transformed into a billowing tent gone adrift among the turbulent sea of rain.

"I take people back in time, before they were born," he said.

"And just how do you do that?"

"Self-induced hypnosis," he answered. "It's called hypnotherapy. You go into a trance, yet the entire time you are fully awake and cognizant."

"Then what?"

"In this guided meditation, you experience your previous lives—when your soul was in another body, another time, another space."

"And how does this help people?"

"It helps them understand the evolution of their soul." Vincent turned from the rainy view and waved his hands to underscore his every word. "Or it helps them cure a pain, trauma or fear. Usually once people understand what caused the problem, it stops. It's extremely effective when dealing with negative thought patterns and false beliefs about one's self."

"You cure your patients for good?"

"A patient of mine had an unexplained pain in his shoulder ever since he could remember. During the regression, he experienced himself in a past life dying from that stab wound, which hurt in the exact same place as it had in his past life as well as in his current life. And when he awoke, the pain was gone. This happens again and again through regression therapy, and the pain never returns."

Raven shook her head, and the points of the silver moon earrings poked at her ivory neck as she spoke. "But Antonio didn't heal. You uncovered secrets he had forgotten, but they came back in therapy, didn't they?"

Vincent shook his head, not wanting to get into the details about DeMarco with someone who most likely was his mistress. He walked over to Raven and looked down at her sitting on the couch. "DeMarco had a troubled childhood, but that doesn't mean that he couldn't rise above it. Maybe he had a hard time living two lives with two women." Vincent sat next to her and tried comforting her by patting her leg. The pained look of Raven's eyes tugged at his heart. "I can understand why he would be attracted to a beautiful woman though," he added, realizing that his need to console her and touch her physically was part of being Italian, part of the knee-jerk response all Italian men have with women.

Raven closed her eyes and rested her head on his shoulder, then placed her hand over his. "Tell me, what drove him to visit his brother one last time? What did Antonio remember in that last session?"

"I cannot continue discussing my patient's sessions," Vincent said, wanting to pull his hand away but unable to resist the warmth of her hand on his.

"Why not?"

"This is not something I can do. It's confidential." Vincent wanted her to leave because if she didn't stop, he might regret his impulses. Her touch made him want her.

Raven squeezed his hand, then let go. "I'll leave, but I'll not leave your mind. He told you about his past, didn't he? What did he say? If you don't tell me, I'll—"

"What?" Wondering if she had just read his mind, Vincent stared at her. He hadn't said anything about leaving, yet she had responded to his thought as if she heard it. "Are you threatening me?" he asked, refusing to allow her to play with him.

"I'm warning you. This is too dangerous for you or anyone else to deal with, unless you have powers to protect yourself."

"You're not serious," Vincent said, laughing for a moment, then choking on his cough when he saw the disdain in her face. "My procedures are perfectly safe. Hypnotherapy is incredibly effective and safe. There's nothing mystical about it—it just enables us to delve into, and therefore use the vast resource, of the mind."

"I'm not talking about your procedures. You don't understand what you are dealing with. I'm talking about real magick."

Raven got up from the couch and grabbed her bag, making Vincent stand up too. Once Raven straightened, she stepped toward him and stood inches away. Defiantly staring, Raven's eyes pierced through his veneer into his deep-seated male instincts. Even the effects of her breathing made him want her—that gentle uplift of her chest as she sucked the air in, then her chest lowering ever so slightly as she exhaled.

43

While intoxicated by a faint smell of some exotic flower, Vincent grabbed the charm on her zipper and unzipped her dress just enough to reveal her breasts spilling out of a low-cut, black bra. He looked up and locked eyes with Raven as he slid his index finger into her cleavage. Penetrating the crack of those succulent breasts, he moved his fingertips in and out—dipping into the pleasures of the flesh. Raven just stood there and let him do it.

Then her sultry, jaded eyes forced him to slide the fingertips of his other hand up her neck to her chin and he bent over as if to kiss her swollen, blood-red lips. He froze as he rhythmically moved his fingers in and out of her cleavage and wondered if he could lower her to the floor right then and there. Instead, he kept sliding his fingers between her soft breasts as if they were having sex by this simple, yet erotic movement inside her beautiful cleavage. Finally, he tilted her chin upward and brushed his lips over hers.

In an instant, she shoved him away. It was a shove that demolished his male instincts when she stepped toward him and slapped him on the cheek—a hard, swift slap.

Yanking the zipper pull back up to her neck, Raven whirled around and headed for the door. Vincent frowned, regretting his indiscretion. He'd never done such a thing in his office before. Knowing he'd been totally unprofessional, he regretted compromising Raven's integrity in his office of all places. Just because she may have been Antonio's mistress didn't mean she was a wanton woman for Christ's sake.

Still frowning, he watched her walk away, and every fiber of her skintight dress responded with a distinctive shift from the perpetual movement of her ample, yet voluptuous behind. He rubbed his cheek and smiled at her shapely legs tapering down from that little black dress, making the ruffled hem flare out as her generous hips swayed with each step. Feeling guilty, Vincent looked down. That Italian machismo forced him to react. He vowed to harness his male instincts from now on because he had been totally reckless. But there had never been a woman like her in his office before—she was too mysterious, too mystical and therefore too attractive to him. Most women didn't even know about the layers of the soul or the spirit, for that matter. The women he knew didn't even care. Knowing his life was a contradiction, Vincent realized that his American heritage made his desires unprofessional and sexist, while his Italian blood made it instinctual and hot.

Vincent looked up just in time to catch a glimpse of Raven descending the stairs. "*Bella donna,*" he called out, stretching his arms open wide, palms up, but Raven kept on walking.

CHAPTER FOUR
DIANA

Aspen, Colorado

Time Warp
January 7, 2004
FULL Moon

The home Diana once shared with Antonio was situated on Red Mountain in Aspen, yet built in the classic Italianate style. The rusticated stonework of the cupola atop the center gable made the Aspen mansion look as if it had been flown in from Italy instead of built from scratch. With wide, overhanging eaves supported by intricately carved brackets and hooded, arched windows, the house was an Old World prototype of Italianate architecture. It was designed by the Grigori brothers from Rome and Diana fell in love with the place at first sight, but now the rambling estate made her depressed because without Antonio, it meant nothing. Upon her return, after a four-month hiatus of intensive therapy, Diana discovered even more hidden secrets in this place she called home. What she once considered her reality had dissipated into the unknown.

In Antonio's office, hundreds of antique, leather-bound books lined the walls of the dark study known as his sacred ground. Black mahogany shelving gleamed from the recessed lighting above, casting obscure shadows that bounced off the gilded tomes, making the dark leather volumes vanish among the golden ones. Heavy tapestry drapes covered the windows, turning the light into indigo ink throughout the room. Diana moved among the shadows, wanting to turn on an overhead light, but there was none.

As she sat down beside her best friend Tess on the couch, she felt like she was having a nervous breakdown. After the past four

months of psychiatric care as an in-patient at the Columbine Recovery Center in the small mountain town of Frisco, Colorado, Diana decided she wasn't going back anymore because not only did that place make her crazy, but this one did too. She couldn't continue rehashing her life with a stranger, but then she couldn't continue wandering aimlessly around this house feeling sorry for herself either. Wanting to give up, Diana tried to keep her emotions in check while her best friend visited. She wasn't going back to the center no matter what anyone said, and now that Tess was here maybe she could help bring back some sense of normality.

But the overwhelming loss of her husband kept coming back, especially here in his study. Normally flames roared in the fireplace, but after Antonio's passing, there were no more fires. Immediately after Antonio's death, Diana told the housekeeping staff to leave the ashes in the fireplace because those ashes were what remained of their last fire together. From the beginning, nightly fires had been their ritual. Even though there was a drought in Colorado and fires were forbidden, Antonio claimed his fires would not cause damage to the forest because the chimney was specifically designed to prevent ash and fire from falling on the roof or nearby groves.

Antonio insisted on preparing the fireplace in the study instead of having the butler arrange it because once the fire burned, the study became their private hideaway for making love. Diana stared at the slate-colored ashes in the fireplace until her vision blurred. Blinking to make the tears go away, Diana struggled with her grief.

Snippets of his irresistible Italian accent and magnetic charm kept playing in her mind. Glimpses of him laughing mixed in with his radiant smile kept reappearing in her mind. Just this morning, she finally decided to retrieve the will so that the lawyers would stop hounding her about it. She'd been putting it off for the past four months, and the lawyers kept telling her there was more, even though Antonio had willed everything to her. But once she found the will in the vault, even that upset her because there was an addendum that she'd never seen, and in that legal document was an entirely different legacy. From the looks of the will, Antonio had lied about his work and his position being confidential. She discovered that he owned a *Villa* in Rome and all the rest of his real estate without any debt, and now everything belonged to her. She'd married a billionaire who didn't need to work for anyone because he had already retired on his assets. But that didn't matter; what mattered was that the man that she once knew as her husband was gone.

Thankful to have Tess beside her, Diana tried to focus on her friend instead of her late husband. Six years ago, Tess had been her nurturing art teacher in Boulder during college, but her teaching role hadn't stopped Tess from becoming Diana's closest friend. After the class with Tess ended, Diana knew she had a friend forever. Diana watched Tess stare at the opening of the vault. The enormous painting, mounted on a swinging door with hinges, revealed the walk-in vault Antonio had shown her the day after they were married.

"I found an addendum to the will—it was hidden in there," Diana said, pointing at the vault. "In this box." Diana gestured at the decrepit wooden box on the coffee table. Running her fingers over the intricate carved glyphs, she wondered what the archaic symbols meant, then picked up the ancient box and placed it in her lap.

Tess looked at Diana, then frowned. "I knew you were upset."

"There were many secrets he kept from me," Diana said, trying to sound strong, yet still fighting back the tears. "In the addendum to the will, there were lots of surprises." Diana's voice trailed off as she thought of the surprises on her wedding day. Trying to stay focused, she opened the box and sifted through the contents.

"Why didn't he tell you?" Tess asked, shaking her head.

"When we married, he showed me that will," Diana said as she pointed to the document on the table. "The one without the addendum. The addendum says we own a *Villa* in Italy that's now mine." Diana rummaged through the contents of the box until she found the keys, then dangled them in the air to show Tess.

"I don't get it. Why wouldn't he tell you?"

Diana threw the keys back into the box and grabbed the letter. "And there was also a note, but it's not written to me. It's addressed to Antonio." She stared at the wax seal that must have been broken by her husband four months ago. "It was addressed to a post box in Aspen so I wouldn't find out. I think he was having an affair."

"Antonio had a mistress?"

"You know as well as I do, he was always traveling, but I didn't know he left the country. Listen to this, *Antonio, please return to Roma immediately. According to Tana, there will be many deaths. Senseless deaths that may not occur if we are together. Four days a week is not enough time. We cannot change the future if you are in the States—you must live here. Please move back to Roma, our home.* And it's signed, *Il Vostro Caro, Raven.* What does that mean?"

On the couch, Tess wrapped her arm around Diana and frowned.

"What does *il vostro caro* mean?" Diana demanded.

"Your beloved."

After hearing those two words, Diana cried and gave up on holding her emotions back. Crying felt good, because she'd fought back the tears all the way through the wake and even the funeral; in fact, she hadn't cried in front of anyone except the psychiatrist who kept digging deeper into her emotions. She'd kept the tears private during all this time, and now she had to let go. Tess hugged Diana while she wept. No words were spoken, just silence. Once Tess let go, she quickly gave Diana some tissues to dry her eyes.

"He must have read it before we went to the party at the Atwoods. See the postmark?" Diana leaned back and sunk into the pillows of the couch, clearly exhausted from the power of intense grief. "Now what do I do? Ignore the fact that my husband loved someone else?"

Tess shook her head.

"He told me he has a brother, who I never knew about until the night of the accident." Diana closed her eyes, trying not to cry again.

"He told me he never had family—then he met you."

"His brother, Luca," Diana said. "Is a *Stregone* like Antonio."

"A what?"

"Male witch." Diana pulled herself together, sat up, then reached for the photo in the box and stared at it. "Antonio warned me about his brother the night of the accident. And after I saw Luca's picture, I had a dream about him."

"Good God, Antonio never told me he was a witch." Tess frowned as she reached for the photo.

Diana looked at the picture once more, then handed it to Tess. "I'm sure it was him, not my husband, and that upsets me because it was an erotic dream." Diana's cheeks felt like they were on fire. "He made me come to him."

"He made you do what?" Tess asked, squinting her hazel-colored eyes at the man in the photo as if she already loathed him.

Since Diana wasn't even sure what happened with Luca in her dream, she couldn't really tell Tess about it. Diana leaned over, elbows on her knees, and messed up her already tousled hair with both hands. That was the problem with her; she couldn't make decisions or grab life and go for it. Instead, she cowered and crept along, making herself miserable with her insecurities.

Diana looked Tess straight in the eyes. "I need your help," she whispered. "I can't go on."

"You need to go to Rome and start a new life," Tess said. "I don't care if witches are there. We need to go anyway."

Diana shook her head. "I can't do that."

"We'll leave immediately. It's already been decided."

Diana froze and looked Tess in the eye. "You're serious, aren't you?"

Tess nodded, bobbing her head so that several curls slipped down into her eyes.

"You want me to go with you to Rome. Why?" Diana felt a knot of fear in her stomach as she placed her hand over the pain that was still there.

"Because you need to face your demons, Di," Tess said. "That's where the secrets are hidden, and that's where you'll find answers. If you uncover Antonio's way of life there, then maybe you'll understand his motivation. We need to understand so that you can go on."

Trying not to slip back into fear and doubt, Diana stared at the simplistic line drawing of Buddha on her friend's tight purple shirt and thought about how, even as a little girl, Diana hated

change. She didn't want to leave Aspen, but after the letter, the *Villa* and the dream, she felt as if she were going insane. Normally it would take days, even years, for her to make any kind of change, but not with Tess around. She never allowed indecision or inaction.

Tess made her Mona Lisa-like smile and Diana frowned. "You need to stop thinking about what you lost and concentrate on what you've found." Tess stood, then placed her hands on her hips as she continued. "You need to experience life in Rome. I know what you're doing—you're obsessing about the past and what you've lost, and that will get you nowhere. I suggest we live at the *Villa*, then hunt down Antonio's brother and the other woman. You know too much but not enough, so now you must know more. Either you remain in this house and go berserk, or you leave the country to unravel the past and heal. I'll come with you to help you get situated."

After five years of knowing Tess, Diana still couldn't understand why Tess remained her friend. Tess was wild, crazy and totally eccentric, while Diana was a conservative Catholic girl and rather boring when it came to adventure. Tess incessantly begged Diana to stop being so closed-minded and live a little.

"I've already made the decision for you," Tess said. "I'll book the flight and make the arrangements. Trust me, you must do this because this is the only way to fully recover and heal the wounds of the past."

Diana shook her head, but Tess continued. "I know, you're still numb from the accident, and you think it's too soon to do anything, but you have to make a change. I know it's a miracle that you lived while everyone else didn't." Tess paused, then swept her hair upward with both hands. "But you have to face reality and find out more about the man you loved otherwise, you'll be depressed for who knows how long."

Diana bit her lip, thinking she'd been alone ever since her parents died in the plane crash. When her dad tried to land their private plane at the Pitkin County Airport in Aspen, an engine failure made him lose control. Over the past four months, she often wondered why both families died in Aspen. Maybe she needed to move far away from this place. She still remembered the day her family died, and she still harbored the pain and the guilt for not going with them on that family vacation. Everyone died in that crash; her mom, her dad and even her baby sister—everyone, except her. It was just like the car accident in the blizzard with Antonio. Everyone died, except her. And she blamed herself because she was at the wheel. If only she had steered differently, then maybe she wouldn't have lost control. Maybe she was cursed. Maybe she couldn't ever love or be loved by anyone because then they'd die. Had Antonio ever loved her? She wasn't sure anymore after the letter from the woman. And now, the only person who loved her was Tess, her best friend. If Tess wanted to go to Rome, Diana would have to follow because Tess was the only one who loved her and had lived through it.

She met Tess in 1999 when Tess taught an "oils" class in college. Her work with oils had been phenomenal, but now her focus was sculpture. Although Diana's technique was similar to Cassatt's, Tess's sculptures were more like Rodin. Tess, erotica painter and college professor at Colorado University, had been the talk of the town. When Diana moved back to her hometown of Boston after graduation, they still kept in touch, even after Tess decided to quit teaching and move from Boulder to Aspen. And now her crowded Aspen shows, where she was known for her erotica art, meant Tess was successful, at least by Diana's standards. She stared at Tess as she adjusted the Japanese sticks poked into the knotted hair atop her head. Even though Tess was almost twenty years older than Diana, at forty-five, Tess looked as if she were in her thirties.

Diana tried to ignore the pit in her stomach as she watched Tess confidently cross her legs in her strategically ripped, low-cut jeans. This woman exuded complete satisfaction and fulfillment even though she didn't need a man and didn't even want one for keeps. But then, Tess had always been the go-getter—a woman who knew who she was and what she wanted, while Diana kept lingering in the shadows of self doubt. One thing they had in common was they both knew wealth, yet they remained devoted to their work as if they needed the money. Finding a rich artist for a friend had been hard, because being rich and being an artist normally didn't happen at the same time. At least they both could afford to leave the country.

"You are going to Rome with me because I won't take no for an answer. And now that you have a *Villa* there, we have a place to stay." Tess walked over to the vault and stepped inside. "Good God, this is awesome. I never knew you had a walk-in vault." Tess fingered the Black Madonna and child showcased in the center of the crypt.

Diana watched Tess carefully touch the statue her husband once coveted. She never understood why anyone would even sculpt a Black Madonna because, as far as she was concerned, both Madonna and baby Jesus had been Caucasian. But when Antonio showed her the piece, he held it in his hands as if it were price-less, then told her about his search for the sculpture for more than a decade until he finally found it in France. Antonio made Diana promise to take care of his Black Madonna if he died because he claimed there was no other like her. Diana intended to ask Anto-nio about the artist, but she didn't get a chance to inquire after An-tonio became adamant about the specifics of the will—the will without the addendum.

Tess shouted from inside the vault as she continued her spiel. "We can show our work at a gallery on *via Margutta*. I'll have our people at the studio check into space for a gallery in Rome. We can have separate studios for both of us in the gallery, one for sculpt-ing and another for painting, but maybe the *Villa* will be the place to work—it's up to you, okay?"

"It sounds like you've already done the research. Did Antonio tell you about the *Villa di Spagna?*"

"No, Di," Tess answered, turning toward Diana and looking straight into her eyes as she spoke. "For several years now, I've wanted to move to Rome and work so this is good for both of us. Our work is critical because that will help you heal. I've noticed that when you paint, you become peaceful and grounded and that process will give you strength. We must focus on our work, then unravel Antonio's secrets together."

"You're serious, aren't you?"

Tess nodded, then turned to open a drawer in the jewelry ar-moire. "Where did you get all of this?"

Diana bit her lip as she remembered the generous gifts from Antonio. Tess held up a string of pearls Antonio had given Diana a week before he died—given to her for no reason at all, just like the rest of the jewelry inside the armoire that Antonio insisted was hers. It was filled with heirlooms, and he kept giving her more jewelry to fill it.

"I've never seen a vault like this in a house before," Tess added. "It was our secret. Talk about being paranoid about security. It's like another world in there."

The vault, filled with furs, diamonds and priceless artwork, had been Antonio's place of reprieve. When he took her into the vault at the beginning of their relationship, he had been thorough in explaining the treasures of the vault, but not so thorough when it came to his secrets.

Wanting to avert her thoughts about Antonio, she got up from the couch and entered the vault to join Tess. Diana blinked when she noticed a seam in the upholstered wall that was shaped like a small door in the deepest part of the vault—a seam she had never seen before. She knelt down in front of it, then pushed at the wall around the seam, wondering why it was there. Pressing her fingertips around the entire seam, she finally felt a button on the left side and pushed it. The camouflaged door opened.

"What's that?" Tess asked, coming up from behind her.

"I had no idea this was here," Diana said, poking her head inside, then flipping on the light switch within. Soft rays illuminated a tunnel carved out of mahogany. She hesitated, and Tess gently squeezed Diana's shoulder. Diana moved aside and Tess fell to her knees, then crawled through the passageway. Kneeling down, Diana watched her friend move quickly down the shadowy tunnel, then followed. The arched tunnel, bathed in golden light, lasted for about fifteen feet, then opened into an inner chamber. Inside the inner chamber, Diana stood and walked over to a table at the far end of the crypt so that she could hold onto the edge of the tabletop in an effort to steady herself. Antonio had kept this chamber a secret even though he must have coveted the things in this place too. The walls of the clandestine chamber were lined with shelves that displayed cryptic volumes, black cauldrons and morbid playing cards. She turned around and gripped the edge of the table harder, trying not to collapse. But the table was not a normal tabletop; it was an altar placed in front of the center of an ornate wooden triptych carved on the wall. The carving was a relief of an old man staring into a crystal ball, and the man was surrounded by detailed carvings of a place that looked similar to the one Diana stood in. In front of the triptych, arranged on the black velvet tablecloth, a knife, stick and bowl were placed in what looked like designated places. Candles, crystal skulls and incense holders made it clear—this was an altar for witches. Diana moaned, and images of Antonio practicing his witchcraft here made her eyes blur.

"I never knew him," Diana whispered. "He never told me."

"How could he not share this exotic hideaway?"

"I'm not so sure I want to discover any more of his secrets."

"This is creepy," Tess said, staring at a framed picture wedged between an ancient scroll and a stack of volumes in Aramaic script. Tess grabbed the picture, then walked over to show it to Diana. "Isn't this Antonio's brother?"

Diana leaned into Tess and stared at the black-and-white photo. "There's no mistaking him, is there?"

"The guy looks eccentric with those heavy, black sunglasses on his pearly white face." Tess whistled under her breath.

"He even looks like a witch, or a vampire."

"What's that in his hand?" Tess asked. "That's odd," she added, staring at the photo, then looking down at the altar. She did it again: stared at the photo, then the altar.

Diana tensed as she realized what concerned Tess. "What's that supposed to be?" she asked, pointing at Luca's hand in the photograph.

"It's a crystal wand. See the way it catches the light in the photo? He's standing at this very altar, holding this." Tess picked up what looked like a crystal stick; it was an object that was exactly like the one in the photo. Waving it in the air, Tess added, "He was standing here, right here where we're standing now."

"Look at his other hand." Diana hesitated for a beat, then gestured at the knife on the table. "He's got the knife too."

CHAPTER FIVE

DIANA

Rome, Italy

Time Warp
February 19, 2004
Late Afternoon

As the driver wedged the Mercedes through congested traffic, Diana struggled with a déjà vu of the accident just five months ago. In the backseat, she gripped the edge of the seat cushion and tried to look calm so that Tess wouldn't notice. In a month and a half, Tess had moved them both to Rome, and now Diana had to come to grips with what her best friend had done. Sitting beside her in the backseat, Tess turned and smiled at her and Diana smiled back. At every intersection, millions of miniature cars and shrilly *vespas* funneled into the gridlock. Problem was, all the drivers insisted on being first in the garbled mess.

"*Togliti dai piedi!*" the driver shouted, pinching his thumb and index finger together and waving it at a young girl on a *vespa* who almost hit their front bumper.

Diana steadied herself, then turned to Tess. But instead of interpreting his words, Tess mouthed, *You don't want to know.*

"Do they all drive like this?" Diana asked.

"You'd better get used to it," Tess answered as they jostled from the curvy road.

Diana bit her lip. Apparently, Romans didn't understand what lanes meant because no one drove in them. But this guy was even worse; he drove on the sidewalk. She tried not to think about car accidents as they sliced through the traffic just inches away from *vespas* on both sides. Ever since the night of the crash, Diana still hadn't shaken her phobia about driving a car. She looked out beyond the traffic, determined to forget the accident and her fears.

"The good news is I've double-checked and the movers have already come and gone," Tess said. "And the decorator did her thing too."

"Decorator?"

"Viviana, remember? She designed our studios and handled everything being shipped to the *Villa* and the gallery. There's been an entire team of people working on it." Tess smiled. "You even said yes after I talked with you about it. I asked you the other day in the library. I just wanted everything we need here because we have that show right away at the gallery on *via Margutta*, remember?"

"You gave someone a key to the *Villa?*"

"You gave it to me, remember? And I had extra keys made. Are you alright, Di?" Tess frowned. "Viviana came highly recommended by a friend of mine in Rome. Don't you remember me telling you this while I was making the arrangements? They were shipping our stuff out, so I had to take care of it on the other end. I just let them handle it."

"Of course, I'm just a bit confused from everything happening so fast." Diana rubbed her forehead and tried to think. "Guess I've been in a stupor since September."

Tess patted her knee. "Don't you worry, it's all taken care of. I just spared you the details, that's all. I wanted our equipment and everything here before we came," Tess said. "Viviana designed a couple of fabulous rooms for our studios, so I told her to go ahead after getting your approval. You don't remember that?"

Diana nodded yes, but the truth was she didn't remember a thing.

Looking content, Tess gazed out the window. "We're not far from the *Villa* now."

"It doesn't matter how far or close it is," Diana said, moving as the car veered to the left, almost sideswiping the *vespa* next to them, "because we're going to be dead before we ever get there." She grabbed the hand loop above her head, then realized that after dying and coming back, she didn't fear death anymore, yet she feared being in Rome.

Tess frowned at the look on Diana's face. "Are you okay, Di?" Tess asked again, putting her arm around Diana.

Diana nodded.

The driver stomped on the brakes, because he almost hit a *vespa*. But then the motorist behind him cursed and practically jumped out of his car when he stuck his head out the window and yelled. Their driver waved his hand in the air again, only this time making a screwing motion against his head.

Stepping on the gas, the driver accelerated and Diana held on tight as the Mercedes shot through the archway of an ancient wall.

"We've just entered ancient *Roma* through the Aurelian Wall. Long ago, the wall surrounded the city, and served as a fortress," Tess explained. "The odd thing is, if you look at ancient maps and even check current ones, it's obvious the Roman Wall looks like it was built in the shape of a wolf."

The brick wall, certainly the most intricate, complex fortification Diana had ever seen, was pure magick once they passed through it. What had once been mundane, run-down shops and residences became a menagerie of sophisticated artistic and architectural expression. On the other side of the wall, the city became another realm: an ancient, yet classical realm of ruined temples, forums and obelisks; of architectural wonders in Renaissance and baroque forms; and of Etruscan and classical Greek style shaped by the Romanesque version of arches, vaults and domes. Diana's heart ached as she felt a deep nostalgia for something ancestral that inherently resides within the soul—something ancient that symbolized the past with its timeless beauty that would last throughout eternity.

"It'll be a miracle if he can just get us to the *di Spagna*," Tess said, motioning at the driver to take another route. "Good God, he keeps taking the scenic route." Speaking in Italian to the driver, Tess pointed to the right as the driver turned left. "Let's take a walk after we're settled in."

After twisting through endless cobblestone streets and almost hitting three pedestrians, they finally ascended a hill where the driver slammed on his brakes just as Tess pronounced their arrival at the *Piazza della Trinità dei Monti*. As Tess searched her pocket for the correct euro, Diana jumped out of the car. Thankful to be on stable ground, she walked to the overlook at the top of the summit.

Painters loitered, selling their artwork alongside an old man selling blood-red roses. Diana stood behind an artist who was sketching a young girl. The artist's subject squirmed in her chair, eager to be finished. Diana walked to the railing and looked down, then recognized the historic Spanish Steps that descended just below the overlook. Masses of people below either lingered on the stairs or milled around the gushing fountain at the bottom. Teenagers loitered on the steps smoking cigarettes, some singing Italian lyrics and tourists snapped shots in the prisms of light created by the terra-cotta sunset.

"Did you say number eight on the *Rampa Mignanelli?*" Diana heard Tess yell. "If that's the one, then it's not a *Villa*, it's a *villina*, but then maybe that's another anomaly like Spanish Steps versus Italian ones."

Tess laughed as Diana searched her bag to find the address she'd written down. As soon as she verified that it was indeed number eight, the driver's face darkened.

Tess shook her head. "He says it's haunted."

Diana followed them to the far side of the *piazza* where another set of steps led downward, but these steps looked like private ones compared to the Spanish Steps that were right alongside it on the other side of the wall. As the driver pointed downward, Diana noticed that the stairway descended into a residence, then veered to the left. Every muscle in Diana's body tensed when she saw the foreboding *Villa* below. *Was this the place where her husband shared his bed with another woman while she remained a faithful, unsuspecting wife?*

"That's number eight?" Diana asked, turning to stare at her friend's solemn nod.

As Tess dealt with the driver, Diana decided to go down the steep steps. In a trancelike state, she heard the driver's reluctant voice fade away. And then, time stopped.

It seemed impossible that the *Villa di Spagna*, tucked midway off to the side of the Spanish Steps yet hidden by a massive wall, was invisible from the crowd of tourists nearby. As she stepped down, the Italian Renaissance *Villa* seemed to taunt her with its haunting presence. Biting her lip, she hesitated, then continued her descent. The rough, milled, terra-cotta stucco looked like it had been washed with subtle shades of reds, nudes and pinks as if Mother Nature had painted it through inclement weather. Perched atop the wall going down, spiked plants potted in urns shaped like winged gargoyles glared as if protecting the place from foreigners, while the tightly closed black shutters of the *Villa* guarded its sinister secrets. Even the deeply carved stone arches that framed the windows echoed the eerie reality of the domain—arches that protruded above the front door and lower windows; arches shaped into relief forms of wild, sensuous roses dripping from wicker baskets. The front door beckoned her with its black gloss and brass lion head knobs. Diana tried to ignore her instinctive fear of the place, then froze once she reached the bottom of the steps.

She turned away in an effort to ward off illness. To her left, the back wall of couture boutiques created even more privacy; on the right, a high cement wall barely contained the wild overgrowth of the courtyard, buffering the *Villa* even further from the popular Spanish Steps. Lush greenery swelled over a black, mesh-covered, wrought iron gate. Large, fiddle-leafed plants and exotic ferns spilled over the wall, and monolithic olive and eucalyptus trees silenced the sounds of the city and made her feel like she had just transcended her world into another.

Diana walked up to the iron gate, then peered through the twisted latticework, but the thorny brush blocked her view. An azalea branch, whipped by a sudden gust of wind, poked her scalp, then yanked her hair as she pulled back. She struggled as the branch tightened its grip.

She jumped when she heard Tess. "Looks like you've got some landscaping to do," she said, helping Diana free her hair from the gnarled branch.

"That's part of the *Villa di Spagna?*"

"Has to be because the wall juts off from the *Villa*. If you peek through the vines, you can see that small courtyard is attached. Are you okay? You look like you're going to faint. Why don't you let me open the door, Di?" Tess held out her hand, and Diana searched for the key in her pocket. "This should be interesting. The driver won't take the luggage inside."

"He refused?" Diana handed Tess the key. "He's not the only one who doesn't want to go inside."

Light faded into dusk as Tess slipped the key into the lock and Diana stepped back. She wanted to stifle the foreboding feeling in her stomach but didn't know how. Instead, she cowered behind Tess and fought the urge to turn and run. Once the door opened, a strange odor invaded her senses. Not wanting to go in, she watched Tess search in vain for the light switch.

"Do you smell that?" Diana asked, wondering if she'd lost her sense of smell, as well as her mind. She wanted to leave this sinister place—do anything but step inside.

"What, in heavens name—"

"That smell. It makes this place even creepier. But there's something else that's wrong. Do you feel it too?" Diana stepped back. "It's intense, as if the walls are closing in on us."

Tess pointed into the darkness and yelled to the driver behind them, "*Bagaglio, per favore.*"

As the driver resisted, Diana woke from what seemed like a deep trance. She blinked, then decided to take control of her incessant fears. Stepping forward, she fumbled around until she found the light switch, turned it on and marched into the house. Knowing she had to fight this cowering side of herself, she needed to face her fears for once in her life. She couldn't tolerate her own spineless reaction that kept re-creating the ghosts in her mind, ghosts of a *Villa* that looked like an entity instead of a house.

"We'll have to open a few windows to get rid of that odor," Tess said.

Diana headed for the stairs. "Anyone here?" she yelled.

She hesitated for a moment, then decided to take the plush, carpeted spiral staircase to the second floor. As she climbed the steps, she stared at a rug in the foyer below that dominated the center of the entryway. Its mesmerizing labyrinth of circular colors in burnt rusts, reds and golds appeared to move as she ascended the stairway. When she looked to her right, shadows on the spiral staircase danced before her in shades of amber from the tear-drop chandelier in the center of the entry. At the top of the stairs, elaborate gilded frames were mounted along the corridor with paintings that looked familiar, yet Diana couldn't pinpoint the artist. She studied a painting of a male nude posed with his legs spread open wide, then recognized the seven-layer technique in the oils, yet she still wasn't sure of the artist. The man's erection, the focal point of the painting, was obvious, yet the artist's signature was illegible. *Could it be Tess's work?* Diana wondered.

Antonio never seemed interested in erotic art, and his home in Aspen never had anything like that in it while she'd been there. Diana shook her head, still unsure about anything her husband did; apparently, she never knew the inner workings of the man. Walking over to another painting, Diana studied the technique, trying to decide whether it was Tess's work by examining the brushstrokes of the nude, yet this time the strokes only captured the muscular curvatures of a male nude's tight behind. Diana leaned over and looked closely at the bottom corners of the piece to check if it was signed but could see only her shadow. The technique sure looked like the canvases Tess used to paint.

She shook her head, marched down the corridor, then pushed open the double doors at the end. But as the heavy doors opened, her resolve turned into dread when she suddenly realized she'd entered the master suite. The exotic aroma that permeated the room originated from a smoldering bundle of dried, leafy sticks tied together and propped up in an incense holder. She froze when she noticed that the smoldering ash hadn't quite gone out. Someone was here.

Diana searched the room for an intruder as she looked inside each closet and behind every curtain. The windows were closed and the only adjoining room was the bath, so she finally decided no one was there. Dropping to her knees, she grabbed the silver dust ruffle hanging below the mattress and flung it up. Diana bit her lip when she realized there was nothing to fear, then stood and glared at the bed.

She refused to believe Antonio betrayed her, yet images of the elegant handwriting in the letter kept coming back. And now that

Antonio was gone, Diana couldn't even confront him with her discovery. If he'd been unfaithful in this room, on this bed, then Diana had to face the facts. She didn't hold back her tears as she defiantly glared at the bed. Not knowing how much time had passed, she brushed her tears away when she heard Tess come into the room.

"You'll be fine," Tess said. "You're a survivor."

Scanning the room, Diana searched for a tissue. Tess squeezed her arm and gently guided Diana toward the bed. Snatching a tissue from the box atop the nightstand, Tess handed it to Diana.

"You need to rest, Di. That was a long flight," Tess said. She grabbed a chenille throw from the chaise nearby, then made sure Diana was tucked in before she turned to go.

"I'm not tired, are you?"

"It's jet lag," Tess said, heading for the door.

"Wait, did you see that?" Diana pointed to the bunch of herbs on the nightstand. The smoldering had stopped and the bundle looked like a bunch of burnt twigs.

"Didn't know Antonio liked incense."

"It was burning when I came in."

Tess raised a brow. "I'll look around. Maybe it was Viviana. You rest." She turned to go, and within seconds she slipped through the double doors.

Diana tried to relax on the bed. But when she closed her eyes, all she could see was Antonio making love on this bed. Feeling sick, she opened her eyes and saw her dark reflection in the black mirror overhead.

Diana jumped out of bed and stared at the mirror in disgust. He must have watched her on top of him in the mirror above. She never knew Antonio liked that kind of thing. During the short period of time she had been with Antonio, he hadn't done erotic things like that with her, except for their love fest on the bed of rose petals when they married. He didn't need any gimmicks with her, because it was already erotic without any props.

Diana searched the room for more erotica, then spotted something strange dangling from a twisted hook on the wall. She walked over and touched the braided leather strips attached to a long, shiny handle. About twenty-two inches long, the leather strips had been braided into nine braids and formed a short bundle.

Turning away, Diana yelled for Tess. She was trying not to overreact from finding sex toys in her husband's bedroom, but these new discoveries of Antonio's other life made her feel confused and depressed. She couldn't stop thinking about her husband coming here every week while he was alive. In the inner chamber by the vault, she found his weekly airline tickets to Rome purchased for the entire month of September. Saddened by the realization that he hid those tickets from her, she needed to face the truth.

The double doors opened and Tess, looking breathless, entered. "What's wrong?"

"Look," Diana said, sweeping her arm out toward the angled mirror on the ceiling, then gesturing at the leather braids that dangled from the glossy handle on the wall. "What's this?"

Tess walked over to the thing and quickly took it off the hook. Gripping the handle, she expertly fingered the pliant braids of leather as she brushed them across her palm.

Tess smiled. "It's a cat."

"What are you talking about?"

"It's used to strike the skin in various sensual places on the body," Tess said, now slapping the leather braids against the top of her hand.

"How do you know this?"

"I've had one used on me before."

Diana collapsed into the chaise, wondering how she could have people so close to her, yet never really know them at all. This side of Tess was a mystery to Diana, and seeing her friend so engrossed with such a violent, abusive toy made her wonder what else she didn't know about Tess. Diana shook her head, certain she kept many secrets.

"It's obscene. This place looks like a den of sexual perversion. My husband didn't do things like that. He was sensual, but not twisted like this. How could he hide these things from me?" Diana quickly looked away, not knowing how to process her new revelation. "How do you know about the cat?" she asked.

"Years before I knew you, I had a lover."

Diana looked Tess in the eye. "You engaged in sado-masochism with him?"

Tess jerked her head back as if in defiance. "You criticize something you don't even understand. It isn't about hurting another or causing pain; it's about trusting and taking someone beyond his or her limit of sensation. It's about playing out one's fantasy in total secrecy and safety."

"Didn't he hurt you?"

"Just a little, but by fulfilling a fantasy, the mind taps into levels where it hasn't been before. Slight pain becomes a stimulant."

"I don't believe it," Diana said, shaking her head but still curious to know more. "He hit you with a leash?" she asked.

"Not a leash—a whip, also known as a flogger, but this particular type of whip is called the cat o' nine tails because the leather strips have been braided into nine braids versus a flogger, which has leather strips without the braids." Tess put the thing back on the hook. "When the cat is used on a person who's blindfolded, slapping specific areas of the body takes the person to another level of sexual stimulation. It's total sensation instead of visualization. And visualizing is extremely overdone in this society, especially when it comes to sex and the body. When you sense something or become stimulated, you heighten the effect of erotica."

"It seems a bit too hard-core for me."

"No wonder Antonio didn't take you there. But it's an exotic world worth traveling to. If you're with someone who knows what he's doing, it creates a whole new experience together. One is bottom, one is top. The bottom receives, while the top orchestrates the experience. You must be able to trust the one in the dominant position—the one called the top. And, if you have that trust established between top or dominant and bottom or submissive, then there is no other adventure that compares to that experience. For me, the best part was when we took turns playing *top* and *bottom*."

Diana bit her lip, trying not to look shocked. Although she was disgusted, she wanted to know more. "How could you even go there? Do you think Antonio did this?" she asked, repositioning herself on the chaise.

"Apparently, your husband had another life here. It's horrid that you had to find out about it this way and not through him." Tess came closer, then sat down on the chaise at Diana's feet.

Diana got up and stood by the window. "You enjoyed this kind of . . . play?"

"It was the best sex I've ever had," Tess explained. "Problem was, I then became jaded. No one else understood this kind of pleasure. Once you experience it and enjoy it, then most people label you as bad, evil or disgusting. If I ever suggested it with a partner, he'd look at me in horror. I never had it like that again."

"What happened to your lover?"

"He left the country once the summer ended, and I never heard from him again."

"Just what does the whip do?" Diana asked, fiddling with the curtain beside her.

"As long as the forbidden areas aren't whipped, it makes you want more. It takes you into another realm of pleasure—a place beyond words."

Diana drew back the gauzy curtain and searched the evening sky for answers. Framed by the mist, the full moon formed a pearl in the sky with platinum moonbeams radiating from its sphere. When the oyster-like shell shapeshifted its form into an omnipresent face, Diana turned away from the window. With its hazy luminescence, the moon had no answers.

Even though the gentle tone of her voice made Diana want to listen to her friend, another side of her refused to hear. Diana's eyes locked with Tess's for a moment, then Diana smiled. "You never cease to amaze me, my friend," she said. "Seems there's a lot more to you than I imagined."

She turned toward the window to look down at the courtyard below. *The courtyard looks as haunted as the Villa,* she thought. The small, grassy opening was decorated with marble statues of more nudes. Directly below, sculptures of naked ladies in erotic poses accentuated every intimate part of the body. From her vantage point above, the statues seemed to float in the air, yet were motionless in the light of the moon. The chalky statutes looked suspended in time as they danced in the private, overgrown garden. One statue looked so real, it moved.

Diana blinked. Directly below where she stood, a naked woman swayed in the moonlight as if in a trance. Opalescent moonbeams accentuated her milky breasts, and her ivory outstretched arms reached toward the moon. Diana clutched the curtain trying to catch her breath as the entire view of the garden spun around in her head until her knees buckled. Without warning, her fingertips slid down the drape and let go as she crumpled to the floor.

PART TWO
THE SEARCH

Stregheria is a passionate Magick. In order to show that they came freely to practice the Craft, Aradia, the fourteenth-century Holy Strega, instructed Italian Witches to be naked during rituals and be sexual with each other. Today's Stregas may not choose to intermingle so freely, but an earthly passion still powers Stregherian rites. It was not and is not a religion for those who are embarrassed by or ashamed of their all-too-human nature. Stregheria welcomes and empowers the many sides of humanity—mind, body and spirit.

Raven Grimassi
Italian Witchcraft

CHAPTER SIX
LUCA

Roma Sotterranea

February 20, 2004
New Moon

"You don't have to do it," Luca said, raising his arms, palms up in surrender. Luca felt the sleeves of his black robe fan out like a dark angel. *Somehow being a dark angel in the Sotterranea seemed apropos,* Luca mused. He smiled at Maddalena, the youngest of the *boschetto,* and hoped she was ready for the ways of the *Malandanti.*

The *Malandanti* had been doing sex magick together in secret for seven years in the *Villa de Marco*—the *Villa* that was buried underground as part of ancient *Roma*—but so far Maddalena had never been invited to those rites. The *Villa* underground was suitable for the rites because it provided the privacy, as well as the space they needed for sex magick. Much like *Hadrian's Villa* underground, the *Villa de Marco* had fountains, chambers, baths, theatres and temples, but it was an entirely different experience from the *Grotto* because the caves didn't have electricity and the pools weren't heated. Luca grinned as he thought of taking Maddalena into the sacred *Grotto* for sex magick instead of using his rustic *Villa.*

When his father was alive, he cherished Maddalena, so Luca waited to indoctrinate her into sex magick ritual. Luca waited because he was certain she would have told the *Sacerdote* about the secret rites of the *Malandanti*—rites that his father never would have allowed. But now there would be no one to tell because everyone did the rites—everyone except her. Janus didn't approve of being skyclad or doing sex magick, so Luca didn't even tell Maddalena about the New Ways while his father was alive. Then, after the *Sacerdote* died, he decided Maddalena was too depressed, so he waited until she recuperated from the loss. Now that his father had been gone for five months, he felt it was time to expose her to the New Ways. In the beginning, he felt certain Maddalena would convert to the new rites; she just needed time. Knowing he must initiate her tonight, Luca wanted to make her feel safe and secure.

"But I want to," Maddy said, shivering even though she hadn't removed her robe yet. "This is my family, because I don't have anyone else. And Janus—I mean, our *Sacerdote*—he was so kind to me. My real father hated me, but not Janus he cared. I never knew a man like him before. I was raised a Southern Baptist, and I hated that religion." She shook her head and her Medusa-like red hair snaked into her eyes. Maddy pressed her index finger against her pursed lips as if she'd just told him a secret. "I started practicing Wicca when I was thirteen, right after I ran away from those fanatical Southern Baptists. I went to New York and joined a coven."

Luca raised his brow. "Did they tell you about us in *Roma*?"

"They told me you left New York to join your father in the underground tunnels beneath Rome, then your entire coven followed you. My High Priestess called you the legendary *Malandanti*. So I scraped up the money by working the street reading palms and tarot. Some rich guy kept giving money to spend time with him, and that's how I got enough to come here. All he wanted was companionship, no sex mind you. But he was nasty—he thought sex was dirty, so he did other, strange things instead."

Maddy looked down when she talked and when she listened, her green eyes riveted on the restless flames of the black candelaba on the alter in the pagan temple of the *Villa de Marco*.

Luca touched Maddalena's silky arm. "This isn't having sex. It's sex magick, the most powerful there is. You don't have to do it if it scares you."

"I'm not scared."

"Janus would be proud of you—bringing the New Ways into fruition." Luca lied, but he wanted her to join the *Malandanti* without hesitation. He nodded and tried to encourage her to open up, feel relaxed and express her emotions. She needed someone who cared because Janus, her surrogate father, was gone. Luca knew he would be Maddy's lover in time; he just needed to get her in the right position to trust him. *Position.* Luca smiled as he thought of positioning her on the altar tonight. Trying not to think of Maddy's naked body beneath her black, shiny robe, Luca was keenly aware that her physical body was beyond mere words. Her curvaceous hips and breasts had always enthralled him. She was voluptuous in all the erogenous zones, yet the rest of her body was petite, taut even. Luca frowned, not wanting to be crude as he lusted for her physical body, but just the thought of her taking off her robe aroused him. With more than a decade difference in their ages, her beauty epitomized youth and freshness, and for a fleeting moment he wondered if she was a virgin because she looked like a teenager. Surely not. Regardless, he wouldn't let her be skyclad with any negative energy about being naked in front of him or the others, because then the magick wouldn't work.

"If it doesn't feel right, then don't take your clothes off," Luca said, sliding his hand up her arm and massaging it.

"We didn't do anything naked in New York," she said, cinching the long, black robe tighter around her body.

When she drew her robe around her, Luca squeezed her arm for encouragement. "Skyclad was the way it always used to be done, but now with all the worries of disease and dysfunction, the naked rites haven't been used as much as in the past. Being skyclad will create the strongest talisman possible. If you do this, you will begin our transition into the new rites. According to the *Gospel,* the sexual power of a woman or a man is the strongest force that can be raised from the body. Christians teach people to repress and be ashamed of nudity, even of their own sexuality, and this belief depletes them of their natural power."

"Will I be more powerful if I have sex?"

"No, this is not about overpowering, manipulating or using people for sex. This is not just for one—it's for all. Our sex magick will create the talisman to protect our people. And tonight, you will join the *Malandanti* in ritual."

"How are we going to make a talisman?" Maddy's big, green eyes opened wider as she spoke.

"We won't make it tonight. Tonight you will be initiated to some new rites—the *Malandanti* will help you through this because we have been doing these things for a long time now. Are you ready to join us?"

Maddy nodded, then froze as if she was unsure. "How long have you been doing this?" She paused. "What does sex magick mean, anyway?"

"I've been doing it over a decade. But ever since I arrived in *Roma*, it was my dream to have a *Malandanti* family do the modern rituals of sex magick here, and now that dream has become a reality. Besides being part of the *boschetto* after tonight, you will be a *Malandanti* too. We need you to join us because we are about to embark on a mission. Sex magick isn't about having sex—it's about harnessing energies raised through sexual activity. It is sex with a purpose."

Maddy put her hands on her hips, then shook her head. "You want me to have sex with you while the *Malandanti* watches, right? Did Janus agree to these rituals? No wonder he called you *malocchio*." Maddy shook her finger at him.

Luca frowned at the sound of the word *malocchio*, or "evil eye," the nickname his father called him. It meant the negative energy from a look, stare or glance. Known as the overlook, it could be used to bring devastation to those who received it. *Malocchio* was typically a look from someone who was envious of another's possessions. In ancient lore, the evil eye could be cast to obtain the property of another. Looking back, maybe his father was right because Luca had inherited his father's *boschetto*, and now they were the *Malandanti*. But nicknaming Luca *malocchio* meant his father suspected something.

"Janus agreed that the Roman Catholic Church needed to be stopped from executing the Second Inquisition, and sex magick is the only possible way to do that. He would be proud of us saving our people, and that's what matters."

Luca nodded to acknowledge Maddy's concern, then waited in silence for her to fully digest what he just said.

Over the past seven years, Luca had developed the rituals for sex magick in the *Villa de Marco*, which was an entire *Villa* buried in the *Sotterranea* beneath the *Castello del Pincio*. The *Villa de Marco*, a place that no outsider could enter because it was accessible only to those who could navigate through the intricate network of underground tunnels, was where the *Malandanti* could keep their ways secret, but now there would be no more secrets in the *Sotterranea*.

Luca put his arm around her to try to stop her shaking. "If you don't want to take off your robe, I understand."

"What's sex magick again?" she asked.

He clicked his tongue, then continued. "The *Gospel* says share your sexuality with whomever you may, in whatever manner you choose, because all acts of love and pleasure are rituals to the God and Goddess. Since sex is a natural, stimulating experience and an expression of love or lust, it's okay to gather power from it and use it for a higher purpose." Luca paused. "We can wait if this troubles you, or do it clothed," he added.

Maddalena, still trembling beneath the thin cloth of her robe, shook her head.

"You don't have to do it skyclad," Luca said again, slipping off his robe and covering Maddalena with it. *It's not that cold in the Sotterranea*, Luca thought. It warmed him that his nakedness felt so liberating and free. "Most of us have difficulties being naked when in fact the body, especially the female body, is an altar."

Maddy froze. Even though she tried averting her eyes, she still looked down when she asked. "You play—I mean, pray at the altar with it?"

"According to the Old Ways, the female body has always been sacred. Consider it an honor to do these rites. I would consider it an honor to be with you skyclad. And your beautiful body hidden in those robes deserves to be honored. In the past, females were the focus of many ancient and magickal rites because the power of a woman to give birth and nourish new life meant her body must be held sacred. Menstrual blood or the blood of the moon was often used for ritual markings in initiation ceremonies and

rites that return departed souls back into their clan. Many rites of long ago involved sexual union. But that's not what we will do tonight. Tonight we shall honor the Great Rite of Drawing Down the Moon for you."

Maddy looked up and locked eyes with Luca. Raising both hands, she unhooked the closure at her neck and threw the fabric off her shoulders until her robe slid to the floor. Struck by the sheer naked beauty of the woman who stood before him, Luca drank every pore of her body with his eyes, then touched her breast, barely able to hold it in one hand. He squeezed her erect nipple, rolling it between his thumb and index finger before letting go. Normally, Luca would never touch someone in the *Malandanti* like that unless it was part of ritual, but he could not resist Maddy's body. She moved toward him, eyes closed, lips pursed, but Luca picked up his robe and put it on, trying to focus on their mission—their purpose for being here. Maddy opened her eyes when he took her hand and returned his smile. He led her through the web of tunnels until they finally reached the cavern where the *Malandanti* awaited.

Once they entered the *Grotto,* Maddalena slipped on the rocky earthen floor, but Luca caught her before she fell. Wondering if she hurt herself, Luca supported her as much as he could, yet she insisted on walking on her own. Maddy's jaw tightened, but there was no limp. He led the way to the center of the group, and the *boschetto's* whispers intensified. Maddy moved in closer to Luca as if she were afraid, but Luca held her tightly, trying to give her strength for what she was about to do. He gestured for the two robed ones to come forward, then Luca had to let her go. He kissed her on the cheek before the robed ones helped her to the stairs leading to the altar. Luca stared at Maddy's sculptured behind as she walked away. Maddy glanced back and grinned at him, and he returned her sweet smile. Luca then focused on the *boschetto.* The *Malandanti* parted as the black-robed ones moved through the mass of people to escort the young initiate through the crowd and up the carved-out steps.

Luca smiled and savored the moment. For seven years, he had obeyed his father's wishes and honored his father's traditional ways as *Sacerdote,* and at last he was ready to begin what he knew was

76

his purpose in this lifetime. Now they would practice with all the modern sex magick rituals from America, then they could begin to execute their plan.

From now on, the rituals would be held here because of its strong imprint from the past. The imprint of the *Grotto* combined with the nearby *Cripta dei Morti* contained a highly charged collection of energy from people who were killed, maimed and executed in the prisons during the Inquisition. The heinous waves of agony remained as vibrational energy that only people attuned to these higher vibra-tions could sense and therefore use in invocation or ritual.

Before he began, he closed his eyes and gave thanks, know-ing he must fully honor this force in order to connect with it. Called an odic force by most occultists, this electromagnetic energy field could be summoned and harnessed by himself and the *boschetto*. Nature generated the force by the earth's rotation, along with the gravitational pull of the sun and moon and the magnetism of the poles. After arousing this energy field, they used these currents of energy to create a new cone of power.

Luca chanted and walked through the crowd. "*Tana, bella Tana. Dea della Luna e del di La, a te invoco e te chiamo ad alta voce.*" He repeated the words as he walked, then continued chant-ing as he climbed the carved-out steps.

When he reached the top of the stone platform that over-looked the *boschetto* below, he motioned for them to join him. The chant intensified with each repetition until the tone sounded as if they were one voice. Luca took his place at the altar between the niche of magickal tools and the stone slab. The rectangular slab was the focal point of the altar, and the arched niche surrounding it contained the tools. The stone slab, placed directly in front of the niche, was essential for the sacred rites. With just enough room to move between the niche and the slab, Luca could then concentrate on either the woman as altar or the magickal tools in the niche behind him. This arrangement enabled him to charge the tools in private with his back turned away from the *boschetto* below, or to perform the rites on the woman upon the slab and face the *boschetto* so that they could not only see the rite but also, if need be, participate.

Luca paused to acknowledge the power of the sacred tools as they shimmered from the bronze-colored candles that represented God and Goddess. Glittering flecks of light made the tools appear to rise above the backdrop of the ebony cloth. In the center, the pentacle had been placed with the spirit bowl atop. An indigo blue flame radiated inside the bowl; its color and intensity signaled the strength of the hidden realm of the invisible. Luca fingered all four elemental bowls placed around the pentacle to honor the creative material from which all things are made manifest.

Clearing the way for the odic force, he gestured to the two robed ones to leave them on the platform and join the *boschetto* below. Standing at the far end of the stone ledge, Maddy looked nervous. She stood overlooking the *boschetto,* hands by her side, defiantly holding her head up as if she were proud of her sexy body. She fidgeted though and kept moving her hands as if she wanted to cover her luscious breasts. Luca grabbed the dagger on the altar, then walked over to her side and raised his hand to silence the chanting. He held up the dagger for all to see the glint of the blade in the candlelight. With respect, he saluted the directional elements of north, east, south and west.

After the salute, he turned away from the *boschetto* and took his place between the slab and the niche, then placed the dagger back where it belonged on the altar. Luca considered himself a spiritual warrior, and even the tools resembled the weapons of a knight. His tools were the sword, vital for a stable mind and cutting through delusion and deception, the chalice for compassion on the warrior's spiritual path, the wand for the intuitive mind necessary for discernment and perception and the shield or pentacle for protection against evil. Luca fingered the carved wood of the wand, the sharp blade of the dagger, the ornate filigree of the chalice and the fine etchings of the pentacle. Saying a prayer, Luca lit the cone of frankincense before him.

Turning to face the *boschetto,* he began. "Once, long ago, our people worshipped in the open fields and upon the ancient sites. Our chants were carried upon the winds. Our prayers were received upon the smoke of our incense by the Old Ones. In time, we were enslaved by the worshippers of a jealous god, and our villages were given over to cruel lords. The Old Ways were forbidden, and we were forced to accept the ways of our oppressors."

He closed his eyes for a moment of silence, then continued. "For us now, it is a time of gathering in the shadows. We have suffered persecution for our beliefs, and many of us have died. Yet we have been reborn among our own again. Always has it been that the cycles of life pass and return again. All things are remembered all things are restored."

Walking in front of the slab altar to look down at the *boschetto*, Luca motioned for them to join him in the chant. "*Tana, bella Tana, che tanto bella e buona siei, e tanto ti e piacere ti ho fatto. Bella Tana Dea delle stelle e della Luna, La Regina piu potente, Appari di fronte an noi.*"

Together they repeated the chant over and over, making a tonal mix of hypnotic sound fill the cavern. The spiral of psychic energy became visible. It seeped from the raw wall of the earthen cave into the *Grotto*, appearing as a fine mist that feathered into a pyramid atop the group, then immersed the *boschetto* in a delicate shroud of vapors that slithered around the black-robed figures. As caliginous vapors rolled out from the crevices of the thinly layered brick, the stonework seemed to squeeze the earthen element between each layer, squishing it, as if forcing the guts of the earth to ooze out. Rough splotches of mortar randomly splattered on the cavernous walls left traces where the earth had already vomited its bowels from the pressure. Once the candlelight dimmed, all five walls disappeared in the mist as the odic force grew.

Luca inhaled the musty smell, concentrating on becoming one with the odic energy as the earthy perfume swept him into the darkness. Entering this realm enabled him to reach into the void to access the powerful forces of the other world. Exhaling, he scanned the faces of the *boschetto*, then briefly looked into as many eyes as he could of those who looked upward.

Now that he was *Sacerdote*, he must prepare them for their mission to destroy the church by introducing them to the rites that would charge the talisman and make it powerful enough to evoke death. Luca raised his hands for silence, then awaited their response. Silence came quickly.

"We are summoned here this evening," he said, turning toward Maddy, "to initiate Maddalena into our family."

The *boschetto* responded by murmuring in agreement. Luca nodded, pausing long enough for them to acknowledge their purpose. When the whispers stopped, he continued. "It has been a year and a day since this one joined us, and now it is time for her to become one of ours," he added, taking her hand and holding it out, away from her naked body to fully present her to the group. He guided Maddy to the place between the niche and the slab, then helped her climb onto the rectangular slab. Maddy wriggled upon the table, then Luca helped her stretch out on the stone.

He felt the vibrant skin of Maddalena's arm and wanted to touch more of her body. Waiting for the voice inside his head to guide him, he frowned when it didn't come. Instead of the calm, commanding inner voice, the voice of *la mia nonna* echoed in his mind.

A man who demanded money for his services pricked Janarra's skin with the bodkin. The dagger-like poker was used for pulling ribbons through hoops or hems, and was even pointed enough to punch holes in cloth. They used the pointed bodkin on Janarra, because the church believed that every witch bore a witch's mark, or a patch of skin that has no pain and doesn't bleed when pricked. The witch hunters visited town after town and earned money identifying the Strega. Somehow they found our sacred Janarra in central Italy. She saw them use fake bodkins to falsify evidence, and she told us their instruments had hollow, wooden handles and retractable points to look as if the bodkin penetrated her skin without pain or bleeding, making it look like they had poked a witch's mark. Janarra told us of other needles with one sharp end and one blunt end, either to draw blood or to have no effect so it looked like they'd poked a witch's mark. The bodkins maimed our beautiful Janarra's soft skin so much that it caused not only physical scars, but mental ones, as well.

Luca reeled from the memory of his grandmama's words and clutched the edge of the slab to stave off the dizziness. Maddalena opened her eyes and sat up, as if she were concerned by his wavering. Luca whisked his fingertips over the features of her young face and vowed to focus on the present.

He thought he had blotted out those stories from long ago, but he could never forget the detailed drawing of Janarra that he found in the diary. She must have been twenty-one. The bodkin tore her skin, including her face, until she was unrecognizable.

With one hand cupping Maddy's breast and the other holding her back for support, he gently eased her back down onto the slab. As she stretched out, Maddalena's large breasts pointed toward the heavens and she closed her eyes. Mesmerized by her erect nipples, he felt the soft skin of her abdomen. Abruptly, Grandmama's words flooded back into his mind.

> *They used a torture device on Fana called the spider, which was a sharp iron fork used to mangle breasts. To this day, Fana's screams can still be heard in the woods because they used red-hot pincers to tear her flesh until it ripped her breasts off her body.*

Luca, trying to gain control over his thoughts, stepped backward, almost knocking over the chalice in the niche behind him. Trying to blot out his rage, he struggled to clear his mind of the bloody images of Fana, who was still alive after they had torn her beautiful breasts off her body.

He loved *la mia nonna,* yet her words combined with the drawings in the journals tormented him and made him want revenge. Staring at Maddy's breasts, tears came into his eyes as he concentrated on the Triangle of Manifestation. Determined to continue, he envisioned the base of the triangle as an imaginary line drawn from nipple to nipple, and the sides of the pyramid as invisible lines pointing to her mouth. Once he saw the pyramid, his mind stilled and he continued. "We are now ready to begin the new rites bequeathed by our elder, Janus," Luca said. "Before he died, he begged me to use the Old Ways where the woman's body becomes the altar, and the body points are kissed in the traditional way." Luca's face reddened as he lied, but he had to make her believe Janus had agreed to the ways of the *Malandanti.* Janus never allowed skyclad because he wanted them to be more like other religions in their daily practices, but Luca would not settle for that kind of mediocrity.

With steady hands, Luca faced the niche and poured the wine into the empty chalice. Turning toward Maddy on the slab, he placed the cup onto her stomach and she flinched. She raised her hands, and he helped her steady the chalice upon her navel. Once she held it steady, Luca began.

He reached down at the end of the stone slab, held her feet tightly together, then pushed her feet toward her torso so that her knees bent upward and her heels touched her buttocks. Gently, slowly, he parted her shapely legs, then moved to her side.

After dipping his fingers into the chalice, he anointed her nipples with three drops of wine, then kissed each one as he recited the invocation. To complete the Triangle of Manifestation, he poured three drops into her mouth and kissed her on the lips. After the kiss, she smiled and flashed her pouty lips at him, so Luca decided to do the five-fold kiss. He began at her feet, anointing and kissing each foot with his wine-drenched lips. He did the same with each knee. And for the last kiss, he walked to the end of slab and stared at the darkness between her legs. Luca anointed her succulent lips with the wine and bent over for the kiss. His lips lingered on her wet juices as he flicked his tongue in and out of her wet pussy. Humming the chant they had all recited together moments before, he moved his head from side to side as he hummed, lips vibrating over her pussy. He only stopped humming when he poked his tongue in as far as he could. After a blissful eternity, he kissed her tender lips softly before he drank his last.

Tearing himself away from her juices, he straightened and turned to face the *Malandanti*, who looked as if they were about to cheer, but remained silent. Raising his hands to dissolve the circle, he closed the rite. "Give us power, O Most Secret Lady, to bind our oppressors. Receive us as your children; receive us though we are earthbound. When our bodies lie resting nightly, speak to our inner spirits and teach us all your Holy Mysteries. I believe your ancient promise that we who seek your Holy presence will receive of your wisdom. Hear us. Recall your ancient promise. Let your glory shine about us. Bless us, O Gracious Queen of Heaven. So be it done."

The *boschetto* echoed, "So be it done."

Luca smiled. "Let it be known that our new member, Maddalena, is one of us."

The *Malandanti* responded with muted tones of agreement. Luca eased Maddy to a sitting position and waited until she was ready, then helped her off the slab. Holding hands, they walked together to the edge of the platform and looked down at the *boschetto* in the *Grotto* below. Luca gently nudged Maddy forward and stepped back. She smiled, then the *Malandanti* shouted words of praise and support. Luca, aware that Maddy's hot juices were smeared on his face, stepped forward again and wrapped his arm around her waist to pull her close to his side. Feeling confident now that Maddalena would convert to the New Ways and become his *Sacerdotessa,* Luca moved his hand to her derrière and squeezed the soft mound of each cheek. Certain the *boschetto* would be anxious for her to join them in sex magick, Luca watched the gaiety below as he massaged Maddy's naked bottom. When Luca noticed the eager faces of the *Malandanti* men, he nodded to reassure them that next time they would all have sex magick together.

CHAPTER SEVEN

VINCENT

Villa di Spagna

Time Warp
February 24, 2004
3:00 p.m.

"With the decorator you recommended, it took us only four days to get situated." Tess placed a piece of rolled clay down the middle of a ball mounted on a stand. Using the heel of her hand to rough in the nose, chin and lips, Tess worked the clay as Vincent watched.

"Four days?" Vincent asked. "That's Viviana for you."

Tess nodded, then looked as if she was about to change the subject. "Vinny, I know you don't see many patients, but I want you to regress Diana. There's something haunting her from a past life, and only you can help."

"How do you know it's a past life?"

"Since she came to Rome, she's been possessed with painting, and now her work has totally changed into something quite remarkable. She paints things about some distant past that she doesn't even recognize, because the images are either ancient or ethereal."

"I'll need to see her work. How did you meet?"

"She painted nudes in one of my classes," Tess answered. "She left right before you came that summer. Diana and I have been like sisters since we met, so after she graduated and moved back East, it wasn't the same without her. We made a point to meet at the art show in Loveland, then decided nothing was going to separate us anymore. I lived in Aspen at the time, so she decided to visit and loved the place, then ended up staying and marrying Antonio."

"Why do you think she needs regression therapy?"

Tess turned away from her work and locked eyes with him for a moment. "Actually, she used to be a wife and an expectant mom until she lost both titles through death," she said, turning toward the clay to sweep it back from the midline of the face with her thumbs and feather it into what now looked like a head. "After the accident, she's left without a family, no one. Except me," Tess added. "She needs to be regressed to know her karma and the destiny of her soul. Regression is the only therapy that will work for her to understand her motivations and desires. Then maybe she'll find peace on her own."

"Must be a difficult time." Vincent raked his hands through his hair and wondered how Diana handled a tragedy like that. "It's been how long?"

"The accident happened in September, so it's been just over five months." Tess shook her head. "Then she discovered so many things she didn't know, like this *Villa,* a brother, Luca, who is a witch here in Rome and a mistress."

Vincent frowned. "Are you talking about Antonio DeMarco?"

"He contacted you?"

"He wanted to be regressed, but he never told me about you or a mistress," Vincent said. "I knew he spent time in the States, but I didn't realize that was his main residence. The only person he talked at length about was Diana, and the reason for that was she came through in his regressions as other people in other lifetimes, so that's what we analyzed. Seems he kept secrets from us all, no? I didn't realize his address was this place, and it's right across the street from my office. It was there in his record, but I never realized it was the *Villa.*"

Throughout Antonio's therapy, Vincent hadn't known his patient lived here. Midway on the Spanish Steps, directly across the street from his office, most Italians didn't even know the place existed because most locals didn't even know about the *Rampa Mignanelli.* The *rampa* or steps weren't well known by people who lived in *Roma* because most Romans preferred using the popular steps instead. The *rampa* was like the elevator on the other side of the Spanish Steps—unknown and almost invisible even to people who lived here.

Over the years, Vincent had noticed how the both the *rampa* and the *Villa* seemed invisible because it was tucked away behind the wall of the Spanish Steps. From the Spanish Steps, a wall jutted off into an enclave with a small, indiscrete gate that led to the *Villa's* private courtyard. The gate blended into the surroundings and seemed to disappear in the backdrop of the famous steps. Although the *Villa* was next to the Spanish Steps, it remained hidden from view except for glimpses of the *Villa's* tiled roof. No one noticed it, except Vincent.

The front of the *Villa* was visible, but only if you took the *rampa* or side steps that led down to the *Piazza Mignanelli* and few tourists took that route versus the famous steps. But Vincent often took the secluded steps from his *attico* on the corner of *Piazza di Spagna* and *via Frattina* because the *rampa* wasn't so crowded.

Vincent scanned the makeshift sculpting studio to pinpoint the cause of Diana's fears in the *Villa*. He was certain the *Villa di Spagna* was haunted by something, he just didn't know what. It was the atmosphere inside that made it seem like the House of Usher. Reflecting the *Villa's* outside architecture of Italian Renaissance, the inside was filled with dark, hidden spaces and narrow corridors snaking from room to room. Moss-colored walls trimmed with black mahogany baseboards and *barocco* crown molding evoked a deep sense of Italian heritage. Lush tapestries covered each chair and sofa, and bronze-colored sheers fluttered in the breeze wafting through the open windows. The Gothic décor of what had once been an extra bedroom, but now was Tess's studio, made the place dark and mysterious. He'd heard many a Roman say the *Villa* was haunted by *Strega*, and that made Vincent even more curious, but maybe it frightened Diana.

"Last night, she woke up screaming in her bedroom," Tess said. "She just stood there naked, with her nightgown crumpled at her feet, as if someone put a spell on her."

"Did she tell you what happened?"

"She told me it was like mind control."

"Did she say anything else?"

"No, she was too dazed," Tess answered. "Later I asked her about it, but she wouldn't tell me more. I think she's afraid."

"Maybe it's the *Villa.*"

"Maybe Antonio's haunting her. I always wondered what made that guy so secretive. If he believed in spirits, couldn't he haunt her after dying?"

Vincent shook his head no. "Antonio loved her too much to scare her. But why would a man hide this place and the erotica from his wife? First answer this for me though, how did Antonio get all those nude paintings?"

"Antonio bought every one. Diana never knew about the paintings because Antonio told me they were a gift. They had nothing of the sort in their other house. Their artwork in Aspen was rather conservative. I didn't tell Diana about selling the paintings because the sale was made before Diana even knew Antonio." Tess frowned at what now looked like a sculpted face in the clay, then etched tiny lines for the eyebrows and lips and stepped back to scrutinize her work.

"You didn't want to keep one painting of me, just for old time's sake?"

"Why should I?" Tess looked up and scowled at him. "When you never called or wrote, I gave up and decided to forget you."

"But you still kept my number, no?" Vincent smiled at Tess's frown. "Why would Antonio only have erotica here and not in Aspen?"

"He told me he bought those paintings for a relative." Tess, now absorbed with sculpting the nose, ignored his question. "I got rid of them because I was letting go of the past. Those paintings were what remained of you."

When Vincent saw Tess's paintings of him displayed on the walls of the *Villa,* he couldn't believe it. Relieved that his face was either blurred or turned away in all her masterpieces, Vincent was glad she honored his request to not paint his face back then.

When he met Tess in Boulder at his regression seminar at the Naropa Institute, he instantly felt the attraction. He used to travel to the States every year to teach in the summer, but ever since Tess moved to Aspen, he stopped going because the summers in Boulder weren't the same without her. He liked teaching at Naropa, because it had an excellent school for regression therapy, and the Institute welcomed his cutting-edge research in the field, but without Tess, he couldn't go back. Living there had been an eye-opener for him though, especially once he knew Tess. The day they met, she'd argued with him about one of his theories, and the rest was history. He had a steamy summer with her painting him nude all the time. She even painted him nude while he slept or when he relaxed after their outrageous lovemaking. Her passion for painting nudes had been all-consuming at the time, and that summer it devoured both of them.

Vincent picked up a sculpted hand on the worktable and admired her work. Upon his arrival at the *Villa*, Tess explained how she had started sculpting after moving to Aspen, and now he realized her technique was already beyond compare. When he met Tess ages ago in Boulder, her favorite medium had been oil on canvas, but as a sculptor she had progressed into an entirely new realm with her work. Among the array of sculpting tools strewn on the workbench, numerous sculpted heads, torsos and hands—some finished and some unfinished—were scattered throughout the workroom. She used to be an avid fan of his research about past life regressions, but it was apparent now that her passion was human forms of clay.

Watching her work the clay, Vincent decided he had missed her without even knowing it. One thing was certain; there weren't any women like Tess in *Roma*. Even though Tess was almost seventeen years older than he was, she still looked magnificent. But he failed her in the end, because he'd been careless about keeping in contact once he returned to *Roma*. And over time, he had forgotten how much fun they had together until now. No other woman satisfied him like she had that summer. Surprised that she kept his phone number, Vincent realized he had a habit of not keeping any woman's phone number unless she was a patient and there was work to be done.

Vincent shook his head as he recalled his indiscretion with Raven just a month ago. He hadn't seen her again either—but then, why would she want to see him after what he'd done to her in the office? Vincent frowned.

"Fine, don't talk about it. I don't want to talk about our past either," Tess said, breaking the silence. "It's Diana who needs our help. She's been under a spell since the accident, and even more so since she moved into the *Villa*."

"I no understand spells," Vincent said, lapsing into his broken English—a knee-jerk response whenever he wanted to entice a woman. It worked, even this time.

Tess looked at Vincent and laughed. "Honest, I really do think she's cursed. Any family she's ever had died on her."

"Let me talk to her. I'll figure it out. But there's one thing I need to know—are you the reason why Antonio found me in *Roma?* He never gave me a straight answer."

"About two years ago, he asked me about regression therapy, so I gave him your brochure about the regression seminars you used to offer at Naropa, and that brochure had your telephone number in Rome. At the time, I saved it because I wanted a picture of your face, but when I didn't hear from you, I gave it to Antonio and let it go."

"I didn't know you wanted a long-term relationship."

"I don't want a long-term anything. You needed to move on, and I wanted to keep the connection," she said. "Once I have sex with a man, I never forget him. I just wanted to keep our friendship—that's all, nothing more. Face it Vinny, I'm not the one because one isn't enough for you."

Vincent frowned. "It's my downfall, isn't it? The Italian machismo has taken over and I'm cursed."

"And I'm over it, but now I need your help with Diana. She needs to be regressed to understand why so much tragedy has happened to her in this lifetime. It must be something karmic over lifetimes. Just promise me you won't come on to her—you'll leave her alone, understand?"

Vincent nodded. "You know as well as I do, that's unethical." Vincent, feeling guilty about his behavior with Raven, kept telling himself he was only human for Christ's sake. But he certainly wasn't about to give Tess a confession on the matter because he felt bad enough without analyzing it further. From now on, he had to ignore his male instincts with any woman in his office. "How did she meet Antonio?" he asked, wanting to change the subject.

"I introduced them. It took me awhile, but I finally managed to make the match. You see, Diana lived in Boston, so I asked her to visit. Sparks flew when he saw her, and they married almost immediately after they met."

"And Diana?" Vincent leaned forward.

"On the surface, it all seemed like a dream," Tess answered. "But there was always a quiet reserve about Antonio. He was very private. Maybe that's why it took me so long to introduce them. I was unsure about him too."

"What do you want me to do with her in the regression?" Vincent knew with Tess's background in regression therapy classes that she'd have an opinion on the matter.

Tess didn't answer at first. She had a habit of ignoring people and had done the same thing during their summer together in Boulder. Normally, she was the one who asked questions, then argued over answers. Vincent figured that was her way of staying in control of the conversation.

Finally, she looked up and glared at him. "I need you to probe the depths of her soul through your therapy." Tess grabbed a wire-end tool and expertly gouged out the sockets for eyes in the clay head.

"First, maybe we should find out what she wants, no?"

"Here's a woman who fails to look within." Tess dropped the tool, then pressed her thumbs into the clay holes to smooth out the sockets. Moving her hands deftly over the clay form, she dramatically swept her thumbs up and out from the bridge of the nose. "She doesn't understand the concept *know thyself.* And now, I'm afraid, she's losing her grip on reality."

"What makes you think that?"

"She's—"

The door opened, and an exotic blonde bolted into the studio—a woman who Vincent immediately recognized as the one in the photo clip from the internet.

"What?" she demanded. "She's what?"

Diana's long, layered hair—straight and messy—made her look wild. Although she looked riled up, she had an undeniable sadness. A petite woman in a short blue-jean skirt, the dark circles under her eyes proved Diana wasn't getting much sleep, and her impatience indicated what may be her inability to cope. But her natural beauty made Vincent warn himself to be careful. Normally women worked at looking beautiful, but Diana had a natural beauty that didn't need cosmetics. Exotic was a better word to describe the woman who stood before him. Tangled hair, jittery hands, restless eyes—eyes that looked like the ocean or more precisely the tide, with a current that could suck you in and take you away. Glancing at Vincent, she stopped dead in her tracks and frowned, then slid her hands into the big pockets of her paint-splotched jacket and turned away.

"What?" she repeated. "She's what?"

"Diana," Tess said. "Please, sit down. I'd like you to meet Vincent, an old friend of mine." Tess gestured toward the chair next to Vincent, but Diana didn't move. "Diana, meet Vincent. Vincent, Diana," Tess added.

Silence. Diana stood with her back toward him as if he didn't exist.

Vincent, finding it awkward to be ignored, stood. Normally, he'd be on his feet the minute any female walked in, but he felt strange being chivalrous with a woman who acted so hostile. He motioned to Tess, then sat back down. Tess guided Diana to the chair next to Vincent and made her sit down. Diana leaned forward, head down, and propped her elbows on her knees. She tousled her hair with both hands and finally looked up and glared at Vincent, hair sticking out in different directions, eyes defiant.

Vincent laughed when their eyes met.

"What are you laughing about?" Diana asked, stone-faced.

Before he could answer, Tess stood between them, then bent down until she was inches away from Diana's face. "Look, Diana, you should consider getting to know Vincent, because he's a therapist."

"You've got to be kidding me," Diana said, slamming her hand down on the armrest. "I told you, I'm done with therapy."

"But he's different, Di." Tess paused. "I met Vinny a long time ago. He lived in Boulder while he taught regression technique and hypnotherapy seminars at the Naropa Institute."

Diana gasped. "Hypno what?"

"He studies past lives." Tess put her hands on her hips and straightened herself, still blocking Vincent's view of Diana. "Since the subject always fascinated me, I actually thought about being a hypnotherapist once too, but I'd rather sculpt than take people back in time."

"You aren't kidding, are you?" Diana said, peering around Tess to stare at Vincent like he was some freak. "How is that going to help me?"

"I'll leave that up to you to figure out." Tess turned away and resumed sculpting. "I need you two to leave now. I'm working." She waved them away with her muddy hand, then formed a ball of clay and placed it into one of the eye sockets. With precision, she rolled out a small coil of clay and positioned it over the eyeball to make an eyelid.

Vincent turned to Diana. "Want to take a walk?" On the way out, Vincent waved to Tess, who didn't even notice. Vincent followed Diana down the hall, then descended the spiral staircase into the foyer. At the front door, he stepped forward to open it and let her pass through first, but then she stopped.

Vincent, sensing her reluctance, decided to urge her on. "How about we talk? Allow me."

He gestured to the *rampa* descending down to the *piazza*, then took the lead. The quiet steps were deserted. Even the bistro terraces, which normally were filled with diners, were silent. It was midday, so the bistros were closed for the *siesta*. As he waited for Diana at the base of the steps, he listened to the sound of her footfalls. Her step evoked doubt, uncertainty, even fear. There was a hesitation in her walk and an overwhelming sadness in her smile as she came toward him.

Vincent turned and continued toward the *Piazza Mignanelli*. After rounding the corner, he noticed the *piazza* was quiet too. Raking his fingers through his hair, he walked toward the *Colonna dell'Immacolata Concezione*. Immediately, Diana came up from behind as Vincent stopped and turned around.

"I don't need a therapist," she said, glaring at him with eyes that looked like they hadn't slept a wink for days.

"Your deceased husband was my client. He had been in therapy with me for more than a year."

Diana's eyes widened. "Why would anyone see a shrink in Rome when there are plenty in the States? For what reason?"

"My work is unlike that of any other therapist. That's why your late husband came to me. I'm not your normal shrink, let alone your average regression therapist. Antonio was interested in resolving his inability to commit and analyzing his karmic connection with you. He thought he had a problem with being in a relationship until he met you." Vincent paused, wondering if she suspected her husband of any affairs, then blocked that thought from his mind. "We just reached a turning point in our therapy when he proposed to you. In the session before he proposed, he regressed to a past life with you in it, and that tragic lifetime affected him ever since. After that, he understood how important you were not only in this lifetime, but in all the others."

"Look, I don't even know if I believe in past lives." Diana frowned as if she didn't want to hear about her husband's therapy. "But I am beginning to believe my husband had problems. You're talking about his inability to commit and his infidelity, right?"

Vincent raked his hand through his hair, not wanting to think about Raven. He couldn't betray Antonio and tell his wife something speculative like that, even though Antonio was dead. Italian men didn't divulge that kind of information anyway. Most Italian men who were married had affairs. In Italy, it was commonplace to have a mistress, as well as a wife. Nevertheless, he couldn't fathom why Antonio hadn't mentioned Raven. Until he met her, Vincent believed Antonio had solved his problems with commitment and didn't need another woman, but now he wondered if Antonio needed more than one woman even when he was married. Maybe that was why he had been so attracted to Raven—because she was willing to settle for the title *mistress* and not be a wife—so that meant she was more sexual, more wanton than others. His Italian instincts were responsible for that indiscretion with Raven, and now he had to watch himself with Diana, as well as any other women who crossed his path in his work. Instincts or not, he must keep his promise to himself and to Tess.

"Antonio never told me about any affairs while he was with you," Vincent said, vowing not to say a word about Raven.

"Did you know about the other woman? I saw her in the court-yard dancing naked in the trees. She looks like a teenager."

Vincent frowned, not wanting to speculate about who Diana saw. "He didn't tell me about anyone else during our therapy and frankly, I never would have guessed, because Antonio discovered that you were with him through many lifetimes, and the tragic one made him incapable of loving any other woman but you."

Diana froze. "What are you talking about?"

"Would you rather me describe it, or would you rather experience the lifetime through a regression?"

"You can do that?"

"It's not always that precise, but over time we will get there," he explained. "My office is close by—it's just down the street." He reached out his hand, but she didn't take it. Vincent gestured in the direction of his office and she stepped forward, then he led the way. Since the day had faded into late afternoon, the shopkeepers were opening their doors and resuscitating the *Piazza di Spagna.* The sounds of the city blended with the distant melody of a violinist playing Vivaldi on the street for spare change. As Vincent walked through the rays of dwindling light, the fading sun made long, misty shadows down the cobblestone street. Elongated facades made each place of business look like a separate building, yet the street consisted of one structure that towered six stories high and was dotted with tall, skinny windows. Sandwiched between a terra-cotta facade and a moss-colored green one, his office was in the ideal location because it overlooked the Spanish Steps yet was entirely private. He even walked to work because his *attico* was just down the street in the other direction.

Vincent picked up the pace, making sure Diana was behind him as he weaved his way through the sea of people loitering at the cascading waters of the *barcaccia.* Vincent crossed the street to the office building and opened the door for Diana. Located between the local *caffè* and a trendy boutique, his place looked like an apartment building on the outside, but on the inside it was filled with offices. He took the lead and showed her the way upstairs, then opened the door for her again to enter. Inside, he gestured at the couch. She scowled at him, then sat in the chair.

"Not there, the couch if you will," he said. "It's just easier, more comfortable for you."

Diana laughed a nervous laugh. She moved to the couch and slipped off her shoes. "Are you going to hypnotize me?"

"It's self-induced, meaning you're fully awake throughout the entire session, yet you are regressed." He squeezed her shoulders and gently helped her lay back on the couch. "You won't do anything against your will, trust me."

He smiled at her smooth, flawless legs and her short skirt hiked up her thighs as she positioned herself on the couch.

"Trust you?" she asked, pulling at the hem of her skirt. "When you look at me like that?"

Vincent shook his head trying to ignore his Italian instincts, then realized Diana wasn't about to accept any compliments from him because American women did not know how to respond to a man who appreciated a woman's beauty. *She just hasn't lived in Roma long enough yet,* he thought. Once she was accustomed to it, then she might eventually understand how the Italian male intellect functioned, or rather dysfunctioned, with a beautiful woman.

He smiled at her and she frowned—well, on the other hand, maybe not.

"Perhaps we should schedule an appointment," he suggested. "I'm not so sure you're ready."

"I'm ready. You can get started." She closed her eyes and relaxed.

Vincent took a deep breath, then started talking slowly with his deep voice, using just the right tone to bring her into semi-consciousness. He was taking her to a place where he was sure she'd never been before in the recesses of her mind. As he spoke, he watched her body movements, especially her closed eyes, for signs that she was regressed. After about twenty minutes of preparation, her eyelids fluttered as if she were watching a movie with closed eyes.

"I want you to go back in time to the place where you found your soul and those who would be a part of that soul as a mate," he said. "Take your time. When you are ready, tell me where you are."

"I'm in a void," she said after a few moments. "Total darkness."

"Look around. What do you see?"

"I'm in a vacuum of nonexistence."

"It may be hard to see, cloudy even, but try to figure out where you are," Vincent said, coaxing her to concentrate harder. "Look down at your feet. What are you wearing?"

"I'm not wearing anything except stars." Diana knotted her brow. "Actually, the stars make up my body. I'm filled with tiny pinpoints of azure-colored lights." Diana giggled, clearly excited by her realization.

"What do you see around you?"

Diana shook her head as if she were uncomfortable. "It's a vacuum sucking everything into a hole. All the things floating around are being dragged into this black pit."

"Is there anyone with you?"

"And the light," she said, gasping before she continued. "It's sucking the light into the pit, along with all the stardust and light particles around me." She whispered, making Vincent lean closer to hear. "No, there's no one else here but me. As the light goes into the hole, it becomes the darkness. It's gone, it vanishes."

"Are you being sucked in?"

"It's like a huge drain, and I'm going down it," she said, shaking her head. "Now it's drawing me near to the edge. But as I get closer, the swirling slows down for some reason I can't explain, like it wants me to peer inside. And I'm fearless—"

"Do you see anything in the hole?"

"No, but this place has something to do with my soul."

"Can you get closer to see what's inside without being sucked in?"

"I'm almost inside, and now I see it. It's hard to describe," she said. "I've never seen anything so bright—there must be a million suns here. It's another universe with planets in every imaginable color. And their moons are in shades I've never seen before like blue, magenta, celadon. I'm being pulled in, and I know I'm supposed to go. I want to go in there, because that's where my soul is."

None of Vincent's patients had ever gone through the black hole before, and after he'd regressed hundreds of patients to this place, he had finally concluded it was the black hole in the center of our universe, the Milky Way. Normally, the patient could only see the hole in the fabric of the universe and never got close enough to see anything inside it, but in Diana's regression, it was different. He needed to take it slowly with her—not haphazardly plunge into this unknown realm without exercising caution. Diana's safety was more important than exploring places he'd never been before, despite his desire to find out more about what was inside the black hole. Vincent wasn't so sure he should let any patient go there, because what if the mind didn't come back after going that far into the beginning of its existence? He decided to take her out of the regression in case the session jeopardized her well-being.

"When I finish counting to eight, you will be awake and fully aware of where you are," Vincent said. Using his hypnotic voice, he gently brought her back to the present. "One, two, three . . . "

On the count of eight, Diana opened her eyes just as he had instructed. After that, he made her wait until she was totally awake and centered in the present time, then he helped her off the couch to sit in the chair.

Diana stared at Vincent, looking confused by what she had seen in the regression. "I don't get it," she said.

Her eyes looked like the blue moons Vincent had imagined she saw in the black hole. "I'm fairly certain they're trying to tell me something," Vincent said.

"Who are *they?*"

"The forces of the universe." Vincent didn't know what made him tell her or why, but he decided to forego the confidentiality he normally maintained with any new discovery. Maybe he did it because he needed to process what had just happened. Or maybe he did it because he wanted to get closer to Diana, since she'd changed from being so hostile to him to being interested.

"That's wild." Diana locked eyes with him—not disbelieving eyes, but fascinated eyes. "What do these forces do?"

Vincent, enthralled by her new attitude, made a concentrated effort to not look into those full-moon eyes again because Diana had a magnetism that kept pulling him toward her. No one ever wanted more; in fact, usually people were frightened when they heard him talk about such things. Vincent fought the impulse to get closer to this woman who was now his patient. She was a client for Christ's sake, and he couldn't make the same mistake he'd made with Raven, plus he made a promise to Tess. Never again would he let his desires take control like they had with Raven. Even though this was Italy, he must have professional ethics with patients. As those iridescent blue moons of this beautiful woman kept staring at him, he swore not to jump into the lunar eclipse again.

"Our galaxy is just one of billions in the universe," he said. "And what we see surrounding our planet is just a tiny spec in the immense flat disk known as the Milky Way. Scientists have recently discovered elements conducive to produce life in the bulging orb that's in the center of our Milky Way—conducive to creating intelligent life. It has to be intelligent, because the stars in that orb are even more ancient than our sun, and they are vibrantly thriving next to planets much like our own."

"Is that where the forces are?"

Vincent nodded. "Just think about it, the sun-like stars in the center of our galaxy were created between four to eight billion years ago, and ten percent of our stars were originally formed from it. So that means intelligent life in the center of our galaxy has had longer to evolve than we have, and it's highly likely that they could have a star similar to what we call our sun in their universe too. With the billions of galaxies besides our own, it's only logical to conclude that other life-forms exist somewhere out there, and there's no doubt those life-forms are more ancient and far more advanced than we are."

"And how does all this fit into your therapy?" Diana asked, leaning forward.

Vincent, pleased that he had Diana's full attention, couldn't believe she had listened to his conclusions without argument or disbelief. He had to tell her about his conclusions, because so far he hadn't been able to share them with anyone.

"When I regress people, I take them back to the beginning of their existence, right before their first lifetime." Vincent hesitated because he couldn't pull his eyes away from hers once again. "I

regress people to a time before they had a body, before they had a face. And every time I do this with patients, they start at the black hole in the center of our galaxy, just as you did. After regressing hundreds of patients to the time before their existence, they end up in this exact place, which is a wormhole or the gateway to another dimension or another time frame in our galaxy. And now, after your regression, I'm convinced that the black hole in the center of our Milky Way is a wormhole to another existence, to another lifetime, and it transports the person's soul into another lifetime either on this planet or possibly on other planets in our galaxy. It's interesting because just recently, some scientists claimed that black holes aren't mysterious drains of mass destruction and death, but may be galaxy sculptors, so to speak, that birth planets and stars into existence. And now I'm certain that black holes are the origin of our Life Force. Black holes birth our souls into existence—I'm certain of this. Life begins in that massive black hole in the center of our universe because that's where our souls are created."

CHAPTER EIGHT

LUCA

Roma Sotterranea

February 24, 2004
Late Afternoon

Pan, the Horned God, stared at Luca in mosaic form through tiles of rust, slate and nude that created a two-dimensional image of the elfin face. With almond-shaped charcoal eyes, a pointed beard and curled horns, the image on the floor of the *Grotto* gesticulated as it spoke to him in the flickering light of the towering candelabrums. Inside a circle edged with vines and animal-shaped *fata*, the spirits of the wood and Pan urged Luca to continue the fight against the church. Pan was a god of the woods who considered caves sacred, and Luca regularly consulted him on matters related to the sanctity of the *Sotterranea*.

Meditating on Pan in the earthen rot and musty odor of the *Sotterranea* assuaged Luca's pain, because his suspicions about Antonio's death had been confirmed and it angered Luca that Raven never told him. Antonio died five months ago, yet no one notified him. Infuriated that Raven had been so disrespectful, Luca still could not understand how she could be so vile. Now, instead of dealing with the agony of losing his only brother, Luca directed his anger at Raven. Luca had only seen Antonio once in the past year, and he felt guilty that he never had the chance to make amends with his brother, but with Raven in the way, he never got the chance to. That last encounter in the *Villa de Marco* had not gone well either, because they ended up arguing over the New Ways again.

After Antonio left the *boschetto,* the entire coven disowned him because of his vendetta against Luca. After accusing Luca of conducting a Black Mass in the tunnels, Antonio told the *Sacerdote.* Luca in turn told his father that he was not conducting a Black Mass, he was just doing ritual skyclad, so Luca turned the accusations around. In the end, his father sided with Luca, then he exiled Antonio from the *Sotterranea.* After that, Antonio left and joined Raven's *boschetto.* Regardless of the past though, Luca felt that Raven should have told him about Antonio.

On one hand, Luca regretted his father's banishment, but on the other, he was relieved to be rid of Antonio because he knew his brother would never participate in sex magick ritual. Over the years, Luca had carefully weeded out those in his father's *boschetto* that he suspected would never do the new rites, then made sure everyone became a *Malandanti* in secrecy—everyone except Maddalena, that is. He waited to initiate her because she had been so close to his father, and she needed time to mourn. By infiltrating the *Malandanti* into his father's coven, he was prepared for battle. Now they would all practice the New Ways of sex magick together as soon as Maddalena was fully indoctrinated.

He called his people *Malandanti* because their purpose was to fight the war against the Roman Catholic Church. In ancient times, *Malandanti* witches were legendary for fighting the wars through ritual battles that had a purposeful outcome. For the past seven years, the *Malandanti* had been preparing for battle, knowing that once the *Sacerdote* died, they could begin the war. But after his brother caught Luca and the entire *Malandanti* doing a sex magick rite in the pagan temple of the *Villa,* everything changed. Antonio almost killed Luca over the matter, and once Antonio brought his concerns to his father, Luca's relationship with his brother ended forever.

Nevertheless, it comforted Luca that Antonio came to him in spirit after he died; although the fact that it took him so long to come back worried Luca. Antonio appeared in spirit hours after he died, which might mean that Antonio needed more time to cross over with his ethereal spirit. Normally, an advanced soul like his brother's would cross over more quickly than the typical person, but Antonio had taken longer than Luca would expect, and that time frame concerned Luca.

People who didn't understand the veil that cloaked the invisible realm always took longer to get to the Luna realm after death, and Antonio should have moved easily through that veil. Moving through it should have been effortless because he understood astral travel, where one can instantly be anywhere at anytime on the earth or in the universe in spirit. Antonio should have traveled astrally to Luna, the realm of the afterlife, but Antonio hadn't received the Rite of Passage for the soul, so Luca wondered if his brother ended up being a lost soul in the *Sotterranea* instead. Luca's eyes blurred as he thought of the times he spent with his brother in their secret library at the Aspen estate. All the journals and diaries they read together changed his life forever because it gave his life purpose. Maybe Antonio would appear in the tunnels again, then they could talk, make amends bury old wounds.

With his father and brother gone, Luca was ready to fight the battle against the church. In order to begin the war, he needed Maddalena to do the new rituals with the *Malandanti* in the *Sotterranea*. Obviously, Maddalena's mourning for Janus was easing. Since she cooperated so nicely during her first rite skyclad, she must be ready for the rituals of sex magick. Out of respect and honor for the deceased *Sacerdote*, Luca had waited, but now it was time. Tonight, Maddalena would have sex magick with the *Sacerdote*.

"Luca?"

Recognizing Maddalena's lilting voice, Luca grinned. "Come, sit beside me." Luca got up as she entered the cavern and remained standing until she sat down, then he sat next to her on the soft cushions of the wrought iron bench.

Furniture was an opulent luxury in the *Grotto*; here couches, chairs, benches and pillows mixed with architectural elements from antiquity evoked a sense of *Sotterranea* splendor. The elaborate, twisted metal of the iron legs and arms on each bench and chair was shaped into branches that blended with the earthen atmosphere of the cave, and massive cushions of rich fabrics softened the iron seats and chair backs. Even the rough floor of the cave had humongous pillows strewn about to invite the reclining pose. Luca carefully selected each fabric at his textile factory: fringes and furs, velvets and silks, snakeskins and ostrich leathers—it all created an atmosphere of warmth and comfort. Because of these comforts, the *Grotto* was the ideal place for sex magick ritual.

"Would you like to help me evoke the sigil?" Luca asked, taking Maddy's hand and turning around to face the wall of etchings, frescoes and signs directly on the cave wall behind them.

Maddy swung her leg upon the seat cushions and turned around too. "What sigil?"

"The sigils on these walls are used in invocation." Luca gestured at the blackish-purple sigil he wanted them to focus on. "Each sigil designates an aspect or the essence of the aspect."

Drawn with thick, purple-blue lines, the sigil they focused on resembled two snakes; one snake was a straight line with a diamond-shaped head, and the other was a curved line that twisted over the straight one. Instead of a diamond-shaped head, the twisted snake had an oval head with a forked tongue protruding from it.

Luca put his hand on her shoulder. "When you stare at this symbol, think about absorbing the image and internalizing the shape and its meaning."

"But what does it mean?"

"Male sexual power."

They stared at the image on the cave wall until Luca felt the time was right, then he continued. "Now, move that mental image to the mirrors and replace the physical manifestation of sexuality into a transcendent one."

He took her hand and led her over to one of the large black mirrors in the *Grotto.* Maddy followed his gaze and stared into the reflection. Rectangular mirrors with frames shaped into iron branches were strategically propped against the cave walls to reflect the entire length and width of the body, and create a multiple image due of the angle of the mirror.

Maddalena rubbed her forehead. "Why are we looking in the mirror again?"

"Don't look at your image, look to the side and try to look past the mirror to what's on the other side. Mirrors take us to the other dimensions. They are the portals to the astral."

Luca watched Maddy's reflection in the mirror as she stared at an endless holographic image of herself. She wore a transparent dress that showed the pronounced curves of her hips and breasts. Luca frowned when she rubbed her arms and shivered.

"Cold?" Luca put his arm around her. "Come, let's sit back down on the bench. The throw will keep you warm."

But after they sat down, Maddy chose not to use the throw. Instead, she nervously fingered with the folds of her dress, and Luca couldn't help notice her leg as the fabric inched up her thigh.

Luca licked his lips before he began. "Do you know why I asked you to meet me here?"

"Did I do something wrong during my initiation?"

"I'd like to tell you what happened during your initiation. Please, just listen very carefully."

Maddy nodded, then kept playing with the hem of her dress until she cinched the fabric at the very top of her leg.

"Together, as a group, we can accumulate the energies raised during sexual activity to manifest our calling," Luca said, placing his hand at the top of Maddalena's naked leg, then massaging her inner thigh.

"Is that why you ate me in the initiation rite? I didn't talk about it with the others, although several brothers asked me if I enjoyed it."

"Come to me if you need to talk about it, because I can help you understand why," Luca said, rubbing her inner thigh, yet wanting to caress her warm pussy instead. "We have to strengthen the rites to protect ourselves."

"Putting your tongue up me makes the *boschetto* stronger?"

"We've been without a *Sacerdotessa* far too long," he said. "And now, if you do as I say, that position may very well be yours."

"You would make me High Priestess?" Maddalena smiled and straightened herself, then put her index finger against her pouty lips. "But I've only been with the coven for a year."

Luca reluctantly took his hand away from her inner thigh, then helped her get up and steered her toward the waterfall. Sliding his hand around her waist, he guided her through the hidden passageway, then helped her step into the *Cripta dei Morti*. Inside, Maddy's face turned the color of his father's ashes because she never knew about the *Cripta*. Finally, he could show her the secrets; finally, she was ready.

"Creepy," Maddy whispered. "This is frightening."

"This is the holiest place in the *Sotterranea*," Luca said, taking off his black velvet jacket and wrapping it around her shoulders to keep her warm. He led her to the crematorium, then took the lid off of the urn that held his father's ashes.

"What's that inside?" she asked, grabbing the edge of the urn to peer inside.

"When Janus died, he asked me to cremate him because he knew we needed his ashes for the talisman."

Maddy screeched as she stepped back. "That's him?"

"His ashes will be our talisman to fight the war. After drawing down the power, his ashes will be used to prevent the Second Inquisition—an Inquisition that is still in the strategic planning process at the Vatican, so the time is right to stop the terror before the torture begins."

Maddy stepped forward and peered into the urn again. Watching her bend over to look inside the urn made Luca aware of her lusty feminine nature, and he instinctively knew Maddy's innate sex drive was what he needed to make the charge of the talisman more forceful. Even though he hadn't tapped into her sex drive yet, with her young, sensual body, her energies would serve the *Malandanti* well when they needed to make a more potent talisman. Maddalena just needed to be stimulated enough so that they could use the forces of her sex drive to create the magick.

"Another Inquisition?" she asked, looking back at him as the blood drained from her face.

Sliding his hand back around her waist, Luca held her tight in case she fainted. "We must annihilate the Roman Catholics before it happens. Once I make you my *Sacerdotessa*, you will be the one to help us raise the energies needed for charging the talisman. With these ashes, we will poison everyone who receives an ashen cross upon their forehead. First, I need my informants at the Vatican to substitute these ashes for the ashes of the palms, then you'll see how ashes of the dead can be used as a weapon. With this talisman on Ash Wednesday, the war begins."

"Me, *Sacerdotessa*?"

Luca nodded, then placed his finger on her fleshy lips so that she would listen as he told her something extremely important. "Antonio's wife, Diana, is here in *Roma*. She needs our guidance because she knows nothing of *Stregheria* and our ways. I need you to help bring her to us, because she is needed to amplify the charge of the talisman."

"Antonio had a wife? What about Raven?"

Luca shook his head. "Antonio always needed more than one woman." Luca licked his lips remembering his childhood and the games they played with Raven. Antonio always got the girl then, but not anymore. "My brother told me that his wife was the Goddess of All Witches in a past life, and that incarnation will amplify the ash and the power to kill. I've been working on calling her because she must join us in our mission. Will you help me?"

Without hesitation, Maddalena nodded.

"Please, follow me." He led Maddy back into the *Grotto*, then guided her to the couch.

"Are you ready?" he asked, helping her sit down, then trying to make her relax. "We must charge a crystal to work its magick, then Diana will be brought into our world. Will you join me to program and encode it with a summons?"

Anxious to begin, Luca marched over to the funerary niche carved into the wall of sigils, then grabbed the black pouch hidden deep inside. His fingers dipped into the pouch and pulled out a crystal rod that was about twelve inches long and fatter at one end than the other. The rod consisted of bulbous shapes that looked like balls that were stuck together. The beaded forms were small at one end, then progressively became larger at the other. In the eerie light of the *Grotto*, the crystal transformed the sputtering candlelight into faceted prisms of purplish-copper bronze.

"Is that your wand?" Maddy whispered.

"Don't be afraid," Luca said, waving the wand in the air. "Once we are finished, you will understand what it means to charge a talisman. As *Sacerdotessa,* you must know these things."

Luca placed the crystal on the couch and smiled at Maddy as he unzipped his trousers. He let his pants fall to the floor before he sat down next to Maddy, turned toward her, then leaned back against the soft cushions of the crescent shaped couch. He stroked his cock, then locked eyes with Maddy. Her innocent eyes widened while she watched his throbbing penis grow bigger and bigger as he squeezed and pulled it. With ragged breath, he rhythmically moved his hand up and down his shaft. Once his cock was rock hard, he licked his lips, hoping she would fall to her knees. But she didn't move.

"Will you help me?" he whispered, taking her arm and guiding her closer to his throbbing cock.

She slid off the couch and lowered herself onto the mosaic floor. Luca handed her the pillow next to him so that her knees wouldn't hurt, then he watched her head move closer to his now gigantic cock. When she was close enough, he concentrated on keeping his juices inside so that nothing gushed out onto her face.

"Will you be my *Sacerdotessa* and help me with the cause?" he whispered, barely able to talk now.

Maddy opened her mouth, grabbed his hard cock, stuck it in her mouth and fervently sucked. Instantly feeling the relief of her warm, moist mouth, Luca groaned. As her lips tightened around his bulging cock, he gently rocked her head back and forth to sustain the rhythm. Forward and backward, up and down his cock. When her head bobbed faster and his cock penetrated deeper, his breathing quickened.

Knowing he must not climax, Luca focused on the purpose for this talisman—to summon Diana. But imagining Diana with the *boschetto* while Maddy made primal sounds as she sucked made it harder to hold back the fluids. After awhile, Luca felt Maddy slowing down. Her tight, wet lips moved up and down his hard cock, yet she teased him with her inconsistent rhythm.

"Are you okay?" he asked, pressing his fingers against the perineum, a point about halfway between the base of the scrotum and the anus. Pressing that area made his desire to ejaculate subside.

He remained hard as he mentally climaxed, then his urgent need to release shortly vanished. For sex magick to work, he had to circumvent any premature ejaculations because smaller amounts of ejaculate wouldn't generate enough power for the charge.

Maddy acknowledged his question by sucking harder, and her red hair bounced from the fervent movements of her head. Trying to gain control over his arousal, Luca stared at Maddy, her lips still on his cock and her eyes opened wide. Luca concentrated on the most difficult part of the ritual called the sederunt or "prolonged session." When done right, the sederunt lasted twenty minutes—that is, if he could last while Maddy worked. If she kept on sucking this hard, he wouldn't last much longer.

"*Dovete venire* Diana, *Dovete venire* Diana, *Dovete venire* Diana," Luca said, repeating the words to summon Diana as Maddy suckled harder with every word.

Finally, the time came, and he knew it wasn't possible to continue the sederunt any longer because he couldn't hold back anymore. He yelled out the summons once more, then sharpened his vision of Diana in his mind. Needing to release the pressure, he gritted his teeth in agony from the bloated pain in his cock.

Before his juices exploded, Luca pushed Maddy aside, then grabbed the crystal. Continuing the invocation, he ejaculated onto the crystal rod. As he spurted his fluids onto the bulbous rod, he visualized Diana in their sex magick rituals. Once he emitted the last drop, he worked the fluids onto the crystal with his hands so that the charge would manifest as the talisman. Smearing the liquids onto the crystal, he envisioned the day Diana would join the *Malandanti* to fight the war. He repeated the summons until he programmed the crystal with the thought. When he was certain the rod was fully charged, he smiled and gave thanks to Pan for the sacramental power he held within.

Ever since he was a small boy, he knew that his fluids produced the Eucharist. These fluids were consecrated by the forces he evoked through ritual and the ultimate power he held inside his body. He naturally produced a sacrament used to destroy or empower whatever he so desired through his own will. Instead of the wine and wafers of the church, Luca's Eucharist had always been

his very own fluids made from within. The *Malandanti* knew how to make the Eucharist too.

To complete the ritual, he banished the area of evil spirits with his command. "I now dismiss any spirit that may have been called to this ritual." He waved the crystal rod in the air as he spoke. "Depart now and go to your homes and habitations, harming none along the way. Let there be peace between me and thee, and may you be quick to come when you are called. May the blessings of the Divine be upon you as you may receive them. I now declare this ritual duly closed."

Turning toward Maddalena, Luca stood and pulled up his trousers, then smiled at her still kneeling on the pillow. "Your sex drive is a great source of power," he said.

"We made a talisman, didn't we?"

Luca nodded, then grabbed the key hidden in the niche and walked toward Maddy. "Please, you must go through the courtyard of the *Villa di Spagna*. Use this key to unlock the garden door of the *Villa*." Luca gave her the key, then brushed his fingertips over her lips. "Leave the crystal on Diana's bedside."

"I don't understand—"

"We just programmed this crystal to make her come to us. We need her because in her unconscious mind, where the information about her past lives resides, she knows how we can win the war. With the knowledge of the Goddess of All Witches, we can stop anything. But this crystal must be in Diana's possession for the summons to work."

"Don't you need me too?" Maddalena asked, putting her index finger inside her pouty mouth.

"Of course we need you." Luca smiled and slid his fingers through her thick, fiery-red hair. "Now you are ready for the rites of the *Malandanti*, my *Sacerdotessa*."

PART THREE
THE STRUGGLE

*Now is the time to do that thing, now is the time to move.
And I know that anything I touch at this esoteric time will
turn to gold. There are no calendar dates for the coming of
the Winds—they swirl and flow as they will and cannot be
contained. A Witch will learn to smell the changes in the
air and notice the differences in her surroundings, and for
that brief moment she must act if she is to benefit from
the extraordinary power that is the Winds of Change. Strong
and terrible, soft and sweet; as they change the structure of
the ether around us, we can use this time to make dreams
come true and unheard of possibilities happen. A very
potent time is then, the time of the Winds of Change, for
this is Our Time.*

Gilly Sergiev
A Witch's Box of Magick

CHAPTER NINE

DIANA

Villa di Spagna

February 24, 2004
Twilight

As Diana descended the steep steps to the *Villa*, the last rays of light diminished into a thin veil of dusk that changed reality into illusion. The illusion transposed everything into something else, like a chimera of Italianate architecture, making the scene look as if it could vanish into thin air with the blink of an eye. Setting down the bags from a shopping spree on *via Sistina*, Diana stopped to rest for a moment and stare at the *Villa di Spagna* nestled in the enclave below. Apparently, she had left the lamp on in her bedroom because the dim light filtered through the gauzy bedroom curtain. Even though Tess had made major changes to the *Villa*, it still gave Diana the creeps. She shivered, picked up her bags and resumed her descent.

As she approached, the gauzy, lace curtain fluttered frantically outside the window on the second story, allowing for a faint glimpse of someone in her bedroom. Diana squinted to see who it was but couldn't make out anything through the filmy lens of dusk.

"Tess, open the front door," she yelled, struggling with the heavy bags, but the figure, now obviously a female, darted away from view.

From the sudden movements of the stranger inside, Diana knew it wasn't Tess. It was an intruder. Diana dropped her bags and almost slipped as she bounded down the narrow steps and collided against the front door. One of her shopping bags crumpled down the stairs behind her, and the porcelain teacups inside shattered.

"Damn," she said, as she searched her pockets for the key. Then she gave up and tried the door, which opened easily because it was unlocked. She raced up the stairs to the bedroom, but the intruder had vanished. Yanking back the curtain, she spotted a young woman running through the courtyard below.

"Hey," she yelled.

The girl froze and turned around slowly. *She was your lover, Antonio?* Diana wondered. How could someone named Raven have such fiery red hair? In an instant, the girl looked up and stared at Diana, then turned and ran away. Certain that girl was the one dancing in the courtyard that first night at the *Villa,* Diana didn't know what to do. She yelled out again, but the girl slipped through the gate into freedom and fled through the crowd on the Spanish Steps.

Diana searched the *Villa* and found nothing amiss, then decided to take a sedative for the first time since she had been hospitalized from the accident. But after filling her glass with water, she stared at the tranquilizer in the palm of her hand and decided not to take it. She hadn't had any medication since her rehab, and those drugs hadn't helped her one bit as she had spiraled down into hopelessness. Diana shook her head. Drugs would just make her problems worse.

Diana tossed the pill in the trash, then walked into the bedroom and collapsed on the bed. Reaching for the phone, she froze at the sight of a strange object—an odd-shaped crystal. Diana used a tissue to pick it up, then washed the grimy thing with soapy water in the bathroom sink. When Diana first spotted the intruder, the girl was standing near the bedside table exactly where Diana found the crystal, so maybe the girl had left it. Diana held the crystal up to the light and gazed at the multifaceted colors of purplish gold.

Setting the crystal back down on the bedside table, Diana grabbed the phone and dialed Tess's cell. After endless ringing, Diana finally heard Tess's recorded voice. Diana slammed the receiver down into its cradle, then stopped and stared at the crystal again, mesmerized by the clear prism in the light from her bedside lamp. She dialed directory assistance, then asked for the only other person she knew in Rome. Once the operator gave her the number, Diana dialed it.

"*Buonasera.*"

"Vincent? It's Diana. I need help."

"Is something wrong?" he asked.

"I've had an intruder."

"Give me a minute. I'll be there as soon as I can."

After slamming down the phone once again, she remained on the bed, then bent over with her elbows on her knees and messed up her hair trying to relax. She stood up and stared at the window facing the courtyard below. The locks had to be changed. Tess was supposed to be taking care of that project, but the way things worked in Rome, it took forever to get anything done, especially repairs or construction. And to leave the door unlocked—that was vintage Tess. She should just do it herself; tomorrow she would install dead bolts. And that iron gate in the courtyard she would just have to find a way to secure that too.

But if she put deadbolts on, then her intruder wouldn't come back and maybe she would never know about the other woman, the one who slept with her husband. Maybe she shouldn't fix the locks because maybe that girl had other things to give her besides dirty crystals.

After moving to Rome, she had more questions than answers. She still hadn't found Luca, even though she had tried every way she could possibly think of. His whereabouts had not been recorded anywhere. Maybe he didn't live in Rome, because no one knew him—not even the telephone company. Diana picked up the crystal, then walked over to the window. The crystal glowed in the moonlight as if it were lit from within. In shades of purplish-copper bronze, the faceted glass reflected the moonlight in awe-inspiring ways. She almost dropped it when the chime rang at the front door.

Leaving the crystal on the windowsill, she rushed downstairs to the foyer. When Diana opened the front door and locked eyes with Vincent, she froze and her pulse quickened.

When she was first introduced to Vincent, Diana tried not to feel anything toward him. But now, there was just too much Italian macho for her to ignore. For one thing, Vincent's ItalianAmerican voice made her want to melt, just as Antonio's voice had affected her. To further complicate things, Vincent's looks made her nervous. He was almost too handsome, if such a thing was possible. Rather than stocky and large like Antonio, Vincent was tall and thin, yet he had a strong build. Vincent's charisma reminded her of Antonio's magnetism, and she wondered if that was the attraction. It unsettled her that she felt this way because she had only been five months without Antonio. How could she even think about another man? Wearing blue jeans and a soft, baggy, white shirt, Vincent held out his hands as if in surrender. Rather than ignore him this time, Diana impulsively embraced him with gratitude now that she was no longer alone.

"How did you get here so soon?" she asked, pushing him away immediately after the friendly embrace.

"My *attico* is very close to you." When Diana scrunched up her nose, Vincent added, "I live just down the steps across the *piazza.*"

"Thank you for coming," she said, gesturing him inside. "I tried calling Tess, but she's nowhere to be found. Her cell must be turned off. Then I thought of you."

"You're shaking," Vincent said, frowning. "What happened?"

"The intruder. I came home and she ran away. She was in my bedroom."

"How did she get in?"

"Through the courtyard."

"Show me."

Diana flicked on the lights in the living room, crossed the threshold and opened the French doors to the courtyard. Outside in the moonlit garden, Diana pointed at the gate in the wall, which was almost hidden from view by the brush. Vincent examined the latch as he opened and closed the door, then shook his head.

"Do you know where the key is?" he asked.

"I have a copy, so that must mean she does too."

Vincent scanned the courtyard, then pointed to an obelisk in the sculpture garden. "Help me move this."

Diana grabbed the pinnacle while Vincent reached for the bottom, then they lugged it over to the gate. Vincent wedged the pinnacle against the latch until the iron door couldn't be opened again.

"You need to change these locks," he said, checking once more to see if the gate was secure.

"We've called the locksmith, but he keeps putting us off."

Vincent laughed, then held out his hand. "Let's call the police."

"No," Diana said, ignoring his outstretched hand. "No police."

"Let me search the house then."

"I know who it was. Follow me," Diana said, leading the way into the *Villa,* up the stairs and into the master bedroom.

Walking over to the bedside table, Diana paused before she picked up the crystal and handed it to Vincent. "She left this."

"What is it?" he asked.

"She's a witch. I found something similar in our Aspen home right after Antonio died."

"You know who it was?"

"I'm certain it was Raven."

Vincent frowned and they were silent as their eyes seemed to converse. "Please, you must rest," he said, guiding her to the bed.

"No, I don't need anything." Diana stiffened but let him steer her toward the master bed.

Vincent pulled back the sheets and helped her climb in. Diana settled into the pillows and watched Vincent pull up a chair. "There. Just close your eyes and relax."

"Do you know a man named Luca DeMarco?" Diana asked, wondering if Antonio had talked about his brother in his therapy. "My husband's brother."

"I never met him."

Diana swung her legs to the side of the bed to get up, but Vincent took her by the arm, then gently guided her back against the soft pillows.

In silence, he moved to the foot of the bed and took off her shoes. Expertly massaging her foot, he whispered when he spoke. "Antonio was concerned about his brother."

"Why?"

"Antonio claimed his brother wanted revenge against the Roman Catholic Church."

Diana gave him a questioning look. "Do you know where he lives?"

Vincent shook his head.

"Did Antonio talk about Raven in his sessions?" Diana watched Vincent flinch as if he were hiding something.

Vincent shook his head again. "No wonder you hate men. A woman like you drives men crazy, because you don't understand their needs."

"I have to find out why my husband kept so many secrets from me, because there's more to it than just an affair." Diana frowned. "What makes you think I hate men?"

"You want to know why he was with another woman? It's easy. It has nothing to do with you or with love. It has to do with necessity. One woman is never enough for an Italian man."

On the one hand, Diana felt the tension melt away as he massaged her foot, but on the other hand, her anxiety increased from Vincent's faulty rationale. "Have you ever loved a woman?" she asked, wanting to know what made Vincent tick.

"I don't think the way you do. Love doesn't exist for me the way you see it. I don't know the type of love you speak of, nor do I even *want* to know it."

"Why not?"

"Because it cannot be for me, as it couldn't be for my family either. Men are not supposed to have just one woman forever," he said. "But then, I do not think women are meant to have just one man either. Please, this is not helping you. My opinions have no bearing here. It is only my way and the way most Italian men think."

"Your parents never loved each other?"

"They fought, they hated, they despised, cheated and lied," he said. "That is why marriage will never work for me. They still hate each other even in divorce. But then, they never loved either."

Diana took off her gauzy sweater and gave him a questioning look, but his eyes seemed cold. "It doesn't have to be the same as it was for your parents," she said, thinking of the love she lost after her parents died, then the love she lost with Antonio and her unborn baby. Certain she was loved by her family, Diana wanted that kind of love again.

"It is all I ever knew as a child," Vincent said. "And it keeps coming back with the women I am with."

"See," Diana said. "It's a choice. You choose them. Maybe that's the problem—you've chosen the wrong ones, ones who are unable to love."

Vincent shook his head. "I'm not sure what I want in a woman, but I certainly don't want love."

"Why not?"

"Because I cannot love them back. I want women who satisfy my desires, not make demands."

Diana kicked at him with her foot, making him pull back from massaging it. "How can you not love, when love is everything? I keep looking for it, and once I find it—either the love dies or the person dies with it." Diana laughed. "True love is not demanding, anyway."

Vincent laughed with her, then looked serious. "Forgive me. I must sound callous. I have talked too much, but then I keep doing this with you for some reason," he said, standing up. "I must go."

"No, don't." Diana said, shivering from the thought of being alone. "Please, don't leave me." She didn't want to sound demanding, but she couldn't let him go, not now. Not wanting to be alone, she had to make him stay somehow. Her thoughts would devour her the minute he left, but if he stayed with her tonight, maybe there would be no nightmares.

Diana held up the duvet and motioned for him to come into her bed. Shaking his head, he must have quickly changed his mind because when their eyes met, he smiled. Vincent slowly took off his shoes and joined her in bed—both with their clothes on, both under the covers.

"How am I to refuse this look you give me? Very unprofessional."

"Just think of it as taking care of your patient," she whispered. "You're keeping me safe at night."

Diana watched his head sink into the pillows next to her, then smiled at the thought of being able to sleep tonight because he would be there beside her. When he settled in, Diana bit her lip and waited. Once he stopped moving, Diana snuggled up next to him and rested her head on his broad chest. A surge of energy pulsed through her veins when he put his arms around her. Then she decided to let go and let this dream become reality.

CHAPTER TEN

DIANA

Vatican City

February 25, 2004
Morning

After shivering for hours from the cool morning breeze, Diana was thankful when the doors of Saint Peter's *basilica* finally opened. What started with a few individuals had now turned into a line that stretched indefinitely as people waited to get into the Ash Wednesday rite at the Vatican. Diana was one of the first to step into the *basilica*, so she figured it would be easy after that. But once she was inside, she discovered that several preopening tours had made the *basilica* almost full already. When Diana reached the center of the *basilica*, directly under Michelangelo's dome, she wondered if she could get any closer to the rite, then discovered she couldn't move for the burgeoning crowd. As part of that crowd, Diana decided she would just have to be satisfied where she was.

Even though she was surrounded by people who looked warm, she felt cold. Recalling what Tess had told her about this place made her shiver even more. According to Tess, the tombs of Saint Peter and other papal dignitaries were directly below the *basilica* in a place called the *City of the Dead*, or the necropolis. Looking up at the towering *baldacchino*, the holiest part of the church, Diana decided that commemorating the papal tombs below contributed to the ghastly feel of the place. There were also other monumental tombs aboveground in the *basilica*, and the one Tess had mentioned was Bernini's gilded bronze that memorialized Alexander VII. For that tomb, Bernini created a gilded skeleton holding an hourglass in his hand of gilded bones, which seemed to set the theme throughout the *baʒilica* that it was only a matter of time before we die.

The dark mood of Bernini's other work, the *baldacchino*, didn't help the ghostly atmosphere of the place either because the bronze structure looked too peculiar to be in a sanctuary. Saint Peter's *baʒilica*, known for comforting the lost and weary, did just the opposite with the towering *baldacchino*. The monolithic canopy, perched on twisted pillars, looked more like the dark night of the soul. A gargantuan structure of ebony bronze, the *baldacchino'ʒ* lurking presence haunted the soul and turned any feelings of comfort into insidious fear. Knowing that the *baldacchino* was situated atop a morbid necropolis below made Bernini's work evoke the death knell rather than inspire the downtrodden.

Regardless of the macabre artistry, there was no denying the sacredness of the sanctuary. After what happened last night, Diana tried not to feel guilty, but the holiness of the *baʒilica* coupled with the ceremonial purpose of the day forced her to reflect on it nevertheless. Because it was Ash Wednesday, Diana decided to attend the service to reexamine her motives and desires in her relationships with men, then abstain from anymore reckless behavior. She crossed herself again, even though she had already done it with the Holy Water when she first entered with the crowd.

During her short time with Antonio, Diana discovered things she never knew about herself. As if Antonio had opened Pandora's Box, Diana realized that her latent desires had been awakened, as well as an energy force within herself that had surged whenever he was around her. Like an electrical current every time they were together, this force between them continued until his death. But it concerned her that she felt that same force with Vincent too.

Vincent reminded her of Antonio, yet they were entirely different. One thing was certain though: the energy was the same. She could hardly explain this potent energy, yet it happened from the beginning, from the very first moment either one of them crossed her path. She wouldn't allow herself to acknowledge the magnetism when she initially met Vincent. Feeling that force again scared her because it happened so quickly after Antonio's death. She was angry the day she met Vincent, because she was afraid that force would come back into her life and turn it upside down all over again. She thought it was better to be angry than be attracted to a man so soon after her husband's death, because going from one to the next just wasn't right. But even after being rational about Vincent, she still wanted him.

Although he hadn't done anything sexual last night, Diana had fantasized about making love to Vincent. Her desires made her feel even more guilty, because she had to keep reminding herself that it had been only five months since Antonio died. Her guilt hadn't stopped her from thinking about having sex with Vincent, though. Diana figured if she were more Catholic, maybe she wouldn't have these kinds of thoughts. Last night, she wanted Vincent to make a move, but he didn't do anything. She thought about making a move the entire night while he held her, but she couldn't. Diana didn't want to be the one to initiate it—she wanted him to. He still hadn't even kissed her although they snuggled, and in a way that had been even worse. She fantasized as he held her until she almost begged him do something, but he had been a gentleman. Thankful she hadn't done anything with him, Diana felt guilty about her thoughts anyway.

The problem was they got along so well. She hardly knew him, yet during the short time they had been together, they laughed, they talked about anything and they had that energy—that invisible force between them. Even though she just met him, she knew that feeling because she had it with Antonio too. But now that Vincent was her therapist, it would be impossible to do anything about her feelings because having a relationship with Vincent would be unprofessional for him. The fact that he was emotionally unavailable made it even worse—it wouldn't even be a relationship. He didn't want one woman, he wanted many, and even then he wasn't open to love. Vincent was unable to love just one woman he had told her, so she could never do anything intimate with him because love made sex so much better. Diana slapped the back of her hand and vowed to stop thinking about sex with Vincent.

Trying to abstain from her wanton thoughts, Diana had to get back to her Catholic roots, and this Ash Wednesday service followed by the days of Lent was a perfect beginning. She skipped breakfast to start the fast, and now she would abstain from thinking about Vincent. Vowing to focus on why she was at the service, Diana turned her thoughts to the ceremony. She had been told it would be different, because the ritual was being held right here inside Saint Peter's *basilica.* Due to the ailing pontiff, Pope John Paul II couldn't travel like he normally did to Aventine Hill. Tess had told her this custom was introduced by Saint Gregory the Great in the sixth century and was reestablished by John XXIII in 1960 with a ceremony outside the *basilica* at Saint Sabina, but today heralded a change in the location of the Ash Wednesday ritual. If the Vatican could change, so could Diana.

Eager to hear the "celebration of the word," she needed to remind herself what the ashes meant and why she would wear an ashen sign of the cross on her forehead throughout the day. The ashes were a symbol of our immortality even after death, and the ashen sign of the cross was to remind us of our sins. This was a time for sacrifice, penitence and reflection on our sinful nature. With one ear, Diana heard the Pope asking the faithful to pay attention to the plight of children around the world, because they were the ones who were often abandoned and needed special care.

Thinking his words were rather apropos in view of the high-ranking officials in churches around the world who had been accused of molesting children in their parishes, yet had been protected by the Vatican by silently moving those errant officials to other parishes, Diana wondered why the Pope didn't mention the sins of the church too.

Diana tried to find a spot where she could see the Pope, but she soon decided that even a glimpse was impossible. Then a woman brushed passed her, effortlessly moving through the chaotic mass of people. She was pregnant and almost at full term. When the crowd didn't meld together after she passed, Diana quickly stepped behind the woman and followed her toward the Pope. Like a reenactment of the Red Sea, the crowd parted as the pregnant woman walked deeper into the *basilica.* Snaking through the mass of people with just a slight murmur to make them notice, the pregnant woman made some people turn and smile, while others respectfully nodded. Diana stayed close to the Italian woman even when they reached the area in front of the Pope.

When Diana realized the Italian woman had just effortlessly walked through the crowded *basilica* of the world's largest church, she fought the urge to tap her on the shoulder and say *grazi*. Diana shook her head, surprised she was close enough to see the Pope's wrinkles. As if he could read her thoughts, the Pope smiled at Diana. As he smiled, a peaceful serenity filled her entire being. Although Diana didn't follow the rules of the church, yet still considered herself a Catholic, seeing the Pope was monumental.

He moved his feeble hand as he spoke. "Exterior gestures of penitence have value if they are expressions of an interior attitude, if they show the firm willingness to move away from evil and take the path of good," he said.

Diana watched him gesture as he spoke and wondered if he was in pain. Although he didn't show any signs of agony in his face, his physical form looked as if he might fall over from exhaustion at any minute. She closed her eyes and said a prayer for his health, crossing herself once again. When she opened her eyes, she imagined the Pope nodded, thanking her for her prayer.

When the people near her began the imposition of ashes, she followed the pregnant woman to the front. Diana watched as the Pope dipped his white-gloved hand into the ash, then drew the sign of the cross on a man's forehead and recited the blessing. Although the man was big, he seemed rather moved once the blessing was finished because he faltered as he walked away, then needed help as he left. Diana watched as the pregnant woman stepped up to the altar to receive the ash. She closed her eyes, then the pontiff"s white-gloved hand made a perfect sign of the cross upon her forehead. Immediately, the pregnant woman whirled around as if she were about to faint, and just as Diana was about to assist, three attendants came to help the woman walk away.

Diana was next. She approached the altar and smiled at Pope John Paul II, then closed her eyes. As the pontiff drew the sign of the cross on her forehead, she heard him say, *Remember that you are dust and to dust you shall return.* But the minute his gloved finger touched her forehead, a jab of pain seared through her body and she instinctively recoiled. One of the attendants nearby moved to help her, but Diana shrugged him off and tried to walk away without falling. She staggered through the crowd as it parted like the Red Sea, then she held her hand over her mouth as her head throbbed with pain.

As she reached the front doors of the church, her headache turned into a stomachache. She rushed out the massive door and down the steps, then hunched over from a coughing fit just as she reached the outskirts of the *Piazza San Pietro.* She tried to hail a cab but couldn't get anyone to stop. Then, she heard Tess.

"Get in, there's no way you're walking home—it's too far." Tess leaned over and opened the passenger side of the car.

Relieved to see her friend, Diana bit her lip as she climbed into the little Fiat. Her stomach pains had gotten worse.

"What's wrong?" Tess asked, helping Diana close the car door. "Is it really that bad in there?"

"No. I'm just sick, that's all. It came on so suddenly." Diana rolled down the window for some fresh air. "I don't know why."

"All that pomp and circumstance would make me sick too," Tess said, doing a double-take at Diana's frown. "Sorry, I know that's your deal, but if they can't decide which cross to use, then they've got problems."

"What are you talking about?"

"The architecture is a mess just because they kept changing the cross. As if it made a difference, when all crosses mean the same thing," Tess said, waving her hand like a true Italian. "The original Saint Peter's was a typical *basilican* form with a Latin cross that included nave, side aisles and a crossing, but then during the restoration, it was changed to a Greek cross. That's when Michelangelo created the dome, but according to Pope Paul V, the Latin cross was more appropriate. Because they just couldn't decide on the type of cross, the architecture suffered."

"Maybe that's it—the restoration project. The fumes made me sick."

"The restoration project was done before the new millennium, not afterward, Di. There can't be any fumes."

"I think you need to pull over," Diana said, leaning out the window, wanting to vomit as the car lurched to the side of the narrow street. She jumped out before the car came to a complete stop, bent over and eliminated everything in her stomach.

Tess jumped out of the car and rushed over to help. "Are you okay?"

"No."

"Want to stay here for awhile until you feel better?"

"We need to go."

"You're too sick," Tess said, helping Diana to the car. "We should take you to the hospital."

"Please, just get in and drive. I'll be okay." Diana climbed in, then closed her eyes as soon as the car started moving. Once the cool breeze whipped through her hair, she felt better—still not right, but better nevertheless. She couldn't be sick because they were starting their new venture today on *via Margutta*.

"We have to set up our work," Diana said, breaking the silence.

"Already did. The gallery awaits us."

Diana turned to stare at Tess. "How did you do that? But first answer this, where were you last night?"

"I had to go out," Tess said. "I had some wine with my new friend, Mario."

"A male friend? Are you serious?" But Diana could see it in Tess's eyes. She was serious, and that warmed Diana's heart. She wanted Tess to find someone ever since they met, and as far as Diana knew, Tess never had a man for long. "Tell me about him," Diana added.

"It's nothing serious," she said, wheeling the car into a tiny parking spot, then jumping out.

Diana followed Tess as she walked down the cobblestone street toward *via Margutta*. "How can you know so soon?" Diana called. "Wait up, I'm sick, remember?" Surprised that her illness had vanished as quickly as it had appeared, Diana was relieved that her pain was gone.

Tess laughed. "I only need a man to satisfy certain needs. Everyone needs a bit of pleasure now and then." Tess walked midway down *via Margutta,* then waved at the woman unpacking crates filled with paintings and sculptures. The front door of what must be their gallery on *via Margutta* swarmed with people browsing through the artwork just outside the shop.

"Is this Viviana?" Diana asked.

Tess nodded, then introduced Diana to the decorator. "With the help of our decorator, who is now our new housekeeper, we only have a few crates left." Tess gestured at the young woman and helped her remove the bubble wrap from a large sculpture. "The nudes I had shipped seem to be intact."

"What a job. There's no doubt with that kind of karma, we're meant to be in Rome."

"We'll get some answers about Antonio's hidden past, I promise." Tess stopped working and smiled, then gave Diana a quick hug. "I'm glad you feel better."

Together they unpacked the remaining pieces and displayed them outside as well as inside the gallery. But after awhile, Diana noticed a slight stomach pain that seemed to come in waves. She tried not to think about it, then popped an antacid into her mouth and walked outside the gallery for some fresh air.

Diana squinted through the glaring sunlight to watch the people milling through the exhibits and dealer displays on the narrow street. Framed in splotches of amber, aqua and verdigris, the scene before her at *via Margutta* came alive with eclectic exhibits and creative displays. Spectators milled through oils perched on easels and makeshift stands, while violins played in the distance. Miniature galleries sandwiched between exotic studios beckoned onlookers to enter, and sprawling vines dangling from antiquated stone walls waved them away in the wind. Elaborately framed windows and small arched doors invited the curious to enter places that looked like the Holy Grail. Tunes from a violinist playing *Ave Maria* haunted the cobblestone street with the ghostly music until kaleidoscope colors lulled Diana's thoughts into a dreamlike trance. Thankful to have her gallery premiere on this exquisite street, Diana closed her eyes and smiled.

In an instant, her stomach pain sharpened. Leaning over, she almost rubbed the ashes on her forehead, but didn't because, according to the church, the ashes should be left on the forehead all day. The waves of nausea worsened, and she eased into a director's chair amid her paintings displayed outside the gallery. Wondering what she should do, Diana realized the pain vanished as quickly as it ensued. She shook her head, then decided stay put for awhile to make sure her sickness was gone.

Since she spent the entire night in Vincent's arms, Diana felt a deep sense of trust with him. Any man who could sleep next to a woman and not do anything had to be someone special. He hadn't even tried to touch her. Last night was the first night she felt safe and secure. Unfortunately, Diana knew it was her insecurities that made her feel anxious and unfulfilled. And then there were the dreams she kept having ever since she saw the picture of Luca in Aspen. Last night was the first time she didn't have those wicked dreams. Feeling guilty, Diana wondered why she didn't dream about Antonio making love to her instead of Luca. She wondered what the church would think about her sinful dreams. Surely sexual dreams didn't mean you were sinning in the eyes of the church. On the other hand, maybe sexual dreams were a sin because sex in general must be sinful if priests couldn't even have it.

The crowd thickened as Diana focused on a man wearing a long, black jacket that flapped in the breeze. With his back toward her, the man's broad shoulders made him seem rugged even though his Italian silk suit made him look like a man of wealth and leisure. He waved his hands in the air with emotion, and his ebony hair furled in the wind. When the conversation escalated into sharp tones, the man wheeled around and stormed past Diana. Wanting to help him, Diana opened her mouth to speak, but no sound came forth when she realized it was Luca.

Diana froze, stunned to see the man in the photo, then jumped up to get Tess's attention inside the gallery. "Keep an eye on our work outside," she yelled. "I'll be right back."

Tess waved and made her way toward the door.

Diana ran down the street after Luca, then spotted his shiny, black jacket flapping in the breeze as he turned down *via Vittoria*.

She almost shouted, but he was too far away. Once she entered *via Vittoria,* she stepped into an undulating sea of people loitering in the couture district. People meandering into the boutiques and staring at the window displays made it impossible for her to catch up with Luca. She tried to nudge them out of her way as she raced down the narrow street, but her pace slowed to a frustrated walk. She saw Luca dart into another narrow street and was able to follow, but the street overflowed with Japanese tourists who blocked her way. The crowd shifted and Diana noticed Luca swiftly weave his way through the district. As he turned left onto *via de Fiori,* Diana bumped into a man playing his saxophone for the people at an outside *caffè.*

"Sorry," Diana said, grabbing his shoulder to stop herself from falling.

The man stopped playing his sax, but he still had the mouthpiece on his lip. Diana continued in what she thought was the direction Luca went. As the crowd thinned briefly, she saw him head down a street named *via Borgognona.* But as soon as she entered that street, she became part of a pulsating mass of people who forced her to slow down again. Shoulder to shoulder, elbow to elbow, she inched her way through the crowd. Even when she tried to push her way through, no one moved. The crowd swelled at the end of the street, making the multitude of teenagers puff harder on their cigarettes, then laugh at their plight. Hemmed in by the crowd, Diana's pursuit stopped until she entered a busy street named *via del Corso.* But by that time, Diana knew she had lost him.

Tears welled up in Diana's eyes from the thought that she would never find Luca in this overcrowded city. After trying everything, it had been an impossible task to track him down. Telephone books, operators and even strangers hadn't helped her locate the man, and now she didn't have the strength to continue her search. She felt the tears stream down her face as she passed an endless stream of people rushing down the street. Lost in Rome, she wasn't sure how to find her way back to the *Villa.* She stood on the curb and motioned to several cabs, but none stopped.

She stepped into a dark avenue hoping she was headed in the right direction, then spotted Luca at the end of the street. But with her side ache and her stomach pain returning, she couldn't run, so she searched for a place to rest instead. A strong, gusty wind whipped down the lane, and its tumultuous force wreaked havoc on an ancient sign dangling above a dark, hollowed-out passageway. The creaking sound drew her near, then she looked up and read the words on the decrepit sign: *Le Vecchia Religione.*

The surreal light inside the small store intrigued Diana because it looked like the twilight was caught in the crystal pentagrams that were on display. Trying to thwart a wave of nausea, Diana bit her lip as she realized this place was for witches. She stumbled through the dark passageway, then grabbed the twisted latch on the heavy wooden door and opened it. The sound of bones rattling as it opened made Diana almost turn and run. Inside, the subdued candlelight blurred her vision, and a mist engulfed her with vapors. She froze, blinded by the smoky mist and blinked until cloudy images of tarot cards, crystal balls and strange figurines came into view. The pain in her stomach seemed to move to her chest, and she pressed her fingers against the base of her throat.

As if she were having a stroke, Diana gasped for air and inhaled a strange yet familiar aroma. Breathing deeply, she realized it was the same scent that she smelled that first day in the *Villa.* Certain the smell made her chest pains worse, Diana tried calling out for help, but before she could utter a word, a dizzy spell overcame her and she reached toward a display table to steady herself. But her distorted view made her hand miss the table and almost fall. Unable to stop the vise grip in her chest, she couldn't breathe. She stepped toward the table, wondering why she couldn't hold onto it, then missed it again when the thing spun around inside her head. In an instant, the entire store whirled around and she eased herself down to the floor for support. Thankful for the solid tiles beneath her, Diana closed her eyes in relief. But the respite didn't last long because once she closed her eyes, the floor became a whirling dervish.

CHAPTER ELEVEN

LUCA

Via Condotti

February 25, 2004
Late Afternoon

Luca hurried down *via Condotti* anxious to view Diana's paintings. After she chased him for nearly forty minutes, it now seemed as if he had finally lost her. He waited until he was certain she had vanished in the labyrinth of cobblestone streets, then slowed his pace and started back to the gallery. When Diana recognized him on *via Margutta,* he had no choice but to flee because he couldn't help her. The moment he saw Diana, Luca noticed the ashes on her forehead and the pallid color of her skin, then knew she was either dying or sick because of the ash. The only one who could possibly save her from the talisman was Raven, so Luca lured Diana through the web of narrow streets near Raven's shop, *Le Vecchia Religione.*

Wanting to save Diana from impending death, Luca hoped Raven could find a cure for the talisman—if there was one. Luca was careful to let Diana catch a glimpse of him here and there along the narrow streets, then made sure she was close enough to Raven's shop before he vanished completely from Diana's sight. Confident she would find the shop and meet Raven before succumbing to the poisonous ash, Luca knew the talisman would take effect soon. Other people with the ash from the Vatican on their foreheads also would succumb soon. Luca estimated that it would take about four to six hours after the ash was rubbed onto the skin for the full effects of the talisman to take place. Then he would know the potency of ashes charged with ritual, as well as ashes from cremating his father, the *Sacerdote of the Sotterranea.*

Luca couldn't help Diana or even talk to her because she wasn't fully "programmed" for instant hypnosis yet, and if she connected his face with his seduction voice, it might change her willingness to "go under." The ability to be hypnotized was always determined by the person's choice to go under, but in this case Luca planned to arouse her desires, then make her want to be "controlled." By sexually arousing Diana in the dream state, he would eventually tap into her desires until she wanted him to do things to her.

Once she let him into her mind, then he would be able to induce her with the three-minute somnambulistic technique. Now that he had perfected the technique, he could take her into a state where she was unconscious yet fully awake, then communicate with her subconscious mind. Once he trained her mind to switch from the conscious to the unconscious state when he uttered a word or two, she would be in the somnambulistic state and would automatically go into a trance at the sound of the words, as well as his voice. In this deep sleep or trance state, Diana wouldn't remember anything, yet would allow herself to experience everything that happened. She let him come to her in her "dreams" because it fulfilled her needs. He wasn't finished with programming her mind to receive him though, so he needed to be careful not to interact with her while she was conscious.

Luca weaved his way through the crowded *Piazza di Spagna,* then reached Diana's new gallery in no time at all. He searched her collection of oils, then finally found the painting that revealed everything.

Scanning the entire surface of the work, which was probably only twenty by twenty inches, he relaxed his eyes and stared at it until he penetrated into the depths of the painting. Using his variation of the magick eye technique to see the hidden image, he tried to discern where two dimensions became three. The shuffling feet of onlookers around him became muffled when the top surface of the painting popped out like a cutout card with images that appeared either closer to or farther away from his sight. As if he were wearing three-dimensional glasses, everything came alive through depth perception. Then the image appeared to move as the globs of oil formed a portal, or an open door into another dimension. The background receded, much like the ones in the magick eye pictures, but this image was different because it produced a tunnel or hole that appeared to go through the picture into another realm or an altered state of being. He recognized this realm readily because he had used portals like these many times before for astral projection or as a doorway to the lunar realms.

The portal beckoned him with its black energy writhing in circles as if it wanted to suck the air he breathed inside its funnel. If he allowed it, the seething mass of darkness might take him into another place and time. He blinked, then stepped back. This had to be Diana's painting because only a Goddess would know the key to the other realms with the stroke of a brush. In a two-dimensional pattern, she created a three-dimensional form hidden inside an image that was created on a flat plane. Known as a stereogram, this hidden image could be seen only by someone like Luca, who had an advanced sense of depth perception and an ability to use divergent vision. By making his eyes relax, he could see images that most people never saw at all.

Concentrating harder, he stepped back to stare at the painting from afar and make the hidden image appear once again. The gray scale became the source for the secret image that created the two-dimensional pattern, but in order to encode the invisible image, an algorithm would normally be used; however, this image wasn't designed with a scientific algorithm. It was done through a natural ability to—

"May I help you?" a voice asked from behind him.

"Who's the artist?" Luca asked, knowing the answer, yet wanting to hear her name spoken aloud. He spun around and saw a striking woman in tight blue jeans wearing a gauzy, transparent top. Her curly hair, piled on top of her head, enhanced her seductive look.

The woman froze. "You're Antonio's brother, right?"

"I am. Who painted this?"

"Your sister-in-law, Diana DeMarco. Did you receive word about your brother's accident?" she asked, furrowing her brow.

Luca nodded, then turned away to stare at the painting.

"My condolences," she said, then paused. "I'm Diana's friend, Tess. Diana has been trying to find you ever since we moved here." Tess kept on even though his back was turned. "Will you give me your number so she can call you? You're not listed in the directory."

"Tell me about her work. Are there others?" Luca spun around, then stared into her sultry hazel eyes.

"Inside." Tess gestured at the open door of the shop. Her cell phone rang just as Luca stepped into the gallery. "I'll be right with you," she added.

As Tess talked on the phone, Luca scanned the gallery for any oils that were similar to the one outside, but soon realized that no other work had the dimensional portal like the first one he'd seen. When he stepped outside again, Tess ended her call and slipped the telephone into her pocket.

"When did she paint this one?" he asked, pointing at the oil he coveted.

"It's her most recent. She just finished it."

"I'll take it." Without hesitation, Luca gave Tess his credit card. He didn't want to waste any time.

Tess carried the painting into the gallery, then finally returned minutes later with it wrapped. Handing him the charge slip to sign, she asked him to write down his address and telephone number.

When Tess handed him the painting, Luca touched her arm. "You both live at the *Villa di Spagna,* no?"

Tess nodded.

"May I visit you there sometime?" Luca asked, then turned and fled without waiting for her reply. Although he heard her say *yes,* he couldn't be delayed any longer. He had no time to spare, because with the hidden secrets embedded in the painting, Diana's work belonged in the *Sotterranea.* There the knowledge could remain hidden with the secret sigils of the *Grotto.*

Once he returned to the *Piazza di Spagna,* he bought the crimson roses he needed from Giuseppe at the flower stand, then ascended the Spanish Steps to the *Trinità dei Monti.* Ignoring the loitering teenagers there, he reached the top, then passed the peddlers selling their wares. Without hesitation, he stepped from the curb onto the street. A chaotic mass of motorists sped by, but Luca didn't flinch. Once he reached the sidewalk, he hurried down *the Trinità dei Monti* at a steady pace for almost a kilometer before the *Castello del Pincio* came into view.

In the beginning, Luca hadn't realized how strategic it was for him to live with his father rather than fight with his older brother about the *Villa di Spagna,* which was Antonio's inheritance. Seven years ago, when they first moved to *Roma,* Luca argued with his brother about the ownership of the *Villa di Spagna* until Antonio forbade Luca to come near it. Even though Antonio spent only half his time at the *Villa* and the other half in Aspen, Antonio never relented after their dispute years ago. Now that Antonio was gone, Luca didn't even want the *Villa di Spagna* anymore because he had his own *Villa* beneath the *Castello*—the *Villa de Marco* in the *Roma Sotterranea.* With his father's passing, Luca now also owned the *Castello del Pincio,* which meant he had direct access to the underground where he could perform sex magick rites anywhere in the *Sotterranea.* So in the end, Luca got what he wanted.

Janus restored the dilapidated *Castello del Pincio* to its original condition when he first moved to *Roma* so that the property was magnificent. Because *Pincio* Gardens had once been owned by his father, they had an arrangement with the city to keep their privacy underground. And that privacy turned out to be fortuitous, because then Luca could access the underground not only through the elevator in the gardens, but also through the portal in the cellar of the *Castello.*

Having an elevator in the gardens had proved ingenious because then the *boschetto* could come and go as they pleased. On the far end of *Pincio* Gardens, right by the clock, a building built in the nineteenth century contained an elevator that had been closed from the public over fifty years ago. The structure, built atop the Roman Wall, once contained a decrepit elevator shaft that led straight down the wall to the bottom of the hill at *Pincio* Gardens. At one time, Janus donated the structure to the public for easy access to Borghese Park at the bottom of the hill at *Pincio* Gardens, but once Janus decided his *boschetto* needed another way to enter the *Sotterranea*, he made sure the elevator didn't work for the public anymore. After closing the elevator to the public because it was too dangerous, Janus had a new elevator installed that didn't open to the street at the bottom of the hill, but rather opened in the opposite direction—into the *Sotterranea* inside the hill.

So late at night, the *Malandanti* routinely unlocked the chains of the iron gate, opened the door of the condemned structure, then entered the refurbished elevator inside. The elevator enabled the *boschetto* easy access to the underground, as well as privacy because the elevator and the structure that housed it were the DeMarco property even though the gardens were public. That was another advantage of living at *Castello del Pincio* because the *boschetto* used the secret elevator, while Luca used the entry in his cellar. He had the perfect situation because the private elevator in the gardens allowed the entire *Malandanti* to enter the underground late at night without leaving a trace, while Luca could descend into the *Sotterranea* anytime he wanted.

In the end, the *Castello del Pincio* had been a more strategic place to live anyway because of the underground access. In the cellar, the portal that opened to the carved-out steps provided direct access to the *Sotterranea* and led straight to the *Villa de Marco*. Since the *Castello* was directly above the *Villa de Marco*, Luca could be there in no time.

The portal to the *Sotterranea* had been purposefully built into the cellar because the *Castello*, as well as the rest of the city, was built upon layers of ancient *Roma*. Many times, entries to the underground were already there, including the stairs because when the levels were made, architects intentionally left an access to the underground. Frequently structures with lower levels opened to the *Sotterranea;* in fact, some structures were even built using the old foundation as the base. When the *Castello* was built, it was built on top of the city below it, and the city below that city was built over another, and so on until there were layers upon layers of ancient cities beneath *Roma*. The underground was either directly below the surface, which meant that layer was from the more recent past, or it was deeper inside the earth, which meant that particular layer originated even farther back in antiquity. Many

Italians either didn't know about the trapdoors in their cellars that led to the *Sotterranea* or didn't *want* to know, especially since the underground was known for being haunted.

As the last rays of light dissolved into the fiery sunset, Luca climbed the stairs to the front door of the *Castello del Pincio*. His grip tightened on the wrapped painting as he unlocked the massive door and marched through the great hall. Without hesitation, he opened the small wooden door to the cellar. Descending the wooden steps, he moved quickly because he was anxious to meet with the *boschetto* at the altar in the pagan temple of the *Villa de Marco*. Tonight they would indoctrinate Maddalena to the ways of the *Malandanti*.

He used the light from the oil lamp to guide him as he hurried down the small, arched passageway that snaked through the earth. After passing through the winding tunnels below the *Pincio* Gardens, a cluster of black hooded ones greeted him.

"*Saluti,*" Luca said, raising his hand as if saluting the elements. In silence, Luca ripped the brown paper off the painting and positioned the canvas atop the altar for all to see, then expertly arranged the red roses in the urn next to Diana's work. "Tonight, we welcome Maddalena into our rites." Luca scanned the faces of the *Malandanti* and noticed that some smiled and others nodded.

"Tonight we intensify our rituals and ready ourselves for our mission. Now that our *Sacerdote* has passed and the mourning has subsided, we can indoctrinate Maddalena. I've waited to do this because it's been hard on her ever since our *Sacerdote* died. He was like a father to her. I know many of you think I've waited too long, and I have told you she wasn't prepared for the rites yet. But now she's ready because last night Maddy helped me charge a talisman in sex magick ritual."

Barely able to see Max's eyes for his hood, Luca nodded at Max's questioning look.

"Tell us of your brother," Max said. "Raven knew he died back in September, yet she never told us that he crossed over. Has she put a hex on us too? Her *boschetto* begrudges us and our New Ways."

"We are too strong a force for mere hexes," Luca said. "As you already know, Raven and her *boschetto* are our adversaries.

Antonio died in America. It was a car accident in the mountains. I was unable to perform the Rite of Passage for his soul, because his wife knows nothing of our ways."

"A wife?" another hooded one asked. "He never told us of a wife. We thought there was only Raven." The *Malandanti* chattered in excitement until Luca raised his hand to silence them.

"There's a reason why my brother married," he said. "She's the Goddess of All Witches incarnate. Examine her painting and decide for yourself. Study it and you'll see the hidden message in her work. With this kind of power, she must become one of us, a *Malandanti*. Come, gaze at the work of the Goddess."

He maneuvered them into a line so everyone could view the painting and made sure they relaxed their eyes to see the hidden images. He could tell by their body movement when they saw the dimensions, and he was pleased that the sight amazed everyone else, as well.

Diana, the Goddess of All Witches, was known in ancient *Roma* as the Goddess of wild animals, hunting and the moon. Her importance throughout Old Europe was documented in the multitudes of vessels and figurines found from the past that depicted the Goddess with her wolf and stag. With her legacy, Luca knew the powers of Diana were limitless.

"My brother told me his wife was Diana, the Goddess of All Witches incarnate," Luca continued. "Because of this, he kept her secluded in America. That's why he kept going back to the Aspen estate—he had another life there."

"There's a message," a dark-haired woman said, squinting her eyes as she stared at the canvas. "She's giving us the key to the other dimensions, isn't she?"

"It's a portal," Luca answered. "The painting suggests that she knows the way to the other realms." After everyone finished looking, Luca hurried them along because he knew that Maddalena would be waiting for them in the *Grotto,* and he didn't want her to be alone. "Come, let us take our torches and form the procession to the *Grotto.* Then we can start our work." Luca grabbed the painting and gestured for Max to lead the way, then Luca followed the procession to make sure everyone stayed together and didn't get lost in the network of tunnels beneath the *Castello.*

One by one, the hooded *Malandanti* each took a torch, lit it and moved in unison out of the pagan temple in the *Villa de Marco*, then into the tunnels that snaked through the earth. Silently marching through the narrow tunnel, the *boschetto* only paused when the tunnel widened, then waited as someone slid a torch into the bracket mounted on the wall. Every time they made this procession, they followed the same protocol so that the light from the torches would help them find their way back to the *Villa* because it was easy to get lost in the intricate network of tunnels surrounding the *Villa de Marco*. Once they devised the ritual of placing their torches in strategic spots along the way, they didn't have to stumble in the dark anymore. There was light from the vents of the excavation that had been done years ago, but that light just wasn't enough.

As the candlelight danced with the shadows in the sunken enclave of a large columbarium, Luca stopped to touch the face of a marble relief atop the priceless sarcophagus of Beatrice Cenci. Looking down at the marble figure of the beautiful young woman who had been murdered by Pope Cemente VIII Aldobrandini, Luca fell to his knees. The relief of her body looked as if she'd been placed there after the beheading even though he couldn't see the seam at her neck.

The ghostly white marble relief of Beatrice Cenci, face down upon a prisoner's bench, captured the young woman in a tragic pose of overwhelming sadness and loss. Stretched out on her stomach, her sculpted head had been placed upon her right hand, while her left hand had been placed upon the close floor beneath her. Palm up, on the floor, the lifeless stone hand epitomized her heartbreaking demise with a rosary draped across her open palm.

Luca touched her cold cheek, and tried to wipe the tears from her marble lashes. Even though Beatrice Cenci's innocent beauty lived on forever in sculpted relief, her heinous beheading gave Luca the strength to carry on his mission.

Beatrice Cenci, the young girl who never stopped believing, never faltered while serving her abusive father, yet died for his accidental death, was a tragedy every Italian endured.

In 1599, local town officials already knew the legacy of physical and sexual abuse that the father had inflicted upon his daughter, Beatrice Cenci, and when he suspiciously died, local officials affirmed the killing was an act of self-defense. However, papal authority manipulated the situation and took advantage of the opportunity to seize the property of the Cenci family. The pontiff who caused the tragic end to this young girl had Beatrice Cenci decapitated while her mother and younger brother watched. After the convictions and executions of the remaining Cenci family members, the land was then ceded to the church. In the end, Beatrice Cenci never confessed to killing her father, and Luca knew she'd been murdered by the church for no other reason than for her money. Starting now, Luca would avenge her death.

An eerie guttural sound droned from the mouth of someone who began the chant. The others joined in, and the incantation became a crescendo as the procession continued, gaining momentum until they reached the *Grotto* and gathered around the sacred well. From now on, they would begin ritual this way, because now they didn't have to keep their ways secret anymore. For the first time, they would have sex magick in the place where it was meant to be done—beside the well, in the heated pools and atop Pan's face.

Surprised Maddy wasn't here yet, Luca searched for her in the *Cripta,* but she wasn't there either. Wondering why she was late, Luca knew he must continue without her. He propped the painting on an easel that was set up in the middle of the only wall in the *Grotto* that had a smooth, frescoed surface—a wall that would soon be known as the wall of sigils.

"I have something to tell everyone," he said, motioning for the *Malandanti* to be seated on the pillows and chairs to form the circle for ritual. Luca stepped into the center of the circle before he began.

"Tonight we initiate Maddalena into the *Malandanti,*" Luca said. "Tonight we must help her with her first rite, and that's why I am going to do it a bit differently tonight—a bit more creatively than usual. Please remember, throughout this ritual, we must help Maddalena because she will amplify the charge with her innate sex drive. Make her feel wanted, make her feel loved, because our future depends on it now. If we don't make this magick together, we will surely die—die from the hands of the church like our ancestors when they were tortured, humiliated and exiled from their homes."

Luca walked in a spiral motion between the pillows and chairs to be among the group as he talked. Several heads bowed as he paused and scanned the cavern of hooded ones assembled around the mosaic image of Pan. Luca moved slowly among the group, occasionally touching a shoulder as he always did before they created the magick.

"Let us remember once again, sex magick is more evolved than the Old Ways, because it is an American practice that uses the innate power of the body in ritual," he began, explaining their ways once again as he always did before this complicated rite. "With this magick, we can use the powerful energies during sexual activity for our mission, our purpose in life. I know you have heard this time and time again, but it is important for you to hear it again. This is magick in its highest form. The teaching is simple—the thought held at the peak of sexual activity and even at orgasm is a magickal trigger that will give us what we desire."

Nodding, he continued. "As always, I am your guide to make sure the energy is directed and focused on our intent," he said. "Tonight, our intent is to summon the Goddess who will help us use the energetic forces to prevent the church from doing what the *Gospel* prophesized. Over the past seven years, we have been preparing ourselves for this moment, and now the time has come. I now know how we can make this magick potent enough to destroy the church. Through the charge of sexual fluids and the ejaculate, we will stop those who are against us at the Vatican."

Luca scanned the caliginous cavern and honored the silence amid the trickling waters of the sacred well, then spoke. "Before we begin, we must draw the sigil on the cavern walls and summon the Goddess," he said. "If you haven't already noticed, her painting was signed with the sigil of the Goddess Manifest."

Luca pointed to a roughly sketched Moon Cross in the lower-right corner of the painting. Two crescents with their convex outsides together made the center of the silver cross. The cross bars consisted of a line down the middle between the crescents, with two other lines that extended from the concave insides of each crescent, one on the right and the other on the left, to make a cross. Each cross bar had a small, straight line scratched through it with a circle at the end of the bar; the rough rendition of the Moon Cross made Luca smile. No doubt, that sigil would work its magick on them all tonight.

"Now we will draw the Moon Cross exactly as our Goddess drew it as her signature upon her work," he said. "Once we paint the Moon Cross on these walls, we will manifest the Goddess."

Luca gestured at the cans of oil-based paint in the dovecote niche, then helped the *Malandanti* carry the cans to the wall. Many times they used oils in ceremony to paint sigils on their bodies, but they had never used the power of the sigil by painting it on the cave walls. Luca joined them and dipped a brush into the thick eggshell paint. Carefully, he formed the sigil on the smooth wall using the washed-out fresco of the past as the canvas. When he finished painting the Moon Cross, Luca noticed that the others had painted the sigil in various shapes, sizes and colors over the faded frescoes on the smooth, white wall of the *Grotto*.

"The Moon Cross represents the Goddess Manifest," he repeated. "This Goddess, who now resides in the Eternal City, will come to us after we summon her through our rituals. The Goddess will help us thwart the evil energies of the church that will destroy us."

Once they were finished, Luca watched the *Malandanti* ease down into the pillows to relax. Some closed their eyes, while others peacefully smiled as they waited for the ritual to begin. "Let us do free-form sex magick in the *Grotto* for the first time," Luca said.

Just then, Maddalena entered the cave, and all heads turned to see her. She stood there and looked down, as if scared to take another step.

Luca rushed to her side. "It's okay," he said, taking her hand, then turning it over to kiss her palm. "After this, you will know what it means to be a *Malandanti,* and you will have what it takes to fight the war against the church."

He steered her into the depths of the cave and eased her down onto a large pillow before he continued. Wanting to make sure everyone was prepared for the intense ritual, Luca paused for a moment. He realized that Maddalena hadn't had the chance to ready herself for what was about to happen.

Max was the first to stand up and take off his robe, then the rest followed his lead—everyone except Maddalena, that is.

Luca watched Maddalena slowly get up from the bench, then stare at everyone undressing in the *boschetto*. Her eyes widened when they all threw off their robes without hesitation. She had never seen the *boschetto* naked before, and Luca empathized with her, yet he didn't know what to do. He couldn't stop what was about to happen, but he couldn't go back either. Once everyone in the *Malandanti* stood naked before him, Maddy nervously tried to un-hook her robe too but couldn't unfasten it. Luca stepped forward and reached out to undo it for her, then he slowly opened the folds of the robe and stared at her curvaceous, wanton body for a moment before he threw back the fabric and the robe fell to the floor. With their eyes locked, he slid his fingertips over the perfect swell of Maddy's hip, then turned to ascend the carved-out steps that led to the altar above.

At the top of the steps, he acknowledged the tools at the altar and saluted the four elements. Then, he walked to the edge of the platform and began the ritual. In silence, he watched the naked *boschetto* gather into a circle in the dimly lit cave and smiled at the sight. In the past, Luca could only have sex magick ritual in the *Villa de Marco* because the *Malandanti* needed to hide these rituals from his father, the *Sacerdote*. But now that his father was gone and Luca was the *Sacerdote*, the rites would be held in the *Grotto* from now on. With the well, the warm waters of the *Grotto* and an even warmer heating system here, the *Grotto* was the place for sex magick. Knowing that his father would never permit sky-clad or sex magick, Luca had honored the outdated ways of the *Sacerdote*. But from the beginning, he performed the rites with the *Malandanti* in secrecy so that they would be ready to fulfill their mission when the time was right.

"We'll start by touching our naked, beautiful bodies," Luca continued. "Open to the energy of every person you touch. Don't stay with one person. Move about and experience as many as you can."

The *Malandanti* began in silence, some touching a face and the lips, others touching a breast and some immediately grabbing someone's cock or pussy.

"Open yourself to love and the understanding that we are all here for a purpose. That purpose is to keep our ancestry alive," Luca continued. "We are the chosen ones to defend the people of the Old Ways through using the new modern ways of America." Luca paused before he guided them farther into the intense rite. "Now, caress the most intimate places with your hands, and move into the magick of stimulation. Be sure to arouse by touching the most intimate places of the body, especially the places that generate fluids, and if there are no fluids there, massage that place until you feel warm juices, then move on."

Luca's words signaled that it was time to take the experience to the next level, and the *Malandanti* did just that. Luca heard several women moan from the signal for heightened arousal; however, the men, as always, were ready to take it to the next level without hesitation. Caresses evolved into erotic massage that sometimes began in safe places, then moved quickly into the erogenous zones. Several people lowered themselves onto huge pillows and began kissing not only on the lips, but also the most private parts of the body. Bianca and Belinda were being aroused by Santo. As Santo fondled Bianca's breast with one hand, his other hand lifted Belinda's breast upward so that he could lean over and put her nipple into his mouth.

"Your goal is to arouse and stimulate everyone you are with, but if you feel the desire to arouse someone else, you must do so now," he suggested. "Keep moving with whoever you want and touch as many of those around you as you wish, so that you are always generating sexual energy through erotic stimulation. This is erotica with a purpose, and you must concentrate on this purpose. Now we must focus on our mission. Summon the Goddess incarnate."

Luca blinked when he saw Bianca and Belinda leave Santo, then kneel down beside Max, who was stretched out on the floor watching Maddy. Maddy was either touching herself or covering her sumptuous body, Luca couldn't be sure which.

Turning back to Max, Luca smiled as he saw the girls ease down and nod at each other before Belinda started sucking Max's cock. Bianca watched as Belinda's sucking increased, and her head bobbed frantically up and down Max's hard cock. Then Belinda released Max and let go. Next, Belinda deftly watched Bianca take over and suck his cock. Not missing a beat, Bianca devoured Max's long cock as her lips moved up and down and her hands massaged his balls. Belinda didn't miss a beat either when Bianca almost made Max explode, then pulled back to watch Belinda immediately take over. Luca smiled at their creativity.

But when he spotted Maddalena, Luca frowned. She was in the middle watching, and no one was near her. As if she were shocked by the turn of events, she covered her fleshy lips with her fingertips and closed her eyes for a moment, then looked up at Luca with wide eyes. Luca stretched out his arms, palms up, as if in surrender, and Maddalena shook her head.

Max groaned when Belinda and Bianca left him as quickly as they had taken turns, and when he opened his eyes, they locked with Luca's. Then he turned toward Maddalena. In an instant, Max leaped up and swooped down on Maddy, who was sitting on a big pillow in the center of the ritual. Max ran his fingers through her flaming red hair, then lowered himself down onto the cushion where she sat. In silence, he fondled her full breasts and gently kissed each nipple. Maddy responded by just sitting there and letting him do it. Luca was proud of her for doing that, but then Max moved to the next level.

Spreading her legs open, Max put his head between her legs and tasted her pussy. Maddalena looked up at Luca with her pouty lips until Luca nodded and motioned for her to continue. She lowered herself down onto her elbows, then groaned. Pleased that Maddy was enjoying herself, Luca stared with awe when Max stopped licking her pussy, then stretched out on the floor. Reaching for Maddy, he pulled her on top. Max made sure his hard cock was inside her as she straddled him, then once she was there, Max fondled her breasts. After awhile, he pulled her torso closer until she was close enough for him to suckle her breasts while she straddled him, then Max started rocking his pelvis.

With the group progressing to this level, Luca knew the sederunt had begun. Everything would become even more erotic now because they must maintain the stimulation. Skilled at the sederunt, the *Malandanti* knew exactly what it took to maintain erection or arousal, and Luca was certain that the men would do whatever it took to ensure that everyone was pleased. After doing these rituals here for seven years, Luca realized the women had it made because if they were tired, it was always the men who kept on. Not that the women couldn't do such a thing; it was just that they didn't have to because the men wanted to keep doing it no matter how long it took. Luca watched Maddy ride Max as her shapely buttocks bounced in the air.

Luca turned his head when he noticed Aldo mesmerized by Maddy's ass. Without hesitation, Aldo left the woman he was with, then stood over Max and Maddy on the floor. Luca frowned when Aldo kneeled between their legs and poked his finger into Maddy's ass until she was ready, then stuffed his cock inside. Initially, Maddy struggled, especially since it took Aldo awhile to get that large cock inside that tiny ass, but once he got it inside, Maddy stopped fighting and groaned. Double penetration. Luca tried to ignore his hard-on as he watched the trio. Max shoved deeper into Maddy's pussy while Aldo rhythmically pumped Maddy's ass on top of the two. When their movements became more and more frenzied, Luca knew he needed to get the trio focused on intent, not self-gratification.

So, he took them to the next level. "Stop what you are doing, and send the energy you feel from yourself and those around you to the Moon Cross. Concentrate on summoning the Goddess. When you close your eyes, visualize the sigil so that it's etched in your memory. You can change partners, alter positions and caress whomever, just keep the sigil in your mind to summon the Goddess while you are moving about. But you must experiment with the erogenous zones of someone new this time."

In rhythmic motion, the group responded to his guidance and moved about until everyone connected anew with someone different in the group. He watched as the *Malandanti* started the entire process over again with a new partner, and when the stimulation became intense, almost to orgasm, Luca steered them to their purpose once again. "Good. Now wherever you are, bring the person you are with to climax while imagining or staring at the sigil, then use your ejaculate or any body fluids to draw over the sigil painted on the cave walls."

Luca smiled when some people had orgasms immediately, while others worked harder and faster for a climax. Searching for Maddy, Luca was certain she would be taken care of from now on since she had allowed double penetration. He'd seen it happen before, and with Maddy being a newcomer and allowing it the first time she joined them, the *Malandanti* men would be after her every time during free form. Luca was certain of that.

Luca scanned the *Grotto* for Maddy, and once he spotted her, he frowned. There she was with two different men, but this time Dante held her up in the air with his hands around her torso, while Maddy's legs were wrapped around Dante's waist. His biceps bulging, Dante moved her up and down as she rode his hard cock. Gino, the same height as Dante, stood and watched until he internalized the rhythm, then stepped up from behind Maddy and slid his cock into her ass on the downward movement of Dante's rhythm. Holding Maddy up with his hands on the back of her thighs, Gino synchronized with Dante's upward, downward movement. Both standing, both helping each other move Maddy up and down, they penetrated her at the same time.

Luca shook his head. Dante and Gino moved her between them faster, up and down, until Maddy screamed out in orgasm. Slowing down only for a moment as she climaxed, the instant she finished Dante and Gino resumed their motion with even more vigor than before. Like two pogo sticks, Maddy started bobbing up and down again as both men steadily pumped rhythmically harder and harder, faster and faster. Finally, Maddy screamed with another orgasm, then Dante and Gino let go and exploded too.

Since the rest of the *boschetto* were already using their fluids to paint over the sigils on the walls, by the time Dante, Gino and Maddy finally finished, Luca patiently waited for the two men to put her down before he continued. Because the oils on the stone wall hadn't dried completely, Maddy, Dante and Gino not only painted their fluids over the sigils, but they also painted the sigil on their most private parts. Then Luca, who had been fully dressed during the entire ceremony, finally descended the carved out steps and grabbed a can of oil.

Dipping his long fingernail into the oil, Luca made the mark of the Moon Cross on every forehead of the *Malandanti,* and uttered the words, "You are dust and to dust you shall return."

After that, they all dressed in their robes and left in silence. He nodded and watched several hooded ones take some torches to light their way, then they gathered together and marched into the depths of the *Sotterranea* in procession, heads bowed. Maddy turned back, surrounded by several men, and Luca's eyes locked with hers, but Luca waved her off. When she turned and left with at least six men by her side, Luca was glad to see her go. He needed some time alone to refocus on what he was going to do now. He couldn't fathom how easy it had been for Maddy to take on two men at the same time. Watching her being done by two men had made him excited, but Luca shook his head when he realized that one man would never be enough for his Maddalena anymore. He knew she needed at least two now because he saw the look in her eyes: she loved it.

Luca knew the ramifications of what Maddy had allowed to happen to her tonight. If she had turned one of them away, struggled longer, fought one off or just said no, the *Malandanti* men wouldn't have done anything, let alone the double penetration with her. Nothing was forced in sex magick ritual. But when she struggled with Aldo for that instant, Luca knew it as well as Aldo did— she wanted him to do her in the ass. And now, she was a magnet for the *Malandanti* men. They all loved it up the ass because it was so tight. After tonight, Maddy would never be left with just one man during their rituals—in fact, she could have as many as she wanted from now on.

After staring at the mosaic floor of Pan's face for what seemed like an eternity, Luca came to the conclusion that Maddy could never be his *Sacerdotessa* now. He needed someone that he alone could satisfy, love and cherish. More importantly, he needed someone who cared more for the cause than for herself. Certain

Maddy had changed after her experience tonight; Luca knew he had to forget Maddy.

Refusing to let Maddy trouble him, Luca licked his lips and decided it was time for Diana to join the *Malandanti*. Tonight he would go to the *Villa di Spagna* and confirm that Raven had cured Diana of the talisman. Then, if she was ready, he would indoctrinate her into the rites of sex magick.

Since he knew how to tap into Diana's wanton desires and do what pleased her most, he could satisfy her. Even though he had only satisfied her sexually in the astral realm, it was time for him to pleasure her in the physical realm too. Now that he knew what she wanted, he could use her desires to induce the somnambulistic state using hypnotic seduction.

Luca was astrally with Diana every night during her dreams, so he had watched her please herself from afar. Although he had only pleasured her in his mind, he was certain she was ready and willing for the real thing to happen. Luca checked his watch and realized he had only had twenty minutes to get to the *Villa*, because he needed to be there at the stroke of midnight.

CHAPTER TWELVE

DIANA

Le Vecchia Religione

Time Warp
February 25, 2004
Late Afternoon

Sprawled on the floor, Diana fought the urge to panic because she couldn't remember how she got there. Cool stone pressed against her cheek while stabs of pain hammered the place between her eyes, making her fear she'd hit her head on something. Unable to see through the vapors circling around her, Diana blinked. When she tried to push herself up, a wave of nausea made her collapse and cry out with pain. Hazy smoke drifted through the shop and blurred her vision. Whenever she tried to move, nausea and dizziness forced her to remain still. It was that smell, the same smell she noticed when she first arrived at the *Villa di Spagna*—that nauseating smell.

"Help me, please, someone help," she said, barely summoning the strength to call out.

Diana's eyes widened when an exotic looking woman with long, wavy hair appeared. She bent over to touch Diana's cheek, and her necklace of rough-cut stone almost touched her face. The woman looked agitated.

Sweeping Diana's hair back, the gypsy stared into Diana's eyes. "What have you done?" she asked.

"I can't—move." Diana tried to push herself up again but then curled into the fetal position from the pain in her stomach.

The gypsy left, then returned carrying a leather pouch. She made Diana whiff some smelling salts that would wake anyone from the dead. After smelling the raw odor, Diana coughed and tried to get up. The woman closed the black leather bag and slipped it into her pocket. Helping Diana to her feet, the gypsy almost dragged her through the smoke-filled shop. The blood drained from Diana's face, but she vowed not to faint again. Swallowing hard, she felt like vomiting as the woman guided her over to a futon in the backroom. After the gypsy helped Diana onto the bed, her sickness worsened markedly.

Diana cried out as every pore of her body ached. Raking her fingers through her hair, she began to sweat. Her blonde strands were matted against her face from the perspiration on her brow. She tossed and turned her head back and forth on the pillow until the woman dabbed a damp rag on her forehead. The icy cloth assuaged Diana's pain as the gypsy rubbed the washcloth harder against her brow. The woman whispered something Diana couldn't understand and swept Diana's hair out of her eyes again.

Just when Diana thought the illness had vanished, she shook from the frigid air, prompting the woman to quickly throw a blanket around her. The gypsy tucked the blanket edges around Diana's body, then ran her fingertips over her shivering jaw. Still whispering incoherent words, the woman busied herself at the circular table in the center of the room, turning back periodically to glance at Diana.

Diana closed her eyes and prayed for the sickness to go away. But she succumbed to the fear of dying when she couldn't move her arms and legs. Her eyelids, locked shut, wouldn't open because the lashes felt like they were glued together. She couldn't even pull them apart with her fingers or use her hands to rub off the feeling because she couldn't lift her arms. Tears formed beneath her eyelids as helplessness overcame her. When her vocal chords wouldn't work, she knew she was doomed. Diana wondered if she was dying and remembered the last time she died. Trying to be strong, she decided to let go and stop fighting it. If she died, maybe she would see Antonio again.

Silver images of passages, tunnels and doors flashed in the darkness of her mind. Strobes of ancient relics, some with an alabaster light illuminated from within, burned into her consciousness, much like the light she saw when she met death that one snowy evening after driving on the mountain road the night she lost Antonio. But this light illuminated architectural elements and pathways, unlike the brilliant light hovering on the hospital ceiling. That light had been a sphere of pulsating beams weaving into each other, much like an atom. She realized that this time the light brought a message with its form. It beckoned her yet again to pass through, to enter or cross over into a place she'd never been before. It offered—a rite of passage, an open door, an entry into yet another place in time.

When a pungent smell reached her nose, she jerked from what seemed like smelling salts arresting her senses. Her body awakened with a tinkling sensation that spread from her head to her toes, a tingle that forced every muscle in her body to respond. She moved her hands and legs, and opened her eyes to the gypsy's penetrating glare.

"What happened?" Diana asked as she tried to sit up. The woman squeezed her arm and gently eased her back down on the bed.

"You need rest," the woman said, moving her washcloth yet again over Diana's forehead, then getting up to wring out the cloth in the basin at the table. She returned to Diana's bedside and patted her blurry eyes with the damp rag.

"I thought I was dying." Diana raised her head, trying to get up again.

The woman shook her head, making the drops of blood-red jewels sway from her earlobes. "You were. You can't go anywhere until the spell is gone."

"Spell? What are you, some kind of . . ." Diana scanned the room and remembered how the witches' shop had attracted her here in the first place.

When the gypsy nodded, she reminded her of Tess, but this woman had a distant look in her eyes—a jaded look, one of mistrust and sadness. Regardless of the woman's crusty veneer, Diana wanted to hug her with gratitude for saving her life.

"What's your name?" Diana asked.

"Some people call me Slade," she said. "Others—"

"I've never known a woman named Slade before," Diana replied. "And I'm certainly thankful to know you. You actually believe in spells?"

"It is not a matter of belief—it's a knowledge. Tell me what happened."

"I don't know what happened."

Slade wrinkled her brow. "Then how did you get that mark on your forehead?"

"What mark?" Diana rubbed her forehead, then checked her fingertips for stains.

"I'll show you," she said, then left the room.

While the gypsy was gone, Diana stared at the shiny silks and rich-colored velvets quilted into a work of art and mounted upon the ceiling above her. In shades of burnt amber mixed with purplish-pink hues of indigo and amethyst, a medieval woman had been sewn together from meticulously shaped pieces of cloth. By her side, a wolf stood and they both looked as if they held the key to some lost wisdom. An exotic quilt of exquisite detail, framed with corners offset by tassels of coppery gold and sides edged in braided cords of platinum threads, made this work a masterpiece. Clearly, this handmade design had been created as a labor of love.

Turning her head to the side, she realized that not only the ceiling was covered, but also the walls were covered with homemade quilts too. Embroidered designs in circles, crescents and triangles intermixed with strange symbolic lines to create the backdrop for a pack of wolves alongside a rugged man wearing antlers and animal skins. After gazing at the archaic symbols that framed the quilt, she recognized the same strange symbols embroidered on the quilts that she'd created with her oils. The ideas had come to her in Rome, and she'd followed her instincts to paint unknown designs like these. These were designs she didn't understand yet had formed through the tip of her paintbrush for the first time here in this city. All along, she'd been unconsciously painting the language of witches.

Slade came back with a large mirror and held it so Diana could see her reflection. A faint sign of the cross marred her forehead.

"That's the imposition of ashes from the service this morning," Diana said, laughing with relief. "It's Ash Wednesday today."

"This mark is not something the church intended," she said, shaking her head. "It's a curse through contagious magick, and it won't cease until the talisman leaves your body."

"It's contagious?"

"No, not the way you think it means as in spreading it to others. It's contagious in that it's something that's spread through someone intentionally putting it there. The illness was reported in the news as a virus, but from the symptoms, I immediately knew it was a curse. I banished it in the Vatican this morning with the same potion I used on you, and it healed those who came back to pray. And for those who weren't there, I have people who assist me in these matters. I'm known as a pellar."

"A pillar?"

"A pellar." Slade placed the smoke-colored mirror on a stand atop the table. "My work is to heal, divine and break spells. Anyone afflicted with the curse you had would need to inhale the herbal potion I made, otherwise, they may not fully recover."

"You think magick made me ill?" Diana asked, staring at the peculiar image in the dark mirror as it reflected a murky corner of the room. Obsidian and indigo shadows in the mirror shapeshifted into a dark form, much like the grim reaper. Diana stared at the strange illusion, wondering if she'd lost her eyesight, as well as her mind.

"It was a curse evoked through contagious magick. It originates from the Law of Sympathetic, which means all things are linked together by invisible bonds. It's sort of like quantum physics, because it's about the things we can't see, yet they still exist. But contagious magick works on things that come in contact with each other, then continue to exert influence on each other even at a distance."

"No sane person believes in magick," Diana said, staring at the strange shadow in the mirror that even moved like the grim reaper. With scythe in hand, the dark figure could easily deliver death. Diana squinted and sat up for a closer look. In the reflection, the reaper became a towering man who stepped out of the ebony darkness of the quilt into the dimly lit corner of the room. Reflected in the dark mirror, Diana could see his image clearly as he watched her. Even though the image in the mirror was dark, Diana noticed his bony hands clasped together in front of him, shoulder-length hair tucked under a hood, and a cloak draped over his tall form. He looked exactly like the grim reaper. Diana opened her mouth to scream, but when she whirled around to look at the corner of the room where the mirror had enabled her to see, there was nothing there.

"It's not a belief, it's a science," Slade said. "It works in conformance to the natural laws of the universe."

"Is someone else here?"

"No."

"In this room?" Diana asked. "Because I just saw someone in the mirror."

"Has that ever happened before?"

"What?"

She nodded at the mirror. "Have you ever seen things in black mirrors before?"

"No."

"It's called scrying." Slade looked at her with a raised brow. "That's a gift. Normally, it takes people ages to divine that way. You have the sight—yours is a natural ability. But then it doesn't require practice when it's innate."

Diana stared in the mirror again, but the reaper didn't return. "Maybe he's hiding behind the quilt."

Slade walked over and pressed her hand against the wall, then patted the entire corner down with her hands to show Diana that the quilt had been stretched flat against the wall, with no room to squeeze anything behind it.

"Scrying can be done with any smooth or shiny surface," she said. "Many diviners use pools of water or crystal balls, any speculum will work."

Diana blinked. "You think I divined seeing him?"

"You didn't divine his presence—you just saw what was already there because the medium, which was the mirror, allowed the invisible to become visible. The mirror gave you the ability to see what's hidden in the realm known as the invisible."

"Do you know who it was?"

Slade looked in the mirror, then spoke. "He's hiding from you now. *Semjaza* is known as a Watcher—a *Grigori*. The Watchers come from the stars—they're beings of light, and they come to help us in the ancient arts. Watchers are linked to certain stars that mark the solstices and equinoxes. *Semjaza* instructs me in the ancient art of healing and helps me manifest the magick of herbs."

Diana scanned the mirror in case the dark figure appeared again, but there was nothing. "He looked more like the grim reaper than a star. How do you know these things?" she asked.

"Because I honor and align with the earth and the universe, I am directly linked with the forces of the universe. Then it's a matter of choice to use the energy for good or evil. Magick is the art and metaphysical science of manifesting desire through the collection and direction of energy."

Hearing the words about aligning with the universe that Antonio had said right before he died made tears form in Diana's eyes, but her sadness quickly vanished when she saw the darkness move again in the mirror. She wondered if the mirror was just playing tricks on her. "Is that how you cured me, through your beliefs?"

"True magick isn't a matter of superstition or belief," she said, sitting on the edge of the bed next to Diana. "One must understand the laws of the universe to manifest something needed or desired. Through using specific tools and established states of consciousness, I can create healing potions and tap into the astral realm to make the potions work. The astral realm is just as real as this one except you can't see it. Its effect is felt through energy currents on this plane. You glimpsed the astral realm in the mirror when the Watcher appeared. Sometimes they make their presence known, other times they remain elusive even to those who have this kind of vision. And as for those who don't even know they exist—the Watchers never appear."

"Look, this is getting complicated. This realm thing is too far-fetched for me. All I want to know is how you stopped my illness."

"When the potion smolders, smoke moves through the air and carries particles with it," Slade explained, pointing to the smoke still curling upward from the cauldron on the table. "It's similar to the way spores are carried through the atmosphere."

Convinced it was just an illusion, Diana turned away from the mirror.

Slade tilted her head to the side, then continued. "*Stregheria* holds the belief that there are many planes of existence, including the one you see with your eyes, or the physical dimension. But it's just one of seven. There's the plane of forces or the elemental plane, the astral, the mental, the spiritual, the divine and the ultimate. You see, there are seven."

Diana smiled at the woman, thinking she'd just lost her with all this talk about realms. Then she noticed the odd-shaped object dangling from a silver chain mixed in with the rough stones around her neck. Diana froze when she recognized the symbol as the one she'd been using with her signature on her work—a symbol that she thought was her original creation.

"What does that charm on your necklace mean?" Diana asked.

"It's the Moon Cross." Slade touched the silver piece and leaned forward so that Diana could hold the exotic charm in her hand. "It's known as a sigil to manifest the Goddess. A sigil is a design that contains the essence, nature or character of a spirit or deity. When the *boschetto* or coven stares at, concentrates or focuses on a sigil, we call forth or evoke that spirit or deity. We use them in our work together in positive ways to help this planet and those living here on earth."

Diana was amazed. That design had come straight out of her head, and she didn't even know what it was. Just then, Diana realized that the throbbing pain and sickness she felt earlier had vanished. Shaking her head, Diana felt like she was in another world. On impulse, she tried to sit up and was surprised by her lack of dizziness. Diana victoriously saluted the air and Slade laughed.

Slade winked before she spoke. "You don't believe a word I've said, do you?"

"I'm Diana." She held out her hand, but Slade turned her hand over to look at her palm. Thinking she might read it, Diana vowed to humor her new friend, but Slade only shook her head. After stroking her fingers over the lines of Diana's palm, Slade let go and frowned.

"Whoever did this to you is using the ways for evil purposes, and I know who it is," she said. "Do you know Luca DeMarco?"

Diana's stomach cramped as the woman stared at her, waiting for a reply. "I've never met him. Have you?" Diana asked. She wanted to trust this woman, but she wasn't certain if she should.

"Let's just say we both believe in *Stregheria,* but I know his ways are evil," she said. "Your eyes tell me you know him."

"Since you're a witch, maybe you knew my husband."

"*Strega.* Believe me, there's a major difference between *Strega* and *witch* in Italy." Slade raised her hand to stop Diana from saying any more. "The word for Italian witchcraft is *Stregheria.* But one word you shouldn't use is *witch.* That word seems to keep perpetuating false beliefs about the religion. Use *Strega.* I learned the craft in America when I was young, so I'm an Americanized *Strega.*"

She pressed the back of her hand against Diana's forehead as if it were natural for her to continue doctoring, then nodded. "Good as new. You're almost back to normal." Slade crossed the room and opened a drawer under the tabletop to search inside. She returned carrying a small photo.

"Tell me the truth. Do you know this man?" she asked, handing her the photo. "You must stay away from him. He wasn't a threat until Janus died. Janus was the *Sacerdote*—High Priest—of a *boschetto* that Luca was part of. But after Janus's death, Luca took over. As *Sacerdote,* he abuses the ways with his Black Mass. Be careful, he might hurt you."

The photo Slade showed her was different from the one Diana had. In this photo, Luca wore jet-black glasses and a tuxedo. Dressed in Italian couture from head to toe, his square jaw and pronounced lips made him look larger than life. The epitome of high class, he portrayed one of the rich and famous with his suave style and mysterious look. Luca didn't look anything like his brother, because her husband had dark eyes, skin and hair, while Luca looked like a vampire. His ivory complexion contrasted with the nude color of his large lips and made him look like he could suck blood from virgins. His dark sunglasses made Diana's body involuntarily tense, and she felt as if he'd just told her to jump into the picture and start doing things—sexual things that drove Diana insane. She pressed her hand against her flushed cheek and turned away from the picture.

"Why would he want to hurt me?" Diana asked, wondering whether she should tell Slade about her nightly dreams with Luca.

Diana looked at his image again—this image that had haunted her ever since she'd seen his picture in Antonio's collection of hidden secrets, this man who came into her dreams at night, this man who made love to her in wicked ways. Luca always pleasured her in her dreams, except for the one night when she slept with Vincent. Diana looked up at Slade's concerned face, then blinked.

"You know him, don't you?" Slade frowned when Diana didn't answer, then continued. "He abuses *Stregheria* by using it for his own purposes to gain power and harm others when it is our creed to harm no one. He uses magick to make people do things they normally would not do, and that is against the tenets of our belief. Come, let me show you something."

Slade helped Diana up, then walked over to a deep purple curtain and pulled it aside. She stepped back so that Diana could pass through into the shop which looked like an apothecary with herbal potions and bottles of strange, withered plants. Displays crammed with multi-colored jars of seeds, leaves and sticks; ancient books etched with intricate gilding on the spines and crystal balls that seemed to illuminate from within filled the store. Freshly made candles of every imaginable color dangled from a rack overhead, and crescent-, star-, pentacle- and pendulum-shaped crystals seem to float in the air, yet were attached by colorless threads to dangle from the ceiling above. Ornate candelabrums spiraled to various heights from the stone floor, and looming stacks of fat, thin and medium-sized books filled the room. High up on a shelf, a pumpkin-colored cat crouched and watched Diana with his olive eyes. The cat crept backward into the dark recess of the bookshelf, and his ominous cat eyes turned into tiny slits of silver light.

Slade whispered something as she walked behind the counter, then pointed to the place where a scroll had been mounted to the wall. "These are the tenets of belief for the *Strega*," she said. "But the underlying principle is one that affirms: harm no one."

Diana touched the crackled parchment before she read the words. "We believe that the source of all things is both masculine and feminine in nature." Diana paused, then scanned down the list and continued. "We believe in psychic abilities and the supernatural as normal conditions that have been suppressed by Judaic and Christian culture, but can be restored through the practice of Old Ways." Diana looked up from her reading. "Normal conditions, you must be kidding."

"Being psychic is an inherent ability within us all. It's there, but most people don't know how to use it."

"You believe in the supernatural?" Diana stifled a laugh.

"Even though it's the root of all religions, *Stregheria* is probably the most misunderstood religion of all, and Wicca has been slandered even more than *Strega*," Slade said, walking to the center of the room and holding her hands up toward the crystals above. "Pagan and folk beliefs existed long before the other religions even began. They used to be the cornerstones of our belief systems, but then our ways were misconstrued into something wicked after the Inquisition."

"What do you mean?"

"The Inquisition tortured Druids, Celts, the *Strega* and anyone else who had a different belief system than Christianity. Then the inquisitors documented, they called it *extracted*, information about our different beliefs under torture. In many cases, the records left by the Inquisition are still what people think document our beliefs, but those records were produced by dishonest people using corrupt methods that purposely annihilated our religion from the world. The Inquisition published lies about our ways, then people believed those lies because, in many cases, that was the only written record that ever existed. Those records were riddled with lies meant to ruin us so that Christianity would be the only religion."

The crystals moved, no they vibrated, when Slade stretched out her arms as if to the heavens with her hands turned up and open. Then she circled around like a slow-moving dervish dancer. As if crystal elements could react to human nature, the crystals started spiraling above her. Initially, when the crystals began to move, Diana thought it was some kind of gimmick and that the crystals were attached to colorless threads to make it look like an illusion.

But then Diana realized that what Slade was doing couldn't be trickery; it was for real. How Diana knew this, she couldn't quite understand. Then again, maybe that's what she wanted to believe. She shook her head because there wasn't a breeze in the room that was moving the crystals. Slade's movements were too slow to generate a breeze. Each unique crystal moved in a circle in the same direction that she did, and all the crystals rotated as if dancing with her as she slowly whirled beneath them. When Slade changed directions, the crystals responded by changing directions too.

Slade stopped whirling, then opened her eyes and watched the crystals as each one slowed down in its own time, some abruptly, some slowly. Slade turned to Diana. "The *Strega* believe in nature, that individuals are connected to the natural cycles of the earth and the cyclic phases of the universe."

"Connected to what?"

"Connected to something beyond. Our religion values this planet, including the people and animals on it," she said, glancing upward just as the cat jumped from the bookshelf onto the counter where she stood. As though on cue, Slade stroked the cat and it crouched down and flipped its tail to the rhythm of its own purr.

"What's his name?"

"Her. Gemma. All phases of the moon as well as the entire universe have an effect on us. The full moon has just been publicized more than the others."

"Do you think God was a woman?" Diana asked, as she leaned over the counter to look at an etched pendant with a Goddess on its face.

"Rather than believing God is primarily male, we believe God is a positive force that can be either male or female. We recognize and honor the divine feminine, something that's been lacking in the last 2,000 years of patriarchal-dominated religions."

"You're not from Rome, are you?" Diana asked, turning from the necklace display to Slade.

"No." Slade hesitated and once Diana nodded, she continued. "We believe humans have the divine spark of their creator within themselves, known as soul and spirit, and we are spiritual beings temporarily encased in physical matter by our bodies."

"But then, you already mentioned that you were from the states."

Slade hesitated for a moment, then walked back behind the counter. "Along with that spirit, we believe in the earth's energy, and we acknowledge places of natural power that exist on our planet. It's a power that exists in material objects too, it's just that most people have forgotten this ancient knowledge. That's why I want you to have this." She took the silver necklace from around her neck, the one with the Moon Cross charm, then fastened the short, silver chain around Diana's neck. "This will be your talisman to protect you from harm," she added.

"I can't accept—"

"Please, just wear it." She patted the silver charm at the base of Diana's neck. "Luca has seen you in Rome. And you've seen him, no?"

Not knowing whether she should accept the gift, Diana didn't know what to do. Convinced it would offend Slade if she didn't wear it, Diana realized she hadn't even thanked the woman. "I should be the one thanking you with a gift, since you just saved my life," Diana said, touching the charm as she spoke. "No. I've never met a man named Luca before." Not wanting to tell her what she did know about Luca, Diana decided not to share what had already happened in her mind with the man.

"Your eyes and your heart tell me something quite different. You are lying, and for what reason, I do not know." Slade grabbed a sheet of paper from behind the counter and started drawing lines on it.

"I'm not—"

"Don't say it when I already know," she said, shaking her head and handing her the paper with her notes. "Take this map, it will show you the way."

Diana stuffed the map into the pocket of her jacket. "Why won't you answer my questions?" she demanded.

"You must leave," Slade said, turning away to walk to the front door. "I have things to do."

She gestured to Diana and she followed her to the front door. Then Slade grabbed Diana's hand and squeezed it for a moment. Surprised by Slade's tender gesture, Diana wanted to say something, but she couldn't find the words. Outside, Slade stepped into the middle of the street and stared at a gust of wind midway down the lane that whirled onto the rough cobblestones, carrying with it dust and debris. She stood motionless, and when Diana tried to speak, she held up her hand for silence. Slade, mesmerized by the spiraling wind, watched it gather force to whisk whatever it grabbed by its current, then swoop down as if to suck more matter into its tunnel of doom. The funnel of wind intensified until the swirling mass looked like a tornado in their midst. It moved toward them, tousling Diana's hair and flinging debris against her lips. As it abruptly stopped, Slade turned to Diana.

"What happened?" Diana asked, wanting to know what was going on in Slade's mind. "The wind. What does it mean to you?"

"*Folleto,* a knot of wind," she said. "They are spirits who travel with the wind. I wanted to listen to them because they are notorious for misbehaving, but it seems they came for a reason. Sexual situations attract the *Folleto,* and they claim you are in one."

Slade looked deep into Diana's eyes, making Diana shake her head in denial.

Diana turned to go, then impulsively glanced back and caught a worried look on Slade's face—a look that instantly vanished when Slade realized Diana saw her.

"*Grazi,*" Diana said, smiling as she waved.

"*Ciao.*" Slade waved back.

After walking several blocks, Diana finally pulled out the map, then realized Slade marked the exact route to get to the *Villa di Spagna.* But how could Slade know about the *Villa* when Diana never told her?

Chapter Thirteen
Diana

Via Margutta
February 25, 2004
Twilight

Light faded into darkness as Diana entered *via Margutta*. From a distance, she could barely decipher the outline of Tess's figure moving like a dancer in the dusk, hands on her hips, head turning to and fro to search the night. As Diana approached, the brickwork behind Tess contrasted with her lithe form, making her loose curls and supple body stand out against the landscape. Right then, Diana yearned to capture the scene, including Tess, with her oils.

"What happened to you?" Tess called out.

"You wouldn't believe it if I told you."

"Try me. Have I ever doubted you?"

Diana smiled. "It's a long story, one I can't even think about right now." Diana motioned at the paintings in her booth. "We need to pack up."

"Let our multi-talented assistant, Viviana, do it. I've already arranged it."

Diana touched Viviana's shoulder. "Thank you for all you've done at the *Villa*. Our studios are perfect."

Viviana nodded, but looked as if she didn't understand a word Diana said. Tess took Diana by the arm and guided her in the direction of the *Villa*. Spinning around, Tess called out, "*Grazi*, Viv!"

"I have something to tell you," Tess whispered in Diana's ear.

"What?"

"Luca bought one of your pieces. The one that you painted in a matter of hours."

Diana would never forget that painting because that was when she started signing her work with the Moon Cross. The sign had appeared in a vision after painting the piece, then she decided to use it as a signature because it just felt right as she painted it next to her name. She painted the Moon Cross in a trance, as well as the rest of the piece. Diana could barely even remember doing it because it all happened so fast. In an instant, she conceptualized and roughed it out, then captured the images she saw in her head with oils on the canvas. That was the first time she felt possessed when she painted, and now it happened every time she used the brush. She debated whether to show the piece today at the gallery because she had finished it so quickly. Although she didn't understand what the images meant when she painted them, it felt right to paint them. Now she knew those instinctual feelings had something to do with the *Strega*.

After being inside *La Vecchia Religione*, she realized that her paintings spoke the language of the *Strega*. Even though she didn't know what most of the designs meant and had never seen them before, she envisioned them in her mind. Most of the strange symbols she painted after moving to Rome were displayed somewhere in Slade's shop.

"He came back?" Diana turned away from Tess's questioning eyes. Convinced that her suspicions were right about her work speaking the language of the *Strega*, Diana wanted to meet the man.

"How did you know he was here?" Tess asked.

"It's a long story."

Tess squeezed her arm as they walked, clearly excited about the news. "I got his address for you, and he told me he would visit us. So now it's just a matter of time until we meet him."

"What's he like?" Two young men stopped to flirt with Tess, but Tess ignored them and just kept walking. Diana laughed when the men whistled as Tess walked down the street.

"It's beyond words," Tess replied. "I'll fill you in once we get to the *Villa*."

The walk was a short one, and once they entered the *Villa di Spagna*, Diana followed Tess inside and flipped on the switch to the sconces in the great hall. Then they both headed straight for the kitchen. Tess gestured to the cushioned banquette beside the window, then washed her hands before rinsing the muscatel grapes. Diana sat in silence, waiting for Tess to turn toward her while she worked at the island in the center of the room. From the look of the modern amenities throughout the *Villa*, Antonio had totally remodeled the place. How she didn't know he'd done such a thing amazed her, but then she never knew about his expenses or even his assets for that matter.

Tess savored cooking at the *Villa*, so Diana let her create the meals they had together. Normally, they didn't eat at the same time; they usually just helped themselves. But whenever they had stimulating discussions, they also had great food. Tess artistically arranged the grapes in a bowl, then popped one in her mouth as she spun around to face Diana.

With lips still wet from the grape, Tess stood waving her hands in the air as she talked. "I've thought a lot about this, but I think we should wait and let him come to us rather than us make the first move. What if he's part of a satanic cult?" she asked.

"He's my brother-in-law who I've never met," Diana replied as she reached for a grape to try to get rid of the taste of herbs in her mouth. Even though she had been fasting for Ash Wednesday, she decided that eating would help stave off any residual sickness that still might be inside her system. "Maybe I should call him and introduce myself."

"He's a brother-in-law known for being a witch, and someone your husband didn't even tell you about. In fact, we need to be more secure, so I'm going to stop leaving the door unlocked from now on, and I'm going to secure all the doors from the inside. Tonight I'll install the dead bolts."

"Antonio told me about Luca the night he died. Dead bolts. I was going to do that. Tell me about Luca. What was he like?"

"Are you alright? It's hard to keep up with you the way you switch subjects so fast." Tess shook her head, then plucked another grape from the bowl and popped it into her mouth. "Strange, eccentric and foreboding—those are the first words that come to mind. What did Antonio tell you about Luca?"

"Did Luca speak of Antonio?"

"No, he hardly spoke at all." Tess shook her head. "Are you avoiding my questions on purpose, Di?"

Finally Diana told Tess about Antonio's words the night he died, then she helped Tess make prosciutto and *bel paese* sandwiches. After dinner, they worked on the deadbolts for the next two hours. Once they were done, Diana realized just how tired she really was from the exhausting day. First her illness after the Ash Wednesday service, then securing locks throughout the *Villa* had depleted her energy so thoroughly that she could hardly stand. She kissed Tess on the cheek before she headed off to bed, relieved that her friend would be just down the hall tonight.

As Diana walked into the master suite, she heard Tess close her bedroom door. Even though the master bedroom was still filled with sexual toys, Diana decided to keep them exactly where they were when she moved in. For some reason she couldn't explain, sleeping here, even with the sex toys, helped her deal with the reality of her husband's secret life.

Tears filled Diana's eyes when she realized how everything had changed after the death of her husband and unborn baby. By keeping herself busy, she'd been able to avoid thinking about her previous life and the love she once had. Diana wiped away the tears, then looked up at the mirror on the ceiling and frowned at her reflection. It was a black mirror, just like the one at Slade's shop, only this mirror was as big as the bed.

She had to forget the past, because she must carry on. After being in rehab and analyzing what happened in the months following the accident, she wanted to be at peace and live a normal life. But being in Rome had unsettled her because it dredged up all of her insecurities about relationships, as well as the secrets her husband had kept from her. Deep down, all she wanted was to love again.

Trying not to cry, Diana walked over to the crystal and picked it up. When she held it up to the chandelier, the reflections from the mirror combined with the overhead lighting created an intense display of rainbow colors that filled the bedroom. Diana waved the crystal wand and the flecks of light shot into every area of the room. As if illuminated from within, the crystal absorbed the light in the room and refracted it into jeweled rays of quivering colors that bounced in every direction around her.

The odd-shaped crystal felt warm in her hand, as if someone had held it not long ago. Diana shook her head and set the rod on the table, but even on the nightstand it had an eerie magnetism about it. She looked at the palm of her hand, still aware of the crystal's warmth, then shook off the feeling by fluffing up the pillows on the bed.

As she took off her skirt and blouse, she thought about wearing something sexy instead of the nightshirt she normally wore to bed. Diana laughed at herself. She was beginning to act as if Luca really did come to her at night, but they were just dreams. They had to be dreams, because she would know if Luca had really been there. She was asleep, yet in her mind she was awake and actually doing those things he told her to do. Even though she tried, she could never wake herself up from those dreams, because she always enjoyed them. No, she loved them.

He turned her on without a doubt. Those dreams created another kind of reality, and that mental reality made her body ache the next day. It was an ache of pain, sexual pain, like it really happened. It's perplexing how the mind works, but it's even more perplexing how the body responds to such thoughts. She'd been having the dreams ever since she found the picture of Luca in the vault.

Diana stood at the vanity clad in her bra and panties and splashed water on her face. She stared at her reflection as she patted away the water. The mark of the cross had vanished, along with the fear in her eyes. Diana looked at the Moon Cross charm Slade gave her. She should have asked her what it meant, but then there wasn't enough time. Diana wondered if she'd ever see Slade again. Looking at the Moon Cross charm at the base of her neck in the mirror, Diana almost took off the necklace, then decided to wear it through the night just in case it really did protect her.

Diana slipped on a taupe-colored, silk negligee that she'd bought in a lingerie shop in *di Spagna.* Biting her lip, she vowed to go to Luca's house tomorrow and visit the man in her dreams. She still hadn't told anyone about the elicit dreams, but then she figured there was no reason to. They were just dreams.

What she couldn't figure out was why they kept getting more erotic. With each succeeding night, he did more to her until now it felt as if his hands actually moved over her body. Every night, he did something different, never letting her do a thing to him. He would tell her to masturbate in different ways as he watched and, as always, she did it in her dream.

Without hesitation, she would respond with complete surrender. Throughout the dream, she maintained pure lust, desire and passion for him, which seemed horrid now that she thought about it. But she didn't have any control because in her dream, she wanted him more than anything. When he suggested something to her, she would do it with pleasure. Diana had never had such provocative dreams. In the beginning it scared her, but now she actually looked forward to dreaming those sensual dreams because it had been so long since she had sex.

Diana stretched out on the duvet. Masturbating in front of her deceased husband's brother in a dream? Where was that coming from? She must really have a nasty mind. Diana shook her head, ashamed of her desires, then laughed at her worries about simple dreams. They were only dreams. She was reacting like they were the real thing. She shouldn't be ashamed of having sexual dreams.

Maybe Vincent could stop her dreams with the regression therapy, but then there was a side of her that didn't want them to stop. Every time Luca appeared in her dreams, she climaxed. Every time he came to her, his sole purpose was to make her orgasm just through his words, through his presence, all the while not even touching her body. Whenever the dream ended, she radiated fulfillment and sexual satisfaction. Why should she stop something that made her feel good? Diana leaned back into the pillows on her bed and stared at her reflection in the mirror.

"Just a dream," she said out loud.

On a whim, she jumped out of bed, then slipped off her panties before climbing back under the covers. Tonight she'd sleep without panties and see what happened in her dreams. Diana felt her face redden as she threw back the coverlet from her body. She was too hot for covers. When her head sunk down into the pillows again, she looked up at the mirror and saw her flushed face stare back.

"You don't scare me anymore."

With a wave of exhaustion, Diana realized it was almost midnight. She sat up and searched for the *Sleeping Through the Night* compact disc on the bedside table before she switched off the Tiffany lamp. The recording had been a lifesaver ever since moving to Rome because if she didn't use it, sleep remained elusive. After listening to this particular meditation, she could go to sleep quickly instead of tossing and turning. Even after dreaming about Luca, she still felt refreshed in the morning.

She was thankful that she found the *Sleeping Through the Night* recording in the *Villa* just days after she arrived. It must have worked for Antonio too. The thought that Antonio probably used it made her even more adamant to do the same. Just knowing her husband listened to it made her want to share the same experience. She slid the compact disc into the recorder, turned off the Tiffany light, then nestled her head back onto the downy pillow, ready to begin the process. The deep, melodious voice reverberated through her body as the words swept her away.

"I want you to picture yourself standing on a terrace, overlooking a beautiful garden," the voice said. "There are five wide steps leading down to a smaller terrace . . . and then another five, down to the garden itself. You are going down those steps into the garden . . . and I will count each step as you go down. As you go down each step . . . you will take one very deep breath . . . and as you breathe out . . . you will become more and more deeply relaxed . . . more and more deeply relaxed."

The voice stopped for a moment, then continued. "Now, just picture us standing at the top of the first flight of steps. One. Down the first step . . . breathe deeply . . . deeply relaxed . . . more and more deeply relaxed. Two. Down the second step . . . breathe deeply . . . very deeply relaxed . . . becoming deeper and deeper.

173

Three. Down the third step . . . deep, deep breath . . . more and more deeply relaxed . . . more and more deeply in trance. Four. Down the fourth step . . . breathing even more deeply . . . very, very deeply relaxed . . . your trance is becoming still deeper and deeper."

The voice paused again, then continued. "Five. Down the fifth step and onto the small terrace . . . deep, deep breath . . . very, very deeply relaxed . . . very, very deeply asleep."

CHAPTER FOURTEEN
LUCA

Roma Sotterranea

February 25, 2004
Almost Midnight

Luca's footfalls crunched on the uneven ground of the *Sotterranea* passageway as he moved through the arched tunnel that stretched for at least fifty feet, then snaked its way into continuous curves as it forked at the end. Through this labyrinth, Luca could find his way to the *Grotto* blindfolded. Inside this earthen hole, a mere six meters below ground, he heard the distant muffling of traffic overhead from *Trinità dei Monti.* Along the narrow corridor, ebony shadows swallowed the eye-shaped niches and cavernous openings with darkness that the lamplight couldn't reach. From the intoxicating smell of raw earth in this subterranean realm, Luca took refuge from the external chaos aboveground. Here, he transcended the physical world into a dimension that only the ghosts who haunted it fully understood.

As he turned the corner, a colossal rat pounced from a niche above, hitting Luca's shoulder as he passed. Luca batted it away, and the rat scampered off in the direction from which he had come. Peering inside the niche, Luca leaned into a thin veil of gray that covered his entire head. Clinging threads of gray gossamer blanketed his face, blurring his vision as a swarming mass of spiders marched directly toward his eyes. Lunging backward, Luca peeled the web from his eyelids as he saw the spiders crawl over the ledge of the recessed niche, some falling onto the path at his feet, others skittering down the wall. Luca stepped even farther back to escape the oncoming mass of spiders, then swiped at the remaining tail of white cobweb in the niche. Luca grabbed the lamp, lit it, then hurried in the direction of the *Grotto*.

After traveling through a long, arched corridor made of layered brick, he peeked inside the *Grotto*. The trickling water of the well beckoned him to rest and mingle with Pan, but he knew he must continue because tonight he needed to initiate Diana into the new rites. Luca walked over to the well and held his hands under the flowing water to tap into the Life Force, the universal mind and the energies that he needed tonight. When the time was right, he stepped back into the passageway.

Luca picked up the pace as the tunnel curved to the right, then straightened as he took the tiny carved-out steps to descend deeper into the *Sotterranea*. Continuing on, after awhile Luca took the passageway to the left and rushed through the narrow, arched corridor where he descended yet another flight of steps that took him down to the deepest layer of the *Sotterranea*.

Relieved when he finally saw the outcropping of rocks, Luca fell to his knees. He scooped up the rocks with his hands and tossed them to the side. Frantically he dug, scraping his hands and wrists against the hard rock until his back ached from the heavy weights. After digging through the pile of rocks, Luca felt the outer edges of the trapdoor. With bleeding fingertips, he pulled the remaining stones away from the entry, then lifted the latch to open the door and climbed the steps that led upward to the cellar. Even though he hadn't been here in a long time, Luca knew how to navigate through this portal even without light. By the light of the moon streaming in through the cellar windows, he marched across the stone floor to the half bath.

After brushing off the dust on his trousers, he held out his hands and stared at the blood oozing from his fingertips. Gauging by the position of the moon in the sky, he realized there wasn't much time. Using the sink, he began the cleansing part of the ritual. He lathered the soap on his hands and wrists, making sure he rubbed his forearms, then cleaned under his fingernails until his hands were pristine and spotless. After thoroughly rinsing himself off, he used clean paper towels to wipe off the moisture from his skin.

After he finished, he examined his hands, especially his manicured nails and made sure they were purified enough for the charging rite. Satisfied with what he saw, he checked the time. Midnight.

Luca climbed the wooden stairs two at a time, then opened the door to the main floor. The darkness called out to him as if beckoning him to hurry. He rushed up the spiral staircase using the moonlight to guide him. When he reached the top, he stood at the doorway and listened to his own voice resonating through the crack of the closed door. Before Diana moved to *Roma,* Luca snuck into the *Villa* and left that burned disc by her bedside because he knew she would listen to it. And now, since Diana listened to the recording every night that meant when he came to her she didn't need to be brought into the somnambulistic state because she was already there—unconscious and ready to do anything he said.

"You are now so deeply relaxed," Luca's recorded voice said. "That everything I tell you is going to happen . . . will happen . . . exactly as I tell you.

"Every feeling I tell you . . . you will experience . . . and you will experience it . . . exactly as I tell you.

"Every instruction I give you . . . you will carry out faithfully. In a few moments, I will count to seven, and when I count to seven, you will listen to me and carry out my suggestions. One . . . two . . . three . . . four . . . five . . . six . . . seven."

Luca crept into the room and stared at Diana in trance on the bed. He silently pressed the stop button on the player, then swooped to the foot of the bed before he spoke in his deepest voice. "Now you are very relaxed. I want to please you, to give you pleasure now. Will that be alright?" Luca asked.

Diana fervently nodded, and then pulled her nightgown up to her thighs as if asking him to go there. "You are so relaxed that you will let everything around you happen, because that will make you fulfilled." Luca licked his lips, and Diana pulled her nightgown up even farther than before. She was deep in trance, the deepest trance possible for a human being. Just by looking at her, Luca could tell she was in the somnambulistic state.

Diana's metabolism and makeup made her the perfect candidate to sedate, because she went under quickly and remained at the deepest level. He was lucky that she'd been so receptive to hypnosis. She had been easy to subdue and train because she'd already been conditioned from listening to his recorded voice. But then, most creative types were easy to subdue. Her trances were deeper than most, and with subsequent trances, her hypnotic experience became even more effective. His induction method brought her into the somnambulistic state immediately now—a deeper place where she couldn't fully remember what happened and couldn't decipher the real from the imagined. Most people had no recollection of what happened while they were in the somnambulistic state.

Because Diana was already in trance and her unconscious mind had taken over, all Luca had to do was keep her there—in the unconscious state. Diana had faithfully listened to his tapes every night, so her mind, as well as her body, was ready to be taken to the next level of experience. Luca came closer, watching her on the bed in trance as he approached. With her eyes closed, she looked asleep, yet her eyelids fluttered and her skin glowed as if she were energized and awake. Luca noticed a silver pendant shaped into the sigil of the Goddess manifest hanging from a chain at her throat and stepped back. Wondering where she got the necklace, Luca needed to make sure the Goddess was ready and willing before doing anything. He needed her to be ready and willing before he could continue, especially since she was wearing the Moon Cross.

"Would you like me to touch you?" he asked.

"Yes," Diana said, nodding her head again. "Yes, please do it again."

In the moonlight, Luca came to the side of the bed so he could be closer to her, then he gently tugged at the hem of her nightgown so that it was around her waist. Watching the folds surrounding her pussy move, he slowly circled his hands above her body. Diana's legs shivered and twitched as his hands moved in the air just above her skin. He followed the aura that surrounded her body, visualizing her orgasm as he moved his hands.

"You can feel the pressure within. It's deep within, deeper and deeper within."

Luca ached to touch her because he had been doing energy work in the astral realm for so long with her. He was ready to progress to the next level, and he already knew Diana was ready too.

"When I count to seven, you will go deeper into trance," he said, still moving his hands in the air that surrounded her body. "One . . . two . . . three . . . four . . . five . . . six . . . seven."

Luca watched her body slacken when he touched her for the first time. He ran his fingertips across the lips of her pussy, then felt the inner thigh of her leg. Wanting to please her to orgasm, Luca climbed onto the bed as he watched her closed eyes. Still co-matose, still in trance, her eyelids didn't even move when he gently moved her legs apart. Massaging her inner thighs, Luca placed his lips over her pussy and flicked his tongue inside her. Diana stirred, and Luca raised his head from between her legs to stare at her.

"Don't stop," she said.

Luca smiled. "You must tell me how you feel. Always. Because I never want to hurt you—only pleasure you." Lowering himself down again between her legs, Luca slid his hand underneath her buttocks and placed each hand on her ass cheeks to raise her pelvis up, then he kissed her pussy once again. Humming as he gently moved his head from side to side, he heard Diana groan. Flicking his tongue inside her, he dug his tongue deeper into her pussy, then pulled it out to hum louder and make his lips vibrate against hers. It was a hyp-notic hum—a hum much like the sound at the end of the word *seven*. After Diana climaxed, Luca took the ritual to the next level.

"With the word *seven*," he droned, "you will become more in trance, more sedated. Your eyes will rapidly become more and more tired, and your eyelids heavier and heavier and the moment you hear the third *seven*, your eyes will remain closed and you will suddenly enter into a deeper state of hypnosis, a place inside you that's deeper than this one. When I say the word *seven*, you im-mediately begin this deeper state of trance."

Luca got up and moved to the head of the bed as he spoke. "Seven . . . seven . . . seven."

Her eyelids fluttered as moved his hands in a circular motion in the air around her body, making sure her energy was right for him to continue. He grabbed the crystal on the bedside table and held it in his hands to warm it, then he walked back to the end of the bed. After making sure the wand was warm, he gently eased the small bulbous end into her pussy as he began to chant. Watching her moan as the crystal slid into her, Luca could tell she would come easily with the crystal. He grinned at the sight of Diana's smile when he moved the wand up farther where the wand widened into bigger balls joined together, and the bulbous shapes moved in and out of her tight, wet pussy. She raised her pelvis and with bent legs, she spread them open for him to see. Her legs were positioned exactly the way he had held onto them when he had kissed her there. Savoring her pleasure, Luca knew he could do this all night.

Sliding the bulbous rod in and out of her pussy, Luca licked his lips as Diana moaned. Taking turns with either the wand or his tongue, Luca worked on her pussy until she became urgent, frantic even. He knew she was near climax with her urgent sounds, so he backed off a bit to keep her in the excited state for awhile. But as he moved the wand deeper inside her pussy, he wondered if she too wanted double penetration just like Maddy.

Using the small end of the wand, he poked at the rim of her asshole as he flicked his tongue on the lips around her pussy. When he finally decided to ease the rod up her ass, Diana let out a stifled gasp, and Luca stopped and looked up at Diana. With her eyes still closed, Diana smiled. Lowering himself between her legs, Luca kissed her pussy, then hummed and moved his head from side to side to help her relax. Luca slid the tiny ball-shaped rod in again, this time humming to make his lips vibrate against her pussy until he could move the wand in and out of her ass as she moaned. Not wanting to hurt her, Luca took it out.

"Don't stop," Diana begged.

Now knowing that she needed double penetration just like Maddy, Luca pushed the wand into her ass, and at the same time poked his tongue in as far as he could too. Moments later, Diana had an orgasm.

Once he drank the last drop, Luca moved her legs together, and made sure she was stretched out on the bed before he covered her naked pussy with the hem of her nightgown. Then he got up off the bed and pressed the play button on the compact disc. Luca's recorded voice floated through the room. "Now listen very carefully to me. I want you to imagine a bright, white light coming down from above and entering the top of your head, filling your entire body. See it, feel it and it becomes reality...

"What you've just experienced is your hidden secrets, your deepest pleasure, your latent desires coming alive inside yourself. When you release your tension, you feel pure pleasure, satisfaction and love. Focus on this pleasure, this ecstasy. Let it wash over you, and feel good about what you've just done, feel good about releasing the negative, tight feelings in your body. Relax your body and bask in all its hidden pleasures...

"Now imagine an aura of pure white light emanating from your heart region, again surrounding your entire body, protecting you. See it, feel it and it becomes reality. When I say *seven* three times, you will go deeper into relaxation... seven... seven... seven."

Luca walked out of the bedroom and closed the door without a sound. With crystal in hand, he descended the spiral staircase, pleased that Diana enjoyed sex magick with him and confident that soon she would become his *Sacerdotessa* of the *Sotterranea*.

Chapter Fifteen
Vincent

Via di Spagna
February 26, 2004
Late Afternoon

In the conference room just below his office, Vincent shifted his weight on the table he sat upon. He looked at the group of students and wondered why he had been so quick to say yes when they asked to consult with him about his past life research. He wasn't sure how open they would be to hypnotherapy.

"We heard about you in the States," a young blonde addressed Vincent, and he stood as she spoke. "We're interested in offering alternative health care that doesn't involve drugs or medication. And we also want to know if regression therapy really helps patients."

"There is no doubt about the effectiveness of regression in therapy," he said. "And I have the statistics with me today to prove it. This therapy is the future because without it we are ignoring the inner working and vast potential of the mind." Vincent motioned to a chair for her to be seated, then took his place at the front of the room. "I also have an entire product line of wellness products that can help you offer alternatives to prescription drugs for your patients. We can talk about that later, if you wish."

"We definitely want information about your products," the blonde said. "We've heard about your doctor network here in Italy, and once we become therapists we'd like to join your network regardless of the boards and associations that frown upon it in the States. But we really came here because we need to know more about soul regression, and we thought maybe you would share some of your groundbreaking research with us before we go back to the States." Still standing, she listened as Vincent answered.

"I'm encouraged to see people beginning their careers in therapy take an interest in the soul aspect of regression," Vincent said, picking up a stack of brochures by some transparencies. "First, here's more information about the wellness products we've been using in Italy." Vincent handed the students the new brochure that he recently designed.

"Thank you," a young man said, looking at the product brochure.

The blonde locked eyes with Vincent, then spoke. "We took this semester off, yet plan to become full-time therapists in America next fall. Tell us about your therapy. Isn't it traumatic to regress someone to a place where they see themselves dying? Doesn't experiencing their death and the trauma that ensues make it worse?"

Vincent again motioned for her to sit down like the rest had, then pulled out the stack of transparencies. "Patients don't just regress to a dying experience, they also regress to joyous events. I have statistics that will show you what happens, and in virtually every case, the patient benefited not only in the mind but also in healing the physical body simply by uncovering what happened in other lifetimes."

Deciding to wait on the overheads, Vincent walked to the window overlooking the Spanish Steps. Just like his office above, this conference room had windows that overlooked the *di Spagna*. Outside, the *piazza* bustled with activity and the lusty breeze made several women attempt to hold down their short billowing skirts, while the men nearby stopped to watch.

"Have you seen or do you know of any adverse side effects from regression therapy?" the blonde woman asked.

Without hesitation, Vincent answered. "No. Past life regressions consistently help people overcome their emotional and physical health problems. No other therapy helps patients discover the specific skills and talents they learned in previous incarnations. With this information, patients can then use their latent, innate abilities as a resource, and thus become more *evolved* and skilled in their current lifetime because they *remember* what they already learned in other lifetimes."

"How can you be so sure that the patient's latent abilities are from a previous lifetime?" the blonde asked, walking over to the window were Vincent stood.

"We've found many children at young ages speak languages they've never been taught, and many even recognize places and events from their past life. In regression, my patients know things that they don't think they know in their conscious life." Vincent moved away from the attractive blonde, then reached for the stack of transparencies on the table and placed the first one on the overhead. "This information gets lost because as we get older, we predominately use the conscious mind and ignore the unconscious or subconscious mind; whereas, children automatically use it because they haven't been programmed by what's in the current reality yet. If you would just take a look at the statistics—"

"But isn't it dangerous to take patients into an altered state of consciousness?" the young black man asked. "Isn't that mind control?"

"It's not mind control. It's self-guided meditation," Vincent explained. "My patients are fully cognizant while they are being regressed." Vincent flipped on the overhead projector switch to show a transparency of his success rate. "Take, for example, the patients I have seen. Every patient was regressed into one or more past lives, and as a result, the majority of patients were either cured of their ailment or enriched by the experience. You can see the numbers here with other past life regression therapists, and in every case these sessions have shed light on the problems the patient faced in this lifetime."

Vincent used his pointer to underscore the type of healings that had occurred as a result of his sessions. There were many achievements of aliments being miraculously cured after a patient saw him for a specified period of time. The number of sessions needed varied with the intensity of the aliment, but each patient had seen results. And with each healing, he'd attributed that phenomenon to a certain type of cell memory, which he'd noted on the transparency.

The blonde, staring at Vincent as she came closer, walked to the front of the room, then sat on the table, clearly not interested in the overhead behind her.

Vincent continued. "Many psychologists, medical doctors and therapists are using these techniques because they have proven to be more effective than drugs or expensive long-term therapy," he explained. "The information we have gained through past life regression techniques is astounding. That's why I'm writing a book on the subject."

"What's the title?" the black man asked.

"*Evolution of the Soul.*"

"How do souls evolve?" the blonde asked, crossing her legs, which made her short skirt hike even further up her taunt thighs.

Vincent tried not to look at the blonde as he flipped off the switch to the overhead projector, since not everyone could see the overhead. The way the blonde was sitting on the table, she had everyone's attention anyway. "It's a spiral," he said, pausing for a moment to look into the distracted eyes of the other students. "The soul journeys through many lifetimes in a spiral. With regressive techniques, we can use our minds to travel to places where we once were in a previous life. If you try regression therapy, you can unlock a stream of incredible stories that are hidden in your unconscious mind."

"And what if they are just that—stories?" the blonde asked. Vincent turned to look at her leaning forward just enough so that he could see down the front of her low-cut blouse. Using her body to passionately speak, her breasts moved with every word. "How can you be sure those aren't from the imagination?"

Vincent locked eyes with the blonde and continued. "I, as well as others, have done research on thousands of patients, and the statistics show that past lives are real. But if you don't want to learn more about your soul and its past, then this type of therapy most certainly will not be available to you because you have to want to go within yourself to get the information. When you examine the lives you have lived, it is like a matrix of interconnected events and involvements that have made you who you are."

The black man whistled. "Are you telling us that the sum of a person's past lives, when pieced together, has meaning and purpose?"

Vincent nodded. "Discovering where your soul has been through past lives is for people who have a powerful urge to go beyond the boundaries of their present psychological, emotional and spiritual selves. It is for those who want to look at the truth about the self. Sometimes people are ready for this type of therapy, and sometimes they're not. It isn't for everybody, although with a skilled regression therapist, you can go back even if you don't believe it's possible."

"How so?" the blonde asked, still leaning over. "Will you regress me?"

Vincent glanced down at her cleavage, then forced himself to turn away from the vixen. "If you like I can do it to you, but there are excellent therapists in the States. Just be certain that you choose a creditable, licensed hypnotherapist," Vincent answered, hoping the blonde wouldn't take him up on the offer because she seemed more than ready for something more than just therapy. "The therapist takes the patient back in time through the tone of voice or the right choice of words, and then, if the therapist is adept, patients are able to use parts of their brain that they've never used before. It's all in the mind—you see, there's a reason why we only use a small part of our brains, because the other unused part resides in the unconscious, intuitive mind. The therapist, through regression, unravels the mysteries of the unconscious or subconscious mind because patients remember what they once knew."

"You mean, the therapist puts you in a trance and hypnotizes you," the black man said. "What if a patient doesn't want to be hypnotized?

"It doesn't work when it's against your will," Vincent explained. "The patient has to want to go there for it to work. The patient must have the desire to be regressed. During the regression, the patient is fully aware and in control. If the patient doesn't want to do it, then the mind doesn't take them there, but if the patient has the desire—"

"What if a patient becomes traumatized after experiencing a gruesome death in a past life?" the blonde asked, sitting up straight now, yet uncrossing her legs just enough for Vincent to have a peek.

Vincent vowed not to look at the blonde anymore. "We have ways of protecting our patients from traumatic regressions." Vincent checked his watch, wanting to finish and get back to his office in time for Diana's appointment. "I personally use a guardian figure, but there are many techniques. Other therapists use white light or imaginary places for protection."

"Isn't it possible to stay stuck in a regression, then become insane because it alters your sense of reality?" the blonde asked.

"Past life regression therapists only guide you through the self-hypnosis," Vincent explained. "It's a harmless, self-guided technique that takes you into a meditative trance so that you can see your past. My patients can wake up at any time because I don't use deep trance as part of my hypnosis therapy."

Vincent walked away from the blonde and moved closer to the other students. "Hypnosis is a heightened state of suggestibility," he continued. "The merest suggestion on the part of a hypnotherapist will often be perceived as reality by the hypnotized subject. For example, if a hypnotist suggests to a subject that she has no feeling in her hand, the hand of a good hypnotic subject will become numb. With a skilled therapist, the subject, no matter how reluctant, can be hypnotized easily. The only prerequisite of the regression is that the subject or patient desires to go there."

Vincent heard the blonde move from the table and walk toward him, yet didn't turn around even though he could feel her stare on his back. "The mind is an interesting thing. If there is a place in the mind where the patient doesn't need to go, then the patient normally will not go there. But if the patient needs to delve into his or her psyche to resolve certain issues, then the mind takes the patient there. For example, if a patient wants to know why she has an eating disorder, then I examine her to see if it was caused by a past life experience."

"Does it work?" the blonde asked as she laughed, then stepped forward to stand by his side.

"I regress the patient to see if the disorder was caused by a past life. Many of my patients have been cured through a simple regression in which the patient remembers starving to death or was without food for many days, thus creating an excessive need to always have food available and her stomach full in her current lifetime. Once the patient has been regressed and remembers this experience, then the dysfunctional behavior usually stops."

Vincent paused and turned toward the blonde, who smiled. Then he continued. "Let me give you a specific example. Imagine I had a patient named Joe. Joe came to me complaining of a pain in his upper thigh that traditional doctors couldn't explain or cure. After being regressed, Joe realized that his pain was from a gunshot wound in his thigh in World War II. Once he relived the experience of being shot through past life regression, his pain vanished."

The blonde moved closer to Vincent. "No matter how much you tell me it cures, I still have doubts," she said, using her hands to smooth out her more-than-tight short skirt.

"Then you should not do regressions or be regressed," Vincent said, nodding to dismiss the group. "This type of therapy isn't for everyone—especially those who are not open to new methods of healing."

Vincent gathered his materials together to signal the meeting was over, and the students headed for the door. Each one thanked him before leaving, and the blonde turned to him after everyone left to ask him if he would regress her before she returned to the States at the end of the week. Vincent got her number and said he'd call. Wondering if he could behave himself in his office with the beautiful blonde, he wanted to keep his promise to himself, but he also wanted to enjoy any fleeting opportunities with an attractive woman.

Vincent watched her hips move as she sauntered out the door. Even though he had recently made a vow not to do anything unprofessional with women he treated, he stuffed her telephone number in his pants pocket, thinking he could use a little action. *How can I keep my vow and ignore her blatant advances?* he wondered.

Cursing his instinctive desires, Vincent dashed up the stairs to his office on the second floor where Diana awaited. He smiled at her standing there, waiting for him. Today, she looked radiant, beautiful even.

Vincent opened the door for her to enter his office. Inside, he immediately walked to the window and ran his fingers through his hair as he checked the view outside. The wind seemed to howl down the Spanish Steps as the same women still clung to their short skirts, but now they laughed with the men who had noticed before. Turning toward Diana, Vincent watched her get settled on the couch, then he began the session.

"How are you doing?" he asked.

"I'm fine."

"Have you had any dreams, incidents or experiences that you'd like to talk about before we begin the regression?"

Diana shook her head, and Vincent watched her bite her lip.

Since getting inside her mind wasn't going to be so easy, Vincent decided to go straight into the regression because maybe that would get her to open up. He cleared his throat, then began speaking in a deep, monotone voice as he started his guided meditation technique. Walking over to the couch, he stood over her and watched her closed eyes as he spoke. He meticulously enunciated each word, speaking slowly and carefully as he told her to tighten, then relax, each part of her body. Surprised how quickly she went under this time, Vincent knew the minute she was ready. He brought her attention to the guardian standing there with her for protection. Then he let her begin the regression.

Diana's lips quivered as she spoke. "I'm in a dark tunnel with specks of light at the end."

"Focus on your immediate surroundings," he coaxed, trying to urge her deeper into hypnosis.

"Or maybe there is no end ..." Diana's voice trailed off as she began breathing deeper, more strenuously now.

He noted the fear in her voice and decided to shift her awareness to something concrete. "Can you look down at your feet?" he asked.

"I have no shoes," she replied, sounding alarmed. "My feet throb, and there's blood between my toes."

"What are you wearing?"

She shook her head as she spoke. "A robe that once billowed, but it's ripped and ragged now. My hair is soaked with blood."

"Concentrate on your breathing," he said, trying to prepare her for any situation.

"I can't breathe," she said, struggling with her words. "I have to run."

"Yes, you can breathe or run if you would like." Vincent's soothing voice filled the room. "Feel as if you are watching what is happening—in control of what you choose to do in this situation. Remember, you can leave with your guardian at any time."

"I've got to get away from them," she said. "Otherwise, they'll kill me. They're sloshing through the mud, coming closer now."

"You can turn around and look if you want," he suggested.

"No," she screamed. "They'll catch me."

"Or, you don't have to be the one running," his calm voice interjected. "You can watch instead . . ."

"Grunting as they run—they're gaining on me."

"You have the choice to control where you are in this reality," he said. "You do not have to be here, and you do not have to be inside this body."

"But it's my body," she cried, pleading for him to understand through the sound of her voice. "They're shrieking, taunting me with their chant."

"I know it feels like your body," Vincent said, guiding her imagined reality. "But you can rise above and watch."

"No," she said, shaking her head. "It's too late."

"Too late?"

"I'm at the end of the tunnel."

"What do you see now?"

"A mob." She whispered the words, making Vincent lean closer. "Waiting for me, at the end of the tunnel."

Vincent frowned. "You can come back now," he said, using his deepest hypnotic tone. "You don't have to stay in this dark place anymore."

"No." She gritted her teeth. "There's no turning back. They're grabbing me, pulling from both sides."

Waiting to pick the right moment to bring her back, Vincent wanted the session to make a smooth transition from the past to the present.

"Their lips move, sneering at me," she whispered. "Charred, dead lips." She sucked in her breath as she steadily wrapped the tail of her crinkly shirt around her hand, wrapping it tighter, twisting it with her wrist.

"What are they saying?" Vincent asked, wanting to know the time and place of the regression.

"*Strega,*" she said.

"What do they want?"

"Yieeah," she yelled, batting her hands in the air with one hand still tangled in the cloth of her shirt. The last two buttons came undone and bared her flat stomach.

"What are they doing to you?"

"They're dragging me," she answered. "They force me to my knees, making my legs slide through the mud and scrape against the stones."

"Can you see where they are taking you?" Vincent asked, prodding for more.

"An altar of branches," she said, rubbing her free hand over her stomach.

"Fallen branches?"

"Stacked," she answered, then paused, making a guttural sound as she exhaled. "Bundled against the post."

"You don't have to be here," he said, providing a way out, attempting to bring her back now if she wanted. "You can leave this place."

"I can't move," she said, wailing her words. Her arm swung up as if trying to free herself. "There's no use. I can't fight it anymore. I must let go."

"It's time to leave with your guardian now," Vincent spoke evenly, deciding to take her out of the trance.

"I'll never leave you, my love." She paused before she spoke again. "My love, he's struggling to free himself from the thugs who are restraining him, making him watch. But he can't move because his hands are tied. He must help our son." Diana's voice wavered as she paused to weep, then continued. "They've captured our son, and are making my baby watch too. My love thrashes with the restraints to help our baby because he's only three. My baby's arms reach out for me. He wants me, but I can't come to him. I see my love look at me one last time as the flames lick at my feet, then he's gone. He disappeared in the smoke."

"That's your soul," Vincent whispered. "It's leaving your body. It looks like smoke because it's a mist, a vapor that exits the physical form as it dies. Your guardian takes you away by making you float up above your physical body as you watch your spirit ascend from the fire."

Her eyelids fluttered as if she were watching a movie with closed eyes. Vincent stared at her face, knowing he must let her witness the body dying in this lifetime. Nine times out of ten, that's how it normally worked. The body released the soul just before death. And each time, the soul floated above the physical form just to witness the body passing. It was a traumatic experience, but vital nevertheless—vital to moving on and letting the wounds of that lifetime go.

"When I finish counting, you will be awake and fully aware of where you are," Vincent said, using his deepest voice to gently move her back into reality. "One, two, three . . . "

Her stony features made him wonder if she had lapsed into deep sleep. As if hearing his thoughts, she lurched forward, sitting up on the couch like a mummy rising from the tomb. Vacant eyes popped open as she yanked her hand free from the tangled shirt.

"That was Antonio!" Diana wiped the tears from her eyes, but the tears came back.

Vincent reached for the tissues on his desk, then handed her a few. "That's what Antonio saw in his regression too. Exactly the same place, the same time."

"Why did they kill me?"

"Burning at the stake. A tormenting punishment and way of exterminating the *Strega*," he answered, shaking his head. "It was used extensively during the Inquisition."

"They're awful to make my husband and child watch. That's a hideous way to die, and so horrid for a small child to see."

"It was a common practice in medieval times. That is the period you saw, no?"

"Yes," she said, buttoning her blouse as she spoke. "And that explains the paintings."

"Paintings?"

Tears formed in Diana's eyes when she looked up at him. "Ever since I've been in Rome, even though I had no way of knowing how to do this, I've been painting designs or symbols of the *Strega.* Even though I don't know what the images mean, the visuals and even the language intuitively come through in my work."

Tears formed in Diana's eyes as she spoke. "I know why Luca just bought my latest work—because it speaks to him," she said. "He must think I'm one of *them.*"

Concerned about her being associated with Luca, Vincent wanted to get closer, so he sat on the edge of the couch and wondered if he could control himself from doing something more if he touched her this time. That one night had been unbearable, and now he wasn't sure he could hold back any longer. Diana put her hand on his shoulder, but when he didn't move, she took her hand away. Wanting to take her in his arms, Vincent vowed to control his desires, then stood. Stunned by the realization that this was the first time he cared, really cared, about a woman he was sexually attracted to, Vincent fought the impulse to run.

CHAPTER SIXTEEN

DIANA

Piazza Di Spagna

February 26, 2004
Nightfall

Still shaken by the regression, Diana weaved her way through the crowded *Piazza di Spagna*, then hesitated for a moment to watch the sunset cast a chartreuse pall upon the people loitering in the streets. Rays of flesh-colored terra-cotta mixed with verdigris gold draped a gauzy mist over the tall facades of the couture district of Rome, creating an alabaster atmosphere of an ethereal dimension. Prisms of celadon light highlighted each face milling past her, much like images from a painting by Toulouse-Lautrec, who was known for his extraordinary ability to capture character. Instead of being joyous and merry, Diana thought the bar scenes he painted created a sense of foreboding.

Even though Toulouse-Lautrec's version of the French bore no resemblance to Italians, the light at this moment distorted reality enough to capture his colors on the human form. Just like his figures, each passerby's gaunt, hollow appearance looked menacing. Faces in greenish hues with grotesque shading around the eyes and mouth looked exactly the way Toulouse-Lautrec accentuated his distorted portraits. Toulouse-Lautrec's use of large areas of flat color emphasized smooth curves on the body such that Diana had always thought his creations evoked something sinister and evil. In each face, in each figure, the strange distortions in his artwork haunted the eye.

Looking down as she walked, Diana couldn't tolerate seeing another macabre face, so she focused on the rough edges of the cobblestone street. Saddened by what she just witnessed in her past life, Diana knew the eyes of *My Love* was Antonio's. Different body, yet the same eyes.

Confused by the recent turn of events, she was still dismayed with the secrets she kept from people she cared about. Hiding the truth and keeping secrets just wasn't her nature. She still hadn't told Vincent or her best friend that her dreams had crossed the line between imagination and reality last night.

The crystal had vanished. Luca had used it on her and then taken it. He had to have been there—she knew he was doing things to her in reality now. Diana shook her head, not knowing what to do. She'd deceived herself as well as those around her. She had hidden secrets—sexual secrets—just like her husband. Tears formed in Diana's eyes, but she quickly blinked them away.

Diana collided with a hefty brunette in stilettos walking her small dog down the cobblestone street. The force of the impact almost knocked the wind out of Diana. "Sorry," she said.

"*Merda*," the woman said, shaking her finger at Diana. "*Lasciami in pace.*" The lady raised her hand as if she were about to slap Diana across her face.

Diana stepped back, shaking her head. "I'm terribly sorry," she said, admonishing herself that she should learn a few words of Italian, at least for the sake of good manners.

Rushing across the *Piazza Mignanelli,* she ascended the steep stairs. Midway up the steps, Diana paused, gasping for air. At a fast pace, the upward trek was virtually impossible for her to complete without stopping. But then she resumed, forcing herself to keep climbing. Straight up and in total seclusion, the charcoal stairway melted into nightfall, creating a chiaroscuro effect of light and dark. As if stepping into a Carvaggio painting, the dark background hovered around her, making the shadows come alive in the dusk. Like Carvaggio, the incomplete shapes echoed the obscure contours, blurring the difference between the visible and the invisible, the seen and unseen.

She reached the top of the stairs and tried to shake off the ominous feeling of something lurking in the night. Her eyes riveted on the black gate beside the front door when she saw something move beyond the iron filigree of the gated courtyard. Diana froze, squinting for a moment, as she tried to decide whether it was a figure or the light of the moon just beyond the drooping vines quivering on the iron gate. Swaying from the slight breeze, the vines beckoned her to come closer. She refused to stare at the darkness beyond the gated courtyard any longer and turned toward the door. Her back muscles twitched as if eyes watched her through the twisted iron bars of the gate.

Moving her shoulders, Diana breathed deep and vowed to change her focus to something other than monsters in the dark. As she stood in the shadows of the *Villa*, she struggled to pull the key from her tight jeans pocket. It slipped from her hand onto the ground. When she bent down to retrieve it, steady, methodical footfalls echoed on the stairs she had just climbed. Involuntarily shaking from the thought of someone following her, she felt the ground for the key since she couldn't see in the dark. The footfalls became urgent, quicker. Her fingertips hit the sharp edge of the house key on the doorstep. She grabbed it, sucking in air as she tried to drown out the sound of the staccato steps coming closer. Whoever made those footfalls didn't need to stop from the upward climb. Whoever it was accelerated the pace with each advancing step as if he were running toward her.

Pinching the key with her index finger and thumb, she jammed it toward the lock, but she couldn't see the keyhole. She tried to get the key in first one way, then the other, but it still wouldn't slip into the hole. Chills shot through her body from the grinding footfalls behind her. She jabbed the key once more into where she thought the lock was. Finally, it slid into the keyhole. Clenching the key, she tried to turn it, but it wouldn't budge. She yanked it left then right, but it wouldn't move.

The heavy steps reached the landing just as she pulled the door latch toward her and the key turned in the lock. She swung the door open, then dashed inside.

Slamming the door, she pushed against it with all her might so that the bolt would slip through the catch. Still trembling, Diana stepped back and listened as she stared at the bolted door in horror. No sound, no movement. She rushed to the living room and peered between the shutters of the window to look just outside the front door. A waxen, zombie-like man dressed in black lurked for a moment on the landing, then abruptly turned away and ascended the steps. Climbing the stairs, it looked like he floated upward. His black outline blended into the shadows, then disappeared into darkness.

"Tess," Diana yelled, hoping her friend was in the *Villa*. "Tess, where are you?"

Trying to calm down, Diana concentrated on searching the kitchen, living room and study, then climbed the stairs to their new workout room. Just this past week, Tess had received the shipment of exercise equipment, then Viviana designed a fitness room the minute it arrived. Diana hoped Tess might be an incentive to work out since Diana couldn't remember the last time she'd done anything athletic.

She opened the door and saw her reflection from a mirrored wall on the opposite side of the room. With the music on full blast, Tess didn't even realize Diana had entered the room. Stretched out on the workout bench, Tess held two heavy weights— one in each hand. She raised the dumbbells up and exhaled as her brow glistened.

"Tess," Diana said, walking over to the sound system to turn down the volume.

Tess finished the rep, then dropped the weights to the floor and frowned. "What's wrong?" Still stretched out on the bench, she grabbed the end of the towel around her neck to wipe her brow.

"Nothing, I just keep thinking someone's following me, that's all."

"Is someone actually following you?" Tess raised a brow.

Diana shook her head. "Has to be my imagination."

"You just had your session with Vinny, right?" she asked. "How did it go?"

"I saw Antonio in a past life, and to be quite honest, I'm emotionally drained. I can't believe how evil people can be. But there's something else." Diana cleared her throat. "I need to talk to you about something."

Tess got up from the workout bench and walked over to an iridescent fitness ball, which she placed in the center of the room. "That's fascinating about seeing Antonio in a past life—you'll have to tell me all about it. I have something to tell you too." She sat on the fit ball and rolled herself down so that the ball pressed against her lower back as she did her crunches. "Who goes first? Maybe I should, since this is a life-or-death situation," Tess said while she crunched up. "They had trouble at the Vatican yesterday when you were there for the Ash Wednesday service. Several people almost died."

Diana blinked. "Almost?"

"They don't know exactly what it is, but it's certainly one hell of a virus. Seems the doctors don't have a cure, but the patients magically heal themselves. They think it's a short-lived killer virus—one where the body almost dies, then miraculously recovers."

Diana shook her head and remembered what Slade told her. As a pellar, she'd administered her healing therapy to those folks by giving them her potions of smelling salts or herbs to inhale. One woman couldn't possibly help that many people afflicted in Rome. But then, no woman was probably like Slade either.

"Has anyone died from it?" Diana asked.

"Amazingly, no." Tess rolled down onto her lower back and began crunching her abs again. She did twenty before she continued. "But they've come close. The pulse fades to almost nothing, then the illness quickly subsides and the patient recovers. They can't explain it."

"What caused it?"

"They have no clue. Did your symptoms ever come back?" Tess asked, sitting up on the fit ball to listen to Diana.

"No."

"What cured you?"

"I think it cured itself," Diana said, not wanting to tell her about Slade because she wanted to keep Slade's shop a secret for some unknown reason. "I need to talk to you about something too."

"I don't know why you continue with Catholicism when the Roman Catholics have so many problems with guilt and sin." Tess got up from the fit ball and walked over to a metal bar propped on a heavy iron rack. She grabbed a metal plate, then slid it onto the bar through a hole in its center. After mounting both of the circular weights, Tess slid a cuff onto each end of the bar to fasten the plates. "I'd stay away from the Vatican," she said, sliding under the bar to position her chest directly underneath it. "It's an antiquated set of beliefs anyway."

"I need help."

Tess looked up, then furrowed her brow. "What's wrong?"

"Have you ever felt like your dreams are real?" Diana didn't know how to approach this delicate subject.

"Yes, I've even traveled in some. It's all a matter of consciousness."

"I'm serious, it's Luca. He's been coming to me in my dreams at night."

Tess gripped the bar. "You've seen him?" She pushed up with her arms, breathing out as she lifted the bar that held the heavy plates at each end.

"No, but after last night, I'm sore. It's like he does things to my body."

Tess slid the bar onto the rack just above her torso and turned toward Diana. After one look at Diana, she scooted out from under the bar and sat so that she could face her directly. "It's been my theory all along that he's coming to you through astral projection."

"In my dream, he touched me, made me climax by putting this thing up—"

"Usually it seems totally realistic, just like a dream can be so real, like you are there—" Tess froze. "He put something up where?"

"The crystal, he put it up me."

"If it's astral projection, then it feels as if it's actually happening, but it doesn't."

Diana shook her head. "Then why is the crystal gone?"

"What crystal?"

"It was there before I fell asleep. The intruder, that girl, left me a crystal, remember?"

"That's weird." Tess frowned. "The bolts were locked, there's no way he could get in. Maybe he came through the astral realm, played with your mind, then took the crystal. Believe me, he could do this without even touching you, yet you can still be sore. That's how powerful thought is—thought-forms are energy—an energy that can be used for good or evil. But the astral is just as real as what we see here in this room, and if you know how to use it, you can travel anywhere to do anything you so desire."

Diana frowned. "What are you talking about?" First Slade did it, and now Tess was speaking another language. But then, Diana had painted in another language so now she was more open to understanding it.

"It's a parallel dimension of energy that he moves in," Tess continued.

"Where do you get these ideas?"

"It's the parallel dimension closest to the physical. Look, one thing is certain. After decades of research and millions of near-death experiences, we still don't have a clue as to the sophisticated form of unseen energy that exists as a highly organized, structured realm that supports the outer physical universe."

"Since when did you start studying near-death experiences and the universe?"

"Since I first started seeing things." Tess glared at Diana as she spoke. "I was about five when I woke up one day and saw another realm, another dimension. I blinked my eyes, but the place wouldn't disappear. There were gauzy curtains fluttering in the wind and streams of light warming my body. And it just wouldn't go away. It was as real as you and I sitting right here in this room, only it didn't exist on this plane."

"You've studied near-death experience?" Diana frowned when she realized that she had never talked with her best friend about her near-death experience when Antonio died. Not knowing why she hadn't opened up, Diana felt guilty for not sharing it with her now. It seemed like such a personal, sacred thing that Diana would never tell anyone about it.

"The unseen, nonphysical dimensions and the outer physical crust of the universe are totally interdependent upon each other. Unseen, nonphysical energy reactions influence our physical reality more than we realize. Physical observations alone are inadequate because the galaxies and matter around us are not the entire universe, but only the dense, outer dimension or molecular crust of the complete universe. The entire visible universe amounts to perhaps less than one tenth of one percent of the multidimensional universe."

Diana blinked, then shook her head. "You continue to amaze me with your ideas, but I don't see how this relates to Luca doing sexual things to me at night."

"These aren't ideas—these are scientific conclusions. I've been convinced all along that he doesn't come into your bedroom—his astral form comes to you. Hear me out, okay? Quantum physics proves how the elemental building blocks of our reality aren't material, but instead are patterns of energy that are interconnected to form an inseparable cosmic web." Tess waved her hands violently in the air, then stopped to frown at Diana shaking her head. "He's coming to you through another dimension, and he may have taken the crystal when he left. If people can use energy to transport themselves astrally, then it's certainly possible to use the same energy to transport an object."

"You're saying that he comes to me like a ghost, then disappears and takes the crystal? Isn't that a bit off the wall, my friend?" Diana laughed.

"It's like E equals MC squared, Einstein knew it all along. Matter is nothing more than a form of energy—a stored energy that's temporarily molded to construct the physical objects around us. Our surroundings are not what they seem. They are vibrating, pulsating loops of energy and vibration and if we can make ourselves be attuned to them, then—"

"Look Tess, can we just have a normal conversation for once?" Diana wanted answers, not some esoteric dissertation. Maybe she would tell Tess about her near-death experience at another time. Right now, Diana wanted to keep it sacred and a secret for some reason.

"Okay, Di." Tess sighed. "I can help you, but first follow me."

Tess wiped her brow one more time before she turned off the strings of Vivaldi and headed straight for the door. She looked like a dancer as she waltzed gracefully down the hall to the bath. Once there, she kicked off her running shoes, pulled her top over her head, then dropped it into a crumpled heap on the floor. Diana stood and watched as Tess bent over topless and cranked on the faucets of the tub. Pulling down her shorts and panties at the same time, she turned toward Diana, hands on her hips, stark naked.

"You need psychic protection," she said.

"And what is that?" Diana asked, knowing this too would be something exotic.

"Just imagine a wall around you, a protective wall." Tess stopped when she saw Diana scrunch up her nose. "Okay, forget it."

"I just don't think pretending—"

"Forget it," Tess said louder as she put her toe into the water, then stepped into the footed bathtub and stood there. "What's up with you and Vinny?" she asked.

"What do you mean, what's up?"

"Look, I just didn't think you'd get involved with anyone so soon."

"What are you talking about?" Diana shook her head. "I'm not involved."

"I set you up with Vinny for the therapy, that's all. I know he's handsome and irresistible." Tess turned to smile at Diana. "And he's very concerned about you. In fact, I've never seen him this way."

"What do you mean by that?"

Tess lowered herself down into the tub. "Vinny's been known for getting involved with many women at the same time."

"I already know how he feels about women, but—"

"I know Vincent's charms." Tess sunk lower into the bathtub until the water reached her chin. "He won't hurt you, or anybody for that matter, he's just unavailable for the long term. When he's got you in therapy, that man can move mountains. I'd just keep it a doctor/patient relationship to protect yourself, okay?"

Diana, confused about what she felt, still ached for Antonio and the soul mate that she had through many lifetimes yet she wanted to move on with her life. "I'm not interested in getting involved. I just need some good friends here in Rome."

Tess nodded. "But the human heart is a strange organ, and I know how Vinny operates with women. Look, just use Vinny as a vehicle to reach inside your soul."

"To do what?"

"Vinny will help you understand your motives, drives and even your destiny—if you let him, that is."

"How does he do that?"

"After he regresses you multiple times," Tess said, staring at her in the dimly lit room until Diana felt goose bumps on her arms from the intensity of her glare. "The places you go in your mind during those sessions will help you understand your soul's purpose in this lifetime. I assure you, he'll figure out what Luca does when he comes to you in your dreams."

Diana stared at the stone floor, not wanting to look Tess in the eye. Her cheeks burned, as she vowed—*no one must ever know.* Because every night the things Luca did intensified, and, deep down, she wanted to know what he was going to do to her tonight.

CHAPTER SEVENTEEN

LUCA

Grotto

February 26, 2004
Dusk

A sea of candelabrums, flickering in waves throughout the *Grotto*, blurred Luca's vision. Focusing on something moving in the dark, he squinted to see through the amber haze leading to the underground tunnel. As if the black hole gathered together in the void then came to life, a form emerged from the tunnel and filled the arched entry. Wearing a hooded, charcoal-colored robe, the figure moved slowly toward Luca in the same way ghosts of the catacombs drifted through the subterranean depths outside the city. Unable to see the man's face because of his hood, Luca creased his brow as the figure approached. The towering man lowered himself onto the stone bench nearby. With his hands clasped together between his knees, the man hunched over in honor of the *Sacerdote*. From his movements, Luca knew it was Max.

"She's at the *Villa* now," Max said. "Gave her a start following her there, though."

"She saw you?" Luca asked.

"Her face, I wanted to touch it." Max rocked back and forth as if in a dream. "She's a Goddess."

"Tell me about her."

Max stared at Luca, then his pencil-thin lips opened and let out a moan. "It was unavoidable. I couldn't stop. She's magnetic, just like Antonio. If only she could join us in sex magick."

"She will come to us soon." Luca smiled at Max. "Give her time to respond to our summons."

"I want to touch her smooth skin and pleasure her with my hands."

Luca nodded, then decided to pick up the pace. "Will you help me carry this?" he asked, standing as he pointed to the crate at his feet. "We must begin."

Luca watched Max carry the heavy box with ease into the center of the *Grotto*, then spoke with Dante and Aldo about their assignments for the evening. As the rest of the *Malandanti* entered the *Grotto*, Luca finished briefing Dante and Aldo, and once the two men understood what he wanted, Luca quickly climbed the steps to the platform above the *boschetto*.

Echoed whispers silenced as Luca turned away from the *boschetto* to focus on the sacred tools on the altar.

"Awaken now, O Spirit of the Old Ways," he said.

On the altar, placed in the center, the bowl of *Strega Liquore* awaited him atop the carved-stone pentacle. Luca used a long wooden match to light the liquid, then waited until the flame shimmered into molten sapphire. He nodded as the fire took hold, noting that its strength clearly indicated a strong presence of deity. Satisfied that the spirits had come, he picked up the appropriate tools before raising his arms. In one hand he held an oak branch of the sacred wand, and in the other he held the *athame*, or Spirit Blade.

"*Bella Tana, dea della luna e del di la pensa per un momento a noi reunite qui nel tuo nome.*" He paused for a moment and heard the *Malandanti* behind him in the *Grotto* below pause as they ceased their chanting with him. "*Tanus, dio del sole e del di la pensa per un momento a noi reunite qui nel tuo nome.*"

Luca rang the bell three times over each of the four elemental bowls on the altar. "I call out into the mist of Hidden Realms, and conjure you spirits of earth and air and fire and water. Gather now at this sacred circle and grant us union with your powers." Again, he rang the altar bell over each elemental bowl three times, then tapped each bowl three times with the Spirit Blade.

Luca turned away from the altar, then walked over to the edge of the stone ledge high above the *boschetto* below. The *Ma-*

landanti all wore the same color robes, so the sea of purplish black hoods indicated that their heads were still bowed in concentration. Luca closed his eyes to gather the energy of the *boschetto* for their work this evening. He sensed a strange energy with discordant waves of vibration.

"We gather here tonight to learn a vital technique for a new power," he said. "I've decided that we will create our own tools for divination tonight, so that each of us will be able to connect to the source to manifest that which we desire. Tonight our focus will be on bringing down the power to charge our new tool that will help us protect our people."

Luca took a deep breath before he spoke. "Would you not do anything as your sister was being tortured? Would you turn your back on saving the ones you love from their nails being torn from their fingers? Would you stand by and watch your beloved ones burn at the stake or be crushed by mounds and mounds of rocks piled upon their bodies?"

Luca paused to let the *Malandanti* absorb his words. "This will happen if we don't prevent it. With our new powers, I assure you, we will save our religion, our faith, our people." Luca gestured to Dante and Aldo. They picked up the crate, then moved among the *Malandanti,* letting each one take a long, silver pouch from the box.

"Through time, there have been many ways to divine things that have yet to happen, things that we cannot see with the naked eye," Luca continued. "We each have the potential to divine through the Akashic Record of time—the record that exists in the magnetic, ethereal plane. The record that holds the energy pattern of all that has transpired on this earth. Called the quantum hologram, this record exists as the pattern of energy that is the very fabric of the universe. We divine through this quantum hologram to see the imprint of the events of the past, present and future."

He moved in a circle on the platform above the *Grotto* as he spoke and held out his hands, palms up, as a sign of surrender to the group. This was a surrender of his innermost thoughts, as well as a gesture of his authority as oracle.

"Scrying is the ancient art of clairvoyance when you concentrate on an object with a reflective surface until visions appear." Luca scanned the cave and searched the eyes of those who looked upward. "Scrying derives from the English term *descry* or *to make out dimly—to reveal.* Nostradamus used bowls of water for his visions, while the Egyptians used blood and dark liquids for centuries. "As we all know, the cauldron makes an effective scrying device, especially when it's filled with water and a drop of silver to represent the moon. What we will do tonight is the same, only now we are using a crystal to divine, rather than water. To do this, we must charge our divining tool with the power to give us the sight to see the Akashic Record of the past, present and future. Once we've done that, we will know how to reverse the prophecies."

Luca paused again. "Reach inside your velvet bag and you will find a crystal. With this tool, we will be able to see clearly."

He watched each *Malandanti* pull out the luminous crystals, and one by one they closed their eyes and performed the gesture of power with the crystal. When everyone finished, Luca continued. "Psychic vibrations are clearer at night, so you should be able to concentrate on your speculum until you see a vision, mental image or impression. Simply absorb this and continue gazing into the rounded tip of the crystal rod. Sometimes these visions are symbolic and must be interpreted, and at other times it's the actual event taking place that you will see. Many times, what we will see is symbolic."

"It's Raven," Max yelled, glaring at his crystal. "She's with the Goddess."

"But be sure to remember what you see," Luca continued. "Just absorb what you see, then we will interpret your visions one by one."

Luca raised the beloved crystal he had used on Diana in bed just last night, then gazed into the brilliant wand. Instantly, blurred images rose to the surface. He relaxed his eyes so that he could see beyond the hazy vision. Once his eyes adjusted, he too saw Raven administering the herbs to Diana. That was when Diana was sick. Luca frowned. The sign of the cross made by the ashes was gone from her forehead, and he knew it was Raven who had indeed cured her. Raven's concoction must have created all those miraculous cures throughout the Eternal City.

If the Sacerdote's ashes are that powerful, then a body charged through sex magick ritual and used as a talisman will make the ash potent enough to kill. The omnipresent voice inside his head whispered to Luca. *Charge the body before turning it to ash, but first add the Eucharist to make it even stronger. Then the talisman will become potent enough for your mission.*

Luca straightened himself after he received the message, then looked around the cave. Tears were streaming down Maddalena's face as she gazed into her crystal. Luca wondered what made her cry, then looked into his crystal for answers. The images sprung forth rapidly, and he instantly recognized Maddalena naked in the center of the circle while her body was charged through ritual. Startled, Luca locked eyes with Maddalena. She met his stare, then blinked. Luca shook his head, unsure about what the vision meant.

"When you are ready, you can put your crystals down," Luca suggested. "I want you to remember what you saw, that is if you saw anything. If you like, you can share your divination with me in private. But since I've just received instruction about tonight, let us act quickly to continue our mission. What we are about to do is new for us, but I assure you this talisman will be far more powerful than the last. Maddalena, can you be in the center of the circle skyclad for us?"

Her tears gone now, Maddy smiled and looked up at Luca, then stepped forward and freely slipped off her robe. Her succulent body glistened from the fiery light of the candelabrums, and she walked to the center of the circle with confidence and ease.

In the center of the circle, she sat down directly in the middle of Pan's mosaic face. "Just stay there and watch this time. The circle around you is called the Philosopher's Ring, and the *Malandanti* are familiar with this ring because we've done it many times before—but this time we will charge something rather different than in the past."

Maddalena opened her mouth to speak, but Luca raised his hand before she could utter a word.

"Please, let us all be skyclad throughout this ritual," Luca said, then paused and watched the *boschetto* disrobe. When everyone finished, he continued.

"We will now create the Philosopher's Ring by forming a circle around the image of Pan on the stone floor," he said, gesturing to the mosaic on the floor where Maddalena sat. "In alchemy, the Philosopher's Ring referred to a circle made of a special substance that gave alchemists special powers. By forming this rite tonight, we become the ring and the substance is the sexual energy that unites us—that substance being the fluids we create. When we form this physical and spiritual ring by performing oral sex to join each other, then we are taking the first step toward making our talisman."

Luca watched the *Malandanti* take up their pillows, then gather around in the circle.

After the circle was complete, Luca began. "It is time. Now we are ready to form the Philosopher's Ring."

Luca watched the *Malandanti* join together in a human chain of oral sex. Bianca started it when she fell to her knees and sucked Aldo's cock, then Dante, lying with his back on the floor, scooted between Bianca's legs. Bianca crouched down until her pussy landed directly in Dante's face. Dante held onto her ass as he feasted, and in an instant his cock was rock hard. Dante's phallic torch made Belinda take notice, so she immediately crouched over Dante on hands and knees to suckle his stick-straight cock. Max joined in by scooting between Belinda's legs as she was on all fours, then Max pulled her hips down until he too, could feast on her pussy. The ring continued until everyone in the circle was linked mouth to genital, genital to mouth. Once the circle was formed, Luca saw the odic energy accumulate.

"You may use your hands and fingers, if you haven't already. Every sensual part of the body can be poked, prodded and licked," Luca instructed. "Feel the energy coming from the mouth of the person giving you oral sex. The energy moves through your genitals and exits through your mouth into the genitals of the person you are giving oral sex to and this continues on throughout the circle to create a current of energy. The energy grows stronger as it travels through the genitals, up the spine and out through the mouth. I can see the energy now. It's whirling around this ring in waves and pulses. Maddalena, can you feel it?"

The naked Maddalena looked up and nodded from inside the circle, then watched the *Malandanti,* clearly mesmerized by the human chain of oral sex.

The moaning started from within, like a chant, then it resonated through the *Grotto* as the ring of naked bodies moved together, sexually linked and totally engrossed in the act of sex. Luca chanted to guide the group to the ritual's purpose, and the guttural sounds of the chant began to crescendo as if in concert.

"Energy builds," Luca continued. "The sederunt begins. We focus on withholding our fluids and wait for the climax until we are together in our purpose. If you are close to climaxing, you may break the chain for a moment and remove your mouth; however, keep stimulating each other with your hands, or preferably with your tongue. We must all concentrate on the meaning of this ritual in order for the magick to work."

Smiling at Maddy, sitting naked in the middle of Pan's face, Luca raised his arms just as a conductor would to orchestrate the music, but he conducted the movement of the *Malandanti* in the *Grotto* below. Maddalena's eyes widened as the activity in the circle became more intense and wild.

Luca scanned the writhing circle, then continued. "Focus your attention on creating the charge we need for our talisman," he said. "Focus on the power to destroy the church—the power to create a talisman that reverses the prophecies."

No one in the room had climaxed yet, although many were close. Several had taken their mouths away and used their tongues instead of their entire mouth. They knew how to keep the chain unbroken yet not succumb to climaxing until it was time. To be connected, the mouth needed to be fully on the genital sucking so that everyone pulled the current through each link.

"Are you ready, Maddalena?" he called out. When Maddy's eyes met his, Luca smiled. "We need you on the floor for this part of the ritual."

Luca watched Maddy's breasts as she stretched herself out on the floor in the center of the circle. Picking up the pace to an accelerated frenzy, Luca continued. "It is time," he said. "Use your entire mouth to pleasure the one you are with and focus on the purpose of the talisman until you all come together."

CHAPTER EIGHTEEN

DIANA

Villa di Spagna
February 26, 2004
10:00 p.m.

Diana meditated cross-legged with her palms facing upward, resting on her bent knees. Pressing her index finger against each thumb, her remaining fingers were outstretched as she envisioned her hands as lotus flowers; in her mind's eye, she became a yogi on a mountaintop. Centered, balanced, peaceful, calm. She sat up straighter in an effort to keep her body alert, and she willed her mind not to drift off onto some tangent of thought. At the deepest part of her meditation, Diana remembered the still waters within by silencing the mind and listening to the inner voice. Her eyes fluttered, not wanting to stay closed anymore because they'd been that way for almost twenty minutes now. She took a deep breath, then finally opened her eyes.

She started her meditating routine the day after she arrived in Italy, and continued doing it because Tess kept bugging her about it. After creating a sanctuary in the corner of Diana's studio, Tess urged Diana to continue meditating because she thought that would help her with her fears. Diana had to admit that she felt better when she meditated. Tess kept telling her it would help ease her qualms about being alone in the *Villa*, but when Diana opened her eyes, the old fears came back as quickly as they had left. She tried not to think about the dark corners of her studio, but the strange light in her studio reinforced her suspicions about what lurked in those obscure places. Her studio was in the attic or, what

Tess called it, the *attico*. It was the top floor of the *Villa di Spagna,* which Viviana had designed to be Diana's work space. Viviana transformed it into the perfect place for inspiration, but the haunting darkness still riled Diana. Through the windows, Diana could see the moon as it illuminated the menagerie of building facades from the couture district.

Diana turned away from the window and headed for her workbench. Rumpled up on the table was the map Slade gave her yesterday. Diana still wondered how Slade already knew about the *Villa,* and she meant to call her today and ask, but the day was over before she got the chance. Making a mental note to go to the shop tomorrow, Diana decided to bring Slade some flowers or a gift of some sort for saving her life—maybe a small painting. Staring at the map, Diana came to the realization that she needed another friend in Rome.

Turning to her work, Diana scanned the studio for her favorite brush. The paintings that were scattered throughout her spacious studio reflected how her work had changed since she moved to the Eternal City. Unable to tote the mammoth canvas of her latest work to the gallery, she had leaned it against the wall of the studio. A splotched stepstool positioned in front of the painting was the only way she could reach the topmost part of her work because it practically touched the ceiling. She had become so engrossed in creating this wall-sized painting that her stepstool had been ravaged from her work, but her easel remained untouched. Intrigued by the way the moonlight streaked into the room, Diana picked up the Kolinsky brush and grabbed her wooden palette, then frantically mixed the colors to create the same effect on canvas.

With the seven-layer technique that the Flemish masters used in the sixteenth century, Diana worked on her fourth layer of this piece. The fourth layer, known as the dead layer, was her favorite part of the process because this layer created something you couldn't see unless you knew what you were looking for. This layer was where she placed the obscurities, the ambiguities and the surreal aspects of the piece.

She dabbed her brush into oils of white lead, light ocher and burnt bone as she focused on creating the penumbra, or partial shadow effect. Like an eclipse between areas of complete shadow and illumination, the dead layer required more than technical expertise; it required cranking up the volume of intuition to get the colors just right. Diana referred to the dead layer as the *sfumato* effect. Da Vinci had used *sfumato* to add a hazy, mysterious quality to his paintings. Translated, *sfumato* meant "turned to mist" or "going up in smoke," and da Vinci and other masters of this technique achieved it by painstakingly applying gossamer-thin layers of paint, one layer over another.

Many masters waited seven days between applications of the layers, but Diana could never wait that long when she was submerged in a piece. She was lucky if she waited twenty-four hours. Using the seven-layer technique, she could apply a bit of color to transform the piece by capturing a different kind of light—light that splashed over the painting as if it were moonlight. By applying thick colors that were a half tone higher, she could make dark shadows, or by applying colors that were a half tone lower, she could make a transparent haze. In this way, she created an uncertainty, an obscurity in the piece that made the real become surreal.

Diana stepped back, then glimpsed a silver flash in the corner of her eye. She jerked her head to the left, baffled by the strobe of light. But nothing was there except the drapes slowly moving with the breeze that wafted through the partially open window. Diana walked over to the curtain, hesitated for a moment, then threw back the fabric. Nothing. She heard a dragging sound like something being scraped across the floor at the opposite end of the room and wheeled around, searching for the source of the macabre sound.

It couldn't be Tess because she was out somewhere, and if it was Tess, she'd be talking to her, not doing something to scare her. Diana scanned the room and saw only shadows. The dimmer switch was turned down on the floor lamps and a golden haze from the silvery moonlight blanketed the studio. Diana flipped on the overhead light switch to see the dark corners. Nothing. A shiver swept over her body as she closed the open window behind the fluttering drape. Shrugging off the jitters, she tried shifting her concentration to her work.

But when she dipped the brush into a glob of oil on her palette, the shrieking sound came again. It was a shriek this time—a high-pitched screech. Diana dropped her brush, then rushed over to the place where she thought the sound originated. Her heart pounded as she heard more rustling, then a slam. She froze. Someone was here. That someone had planted the crystal, then taken it away and now whoever it was continued to play with her mind. Fear gripped Diana's body until she stood before the window on the far side of the room, unable to move. Then she saw it. As the drape fluttered in the wind, she could see an open vent in the highest gable of the *attico.*

Diana had never seen that vent before. The breeze was slamming the vent open and closed. Shaking her head because she knew her stepstool would never be high enough to reach up that far, she decided to ignore it. Just knowing where the sound originated helped ease her mind. Surely no one could squeeze through a hole like that except a witch or a vampire, and Diana didn't believe they could fly. She laughed nervously to herself. Even if vampires did exist, she was sure they didn't have the power to haunt your very soul.

Trying to assuage her jittery nerves, she concentrated on finishing the dead layer. She picked up the paintbrush and dabbed it into the mixture of oils, then added the transparent layer onto a hidden snake fading in and out on the canvas.

Since she arrived in Rome, nighttime continued to inspire her best work. Moonlight shimmered through the window and illuminated her brushstrokes of color on the canvas. With just a few strokes, the snake came alive with subtle, transparent color. The snake was just one of many images she'd created in her mind compared with an image of a person or landscape like she used to paint. Yes, her work had changed. Now she painted images that originated from the deepest part of her soul. Whenever she painted, it was just like meditating; if she stopped and closed her eyes, the images appeared, and if it wasn't images she saw in her mind, she just knew somehow because every cell in her body responded to the thought. When the work was done, Diana didn't have a clue what the images meant. The imagery in her paintings baffled her. She'd seen some of these symbols in Slade's shop, but today the images had evolved into something much greater. Yet she still did not understand their meaning. Something as detailed as this must have meaning; they looked like snippets of Latin, Greek or some symbolic picture of ancient times.

Diana shook her head when she thought of how these images possessed her until she captured them with her oils. She felt compelled to get these images out of her mind and onto the canvas, because otherwise she couldn't eat, sleep or live. Whenever she started a project, her obsession with completing that work became more intense. At least it was her work that possessed her, not some outside force or fear of confronting her demons of the past. Just good old wholesome work kept her from sleeping and being ravished by Luca in her mind at night. Diana shook her head and frowned at the thought of her illicit dreams.

Hearing another haunting sound, Diana threw down her brush. Trying not to panic, she bolted out the door and raced down the spiral staircase—all three floors—until she reached the entryway. Once outside, she quickly descended the steps of the *Rampa Mignanelli.* A warm wind played with her hair, and when she reached the bottom she slowed down and walked straight toward the crowded *piazza.* The breeze fluttered against her bare arms and gave her a chill, yet she kept on. Walking toward the corner of *Piazza di Spagna* and *via Frattina,* she stopped and looked up at Vincent's place at the top of the towering structure before her. Tess had called his place an *attico* too. Since Tess had pointed it out the other day and told her it was the most magnificent penthouse suite she'd ever seen, Diana wondered if he was there now. He was probably gone because most Romans stayed out until all hours of the night. The night usually began at ten every night in Rome. Thinking she saw light through the trees at the top of the building, Diana walked over to the front door. Once she saw his name on the ringer, Diana hesitated. Giving into an impulse, she pressed her index finger on the buzzer not once, but five times.

Finally, a buzzer sounded and Diana opened the door, not sure what to do next.

She bit her lip and stepped inside the elevator, then pushed the top button. When the ancient relic reached the top and the doors opened, she walked down the hall and entered an open door of a place that looked more like the interior of a *palazzo* than an attic. The ruby-colored hibiscus blooms swayed in the breeze from the French doors that were opened wide, and the terrace wrapped around the entire room.

Mink-colored, overstuffed chairs and bulging terra-cotta sofas filled the living room with niches that invited relaxed conversation, and potted palms of outstretched leaves bobbed in the soft breeze. Nodding fronds waved as if to beckon one outside for further comfort. Every wall was a French door that opened wide to the terrace that wrapped around the entire *attico*, making inside merge gracefully with outside. From every angle, a glimpse of the living space outside made it seem like you were outdoors. Diana had seen places like these from the streets of Rome far below, but had never been inside one.

The plants inside and out made the place exotic, and the living space was vibrant with nature's beauty. The eclectic interior of Asian artifacts, oriental rugs and furniture designed in the Roman style made Diana wonder if she knew this man called Vincent at all. She had pictured him living in a messy, dark bachelor's pad, but this place looked like it was owned by a man of the world.

Vincent walked in rubbing his eyes and wearing baggy pants that had to be his pajamas. The caramel-colored pants had tiny white stripes and were held up with a drawstring that tied low on his hips. His bared, muscular stomach made Diana blush. He wore no sleep shirt and made no effort to put one on.

"I'm sorry to bother you," Diana said, looking at her watch. Ten thirty.

"I'm glad you're here. I decided to call it quits early tonight." Vincent said. "That's not like me at all. Come outside, to the *terrazzo*." He gestured toward the double doors, and Diana followed him through the potted ferns and trees just outside on the terrace.

"No one in Rome goes to bed at this hour," Diana said, laughingly as she sat down on a cushioned sofa. Vincent chose the overstuffed wicker chair closest by, then locked eyes with her before he spoke. "Are you okay?" he asked.

"I'm afraid of the dark," she said, nervously. "I know that seems silly, but it's true. Sounds like I'm a child or something, but it's what I can't see that I'm frightened of. I'm not afraid of dying. After the accident, I don't fear death anymore—not since I died and came back. It was what Tess calls a near-death experience. I'm not afraid of death because now I know that when you die, you are taken care of. I didn't want to come back, did I tell you that? It made me come back." It felt good to share this intimate experience with Vincent, and Diana was relieved to talk about it.

"It—being what?"

"A presence, an energy form, an all-pervading light that communicated with me."

"How? By talking?" Vincent leaned toward her.

"No, by transferring thought. It could read my mind, and I could read its—"

"You mean like God or something?" Vincent asked, frowning. "So if you aren't afraid of dying, then what's there to be afraid of?"

"It's the evil that scares me. There's something in that house, the *Villa.* I heard it tonight. A screech in my studio that sounded hideous. It came from up in the highest part of the attic. I found a vent that I think made the noise, but I still can't account for the shriek. And besides the sounds, these strange happenings keep getting worse. I assumed it was Antonio's mistress who did those things because she had a key. But there are other things, like my dreams."

"Slow down," Vincent said as he patted her leg. "I'll go over and fix that vent, okay?"

"And then my work," she said. "It's like I'm possessed when I paint. And I don't even know what those images mean, but they come to me so quickly that I can't stop working until I'm finished with the vision."

"Images of what?" Vincent asked, leaning forward.

"Scripts, ancient things. Writing that looks like Latin, Aramaic or Greek. And the designs range from snakes on parchment to exotic moons in the universe. It's bizarre, but I know it has meaning."

Vincent furrowed his brow. "It may be your cell memory."

"Sell what?"

"Your cells retain the knowledge of your past lives even though you consciously don't, and that knowledge can be tapped through the creative process or by digging deep into the mind with regressions."

"Well, I don't like it one bit when it starts to take over, although, my work is thriving with ideas. Problem is, I don't know what's happening to me. And it's getting worse. I can't even sleep. Maybe it's the *Villa*."

"Please," Vincent said, as he shook his head. "Slow down. We'll figure it out. You just need to talk about it and understand what's hidden in your unconscious."

Diana looked down at Vincent's dark chest, then blinked. She admired those broad shoulders and rippled abs. His physique was phenomenal, and his eyes were alluring. Those eyes that were now staring at her could make her melt if she allowed it. Just one more time, Diana thought. She couldn't do another dream with Luca, not tonight. If she could just sleep with this man one more time, maybe she could start sleeping alone again. The one night that the dream hadn't happened was with Vincent, so maybe she could get some rest tonight if she slept with him again.

"Can I spend the night?" she asked.

"Here, in my bed?" Vincent smiled.

"I just need to be with someone because I can't be alone right now."

"And I suppose you want me to hold you again this time." Vincent leaned back against the cushions of the wicker chair, then clasped his hands behind his head and grinned.

"No. I'll just use the couch in there." Diana pointed to the living room.

"I see. Holding you doesn't help?" he asked. "You don't like being in these arms?"

He stretched out his muscular arms, and Diana shook her head at the sight, then he laughed. Vincent stood, then took her hand and guided her inside the *attico*. He kept walking until he reached what had to be the master suite, which made all the other rooms wane compared to this one.

Massive bedposts carved with African etchings combined with an ebony silk bedspread flecked with gold exuded the *palazzo* effect. Egyptian urns and unusual artwork placed atop shelves, columnar stands and arched insets in the wall made it look a museum, yet it felt like stepping into another reality. With the ivory-colored roses arranged in massive bouquets throughout the room, it looked like he expected visitors or had made preparations for a party—a bedroom party.

"My housekeeper, she loves roses," Vincent said as he smiled.

"It's beautiful, but I can't sleep here—" Diana started backing out of the room.

"I won't do anything, I promise," Vincent said, taking her hand and pulling her back into the bedroom before grabbing the nightshirt on the bed. "Here, wear this. I can't keep it on." He gestured to the bath, then left through the French doors that led to the *terrazzo.*

"I'll pour you some *grappa.* I'm having some." Vincent stood with his back toward her as he rummaged through the wine glass menagerie at the outside bar.

"Okay," she said, staring at his muscular back. She held up the nightshirt to see just how oversized it would be. Satisfied, she stepped into the master bath and closed the door. She stopped and stared at a multitude of her own images in the mirrors that slanted just enough to make the reflection jarring. Mirrors covered every wall, including the ceiling. She took off her clothes and slipped on the nightshirt, then stared at her reflection in the mirror above the black marble vanity. She even looked scared. Diana realized that she needed to get stronger, not weak like some frightened child. But at least tonight she wasn't going to be alone. Maybe tonight she could let go of her fears and stop the wild dreams of Luca one more time by being in Vincent's arms.

She stepped into the bedroom just as Vincent entered with two fluted glasses filled with the red liquor. But when he saw her, he immediately put the glasses down and took both of her hands in his.

"Are you alright?" he asked, squeezing her hands. "Please, sit down before you faint." Vincent led her to a loveseat facing the bed. "Talk to me." Once she sat down, he did too. Close beside her, with his arm resting on the back of the couch, Diana flushed at the sight of him sitting there with his shirt off and the drawstring pants that barely covered his hips.

"It's the dreams. I think they're some sort of mind control." Diana wanted to tell him everything, get close, to share her innermost thoughts with him. It comforted her that he wanted to help her by listening. Even though he was her therapist, she considered him more a friend than anything else. "These thoughts possess my mind. Even my paintings are affected by the curse. I've changed so much that I think I'm going crazy. Ever since I arrived—"

Her words, crushed by Vincent's lips pressing against hers, were never spoken, and his arm no longer rested on the couch behind her. He drew her toward his manly, brawny chest and Diana closed her eyes to savor the kiss. That was when she decided to freefall into his exciting, yet unpredictable world.

PART FOUR
THE BREAKTHROUGH

No one knows the precise reasons for the construction [of bones stacked to form walls and entire skeletons assembled as if they were the living dead], surely before 1793, of this very unusual cemetery. It seems to have been created by the Cappuchine monks, who had escaped from France. This place was a very important stop along the itinerary of some illustrious travelers such as Goethe or the Marquis de Sade. According to some reports of the times the Marquis de Sade did not at all appreciate the cemetery but, it should be remembered, of course, that this hypogeum was conceived with the idea of highlighting the virtues of humility and poverty.

Every detail of the compositions is a hymn to the virtues of heaven, a chorus of disgust for the comforts, softness and conveniences of the rich.

All the skeletons came from the common grave of the church of Via dei Lucchesi where, in 1631, 4,000 Cappuchines were exhumed. Through this incredible cadaver-like deformation, each figure transmits to the visitor the tragedy of death, inviting him to pray and meditate.

Carlo Pavia
Guide to Underground Rome

Chapter Nineteen
Vincent

Vincent's Attico
February 26, 2004
11:00 p.m.

When their lips touched, Vincent pulled Diana's body toward him. Her lips, soft as silk, responded as he held her close. Not only did her lips respond, but her entire body melted into his as if she wanted more. Instantly, he wanted more too. Normally, it took something forbidden or deviant for Vincent to become completely aroused, but with her pliant, full lips and wanton body, she was hard to resist. One kiss and he was rock hard and ready to ravage her in bed. That never happened to Vincent without being enticed by something illicit, but Diana didn't need to use any sexual ploy to get him to react. Diana zapped him into some unexplored realm in his mind simply by being herself. As if it would never end, Vincent forced himself to pull back and look at the woman who aroused such a tumultuous response simply through a kiss.

Feeling strange, Vincent got up from the sofa and reached out his hand. "You must rest. Come to bed." He led her toward the bed and pulled back the silk duvet. When she didn't climb in, he frowned. She tilted her head, staring with her deep ocean eyes, but Vincent couldn't look into those searching eyes just now, because he had to squelch what he was feeling. He wanted to quiet any emotion because that had always been a red flag for him. Vincent gestured at the king-sized bed as he pulled back the duvet even farther, then helped her slip inside. Her hair, tousled and wild, looked as if she'd already been ravished. That was exactly what

Vincent wanted to do to her right now. All the while, he was telling himself he couldn't.

"Something wrong?" she asked, settling herself in bed, then running her fingers through that tousled blonde hair while she batted her long lashes.

Vincent never responded like that right away. It wasn't like him to react so intensely with a woman. Usually it was him orchestrating that response in the woman rather than vice versa. He needed to get a handle on his emotions; after all, she was in therapy with him, and sleeping with a patient wasn't something he did with anyone who stepped into his office.

"Nothing," he said. "I just want you to relax and get some sleep, that's all."

"That kiss. Why?"

"I don't know why." Vincent turned to go, because he wasn't sure he could stop himself anymore. *With no other clothes on except my nightshirt and sleeping in my bed is not a good combination,* Vincent thought.

"Just like the others."

Vincent froze and spun around to face her. "What did you say?"

"The other women," she said. "But the other women don't talk to you about their dark places, let alone the other universes where souls are made, do they?"

Vincent collapsed onto the sofa and eased back into the downy pillows to look at Diana nestled in his bed. "Usually people feel safe when they don't explore the hidden recesses of the mind because delving into the unknown can breed fear," he said. "Many people want to remain in the dark about the things that are buried in their unconscious. In fact, most people prefer to remain oblivious to anything that remotely touches upon the source of their hidden secrets. But your first regression must have been to the time period when your soul traveled into another universe, because that's the way it travels—through black holes and into the light at the end."

"*It* being *what?*"

"The soul."

"I see." Diana smiled. "Well, you and Tess should get together then because she has quite a theory about the universe and parallel dimensions. I didn't get to ask her about black holes, though. But believe me, it doesn't matter because you both have me thoroughly confused."

"In a regression, I take my patient through what's known as the point of entry. The point of entry is a death or a traumatic experience that leaves a mark on the soul, but it can also be something joyous like love. Normally, it's an earthly memory that is strong enough to affect your soul, but in your first regression, your spirit mind chose to go back to the original soul and its entry into this universe." Vincent waved his arms as he talked to reflect the passion he had for his work. "Sometimes the point of entry entails the white light, like the one you saw after the accident, not the dark tunnel we go through to get there. This is the first time I've had a patient see inside the black hole in a regression though. It's the spirit mind that takes us there because it has journeyed through all your previous lifetimes. It's not a physical entity—it's a spiritual or ethereal one. And it has what's known as a cell memory."

"Cell memory?" Diana repeated with a laugh. "I have a hard enough time with my brain's memory."

"Our reality isn't limited to what our conscious minds remember. Our conscious minds are flawed and forgetful, but they are also protective of what we think we already know. Most people believe what they want to believe, interpret facts the way they want to see them and remember experiences based on what we want those experiences to be in the scheme of our lives. But if experience is limited to our conscious mind, then where was that conscious mind when we were in the womb, when we were being born and when we were ages one through three? Where was our mind and the reality that surrounded our thinking during that part of our life?"

Diana shook her head, and her eyes looked glazed.

"See, it's too soon to tell you these things," he said. "Why don't we talk about this another time?" Vincent stood, waving his hand in the air to dismiss the matter.

"Please," Diana held out her hand to him, and he walked over and placed his hand into hers. "Don't go. I don't mean to sound apathetic. It's just too bizarre that both Tess and you talked to me about this very subject within the last eight hours. It's as if you were thinking the same thoughts. Have you two talked about this?"

Vincent shook his head, then squeezed Diana's hand as he fought the impulse to take off that nightshirt and make love to her all night. The way she looked—so wild, so exotic. Those deep-sea eyes and that windblown blonde hair were too enticing.

He released her hand and turned to go. "I'll come back and check on you later, okay?"

"Wait, Vincent—"

He kept walking even when she called out again. He knew that if he looked into those ocean eyes once more, he'd kiss her again—harder this time, and then he'd slide into bed. But there was no way he could do that because then he might do something he'd end up regretting. She was his patient for Christ's sake.

"You rest." Vincent gave a not-so-convincing nod in the direction he was walking and didn't turn back before he slipped through the door into freedom.

He stood in the hallway for a moment, then took a deep breath and tried to redirect his thoughts. No woman had ever made him feel that way, and it bothered him to think that this one was rocking his world. No, he couldn't let any woman do that. He had too many things to do. And besides, Vincent always had a variety of women to choose from, not just one.

Vincent stared at the key dangling from the opening of Diana's purse. It must be the key to the *Villa*. Maybe he should go there and take a peek at her work, because once he saw the paintings, he could assess Diana's unconscious or creative mind and make a better assessment about what was going on with her. Why not fix that vent right now too, and get his mind off the woman who was sleeping in his bed? He couldn't be in the same place with her all night, because he knew, without a doubt, exactly what he would do. He had to get away, far away from his desires to be with her.

Vincent grabbed the key, then found some trousers and an old shirt in the foyer closet before he practically sprinted out the door. Once he stepped outside, he glanced at his watch. It was eleven-thirty, and the night was just beginning. He felt energized. It must be the adrenalin from a kiss like that, he figured. He had almost lost all rational thought when he kissed her. He couldn't imagine having sex with her—what would that do? Probably electrocute him.

Vincent laughed out loud as he strolled through the crowded *Piazza di Mignanelli.* Once he crossed the *piazza,* he dashed up the gray stone steps that led to the *Villa.* If the moon weren't so luminous, those steps would be hidden by darkness, but the eerie glow provided just enough silver light to guide him to the top. He slipped the key into the lock easily, then flipped on the light in the entry. Dashing up the spiral staircase, Vincent finally stepped into Diana's studio and whistled at the sight.

The large canvas that Diana had been so obsessed with looked like no other artwork he had ever seen before. The images glowed with graduated colors of golds, maroons, blacks and burnt reds. A language he could not identify spoke volumes through each image of various phases of the moon, celestial bodies and other worlds as well as the variety of exotic signs and symbols from ancient times. As if the light had seared through it, the large oil looked like galaxy clouds intermittently scattered on canvas. If there ever were a celestial map to the universe, this painting captured it.

The alchemy of color along with astrological signs was superimposed over ancient symbols that included a human eye in the center of what looked like a Mayan or Aztec calendar. The entire piece evoked a sense of mystery or awe through its vivid colors. Constellations mapped out over waves of galaxies and celestial orbits in this unfinished painting made it appear that Diana was more astronomer than painter. The piece looked as if Diana had painted parchment on decrepit wood, yet she had created the illusion that the parchment had peeled off as it aged. Over the peeling layers that created the entire background, Diana had painted slithering snakes, naked figures, radiant suns, luminescent moons and exotic planets intermixed with painted scrolls of archaic inscriptions. Scrolled fonts painted into words along with faded, intricate diagrams and charts gave the work a timeless quality. Vincent had a strange, reminiscent memory of having seen this before—maybe in a past life.

Yes, Vincent was certain Diana had seen these things before in a previous life, probably many. The studio, filled with these strange images, made Vincent wonder just how many past lives Diana had experienced. After looking at her work, Vincent searched the room for the open vent. When he found it, he grabbed a broom in the utility closet, then carried the stepstool over to close the vent. Once it slammed tightly closed, he heard footsteps in the hall.

"What are you doing here?" Tess said, entering the studio.

"It's Diana," he said. "She rang my doorbell, then needed some company. She ended up staying there for the night, so I thought I'd stay here. Is that okay with you?" Vincent smiled and looked her over. "You look inviting tonight."

Tess moved her hands over her hips as the clingy fabric tightened across her flat stomach. "I've been having fun here with so many—"

"Men? The same Tess I always knew," Vincent said, whistling under his breath. "Erotic. Illicit. Forbidden. All the things I love in a woman."

"What do you think of Diana's paintings?"

"Okay, change the subject then. They're profound. I've never seen anything like them before."

"She goes into a trance when she paints, Vinny." Tess leaned toward Vincent, and he smelled the scent of jasmine in her hair. "And if she becomes blocked while painting, she closes her eyes like someone is talking to her. When she opens them, she frantically begins painting again. It's like she's getting messages from somewhere inside her head."

"Yes, they look like messages," Vincent said, thinking about the mixed messages he gave Diana tonight. He shook his head and vowed to forget his earlier arousal.

"Wouldn't you like to know what they mean?" she asked.

Vincent watched Tess's blood-red lips move. When she talked, those luscious lips accentuated her open mouth as if she wanted to entice him, to draw him near. Watching her open her mouth reminded him of how she used to—

"What have you discovered through Diana's regressions?" Tess asked.

Vincent shook his head, trying to focus his thoughts on the words, not the lips. "What?"

"Is something wrong?"

"I was just thinking about her regression as a *Strega*," Vincent said, feeling guilty because that wasn't true at all. Not long ago, he was thinking about sex with Diana in his bed, but now he didn't know what he wanted.

"She regressed to a *Strega?*" Tess asked incredulously.

"That's where all this is coming from." Vincent gestured at the paintings in Diana's studio.

"Being a *Strega* in a past life explains her attraction to Luca," she said. "And her fascination with those exotic images in her paintings, no?"

"Attraction?" Vincent tried to stay focused on the conversation instead of Tess's juicy lips.

"And tell me about you and Diana," she said. "What do you think of her?"

"I've never met a woman like her before."

"You haven't done anything unprofessional with her, have you?" Tess asked as she pursed her lips as if she was blowing a kiss. "Considering our escapades together and your track record with women—"

"Of course not," Vincent interrupted. "I have never had an affair with a patient, and I don't intend to either."

"But you try to get every pretty woman you meet into bed," she said, pointing a finger at him, then putting her hand over the cleavage of her low-neck dress. "Look, I don't want to hurt my best friend here. I just assumed you wouldn't be interested because she's your patient, and since we've had this tryst together in our past, it makes it a bit complicated. Diana is confused and lonely right now, so she's off-limits, unless it's just a friendship, understand?"

"Believe me, I don't get involved with patients." Vincent turned away from Tess, not wanting to talk about Diana anymore.

"This is important to me, Vinny. I don't want you fooling around with her and then dumping her like you do with every woman. She's already been hurt too much."

"I'm not going to hurt her."

"Promise?"

"Promise."

"What's wrong?" Tess stepped closer and took his hand.

"Come, follow me." Vincent squeezed her hand and pulled her toward the doorway.

"Where are we going? Is Diana okay?"

Vincent slowed down and took her other hand. "She's fine. I gave her my place for the night because she was too scared here, then I decided it would be better if I wasn't there, so I came to see you," Vincent explained, knowing that explanation wasn't quite right, but it sounded good for the moment.

"I came home because I was worried about her," Tess said. "How did she end up at your place?"

"She rang the doorbell, then we talked and I tucked her in." Vincent turned toward the stairway downstairs again, pulling Tess along with him. "Don't worry, she'll be fine there. It's this place that gives her the creeps."

Vincent almost dragged her down the stairs, and when he finally opened the door to the master suite on the second floor, he walked to the far side of the bedroom and took the whip down from the wall, not missing a beat. "Have you used this yet?" he asked as he ran his fingers through the leather braids.

"What are you talking about?" Tess blinked. "Why should I?"

"Because you like it."

"What makes you think—"

"We can make love like old times," Vincent said, smiling what he knew was his devilish smile, then cracking the whip to see if she'd flinch. "I need to do it because there is no one like you, Tess. Please, just one more time. I've never done it with anyone else, because no one else would let me."

"I've started seeing someone," Tess said, shaking her head, then smiling. "Although he will never be as erotic as you. No one does the things we did together. Can you believe it? You jaded me."

"As you did me with me. That's why we must do it again—so we won't forget."

"No way, Vinny."

"Come on," Vincent said, stepping toward her with the whip in his hand and making the leather tails rustle against his trousers as he moved. "Just do it one more time. For old time's sake."

Tess laughed. "You haven't changed."

Vincent slid the leather braids of the cat into Tess's cleavage before he kissed her neck. Ever since he met Raven Slade, he thought about doing it again. And now he couldn't wait to do what Tess used to do with him.

While he swished the leather strips of the cat in the air, he brushed his fingertips over the soft skin that bulged from her tight, low-necked silk dress. Just the noise of the strips made goose bumps appear on Tess's flawless skin, and he knew that she too was thinking about what they were about to do. When he kissed the soft bulge of her breasts, he slid his fingers down her cleavage and moved them up and down, feeling the soft skin of both breasts rubbing against his fingers. Soft, pliant skin—skin that responded to his touch.

When Tess moved toward him, he pulled at the shoulder strap of her skimpy dress. He wanted to slip those straps off her shoulders so that her dress would slide to the floor and he could see her magnificent body again. But no, not yet. He must savor this moment with her in that sexy, skintight dress. He might keep it on for awhile, then use the whip.

"Beautiful," Vincent said, still fingering her cleavage. "Your body, *magnifico.*"

He cracked the whip in the air, then dropped it to the floor to focus on her breasts. His hand glided over first one breast, then the other bulging over the top of her dress. He moved his hand deeper down her bodice until he felt her erect nipple. He squeezed first one, then the other before taking his hand out of her neckline. She groaned, then closed her eyes and arched her back as if she wanted more. Knowing she was more than ready, he nibbled her earlobe before bending down to pick up the cat from the floor.

Vincent slipped one strap off Tess's shoulder, then snapped the pliant leather braids of the cat-o'-nine-tails in the air. Wanting to create the perfect scenario, Vincent scanned the room, then headed for the closet. He searched through the clothes until he finally found what he needed. As he stepped back into the bedroom, he heard Tess laugh. On all fours in the middle of the bed wearing only her black stockings, string thong and lacy push-up bra, Tess looked up at him with a mischievous smile.

Vincent, head reeling from her erotic pose, held up the scarf he found in the closet. "Naughty girl. Because you've been so bad, you must now wear a blindfold when I spank your ass."

CHAPTER TWENTY

LUCA

Grotto

February 26, 2004
11:00 p.m.

Maddalena's naked body glistened from the charging ceremony. Reflective pools bounced light off the cave walls and created iridescent strobes of sparkling candlelight against the sheen
of her skin. Gleaming with moisture, her dewy skin radiated from
the flickering light of the candelabrums in the *Grotto.*

"What happens now?" Maddy asked, shivering even though
Luca had turned up the heat in the cave for her.

Luca put his robe around her shoulders and wondered how he
possibly could kill her. He wasn't sure he could do it. He turned
away from Maddy and wondered what he should do next. Water
bubbled down the rock walls into the pools of the *Grotto,* making
a soothing sound. After a moment, Luca decided he couldn't go
through with killing her. Luca turned toward Maddy knowing that
he would never kill her because he loved her.

"Don't you want to do it too?" Maddalena asked, scrunching
up her nose as she spoke. "How can you watch and not do it? I mean,
after seeing all that, I'm dying to have sex. Why don't we do it?"

Feeling the warmth of her stare, Luca couldn't believe what
he heard. After all these years of orchestrating sex magick ritual
in the *Sotterranea,* no one had ever thought about his needs. Without hesitation, he came to her. Taking her into his arms, he felt as
if he could explode, and he knew this time he would release the
tension without holding back for ritual. In a frenzied moment, they

smothered each other with kisses, and Luca wanted her more than he'd ever wanted a woman before. Her hands slid everywhere on his body, and his cock pulsed with energy as he started to lower her onto the mosaic floor. In an instant, she stopped and put her finger to her pouty lips.

"Why don't we do it on the table by the altar?" Maddalena asked. "Then it will be even more special." Maddy, giddy with excitement, giggled.

Luca, stunned by the sudden change of plans, obediently nodded and brushed his fingertips over her lips, then gathered up the robes so that he could soften the stone slab for Maddy.

She dashed up the tiny steps without him, and he hurried to catch up, eager to begin their love fest. He watched Maddy above as he ascended the narrow, carved-out steps from below. Maddy, after climbing the steps two by two disappeared from sight at the top of the platform, then screamed. In an instant, she fell from above and when she landed, Luca stared at her crumpled body on the mosaic floor. Motionless on the floor, Maddy's face was hidden from view. Luca rushed down the steps toward her and immediately knelt by her side. But once he saw her eyes, he knew there was no hope. Luca's eyes blurred with tears as he realized that his thoughts may have caused her death. Luca knew the power of thought could manifest death, and that may have been why she died. The forces beyond were making him stay focused on his mission. Feeling the sudden and absolute loss of his beloved Maddalena, Luca bent down and kissed her softly on the lips.

"I wish it didn't have to happen," he said aloud, trying not to give in to the anguish he was feeling. He needed to be strong for what he was about to do. "I am certain, this happened for a reason."

Luca turned away from her, then walked over to the pools. Stepping into the pools of the *Grotto,* he splashed the warm water over his naked body, then tried to wash away his sadness. Cleansing was part of preparing himself before cremating her to make the talisman. Especially in death, cleansing himself and banishing the area of evil spirits cleared away the harmful energies that may have come through when she died. Once he finished cleansing, Luca walked over to the hidden niche and retrieved the bottle of pennyroyal. Slowly, he approached Maddalena's body, then fell to his knees. He anointed her forehead, chest and the place below the navel, then started the Rite of Passage.

"Now you begin the sacred journey to the Realm of Luna," he said. "Now you know the mystery that is forgotten in this life because you have attained the greatest of all initiations. I do not bind you to this world with my longing for you, nor do I burden your spirit with my sorrow. I release you, Maddalena, the same way a parent must free a child who has grown."

Luca took the scroll from the enclave and recited the *Descent of the Goddess,* then acknowledged the deities summoned during the rite. He concluded with the funeral prayer.

"I wish you well on your journey," Luca said as he touched her forehead and chest with the oil again. "I know that the sorrow I feel is of my own making. There has been no loss for me, since I shall meet you again in a future life to come."

Luca gathered her body into his arms and carried her through the passageway and into the *Cripta dei Morti.* Fighting back the tears when his eyes met the blackened holes of his ancestor's skulls, he held her in his arms and kneeled before them. Bowing his head, he looked at Maddalena's ashen face and offered her to the gods before him. He rose after making the offering clear, then carried her to the crematorium.

Grabbing one of the torches bracketed on the cave wall, Luca held the flame high in the air as he spoke. "May the realms of Luna give you all that you desire, and may you find peace, pleasure and reunion with those who have gone before," Luca said, lighting the funeral pyre beneath Maddy. It was a pyre that he had prepared long ago. "Farewell, Maddalena, farewell."

Once the flames took hold, he stepped into the *Grotto* to meditate with Pan's image on the mosaic floor because he didn't want to be in the *Cripta* when Maddy's spirit left her body. Trying to forestall any hauntings from tormented spirits, Luca willed Maddy's spirit to be in peace. She had agreed to contribute to the cause against the church, so her death had to happen. Nevertheless, Luca regretted her passing because he'd grown fond of her unbridled passions. He wept as he thought of her beautiful body burning in the *Cripta.*

After what seemed like an eternity, Luca looked up and nodded when he noticed that there wasn't any more smoke coming from the pyre. He hadn't had any problem with his father's cremation, and now that he knew how the crematorium worked, he felt more comfortable with the process. The vents and ducts sucked the stench upward and ventilated the chamber, much the same way a chimney sucked smoke from burning embers. Yet there was still that temporary odor that took a few hours to go away.

After waiting long enough for her entire body to burn, Luca entered the *Cripta* and walked over to the crematorium. Staring down at Maddalena's remains, Luca wondered what made her ashes different from his father's. Luca noticed a haze around her remains and knew that hers were potent because of the charging ceremony they had done in the Philosopher Ring. His father's body hadn't been prepared with sex magick ritual, but Maddy's had been. Maddalena had gone through the charging ritual before cremation, so her remains were infused with the intent needed to prevent the Second Inquisition of the church, and that would add yet another layer of energy to the talisman.

Luca grabbed the dagger to begin the gesture of power and concentrated on manifesting his intent to exterminate the Roman Catholics. Picking up the wand with his left hand, he extended both arms outward; in one hand he held the dagger, and in the other, the wand. Then he moved the tools down and made a semicircle in the air in the shape of a crescent. He brought both arms up together, crossed, above his head. Still concentrating on the intent, he moved his arms down until the point of the dagger and the blunt end of the wand touched the ashes.

After invoking the power, Luca wore gloves to whisk all the ash into vials. Then he inserted the vials into carrying cases with soft pockets, rolled up the cases and stuffed them into a large briefcase. Needing a moment to honor the Watchers in the *Cripta dei Morti,* he stepped over to the altar and communed with the guardians about Maddalena's spirit. Her spirit had indeed left her body, and now all he needed to do was perform a banishing. Luca nodded at the robed skeletons standing before him at the altar, then completed the ritual. After he was certain all negative energies were banished, he gave homage to his ancestors once more, then took the passageway out to the *Grotto.*

Slipping off his gloves, he communed with the water spirits through his hands. Dipping both hands into the water, he closed his eyes and concentrated on the flow. After clearing his mind, he focused on his call to destroy the church. Certain that this was the right thing to do, Luca left the *Grotto* feeling refreshed and ready to carry out his mission. The eerie light in the tunnels became dim when he reached the midway point between the *Castello del Pincio* and the *Grotto.* There, Luca slipped through a small opening with stone steps that led to the surface above. He felt his way because it was too dark to see as he ascended the steps, but once he reached the top, he raised his hands above his head until his fingers touched the metal lid. Pushing the round metal plate, he used his legs to gather enough strength to open the manhole. Once the lid popped off, he slid the cover to the side and listened for traffic. After midnight, there was still traffic on *Viale Trinità dei Monti,* but at least it was intermittent. He waited for silence, then catapulted out of the manhole in the middle of the street without a hitch.

Sucking in the brisk night air, Luca brushed the dust from his jacket, then quickened his pace to get to the church. Grabbing his cell phone from the inside pocket of his jacket, he called his driver and instructed him to wait outside the *Trinità dei Monti.* Scanning the street, Luca was certain no one saw him when he darted into the dark shadows around the church and headed for the back entrance.

It'd taken him a long time to secure keys to the churches, but through various connections of the *Malandanti,* Luca had been able to make copies of keys without anyone knowing. Using the penlight in his pocket, he found the back door, then slid the key into the lock.

Once inside, he used the tiny shaft of light to guide his way into the cathedral. Just before he reached the door to the main entrance of the church, he stopped to peer into a basin of Holy Water—fresh Holy Water. Reaching into his pocket, he took out the packet of vials and unrolled the cloth. He opened a vial, then carefully poured the ashes into the water. The ashes swirled around in the basin, then settled at the bottom. They blended with the veins of gray in the old marble basin until they looked as if they weren't even there.

Luca smiled as the ashes disappeared in the Holy Water. He rolled up the packet of vials, then stepped back into the darkness. He had to visit the four *basilicas* of *Roma* tonight: *San Paolo, Santa Maria Maggione, San Giovanni* and *San Pietro.*

Later on that night he realized without his driver, he could not have done it so quickly. It took him an hour to meet his contacts, and make sure the other *basilicas* were taken care of, then at one in the morning, he reached the last. And this *basilica* would be the greatest achievement of all—the *Basilica di San Pietro.*

Luca glanced at his watch, knowing he needed to be on time to meet his informant at the Vatican. Getting the ashes into the Holy Water there would be his responsibility, just as it had been for Ash Wednesday. The bishop would meet Luca at the *piazza,* then he would do the job of tossing the ashes into every basin there. Once Luca's driver pulled up to the *Piazza San Pietro,* he jumped out of the car. Fingering the last vial, Luca searched for his informant, then crossed the *piazza* toward the entrance of the *basilica* to meet him. A dark figure stepped out of the shadows, startling Luca, but he immediately realized it was the bishop he had planned to meet. Without words, Luca slipped the vial into his hands as they looked like they passed each other in the night, then Luca turned and headed back to the Mercedes where his driver awaited.

Just then, Luca realized that something was horribly wrong. He scanned the *piazza* with the premonition of someone evil watching him. Luca used his remote vision and tried to detect who was threatening him, but all he could see were shadows in the moonlight.

He picked up the pace, wanting to reach his driver before something happened, but the presence came up from behind, then spoke.

"Why have you come?" It was Raven's voice.

He turned and there she was—dressed in black, wild hair blowing in the gusty wind, looking haunted.

"Your evil potions will not succeed in killing anyone this time either," she said.

"How can you be so sure?"

"Because I know the cure," she said, walking toward him as she spoke. Her shawl, loosely wrapped around her, fluttered in the wind. "And it works."

"You don't even know its power yet."

Raven stepped toward him as if she were about to kiss his lips but drew a knife instead. In an instant, the blade pierced through Luca's shirt into his chest. Leaving the dagger inside, only for a moment, she suddenly yanked it out from his body, then hid the bloody weapon in the folds of her shawl. Luca groaned and pressed his hand tightly against his wound. Quickly stumbling toward his Mercedes, Luca's driver rushed to his side to help him inside the car. Looking back as the car sped away, Luca saw Raven watch him go. She stood tall, her frozen features like stone in the moonlight while her hair wildly whipped in the wind. Her shawl fluttered and furled around her but she did not move.

His pain worsened during the ride to the *Castello del Pincio,* and Luca called Max on his cell phone for help. Once he reached the *Sotterranea,* he hobbled through the *Villa de Marco* and headed for the *Grotto.* As he slipped through the tunnels of the *Sotterranea,* the pain subsided.

He struggled to reach the *Grotto,* where he took the passageway into the *Cripta dei Morti.* Once there, he prostrated himself before his ancestors. When he died, Luca wanted his ashes strewn here because this place was his only reprieve from the living. Luca closed his eyes and remembered the legacy of the *Cripta.* Long ago, a group of healers had taken the bones of the tortured from funerary niches and dungeons and assembled them in piles to make artistic backdrops of skulls, femurs and practically every bone in the human body. Stacked one upon another, these bones signified the inevitable death of all.

The skeleton that was mounted on the cavern wall told the whole story. This skeleton had one hand holding a scythe and the other holding the scales of justice. Around the skeleton, small bones of the same shape were mounted together to form an oval frame. Luca got up and touched the scales of justice that the grim reaper held, then fingered the scythe of death. Nodding, he acknowledged that this was our common denominator. There were no riches in death; only the spirit remained.

The skeletons at the altar seemed to nod their approval at his reverence for this sanctuary. Tears filled Luca's eyes as he stood in the chamber—this chamber that revealed the truth of death, death and all its implications for the body. This was not about death with riches and burial rites, but death in its raw state of bones and dust.

Luca kneeled at the altar and looked up at his ancestors. The three skeletons were propped up and posed as if they were doing ritual. The Alchemist and Druid were bending over as if in reverence, while the *Strega* in the middle conducted the Black Mass. Dressed in black robes with the hoods pulled over their skulls, the *Sacerdote* of ancient times looked directly at Luca. Beneath the altar, at the feet of the three robed ones, there were three graves with markings that described their torture.

Hundreds of skulls stared at Luca as he showed them his wound. Black holes, noses with sunken triangles and mouths with only the upper row of rotted teeth watched Luca as he inched his way closer. Femur bones stacked one on top of another created makeshift columns between the rows of skulls. Once he came as close as he could to the altar, Luca stared at the skeleton of the *Strega* in the middle that stood with arms bent, holding the pentagram against his chest. Dressed in a black hooded robe, the skeleton's jaw had been wired together, yet there was a huge gap where his teeth had rotted in the middle.

The skeleton leaned toward Luca and he stepped back. Gripping his wound, he stared at the hooded skull. It moved closer, and Luca felt its putrid breath against his brow.

A rustling sound made him jerk back in horror. But when he looked up, he saw Max. "What are you doing here unannounced?" Luca demanded.

"You told me to come," Max answered.

Max pulled Luca up from kneeling on the ground, then helped him to the bed of bones. As Luca stretched out on the stacked femurs, Max knelt down next to him and attended to his wound.

"Who did this?" Max asked.

"Raven. She tried to kill me."

"Tell me what to do."

"You must eliminate her. She wants to stop us." Luca winced at the pain, then closed his eyes before he continued. "Use the last of the ashes in the urn—the urn in the secret niche of the *Grotto*." Luca gestured for him to go through the passageway. "Leave now and destroy her."

"Ashes?"

"The ash kills on contact," Luca said, looking down at his wound. Relieved that the cut wasn't deep, he noticed it had stopped bleeding. "Throw it in her face."

"I'll go," Max said. "But first I'll send someone to help you."

"Just find Raven before she kills us all."

Although Luca was certain Raven would not go to the authorities for fear that her coven would be discovered, Luca was concerned nevertheless. She knew about the ashes before, and now she would try to stop him again. He should have silenced her long ago. But there was Raven's *boschetto* to worry about. Luca didn't want anyone in the Old Religion against him now.

But after tonight, terror would prevail in the church and its parishioners—a terror that would instigate the beginning of their demise. Once he instilled the fear, then he would scatter the ashes into the source of the Vatican's drinking water. After he put ashes in the water that flowed at Vatican City, Luca would eliminate everyone there. But he needed more ashes, because tonight he had used up all that he had.

As soon as the Vatican officials were out of the way, he would find the *Scrolls of Aradia* hidden in the libraries there—scrolls written by *La Bella Pellegrina*, The Beautiful Pilgrim, the one who created the very tenets of his beliefs. But her teachings were distorted by the church during the Inquisition, because instead of recording the truth, the inquisitors recorded their false beliefs about people with religions different than Christianity. Since the church used corrupt measures of torture during their questioning, the records of the Inquisition were inaccurate and fraudulent. Once Luca found the *Scrolls of Aradia*, then he would live by the original teachings. The information recorded during the Inquisition was "extracted" from his people using "engines of torture." Luca shuddered at those quoted words, because they were directly from the records of the Inquisition.

The church confiscated the *Scrolls of Aradia* when they captured *La Bella Pellegrina,* and the scrolls were never seen again. Luca, convinced that the Vatican still had them, would find those ancient documents, and then he would have what was meant to be the legacy of the *Stregheria.*

The Inquisition became part of the law after the papal edict was made that witchcraft was heresy, and the inquisitors tortured the *Stregheria* until they "confessed" to "consorting with the devils." For the *Strega,* the only devils were the ones the inquisitors conjured in their minds. Devil worship, sacrifices and even more came out of the records of the Inquisition, because that was how the church justified the deaths of his ancestors and the church's hatred for his beautiful religion. The Inquisition records were still public, so the perceptions of the *Strega* were still evil and distorted to this day. But once he found the *Scrolls,* he could prove that the tenets of their beliefs and practices didn't involve poisonings and sacrifices. He followed Leland's words about poisoning because that was the only thing he could do to fight the war. Deep down, he knew warring wasn't part of his religion. Deep down, Luca knew war and killing didn't help anyone in the end. He just had to stop the Second Inquisition.

Once he brought justice to those who had wronged his ancestors and terrorized his people, then he would restore the teachings of Aradia. With the original scrolls and not the corrupted version that had been produced by the heinous judicial proceedings and morbid interrogation tactics of the church, he would clarify the magnanimous intent of the Old Religion to the world. *Stregheria* was about taking care of the earth and honoring the universe as well as the body, not destroying life and creation with incantations and spells. He stared into the black holes of the *Sacerdote* at the altar, who had straightened his form and stood taller now. Realizing that the ancient *Sacerdote* of bones in the *Cripta dei Morti* acknowledged his pursuit of truth and revenge, Luca smiled in the face of death, and knew what he was about to do to the Roman Catholic Church was justified.

CHAPTER TWENTY-ONE
VINCENT

Villa Di Spagna

February 27, 2004

1:00 a.m.

Vincent looked up at the mirror and saw Tess's perfect behind. He stroked her back, then tried to undo her bra.

"No," she said, turning around to gently push his hands away. "You have to watch. You can't do anything yet. I'll be the bottom in due time. I'm not doing it blindfold because I want to see everything."

Tossing the silk scarf on the nightstand, Vincent savored talking during their playfulness; it made him concentrate on the rules of S and M—rules they never violated because if either of them did, they could get hurt. Rules were necessary for both of them to experience new thresholds of excitement. *The most erotic part of the body is the mind, and this type of play takes fantasy into another realm,* Vincent mused. Now he knew Tess wanted to be the bottom tonight, which meant she would be the one to receive the flogging while the top was the one doing it. Vincent didn't care whether he was top or bottom, because he liked both positions when it came right down to it. But men were known to prefer being top because it was more active than the bottom. Vincent walked over to the decorative silk ties hanging on the wall, grabbed four of them and turned to Tess positioned on the bed.

"You like?" Vincent asked, holding up the ties with a questioning look.

Tess nodded. She turned around for him to undo her bra, and once that was off, she slipped off her stockings and panties, then rolled onto her back in the middle of the bed.

"Tell me when I tie them tight enough," Vincent added.

With Tess's feedback as he knotted each cord, Vincent tied her ankles and wrists to the bedposts, then grabbed the cat o' nine tails. From the beginning, they tied up the bottom because being untied meant being able to move, and that made it difficult to stay away from the places that shouldn't be whipped. The only way to make the bottom stay put was by tying the person down. Bondage made it exciting, because then it was more erotic to be flogged, and the whippings were easier to take when you were tied up.

Years ago, when they first started this sexual play, they both practiced using the whip on a pillow to learn the various forms of striking. They had practiced for hours, whipping the pillow to make sure they could hit the target and not let the leather braids "wrap" around so that they could hit a forbidden area. Striking exactly where one intended was a critical part of not hurting the bottom. Another critical part was being able to agree upon the right word to signal to the top that it was time to stop.

As they got better at doing strokes like the figure eight, windmill or the caress with the leather braids, they began experimenting on each other and providing feedback on each of those strokes. Vincent never forgot the touch he needed to use on Tess. He also never forgot the forbidden areas, even though he had not done S and M with anyone else ever again. Face, neck, lower back, spine, backs of hands, tops of feet, knees, shins and hips were areas he never whipped. Flogging those areas could hurt anyone.

Flogging specific areas for sensation made the mind spiral into a frenzy of pleasure though. The sensual places for him had been the shoulders and upper back, the crown of the ass and the thighs. Tess liked the sensual areas the best—ass, breasts and lips of the magnificent flower between her legs. Another great place for her was the top of the back of her legs, right under her ass. That was precisely what he wanted to flog tonight.

Vincent grabbed a floor lamp, then carried it over to Tess tied up on the bed and tilted the lampshade so that the light would shine exactly were he wanted it to. Using the light to spot Tess on the bed, he created a shadow on the wall—a shadow that captured both Tess and Vincent's relief in darkness.

Tess smiled, then let out a deep laugh when she turned her head to watch the shadows move on the nearby wall.

"Have you done this here before?" he asked.

"Only in my mind."

"It's the perfect erotica, and you are the perfect woman to receive it."

He'd never forgotten those places she had whipped when she was top long ago, and that kind of sexual play had been exciting because she had taken control over the entire situation. But tonight he would take control, and frankly, Vincent relished the idea. The times he had been top with Tess were etched in his memory forever, and finally now he could do it again. A surge of anticipation shot through his veins as he practiced a light caress and glided the leather braids over her arms and legs.

He pivoted his wrist in a circle, making the tails of the cat go around and around her stomach area. Called the windmill, he began the movement slowly, then sped it up and finally changed direction. Gently using the soft leather braids to lightly touch her skin, he moved the tails of the whip down each leg, then struck the soles of her feet. With each strike Tess moaned, and Vincent looked up to see her biting her lip.

He raked the braids over her chest and made the tails form figure eights on her breasts, striking the whip at the upper part of the loops. When Tess moved her head from side to side, Vincent stopped.

"Are you okay?" he asked, leaning over to look into her eyes.

Tess nodded, then gasped for air as if she'd just run a mile. "I've missed you, baby," she whispered.

Vincent held the handle of the cat in one hand and grabbed the ends of the tails with the other. Without moving the handle, he pulled back the tails until they were taunt, then let go of the leather braids so that they snapped forward directly onto Tess's erect nipple. She screamed.

Vincent froze. "Did I hurt you?"

"No. Apparently you've forgotten how vocal I am while we play."

"Yes, I have forgotten," he said, taking a deep breath, then pulling back the tails like before, snapping the leather braids at the other breast and directly hitting his target. This time, he didn't stop when she screamed. With her head turned toward the shadows on the wall, she moaned each time he lifted the whip.

He used a standard strike on her breasts, directed at her nipples, at least a dozen times, then slid the braids over her stomach down between her legs. As gently as he could, he snapped at her flowering rose, then bent down and kissed it, using his tongue to lick the place he had just struck. Then he flogged her rose with a standard strike at least ten times. From the look in Tess's eyes, she had gone into a trance. The screaming had stopped, but she continued to moan and her eyes were glazed over, even though she still stared at his shadow on the wall. Using his free hand, Vincent slid his fingers into her beautiful flower, then his tongue to taste her juices before he stopped.

"Want to turn over?" he asked.

Vincent untied the cords. She gave him a questioning look as he guided her to the chaise by the window, then he dragged the floor lamp over so that she could again see their shadows on the wall.

"Here, bend over," he said, helping her bend down so that her head and torso dangled over the back of the chaise, while her legs were spread apart on either side of the cushions on the chaise.

He tied her forearms to the legs of the back of the chaise. Then, using plenty of rope, he tied her ankles to the front. With her behind in the air and her head down, Vinny worked on the area between her legs as he slid the tails up through her crack over and over again. Then he glided the tails to the sweetest spot of all: the area right below her cheeks and precisely at the top of her legs. Moving the leather braids with the caressing motion, he glided it back and forth horizontally across her legs until he heard her groan.

"Please, Vinny," she said. "Please, do it harder baby."

Vincent smiled and kept doing the same thing, yet used a softer, slower motion. He wanted her to beg because he knew that would bring her to a new threshold of pleasure. He continued teas-

ing her with the leather braids until her pleading turned into demands, then he struck the skin hard at least a dozen times. When
splotches of red appeared, Vincent stopped. He slid the tails of the
cat up through her crack once more and gently moved the braids
to the muscles of her back to assuage the tension. He struck the
meaty portions of her upper back but stopped once again when her
skin turned red. Then he glided the tails down to the crown of her
cheeks, where he slapped her ass with repeated hard strikes, one
after another.

"No, please, Vinny."

Vincent stopped. "Did I hurt you?"

"Wait, just a minute," she said, breathlessly.

"Sorry."

While he waited for Tess, Vincent played with the whip so that
it made a swooshing sound in the air. He intentionally made this
sound because the erotica of the cat was mostly psychological. The
mind tormented itself with anticipation and fear of what the next
sensation would be, and by cracking the whip in the air, the body
reacted as if it were still being hit. If Tess had said "stop," Vincent
would have quit using the cat altogether, but she'd said "wait" and
that meant she wanted to continue. According to their previous
agreement on the right words, they both knew what to say to make
sure the bottom never got hurt.

"Ready," she said, gasping for air. "Just needed some time
to breathe."

Her voice sounded as if she were in a trance. Vincent knew it
wouldn't be long before she would enter another level of excitement. He used the windmill stroke on her ass, turning the tails
around and around on her cheeks. He knew that after the heavy
flogging of her ass just moments ago, she would feel a tingling
sensation and heightened trepidation of what was next.

Vincent raised the whip, then stopped in midair, staring at his
target, knowing that Tess was watching his shadow on the wall. He
heard Tess gasp when he swiftly brought his arm down and cracked
the leather against her buttocks. Once again, he brought the cat
up, then paused before bringing the cat down to strike. He moved
his arm in sync with a steady rhythm and picked up the pace to

quicken the beat. Tess started writhing in the chaise, moving her ass back and forth, making it harder for him to hit the crown of her ass cheeks. Tess moaned as he struck again and again. When the redness appeared, Vincent raised his arm and changed his strikes to another area with harder hits, but with longer pauses between each hit.

He heard a sound from behind—not from Tess, but something behind him. He turned toward the doorway, where he saw Diana staring at them in horror. With the cat in midair, Vincent froze. Instantly, Diana turned and ran.

"Diana!" he yelled.

Vincent dropped the cat and ran after Diana, but at the end of the hall, he stopped and turned around. Feeling crazed, Vincent sprinted back to Tess because he couldn't just leave her there bare naked and tied up on the chaise.

CHAPTER TWENTY-TWO

DIANA

Via Di Spagna

February 27, 2004
2:00 a.m.

Gathering her strength, Diana tried to stay focused on her destination through the maze of dark, narrow streets. In a stupor, she vowed to keep moving so that she didn't have to think about Tess and Vincent anymore.

Tears welled in her eyes again as she realized that those two belonged together. The tears slid down her face, and she shuddered as a chilly breeze blew through the fabric of her skimpy jacket. Diana turned down an obscure, murky street that looked like the right one. The eerie shadows of the doorways and arched passageways leading into darkness on her left and right changed into something even more ominous on this street. Cold, vacant windows interspersed with doorways into darkness made the deserted lane seem as if the storefronts moved closer toward her on both sides as she walked farther down the street. Feeling like the buildings would close in on her at any moment, Diana tried to stop shaking. She pulled her jacket around her as darkness became the moonlight.

When the dim lights of *Le Vecchia Religione* came into view, a pigeon swooped down from the rafters of the tiled roof and almost nicked her head. She watched the silver pigeon fly away and climb higher in the sky until it crossed the crescent moon.

A breeze tousled her hair, making a chill crawl up her spine as she hesitated before entering the shop. Taking a deep breath, she stepped forward and looked through the windows at the amber haze inside. Grabbing the latch, she tried to pull open the door, but it was locked. Peering through the window, she could see that no one was there. A display of daggers in various shapes and sizes with strange symbols either engraved or etched on the handles illuminated by the overhanging lights of multicolored lanterns reminded Diana of the way she painted light and, what she had thought at the time, were her original designs. Not only did the daggers have these etchings, but also the cups and bowls, sticks and brooms and even the silver and gold pendants were shaped into these forms. Forms exactly the same as the ones she imagined, then painted in her work.

Taking a closer look, Diana noticed how the crystal balls large and small in jewel tones mounted on stands throughout the window display along with the overhead lanterns created a strange, luminescent glow that made everything inside look magickal. Shelves cluttered with exotic bottles filled with capsules, powders and oils reminded her of how the place looked like an apothecary, but this place and the potions it contained were something entirely different.

She tried the latch again, this time pushing instead of pulling, and the door opened. Bones clattered overhead as she entered, and Diana looked up at a chime made of tiny bones tied to strands of various lengths.

Diana heard murmuring in the back and froze. Chants, incantations and other sounds came in waves from the rear of the store. Melodious tones floated through the room, and the reverent atmosphere reminded Diana of what it felt like to be in church. Diana peered through the crack of a purplish-black velvet curtain to see what was going on.

The only light, flickering candles of every shape and size, created eerie shadows, and she felt her eyes blur from the smoke of heavy incense. With the embroidered black quilt as a backdrop to the dimly lit space, Diana wasn't sure whether what she saw was an illusion or something real. Shapes in the darkness moved, and Diana realized that many people were gathered around Slade dressed in a black robe. Slade's beautiful face was the only thing

that seemed real because the rest of the scene looked like something surreal. She also knew the table that Slade stood behind
wasn't a figment of her imagination—it had to be real too. But atop
the ebony tablecloth, a blue light glowed in the bowl in front of
Slade, and the people surrounding her radiated a glow or a mist
as if creating a shroud of haze to hide their secrets. Slade, standing in the center of a circle of thirteen or fourteen people, held a
small, pliant, leather-bound book in her hands. Everyone around
her also held books that looked the same as hers and they read
from them periodically in response.

"Blessed be," Slade said.

"We believe that the Source of All Things is both masculine
and feminine in nature," the group chanted.

"And so it is," Slade nodded.

Silence.

"Blessed be," Slade said.

In unison, the group chanted their response. "We believe in
psychic abilities and the supernatural as normal conditions that
have been suppressed by Judaic and Christian culture but that can
be restored through the practice of the Old Ways."

"And so it is," Slade responded as she nodded again.

Silence.

Again, the group chanted back. "We believe in magick as a
manifestation of energy that is directed by the mind."

"Blessed be," Slade replied, then continued. "And we believe
in earth energy, meaning we acknowledge places of natural
power existing on our planet. We hold that the same is true for
natural objects."

"And so it is," the group replied.

Slade looked directly at Diana without nodding or acknowl-
edging her presence, yet Diana could see that her eyes invited her
to stay. Diana nodded and Slade smiled as the group continued in
unison.

"We believe in the Law of Action and Reaction, and what we
do affects others," the black-robed group said. "And what others
do affects us. Therefore, we strive to live in peace with those
around us."

"And the gifts when we follow the Old Ways, let us recite them together," Slade said, waiting until the group had turned the pages of their tomes to the right place.

"Along with the Divine Spark of the Creator, we have the power to bring success in love," they recited together. "To bless and consecrate, to speak with spirits, to know of hidden things, to call forth spirits, to know the Voice of the Wind, to possess the knowledge of transformation and divination, to know and understand secret signs, to cure disease and to bring forth beauty."

"And let us remember who we are as we conclude this gathering," Slade said.

"Blessed be," the group replied.

After pausing for a moment, Slade scanned the room. "Are there any more questions about tonight's subject?" she asked. "The four worlds of creation can be a tough concept, but necessary nonetheless to understand if we are to experience it."

A dark, curly haired woman raised her hand and Slade nodded. "Can you explain the dimensions again?"

"There are seven dimensions within the four worlds, just as there is a physical dimension or plane of existence that we are experiencing right now. There are also astral or spiritual dimensions, with each plane being a reflection of the one above it. As above, so below."

"What are the seven planes again?" the dark-haired woman asked, looking confused.

Slade stepped forward as she spoke. "The ultimate, divine, spiritual, mental, astral plane, the plane of forces or elemental and the physical plane. The physical is the lowest of all the planes, and the ultimate is the highest. Once all the planes are understood and internalized as another reality of experience, then we can either use the energy of the plane or move within the plane's energy."

A heavyset man stepped forward before he spoke. "And how do we channel and use these dimensions in our magick?"

"The dimensions react like a row of domino pieces; one triggers the other, and a chain reaction takes place," Slade said, turning to face the man who asked the question. "This is the law of physics and metaphysics. It's the essence of the working of all planes—each one vibrating in response to the next."

"But how do we use them in our magick?" he asked.

"Above the plane of forces is the astral plane, which is an etheric housing formed through the thoughts of humankind's collective consciousness," Slade explained. "This is the place where the heaven and hell of religious belief exist, which is fed by the minds of the worshippers on the physical plane. And it is in this plane that we can form images of what we desire, as well as what we fear."

The man stepped forward and used his hands as he spoke, making the sleeves of his robe move with him. "But I want to know how the magick works with the realms," he said.

"The magickal art is one of creation," she said. "The material we use is the astral substance. Within us resides the power to create thought forms. The stronger the emotion is, the more exact the thought is, and so too is the corresponding astral response."

The dark-haired woman looked agitated and waved her arms in the air. "But how do we evoke the magick?" she asked, glaring at Slade as if she demanded the answer.

"Magick is to cause change and movement. To make changes in the physical world, you must first cause them in the astral world." Slade scanned the room, then locked eyes with Diana. "That's why we perform ritual magick—to raise and direct energy of thought forms into the astral plane. The symbols, gestures, colors and ritual manifestations are all methods used to communicate with the astral plane. With these thoughts and rituals, we can become channels for the higher forces of the other planes. Ritual energizes these thought forms and channels through these connections with the higher planes. Like responds to like. You think, therefore you are. And if the forces of these planes are aligned with you, then you can manifest that which you desire in magick. Being aligned with the universe evokes the magick."

"Does Luca have the forces aligned with him?" the jet-black-haired woman asked.

Slade nodded. "I'm told the *Malandanti* only does sex magick ritual now that Janus is gone. Luca claims a right to the tunnels and caverns beneath the *Castello* and the *Pincio* Gardens. He has blocked the portals into the underground, including the one that used to be at Antonio's *Villa,* and claims the *Sotterranea* is his property. He's destroyed all other entrances except his secret portals."

Diana jumped when she heard Antonio's name and her eyes locked with Slade's. Wanting to know what Slade knew about Antonio, Diana frowned. With questioning eyes, Diana stared at Slade, but she turned away when a man spoke.

"Why don't we just destroy Luca in the underground?" the man asked, waving his fist in the air as he spoke.

"I tried to stop him tonight, but I couldn't," Slade said. "We must hurry if we are to help heal the sick. Serious illness surely will happen because Luca was at the Vatican just this evening. This time, I'm not sure about the potion to cure the sick because I don't know what Luca has done to charge the talisman. If we try using the elixir I've made as the antidote, then we might be able to help them."

The man stepped forward. "How did you know about Luca's plans?"

"I divined it," Slade answered. "He appeared in the obsidian mirror, then my pendulum revealed the time and place."

"Does he have the forces of the planes aligned with him as he continues to inflict illness, even death?" the man asked.

"Luca cannot have the forces of the universe with him, because the universe is an ever-evolving place," she said, frowning as if explaining was difficult, then continued. "But his thought forms, when used in magick, can and will continue to destroy. We just have to be more focused about our source of magick than he is. Luca believes he is justified even though killing or hurting someone defies the tenets of our belief. According to Antonio, Luca feared the church would bring about another Inquisition, so he believes that what he's doing is right."

Once Slade mentioned Antonio's name again, the group bowed their heads as if in prayer, and many shook their heads in mourning.

"How can we stop Luca from doing it again? He needs to be eliminated," the man said. "Mere antidotes alone will not stop him forever."

When the phone beside Slade rang, she quickly picked up the receiver and listened. "It's happened. There's been a death already. I'm not sure it will work, but everyone must take one of these." Slade showed them an apothecary's bottle with powder inside. "Just burn the elixir atop the charcoal, and make sure they breathe the fumes."

She paused and looked around the room, then continued. "Now you must go and heal—quickly." Motioning toward the door, Slade looked directly at Diana. "Be true to your own understanding and turn away from those things that oppose the good in you or are harmful to you. Hold reverence to all within nature. Destroy nothing, scar nothing and waste nothing. Live in harmony with nature, for the ways of nature are our own ways. And so it is."

When they started to leave the backroom, Diana snuck behind the counter and hid behind the countertop in the shop. She listened as the group shuffled into the shop, then peered around the counter and watched them remove their cloaks to reveal an exotic mix of clothes underneath. Even though a few spoke broken English, several spoke fluently in both Italian and English.

Once everyone left, Slade walked behind the counter and held out her hand to help Diana up. "What's happened?" Slade furrowed her brow and steered Diana into the backroom. "Did your illness return?"

Once they entered the backroom, Diana stopped and looked directly into Slade's olive eyes. "How do you know Antonio?"

The bone chimes rattled, and Diana jumped from the sound. Slade rushed to the front, motioning for Diana to stay.

"*Buonasera*," she said to the visitor. "*Mi scusi, sono occupato.*"

After that, everything happened too fast. For a moment, Diana thought someone from Slade's coven had come back, so when they spoke in whispers, she thought nothing of it. But when she heard a scuffle, Diana rushed to the curtain to see what happened. A tall man stood over Slade, who was sprawled on the floor, and Diana almost screamed at the sight. The man's bony face and sunken eyes looked like the visage of a ghost. He scanned the room, turning toward the curtain where Diana stood.

Diana moved away from the curtain, then rushed farther back into the room fearing that he saw her. His steps came closer, and when she heard him yank the curtain open, he stopped. Hiding beneath the table among the heavy folds of the tablecloth, Diana heard the man shuffle around the room, then check the back door.

She froze when he approached the table and the toe of his shoe slid under the edge of the black tablecloth, then she heard him grab something from the tabletop directly above her head. His footsteps headed toward the workbench in the back, and Diana lifted the tablecloth to see him carrying Slade's dagger from her altar high in the air—ready to strike.

When the man walked toward the far end of the backroom and opened a closet, Diana bolted out from under the table and rushed toward the curtain door. But when she reached it, the man hurled the knife and barely missed the top of her head. Diana screamed and ran through the curtained opening, through the shop, then yanked open the front door. Outside, she stumbled into the cobblestone street and ran as fast as she could. When she heard the man coming up from behind, she ran faster down the deserted lane into what felt like the dark night of her soul.

Chapter Twenty-Three

Luca

Grotto

February 27, 2004
2:00 a.m.

Pressing his hand against his bandaged wound, Luca faltered as he stood upon the ledge high above the *boschetto* standing in the *Grotto* below, then clenched his jaw in pain and straightened. Raven stopped him once, and surely this time she couldn't do it again, but he wouldn't know for sure until Max arrived.

Since Luca needed more ashes, he had already decided to make the ultimate sacrifice for the cause. Instead of making Diana his *Sacerdotessa,* Luca would use the Goddess to fight the war. After seeing Diana's painting, he knew she was the Goddess of All Witches in a previous lifetime, so all he needed was her potent ash to fight the war. Since he had used all Maddy's charged ashes at the *basilicas,* he needed another talisman with an even more potent charge. Once Diana responded to their summons, he planned to have the *Malandanti* charge her in the Philosopher's Ring, and inseminate her with his Eucharist. Once they finished that ritual, they would then cremate her and make her ashes the talisman. After that, all they needed to do was add it to the filtered drinking water at the Vatican because anyone who ingested those highly charged ashes would surely die. With the intense charge of the Goddess's ashes in the waters that flowed at the Vatican, Luca would surely win the war against the church. Wanting to tell the *Malandanti* about the ritual to charge Diana's body before cremation, he forced himself to continue even though the throbbing pain of his stab wound had been increasing since he began.

Scanning the *Grotto* from the platform above, Luca wondered if he had banished all the evil intent away or whether it still remained. Wanting to rid himself of negative energies, Luca inhaled the musty smell of earthy decay before he resumed speaking to the skyclad *Malandanti.*

"From the words of the *Gospel,*" he recited the words as he always did before the rite, "remember that the sexual energy of a man or woman is the strongest power that can be raised from the body. Christians teach that sexuality must be repressed, so their teachings rob people of personal power. Do not be confused by the duality of sex, for it can be either physical or spiritual. It can also be both. But remember to share your sexuality with whomever you may, in whatever manner you may, because all acts of love and pleasure are rituals to the Goddess and the God. Be not like the Christians who teach shame and modesty and false morality," he said, holding his hands out in surrender. "Blessed are the free. You have heard the Christians condemn adultery and claim that the spouse is the property of the other. Yet no one may rightly dictate the will of another. Do not confuse love with sex or sex with love. Remember, pleasure belongs to everyone and rightly so. Therefore, harm no one through your own will and do not place your will above that of another. There are exceptions to these words, because it is written as such."

The shouts of agreement from the *Malandanti* made Luca hold up his hands, then double over with pain, yet he continued.

"The voice of the Goddess instructed me to use Maddalena, and Maddy succumbed to the calling," he whispered, blinking away the tears in his eyes. "We needed more ashes for our purpose—our mission—because all the ashes of our past *Sacerdote* were used for the Ash Wednesday mission. After the Philosopher's Ring with Maddalena, Maddy and I were about to make love. But the universe had another plan, because I had already asked Tana and Tanus for more ashes, and that request made our Maddalena slip and fall from where I stand. Maddalena died the instant she hit the stone floor, right there." Luca pointed to the mosaic of Pan's face on the floor of the *Grotto*, then searched the concerned eyes of the *Malandanti*. "I cremated her in the *Cripta dei Morti*, in the same way that we did our *Sacerdote*, then used her ashes in the basins of Holy Water at the Vatican and the *basilicas* throughout the city. Maddalena died without pain. She was given to us for our cause, because we needed her for our mission."

The *Malandanti's* silence made Luca descend the stony steps so that he could be closer and so he could convince them that they needed to intensify the fight with taking people's lives if need be. "But now we need more ashes," he said, taking his time coming down the steep steps. "And now I know what it takes to charge a talisman so potent that it kills immediately, because the talisman of Maddy does just that, especially when it's ingested. So our next one will be poured into the drinking water at the Vatican."

The *Malandanti* looked anxious, but no one was afraid or dissented because Luca had already programmed the *boschetto* to have a firm belief in patriotism. No one could protest when the call came to fight the war because protesting meant that person wasn't loyal enough to the cause to save their brothers and sisters from the Second Inquisition. Patriotism had been something he had instilled in the *Malandanti* at the beginning because he knew with a firm belief in loyalty that everyone in the *boschetto* would feel the pressure to fight and defend their people, even if that meant killing people who disagreed with their cause. He knew the *Malandanti* were prepared to take lives because that was expected in fighting a war. Luca had already programmed them to kill the terrorists who were about to take away their freedom, so now it was just a matter of issuing the orders for the *Malandanti* to execute his plan.

Just as Luca reached the bottom of the steps, Max entered the *Grotto*. Max took one look at the skyclad *Malandanti*, then disrobed and joined the group in the circle around Pan's face. Luca approached Max, then squeezed his shoulder as he continued.

"If we don't do this, the Second Inquisition will surely come. The *Gospel* prophesized a Second Inquisition, and to prevent this from happening, we must make sacrifices—sacrifices of our own lives if need be. Maddalena was willing to sacrifice her life for our mission. And now Max must have news of *his* mission to sacrifice Raven for the cause. Tell us, Max, what happened?"

"Raven almost killed our *Sacerdote* tonight," Max yelled. "She stabbed him after Luca secretly gave the ashes to our informant at the Vatican. Our informant poured the ashes into the Holy Water at Saint Peters, but Raven may have found the cure to thwart our plan. As she did with our talisman on Ash Wednesday, Raven administered her antidote to all she could by burning a powdery elixir near the beds of the sick. But this time Raven won't stop the talisman, because now there is no Raven."

Luca rubbed the bandage to quell the shooting pains in his ribs. "Since Raven knew of our mission tonight, we had to make sure she didn't stop what I put in motion," Luca explained. "If given enough time, she would have found the remedy for our next talisman like she did before. Max, are you certain she's dead?"

"I threw the ashes into her face, and some of them ended up inside her mouth," Max replied. "She could not live through it, I am certain."

The *Malandanti's* concerned voices made Luca even more convinced that what they were doing was justified.

"Absolutely positive?" Luca asked, raising his hand for silence. "This had to be done for the cause."

Max nodded. "It would be impossible for her to live with that much ash on her. The ashes were on her lips and inside her mouth."

Luca frowned, saddened to see that it had come to this. But Raven's treachery had to be stopped, because she might ruin their plans. Luca beckoned them to join hands, sit in the circle and come together in peace.

"Please understand, fighting this war is not against our creed. It's what we must do to protect our people. This is a war on terrorism against our people." Luca reached for the *Gospel* and read the words. "The *Gospel* teaches the art of poisoning and malevolent acts against our oppressors." Luca flipped the pages of the text until he found the right place, then continued. "And thou shalt teach the art of poisoning and poisoning those who are the great lords of all. Yea, thou shalt make them die in their palaces and thou shalt bind the oppressor's soul," he said, pausing to look up. "When a priest shall do you injury by his benedictions, ye shall do to him double the harm."

Luca spotted Aldo frowning before he spoke. "Leland wrote that version," he said. "And it isn't the original text of *Aradia*. He wrote that because the Etruscan woman gave him errant information—"

"We need to honor Leland's version if we are going to stay focused on our mission." Luca stopped for a moment, not wanting to argue with Aldo, then stood and carefully placed the *Gospel* inside the carved-out niche. "Together we will execute this plan, because tonight we will create the strongest talisman possible for our mission. Please, let us come together before I tell you what we are about to do."

When everyone bowed their heads, Luca continued. "And so ye shall be free in everything. And as the sign that ye are truly free, ye shall be naked in your rites, men and woman also. And thus shall it be done. Entirely naked, men and women who shall dance, sing and make music together."

Pausing before he spoke, Luca wanted to choose the right words. "Maddalena's ashes had an intense charge because we did the Philosopher's Ring together that night but I wanted to take it one step further. After everyone left, I wanted to amplify the charge even more, but didn't get the chance."

Scanning the attentive faces of the *Malandanti*, Luca wondered what they would say about him using his Eucharist, but then he dismissed any doubts and continued. "With the Goddess of All Witches in the center of the circle, I shall add the Eucharist and inseminate her. Once she carries the Eucharist inside her body, we will charge her, then someone needs to make sure she is ready for the funeral pyre."

Luca didn't want to be the one to kill Diana, and he wasn't sure who would be willing to carry out that last part of the mission. He didn't think that he could ever kill anyone, especially someone with the lineage of a Goddess, but he hoped someone else would.

"Who can make sure she's ready?" Luca asked. "Is someone prepared to kill for our cause?"

Max was the only one to speak. "Since I've done it before, I can do it again. I'll do it to fight for the cause. I assure you, she will die after we charge her body."

Relieved that was settled, Luca ascended the steep steps up to the altar and grabbed the wand, then tried to salute the four directions, but he couldn't raise his arm fully because of the pain from his wound. "We are the hidden children of the Goddess," he said. "From generation unto generation, we have passed the knowledge and kept the Old Ways. And so for us, it is a time of remembrance. We gather this evening to honor our past, secure our future and receive the essence of the Old Ones. As it was in the time of our beginning, so it is now, and so shall it ever be."

"Blessed be," the *Malandanti* responded.

"We need the ashes of the Goddess of All Witches because that is the only talisman powerful enough to destroy those who live in Vatican City—the highest officials of the Roman Catholic Church," he said. Luca raised the wand, still charged with the Goddess power, then doubled over in pain. "Let us begin our cleansing ritual before the sex magick begins. Now we will bathe in the pools by the well and prepare ourselves to charge Diana when she arrives. After divining with my crystal wand, I am certain she will answer our summons tonight."

Luca disrobed and joined the *Malandanti* in the pools by the well. Needing to wash his wound in the clear waters, Luca smiled when Max and Dante helped him climb into the warm water and wade over to the well in the center. Once they positioned Luca atop the rim of the well, he addressed the *Malandanti* encircled around him. "Let us begin."

Chapter Twenty-Four
Diana

Piazza del Popolo
February 27, 2004
2:45 a.m.

Exhausted from running through the labyrinth of deserted alleyways, Diana glanced back, fearing the madman was still there. Desperate to save Slade, Diana turned back, but strange silhouettes lurked in the dark. The faded lamplight made it too difficult to see anything behind her. Footsteps echoed close by as Diana quickly cut through a side street, then made her way through a narrow cobblestone street. She entered a crowded *piazza* filled with gaiety and laughter from people loitering from the late-night clubs and wondered if the madman was watching her among the faceless crowd. On the outskirts of the *piazza*, Diana found a narrow corridor that led to yet another deserted street.

After running for what seemed like hours, Diana decided she'd lost him. Without a minute to spare, she rushed directly back to Slade's shop, stopping only once to ask directions because she was lost. As soon as she arrived, Diana opened the door of *Le Vecchia Religione* with its rattling bones, then almost collapsed with exhaustion until she saw Slade sprawled on the floor in the exact same place as before.

With gray soot on her face, Slade's features looked as though they were sculpted out of stone. Diana fell to the floor and kneeled down beside her. It had to be the same toxic ashes that Diana had on her forehead that Ash Wednesday, but this wretched ash had gotten inside her mouth, and it covered her entire neck. Diana touched Slade's unscathed hand, and its warmth gave her hope. "Slade, wake up," she said. "Tell me how to stop this poison."

Diana rushed to the backroom, grabbed a towel, then doused it with cold water. Not wanting to lose a second, she quickly attended to Slade. Careful not to touch the toxic dust, she wiped the ash off her mouth and listened for breathing, but there was no sound. Careful to not touch any ash, she checked for a pulse and didn't feel anything. She pushed the hair away from Slade's eyes and washed the dust off her entire face, just as Slade had done for her. *She saved me once, and I must do the same for her,* Diana thought. She pressed her fingertips against the side of Slade's throat, but still there was no pulse.

"Please, don't die." Diana brushed her hands over the lifeless face as tears welled up in her eyes.

Leaning over Slade, she listened again for breathing and this time heard a faint sound. Desperate to bring her back, Diana decided to call an ambulance. But just then Slade moaned. Diana grabbed her by the shoulders and lifted her up into her arms, no longer caring about the toxic ash. Slade was alive.

"Wake up," Diana said. "Please, come back to the living." Slade blinked her eyes as Diana pressed the washcloth against her brow.

"It's Luca's Black Mass. His way has nothing to do with the Old Ways. The rites are demented and intended to harm. No *Strega* uses sex magick, only Luca. It's against our creed—making magick for evil purposes. He shames us all."

Diana could barely decipher her words. "Please, don't talk," she said. "You're in pain. Can't you tell me these things after we've taken care of you? Tell me how to stop this poison in your body."

"Ours is a harmless faith that connects us with nature and the universe. Our magick does no harm," she whispered. "This magick is not meant to be used to harm because it's from our creator, but Luca uses it as a weapon because he believes it's for a benevolent cause—his war against terrorism."

Diana's heart ached as she remembered Antonio talking about connecting with nature and the universe just before he died.

"Sex magick is not a European practice—it's from America." Slade struggled with the words like it hurt to talk, but she continued as if she wanted Diana to remember her words. "My people do not do this type of ritual. Our rituals are only for the good of others, not to destroy them in their holy places."

"Ritualistic sex?" Diana blinked. A panicky feeling surged through her body when she connected ritualistic sex with Luca. "What are you talking about?"

"He uses sex magick to charge a talisman that kills. And the talisman consists of ashes from the dead." She coughed until blood stained her lips. "Using sex to destroy is not sacred to us. Magick is not used to harm because it is used to connect with the Life Force—"

"You're bleeding."

She ran to get a clean towel, but when she came back, Slade hadn't moved.

Fearing she lost her, Diana listened for her breathing, then Slade surprised her by opening her eyes.

"Stop him," she said. "He's planning to destroy the world as we know it. He's made another talisman and will keep making them until he kills everyone who doesn't follow him. Once he knows how to make the talisman kill others, he will use it again and again until there's no one left except him and his *Malandanti*."

Her gossamer eyes made Diana's heart ache, and Slade's urgent tone made Diana fear that these words were her last. Like someone waking from a deep sleep or warning of imminent danger, Slade squeezed Diana's hand as if she were hanging onto a limb that could break at any second.

"We can't do anything until we heal you first," Diana said. "Tell me, where is that powder you gave to your people? Do you have any I can use here?"

"There is no cure when it's ingested. It was absorbed into my system when the ash got into my mouth."

"You're a *pellar*, remember?" Diana shook her head. "One who heals. You told me this the first time we met. Remember the powder in the bottles that you showed your people tonight?"

Slade's mouth slackened. Diana felt her entire body go limp in her arms. The poison was sucking the life from her. Slade closed her eyes as if giving in to death. Diana watched her eyelids flutter like she was seeing something when they were closed.

267

"I'm calling an ambulance," Diana said, easing Slade to the floor so that she could get up.

"You can't stop this. No doctor can help."

"You aren't going to die. How can you be so sure when you cured me of the same thing?"

"It's not the same thing. This time it is more potent than what you experienced, and when it goes into your mouth, it's fatal." Slade closed her eyes. "I'm dying."

"Please, just hang on until—"

"Death is a veil that parts from this world into another. Have the *boschetto* secretly bury me in the courtyard out back," she said. "Then be their *Sacerdotessa* and help them deal with the loss. They will be without me, and that means no one will guide them because I am their *Sacerdotessa*, but you could replace me, if you so desire, because you already know the ways through your past life as a *Strega*. All you have to do is recall them through meditation and trance."

"*Boschetto? Sacerdotessa?*"

"Coven. High Priestess."

"How can you know these things about my past life? And trance—what do you mean? Why would your people trust me?"

"I've willed this shop to you. It's yours."

"Why me?" Uncontrollable sadness made Diana want to curl up into a ball so that she could avoid the death of yet another person she hadn't been able to save. "I don't even know these people you talk about."

"They were all here at the gathering. Call them. Use the black book." Slade nodded toward the counter. "Call any one of them, and they will summon the rest. But whatever you do, don't ring the authorities, because they will surely put an end to the *boschetto* and arrest them all."

"Your *boschetto* doesn't even know me, and for that matter, *you* don't even know me."

"No one else can do this except you. Let them gather here, then help them get beyond my death."

"*Get beyond* what? I don't know anything about dying." But as soon as Diana uttered the words, she realized that dying was something she did understand. "How can you know that about me?" she asked. "Who told you I died and came back?"

Slade tried to smile but couldn't. "I see many things without being there. It is a gift we all have, we've just forgotten how to use it." Slade coughed, but this time it sounded strange, like the sound of the death knell.

"Slade?" Diana put her hand on Slade's washed brow, just as Slade had done once for her. It was warm. "Please stay with me, Slade. Just stay awake until I figure out what to do here."

"It's Raven," she whispered, barely hanging on to life. "Raven Slade."

"What did you say?" Feeling dizzy, Diana tried to interpret what she just said, but Slade's low voice distorted the words.

"I'm Raven." She closed her eyes and smiled, then her body slackened.

There was no doubt that death had come. Yet Diana grabbed Slade's—no, Raven's—wrist and checked her pulse. No beat. Nothing. She listened for the sound of her breath, but there was only silence. Frantically, Diana looked for another apothecary's bottle like the ones Raven had given to the *boschetto* earlier that evening. After ransacking the counter, she hurried into the backroom and found one on the workbench. Rushing back to Raven, Diana grabbed a small cauldron behind the counter, then lit the piece of burnt charcoal and placed it in the bowl. When she threw the powder on top of the burning coal, green smoke billowed throughout the room. Holding the cauldron with both hands, Diana waved the cauldron in the air surrounding Raven. But when Raven didn't move, Diana didn't know what else to do.

Still reeling from the discovery that this beautiful woman was her husband's mistress, Diana realized at that moment that she didn't care about the past. All she wanted was to bring her back. Remembering Raven's warning not to call the police, she hurried into the backroom again and rooted through an endless array of concoctions that were scattered on the shelves. Raking through the piles of herbs strewn atop the table, she knocked the dried branches onto the floor. Belladonna, rue, elderberry. It was mind-boggling to see all the roots and herbs. Suddenly Diana froze. *I've never used herbs before,* she thought. *So how did I just know that?* It was like a voice had spoken to her. She grabbed a dusty bottle on the shelf and read the label: bloodroot. Diana pulled out the cork and smelled the contents. Gagging from the odor, Diana coughed from inhaling so deeply. That certainly wasn't the smell that had revived her the day Raven saved her.

She grabbed another bottle from the shelf, opened the lid and slowly brought it to her nose to inhale. Since this wasn't working, Diana closed her eyes and tried to envision what she needed to make a miracle. Just like when she painted—maybe the images, or in this case the smell, would come for the right ingredient to cure Raven. Or maybe Raven would send some magick her way if she could just concentrate on it. Raven had performed a miracle when Diana was paralyzed on the table and couldn't move. In Diana's mind, Diana had died, and if Raven hadn't brought her back, Diana was sure she would have stayed in that place with the light forever. As for breathing, Diana didn't think she could breathe that day, and maybe her heart wasn't beating either. She would have died on that table if Raven hadn't saved her with that smoldering potion of herbs.

Diana looked up at the dried bunches of herbs hanging above and tried to imagine which one Raven had used to bring her back. They all looked the same, but each one had a specific color and distinct smell. Desperate to do something, Diana realized that all she had to do was smell each one and match the aroma. She would never forget that scent—that bittersweet odor that stopped her from dying. Diana scrambled onto the worktable to sniff the shriveled bunches of leaves, pods, flowers and stems and decided each one was incredibly different than the next. Once she inhaled what seemed to be every bunch, she grew confused because the smells had blended together into an indistinguishable odor. Her nose could no longer differentiate the various scents. She shook her head, then spotted a curly leafed bunch in the far corner. Diana snatched the bunch and drew a deep breath. The poignant odor made her remember the smell that she inhaled on that fateful day—Ash Wednesday.

She gripped the dried bundle, then yanked the bunch until the string broke off the rack. Cradling the dried bouquet in her arms, she jumped down from the wooden table and grabbed a handful of matchsticks on her way out.

When she stepped into the front of the store, Diana noticed that the green smoke had dissipated, and Raven hadn't moved. Standing over Raven, she lit the herbs, then blew on the fire so that it would smolder. A black cloud billowed forth as she waved the smoky torch around Raven's body. After fanning it under Raven's nose, Diana dropped the bundle, stomped on the smoldering twigs and fell to her knees.

"Wake up, Raven." She shook her, trying to make her wake up, but Raven didn't move. "Please, don't die."

Diana checked her pulse once more, but there was no beat. She brushed her fingertips across Raven's cleansed forehead, while admiring the striking face that could only belong to a woman named Raven. Then darkness came down like a veil that surrounded Raven's body, and Diana blinked to clear her vision. But the veil would not disappear. She blinked again in an attempt to focus, but she finally gave up and let the tears slide down her cheeks.

In death, she forgave Raven for being with Antonio. In death, there were no wrongs. It didn't matter that Raven had loved her husband; what mattered was that she was dead. Her senseless death made Diana's anger for this other woman melt away. Death had brought wife, mistress and husband to another, different level—it somehow united them all.

She opened her eyes when she heard Raven's voice. Certain it was Raven, Diana stared at Raven's lips, but they didn't move. Not sure what the voice had said, Diana held her breath and listened for it to come again.

"Listen to the wind and intuit its message," the voice whispered. It was Raven.

Haunting music filtered through the shop and made her shudder—but hearing music wasn't possible, because there were no windows to the street in this backroom. Diana scanned the shop for a music box or something of that sort, but the source of the ethereal music was from a circle of stones displayed in the front of the shop. She stopped and listened to the blend of strings and flutes with a sultry female murmuring Italian verse. When Diana reached the counter of the store, the music stopped.

Diana blinked, then wondered if she had lost her mind. Hearing voices, then music playing in a circle of stones didn't seem too logical to her, but now she was beginning to expect the unexpected. She didn't know what to do. *Do what Raven told me to do,* Diana thought.

Without hesitation, Diana grabbed the little black book on the counter and dialed a telephone number that had been scrawled in elegant handwriting on the first page of the book. She waited until a sleepy voice came across on the line.

"*Ciao.*"

"My name is Diana—"

"What's happened?" the woman's voice cracked, making her whisper instead. "It's Raven, isn't it?" she asked.

The Italian American accent sounded like Raven's. "She's been killed," Diana said, trying to keep her voice steady.

"I will take care of her and the *boschetto.*" The line went dead.

Diana stared at the phone for a moment, then brushed away the tears. Desperately searching through the book for Luca's address, Diana found it listed as DeMarco of *Castello del Pincio* with the words *Roma Sotterranea* written beneath. Diana suddenly realized that he lived not far from the *Villa;* the *Pincio* Gardens were just down from the church of the *Trinità dei Monti,* but she wasn't sure about the location of the *Castello.* Certain she would find the place, Diana rushed out the door and into the streets of Rome, determined to stop the killing. Vowing not to go to the authorities because they would probably arrest her and call her insane, Diana knew she could do it alone.

After rushing through a matrix of cobblestone streets, she finally reached the *Piazza di Spagna* and ascended the Spanish Steps, then headed for the *Pincio* Gardens. After several blocks, she realized what *Castello del Pincio* meant.

Without warning, the monstrous *Castello del Pincio* loomed before her, and she knew instantly that the monstrosity was Luca's castle. Fighting off the urge to turn and run, Diana stared at the statues of white, sculpted busts scattered throughout the park. The ghastly heads looked like sentries guarding the forest of hell. The heads stared at her, taunting her approach. Diana bit her lip and followed the footpath to the mansion ahead, reeling from the premonition that the heads had turned to watch as she passed. Glancing from side to side, they seemed to lean in closer as she walked by. She did a double take at an eerie white face, thinking the features moved, but when she came closer, its chiseled features snapped back into place. The night was playing tricks on her eyes.

She ran toward the *Castello,* and once she reached the stairs that led to the front door, she stopped to catch her breath. Turning back once more, she was certain the heads moved closer again. Diana raced up the steep steps to the front door and slammed the knocker. It echoed through the woods, and she heard rustling behind her. She whirled around but saw nothing, then stifled a scream as she frantically tried to open the door. The hinges on the door wailed as she opened it, and she slipped inside. In an instant, the door slammed behind her. Startled by the slam, the silence that followed made Diana listen to the sound of the wind just outside the door, and once she gathered the courage, she turned to face the hallowed walls of a great hall.

Undulating waves of the chills made Diana shake uncontrollably while she tried to breathe in what seemed like a deep freeze. As she rubbed her arms for warmth, she focused on her surroundings. Ebony moonlight streaked through the yawning windows at the far end of the great room, just as the clouds broke up in the night sky. The moonlight slithered through the haunted room, giving it an eerie cast as if it were a prelude to what was to come. Diana searched for a light and finally found it by the door, then flipped the switch. White light from the sconces blinded her as she rushed up the steps two at a time. But she froze when she realized how stupid it was to pursue Luca unarmed and go upstairs—because access to the underground would certainly be beneath the *Castello.* She rushed back down the stairs, then ransacked the kitchen until she found a butcher's knife.

Flashing the blade in the air, she decided to rely on her instincts this time. Her instincts had been the only thing in Rome that had consistently helped her in times of need.

She scanned the kitchen, knowing that an access to the cellar would most likely be here, then spotted a small, wooden door
under the back stairs. Opening the small wooden door to the cellar, Diana found the light switch and stepped down. One teensy
light bulb created deep shadows on the stairs, then melted into a
dark pit at the bottom. She descended the steps and searched for
another light below.

Guided by silver moonbeams from the lower level windows,
Diana frantically groped at the cement wall for a switch. Unable
to find one, she spotted a lantern on the worktable, which she lit,
then held high in the air. As she cast the light into the dark corners to try to find an opening to the underground tunnels, she realized that the place looked like a dungeon. All it needed was the
bones to prove it, and if she looked hard enough, they might even
be there. She shook her head in an effort to try to clear her
thoughts, then jumped when she saw a black, cocoon-like object
suspended from the ceiling that looked like something that would
be used in a torture chamber.

She frowned, knowing she must quell her fears and focus on
finding the entrance to the underground. There weren't any doors
that led to a tunnel, nor were there any cave-like openings in the
foundation. Diana finally stopped, put the lamp down and pressed
her fingers against her forehead as she tried to use her intuition
to "see" where Luca had gone. Intuit. Allow the visions to come.
*Just stop the thoughts and let my inner voice guide me—allow the
silence to take over and see what comes forth,* Diana thought to
herself. Scanning the cellar, Diana rushed to the window, then
climbed on a table to open the sliding glass. Turning her head to
hear, she listened for the voice of the wind. The cool night air
touched her cheeks, but this time it didn't make a sound.

Diana shook her head. She had never been able to psychically
intuit anything before, so why did she think she could now? Why
did she think she could retrieve information about someone else's
actions when she could hardly remember her own? Diana bit her
lip, knowing she was trying to do this now because she knew it was
possible to do. It worked, and people like Raven knew how to do it,
so she could do it too. Ever since the self-guided hypnosis with Vin-

cent, she'd used her intuition more and more. Her paintings were proof that her instincts told a story far deeper than she had ever known. And her instincts were even greater when it came to understanding the ways of the *Strega*. Diana used her intuition when she painted, so why couldn't she use it to help her now? Even Raven spoke of it in death.

Diana gasped when she saw something moving in a dark corner of the cellar. But as she came closer, she realized that a mirror had caught the light, and it was her reflection she had seen. But when she reached the mirror, she could see that the movement wasn't her reflection after all; it was something else. Parts of the dark had shifted, and her reflection looked surreal—as if it weren't her, but rather someone else.

"Raven?" she yelled. "Is that you?"

Diana stood in front of the mirror and stared at her own image. What was wrong with her? She knew she was crazy to think there were ghosts in this cellar. Diana frowned at her reflection, then she pressed her hands against her head, trying to get her sanity back. She needed to focus her thoughts. Raven died in her arms, and now Diana felt like Raven's ghost had slipped inside her mind because she was beginning to think like Raven. Raven was the one who could see things that weren't there, not Diana.

Glaring at her reflection, she tried to ignore the creepy music floating into the cellar. It was the same tune she heard moments ago after Raven died. Wafting in the distance, the haunting sound drifted like it came from another land, another time. And now she was hearing things that weren't there. Maybe she was crazy. As if her brain had transformed into a wireless network, maybe she could now hear things that were there in the atmosphere as vibrations, yet instead of being silent to the human ear, she now had the ability to hear and decode it. It felt as if she was picking up sound waves and could now tune into a frequency or connect with the workings of another computer the way a wireless network does. Thinking that she'd changed, Diana felt like Raven had taught her how to listen to things that weren't in this dimension, yet were in another.

Green specks in the reflection made her lean forward for a closer look. Trying to figure out where the flecks came from, she touched the spots on the mirror wondering if they were painted on the surface. Or maybe the spots were simply misplaced light—just like Diana, misplaced by the sequence of events. She rubbed harder at the spots, still unsure what they were, and the entire mirror moved. The mirror moved. It was on hinges. Diana pulled the mirror toward her and opened it until an automatic light revealed an entryway that stared back at her—a carved-out opening in the stone wall of the cellar that taunted her to descend the steep steps that led into the underground. Diana fought the impulse to turn around and run. It was up to her now. There would be no turning back. She had to stop the madness—stop the senseless killing.

Diana grabbed the lantern in case the light didn't work farther down inside the tunnel and wedged her way into the opening as she held the butcher knife up high, poised to attack. She carefully stepped down onto a tiny carved-out ledge in the stone. She dreaded entering this underworld of evil, a place created by Luca and used for his Black Mass. Her breathing quickened as she tried to control the fear that was spreading throughout her veins. Crazy or not, she had to keep moving because she had to stop Luca, no matter what the cost.

Disgusted that she had once longed for this man in her dreams, Diana knew one of Luca's people must have killed Raven. Certain Luca resided within these depths of hell, Diana vowed to stop him from killing anyone else. With his magick, she was certain he was powerful enough to kill every living soul on this planet. After taking another step downward, Diana froze when she realized this subterranean passageway led into the depths of hell. In this underworld, Diana was certain she would surely meet the devil.

CHAPTER TWENTY-FIVE
VINCENT

Villa di Spagna

Time Warp
February 27, 2004
2:00 a.m.

"So what's going on?" Tess asked, glaring at Vincent as she slipped into her dress. "I lost her," Vincent replied, tucking in his shirt. He looked at Tess, then realized she wanted more information than that. "What do you mean—*what's going on?*"

Tess frowned. "Why would she react that way?"

"I don't blame her for running away. After seeing us—"

"It's not that earthshaking. We're adults. I could see her being shocked, but not running away like that," Tess said, shaking her head. "There's more to it than that. What are you hiding? Have you been intimate with her?"

"Are you serious?" Vincent flipped off the switch and hauled the floor lamp back over to the sofa. "She's a patient."

"Something's wrong," Tess said, raising her voice. "I could tell by the look on her face."

"What look?" Vincent avoided Tess's incriminating eyes as he looped the decorative ties around the twisted hooks on the wall.

"There must be more."

"Maybe she needs a regular therapist. And since Italians don't have any problems, therapists are hard to find in *Roma*." Vincent looked back at Tess and smiled, hoping she caught his sense of humor, but she frowned instead. "It's apparent that regression therapy isn't enough for her. My area of expertise is the phobias, pains or fears caused by past lives, not analyzing day-to-day problems."

"Go ahead, be that way," she said. "Blame it on her, when it's really you."

"I've only seen her a few times," Vincent said as he shook his head and picked up the whip. "It's too soon to diagnose—"

"Good God, Vinny," Tess said, grabbing her bag. "Don't you get it? Diana's in love and I've got to help her understand that it meant nothing between us—we were just playing around."

"What do you mean by *in love?*"

Without a word, Tess marched out the bedroom door.

Vincent fingered the leather strips of the cat, then finally came to his senses and tossed the whip aside to follow her. In an instant, he raced down the steps, into the *piazza,* and caught up with her just as she crossed the *Piazza Mignanelli.*

"Tess, wait up," he called out, and as soon as he was close enough, he continued. "Please, talk to me."

Tess acted as if she hadn't heard, then froze and slowly turned around. With high heels and an even higher slit in her dress, Tess looked ready for the nightclubs tonight.

"You are lying to me," she said, pointing her finger at him.

"What do you want from me?"

"There's more, I know it. Call it woman's intuition, but you're not telling me something."

He shook his head, then looked down.

"What do you think you're doing?" Tess raised her voice to a piercing decibel. A couple that had been making out by the *colonna* stopped and turned to stare. "Every time you have sex with a woman, your chemical makeup changes. You merge with the one you do it with whether you want to or not."

"I didn't have sex with her," Vincent said, holding out his hands, palms up, as if in surrender.

"Then somehow, some way, you got into her energy field, and now it's different between you two."

"We've just met. There is nothing between us."

"It doesn't matter, Vinny," she said. "What matters is that you've gotten inside someone's heart, and now you should try not to break it."

Tess turned on her heel and hurried toward the *Villa di Spagna.* "I've got an idea," she yelled.

Vincent watched her leave, and soon became mesmerized by the rhythmic movement of her hips in her slinky dress, Vincent stared until she turned the corner. He glanced over at the couple who'd been kissing nearby. No longer kissing, the couple apparently had been watching them the entire time. Smiling, the man motioned toward the direction that Tess went. With a nod, Vincent ran after Tess.

Climbing the steps two at a time, he caught up with her as she ended a call on her cell phone. "Diana rang," she said. "My caller ID picked her up. She didn't leave a message though." Tess sighed, then slipped the phone into her purse.

He walked alongside Tess until they reached the top of the *Rampa Mignanelli.* Vincent frowned, then realized he had to tell her. Breaking the silence, he whispered. "Okay, so we kissed."

Tess moaned, then turned toward him. "Do you realize what you've done? One kiss, one touch of the skin in the right place, can change a person's life forever. You go deeper into someone's psyche and affect that person because of your actions. Are you crazy? She's your patient."

"It was just a kiss," he said, shrugging his shoulders. "It was nothing."

"That's what's wrong with you." Tess opened the door to the *Villa,* then slammed her bag onto the bench in the foyer.

"What do you mean, *what's wrong?*" Vincent watched Tess rush up the stairs, then followed.

Once Tess stepped into Diana's studio, she started rummaging through the place.

"What are you looking for?" Vincent asked, wondering why Tess was so mad at him when he didn't think he had done anything wrong.

Searching through a stack of books, Tess looked up and frowned at him. "Her phone book," she said. "Maybe it's been left open to the place where she went. Or maybe—"

Tess froze, then snatched a crumpled sheet of paper from the worktable. "She must be here, at *Le Vecchia Religione.* Ever heard of it? See, the letterhead has the address for the shop, and the map has the route from the shop to the *Villa* drawn on it. This map wouldn't be laying here if she hadn't used it recently. She has nowhere to go, no one to turn to, because she doesn't know anyone in Rome. Maybe someone at this shop knows her. I'm going to find out right now."

"Do you realize what time it is?" But Vincent took one look at the map and decided it was worth a shot. "Let's go," he said.

When they reached the foyer, Tess headed for the kitchen to turn off the portable TV, and Vincent waited for her in the hall. But after hearing the bulletins on the local channel, he knew why Tess didn't return. When Vincent entered the kitchen, he froze. The city was in a state of emergency because of a disaster at the Vatican. Some people had already died, and health officials still hadn't determined the cause. Without an explanation for the deaths, officials were afraid it was another virus or even contaminated water in Vatican City. Although they had tested the water and it hadn't been poisoned, they still hadn't determined why people were dying. And now there were reports around the city about deaths in the *basilicas* and other churches. Then a newscaster reported that officials were considering the possibility of terrorists.

They had already tested for contamination in the Holy Water, but it tested normal. The latest report was that it might be the same virus that occurred on Ash Wednesday, but this one was stronger. The only common denominator was that it was happening to people inside the churches throughout the city, and those people used the Holy Water.

"Good God," Tess said. "It's just like Ash Wednesday."

"You mean that virus they never figured out? But no one died from that."

"On Ash Wednesday, Diana got sick after attending the service, but she recovered. She was different than the others because it didn't affect her as badly. But this time, she must be terrified, especially if she attended the late mass. Maybe that's what brought her to your house—to ask for help."

With those few words from Tess, Vincent spun into action. He didn't want anything happening to Diana, and now they had to find her. "Did she go to church today?" he asked, moving toward the front door.

Tess furrowed her brow. "Not sure."

"You search this floor, I'll check her bedroom. We need to make sure she didn't come back to the *Villa* while we were gone, even for that instant."

Tess nodded, looking dazed. Normally nothing derailed her, but for the first time, Vincent knew she was frightened.

Vincent raced up the stairs and down the hall to Diana's bedroom. "Diana?" The sound of his words echoed in his mind, and he wondered how long it took before people died after contamination. *She could already be dead,* he thought, picking up his pace as he moved down the hall. He checked the entire *Villa*, but she wasn't there.

Once Vincent met Tess in the foyer, he noticed she had slipped on more comfortable shoes, then they stepped outside and climbed up the stairs to hail a cab at the top. When they reached the other side of *di Spagna,* the narrow streets turned dark and gloomy, and the cab turned down the deserted street of the shop. When the car stopped, Vincent jumped out and then opened the door for Tess, trying to hurry, yet still determined to be a gentleman. Without lampposts or streetlights, Vincent searched in the darkness for the correct address. In the end, he identified the place by the odd storefront window.

Entering through the gothic archway, he rapped on the wooden door and waited for an answer. At this late hour, he knew the place couldn't possibly be open, yet the shop glowed inside with amber light. It was a boutique filled with weird paraphernalia. There was no answer at the door. He tried the latch, opened the door and stepped inside. With Tess close behind, he entered the strangest place he'd ever seen.

Feeble rays of amber light illuminated displays of crystal skulls that glared at him as he walked through the shop. Burnt crimson light that reflected from the crystals dangling overhead made the place even more eerie, and Vincent blinked from the strange rays that contrasted with the amber glow of the recessed lighting. He stopped cold when he saw an altar before him. Bathed in the amber light, the altar table displayed a quilted cloth with the design of a man's body with the horns of a stag holding a pentagram in one hand

and a snake in the other. With hoofs for feet and horns sprouting from his head, the image unsettled him. Wolves surrounded the strange looking figure. Vincent turned away from the image and spotted someone crumpled on the floor behind the counter. When he kneeled, Raven's face made him cry out in pain. "No, it can't be," he moaned.

Her elegant features looked like a work of art modeled from clay, yet the tinge of her pallid blue skin, smeared ash from someone trying to wipe it off, told another story. Vincent kneeled down and reached for her hand.

"Don't touch her," Tess yelled, coming up from behind and grabbing his shoulder. "It's the ash. You might die."

"Let me check her pulse—there's no ash there."

Tess fell to her knees. "Poor thing. It looks like the same residue Diana had on her forehead after the Ash Wednesday service. It must be some kind of black magick."

"Why Raven?"

Vincent heard Tess as she got up, moved around and searched the shop. Grabbing the quilted cloth of the half man, half stag, Vincent gently covered Raven with the large blanket, then reverently touched the part that covered her head.

"Found it," she said, groaning as she looked at a small black book on the counter. "It's opened to Luca's name. Do you know where this address is, Vinny?"

Vincent took one look at the address and knew right where it was. "It's down the street from the *Villa.*"

Just then, bones rattled as someone opened the front door to the shop, and Vincent put his finger to his lips to silence Tess. Saying a blessing for Raven and touching her head once more, Vincent grabbed Tess by the arm and rushed out the back.

Guiding Tess through the narrow lane, they made their way around to the front of *Le Vecchia Religione* and watched a small band of what were obviously witches entering the shop. Taking Tess by the hand, Vincent practically pulled her through the streets of Rome, sickened by Raven's heinous death. Filled with sorrow over the beautiful woman's demise, Vincent's pain turned into anger, and he vowed to stop Luca's madness. Fearing Diana was caught in his diabolical web too, Vincent finally understood the gravity of the situation. He admonished himself for being inconsiderate toward women in the past and vowed never again to take advantage of any woman who crossed his path.

They hurried in the deserted streets of the *di Spagna,* and Vincent finally let go of Tess's hand as they reached the Spanish Steps. Waiting for her at the stop of the stairs, they rushed down *Trinità dei Monti.* Hearing Tess slow down behind him, he circled back and took her hand again.

"Go ahead," she said. "I'll catch up."

After sprinting the entire block, Vincent finally spotted the macabre *Castello del Pincio,* then marched up the stairs to the front door and stood there. When Tess came up from behind, he opened the door, which led into an expansive dark hall. Vincent stepped inside and waited for a moment until his eyes could adjust in the dark.

Turning back to Tess, he took her hand, then guided her toward what he thought might be the kitchen. "That black book," he whispered. "In the address book, Raven made a notation for Luca's entry about the *Roma Sotterranea.* Do you know what that means?"

"Rome underground?"

"He's in the underground, which probably means his entire cult is down there too. I've got to find the entrance. It should be in the cellar."

Tess groaned.

"Stay here. I'll come back for you," Vincent said.

"No way."

When his eyes finally focused in the dark, Vincent found a door in the kitchen. "I'm certain it's down there because that's the only way to get to the underground." Vincent pointed to a small, wooden door illuminated by the silver crescent of the moon shining through the kitchen window. "Stay here. Call the police if I don't return within the hour."

"I'm not staying. I can't be here alone, it must be three in the morning."

Vincent looked at his watch. "It's four a.m."

Tess shook her head. "I'm with you."

Vincent opened the small door to a light bulb that had been left on that dimly illuminated the stairs down into the cellar. He carefully descended the wooden steps into the lower level of the house. When he reached the bottom of the steps, Vincent whistled under his breath at the cellar that looked like a torture chamber. As he walked further into the recesses of the cellar, the light at the top of the stairs diminished into nothingness, and Vincent searched the walls for a light switch.

When Tess found an old gas lamp in the cabinet, she cried out with frustration and handed it to Vincent. "I'm shaking too much."

Using the wavering glow of the lamp, Vincent scanned the cellar. He'd heard rumors about openings to the *Sotterranea* in the lower levels of various places throughout *Roma*, rumors that the *Sotterranea* was haunted by the dead of those who had gotten lost, then died of suffocation in the intricate cobweb of tunnels below. Vincent pushed away the thoughts and focused on the stony walls of the cellar. Nothing even resembled an entrance. But when the lantern illuminated something in the corner, Vincent extinguished the light.

"What the heck?" Tess yelled across the room, knocking over something that broke.

Vincent, mesmerized by strange specks that caught the moonlight, realized there was a mirror in the corner. He peered into the dark pool of glass and studied the two emerald spots in the reflection. The jade circles blinked. Vincent stepped backward and stumbled when Raven's transparent image floated to the surface of the mirror. Her penetrating eyes locked with his, and for a moment he felt paralyzed.

"No way," he said, raising his hands to prevent her from jumping out of the mirror, but she didn't move. She blended with the darkness yet contrasted just enough to see her silhouette. Realizing she had to be behind him, he whirled around. When he saw it was Tess, Vincent shook his head.

"Something wrong?" Tess asked, sounding concerned.

"I must be mad." Vincent pivoted back toward the mirror, but the jade specks were gone. Angry at himself for imagining things, he kicked the oval mirror. But the mirror moved toward him, and he realized it was a door that opened outward. Once he opened the mirrored door wide, a light automatically illuminated a gaping hole with steps leading downward into the ground. Vincent whistled under his breath.

From where he stood, tiny steps carved out of stone began at his feet and descended straight down into the shadowy abyss. The passageway, carved in the stony ground, formed a tall, narrow archway.

"I've never seen anything like it before," Tess said, clenching Vincent's forearm in a death grip.

"It's the *Roma Sotterranea.*" Vincent whiffed the oppressive atmosphere of the earthen fumes below and grimaced from the overwhelming stench of mold and decay.

"We're going down there?"

"Luca's realm." Vincent grappled with the thought of Diana lost somewhere down there. But his thoughts were answered by a dissonant wail that floated upward and taunted him with the sound of his own words.

Luca's realm, the echo wailed.

CHAPTER TWENTY-SIX

DIANA

Roma Sotterranea

Time Warp
February 27, 2004
3:30 a.m.

It was the being alone part Diana hated. And now without Vincent or Tess, she needed to be strong. Diana slipped on the tiny, carved-out steps and dropped the lamp, then watched it tumble to the base of the stairs. When her foot slid past the next step, she dropped the knife and clawed at the earthen walls to prevent herself from tumbling into the chasm of darkness below. Grasping both sides of the narrow tunnel, she frantically tried to stop her fall, but the ancient layers of rock and mortar crumbled through her fingers. Finally, her foot landed on a sunken ledge and she sighed with relief that she hadn't fallen into a crumpled heap at the bottom. *No one would ever find me,* she thought. *No one in their right mind should even be down here.*

But the decrepit brickwork and piled debris with its exposed layers of built-up silt, mortar and brick told another story from another time—not this time, but an ancient time. These layers of antiquity were once empires built by kings but ended up as layers of earth buried beneath the city of Rome through the passage of time. Diana bit her lip trying to shake away the phantoms of the past that awaited her below.

When she reached the bottom, she picked up the lamp, then tucked the knife in the back pocket of her jeans. She looked left then right, confused as to which way to go. Both directions had been excavated, but it was difficult to see far when the tunnels

twisted and turned through the earth. Something slithered past her foot and she kicked it away, then fought the urge to run up the stairs to be aboveground again. Turning back wasn't an option, because then she would never stop the root of all evil—Luca. She had to thwart his plans, his talismans. Gathering her resolve, she turned left and continued on.

When the passageway curved to the right, she approached a sunken enclave. Enclosed by layers of thin bricks intricately woven together, an altar covered with solid drippings of multicolored candle wax that had fallen from the votive pedestals above made Diana stop and examine the strange altar. In the center of the altar, a bunch of herbs had been tied together and carefully placed among the other strange objects on the table. She picked up the small bundle, then noticed the end was burnt. In an instant, she dropped it. Maybe Luca burned herbs to make his poisonous ash.

Enthralled by the fine details of the frescoes surrounding the altar, she noticed the delicate artwork painted with birds, animals and primitive shapes, and realized the underground was probably filled with hidden treasures such as these. Clearly, this was a place of worship long ago, and now it was still being used as a sacred space because a spectacular arrangement of fresh roses had been left here not long ago. Diana leaned forward to smell the roses, then checked the details of the ancient fresco as she steadied herself on the ledge of the altar. Instantly, her fingers sunk into a pool of freshly fallen wax. Stepping back, Diana stared at the imprints her fingers left—someone had been here recently. Shivering with the thought of Luca hiding in these depths, she wondered if he prayed, and if so, to whom.

She spun around and stepped into another narrow tunnel, which had torches to light the way. Diana left the lamp on the ground in case she might need it later, then tried to shut out the sound of slithering night creepers as the stones crunched beneath her feet. At this deep level, she couldn't hear or feel any noises aboveground; in fact, all she felt was fear. *There's no way out if I get lost,* she thought. Gripping the knife in her hand, she purposely concentrated on placing one foot in front of the other so that she couldn't think about turning around. She shook her head, wondering how she could possibly stop Luca. If he was with his coven, then surely the element of surprise would work in her favor.

The tunnel opened up and curved to the left, then veered to the right. Up ahead she saw an amber light glowing in the distance. Then an odd sound made Diana stop cold. Foreign sounds droned through the tunnel, and someone called out instructions with a voice that was hauntingly familiar. The hypnotic voice guided them in the chants, then everything stopped. They were silent. Diana inched her way closer to the ominous glow ahead. Holding the knife high in the air, she remained poised, ready to strike.

"Instead of issuing the summons when we reach the climax, this time we use the liquids on the talisman, the body, so that it is fully charged, just as we would charge a crystal wand."

Diana slipped on the stones underfoot when it dawned on her that it was the voice she'd heard in her dreams. It was Luca's hypnotic voice—a voice that immediately made her want to "go under" from its melodic sound. She fought the desire to close her eyes, fall half asleep and listen. Sucking in her breath, Diana vowed to concentrate harder and not let his voice take control of her mind. She crouched closer to the ground as she approached the opening. Catching a glimpse inside the arched stonework, amid the candelabrum of flickering candles, she saw a painting propped on an easel inside the cavern that was the painting she created not long ago—the painting Luca bought.

"After I inseminate her with the Eucharist, you will all be responsible for charging the body using the fluids on your hands. Just as we do with the crystals," Luca's voice continued. "Then it will be your turn, Max. Let us begin. Gather into the circle now, it is time for the Philosopher's Ring."

Diana could see only a portion of the cave, so she put the knife in her back pocket and decided to look inside and then determine her approach. Pressing her back against the cold wall of the tunnel, she waited for the right moment to peek inside.

Splashing water and hushed voices floated from the cavern, and Diana edged closer to the opening. Then the sounds changed dramatically. Moans and wailing from inside the cave made Diana eager to see what they were doing, so she took a deep breath, then slowly peered into the cavern. Amid the sparkling waters bubbling through the layers of rock, a ring of naked bodies on a mosaic floor formed a circle that was connected through acts of oral sex. Each person in the circle did oral sex and received it so that one person gave it to another while receiving it from someone else. The circle alternated gender: a man, then a woman, so that each one was doing mouth to genital, genital to mouth. Cloaked in black, Luca stood atop a slab of stone that jutted out from the cavern wall high above them.

Luca immediately saw her, and she tried to turn and run, but he quickly used his hypnotic voice. "You must remember the word seven," Luca said. "Seven . . . seven. And what that word means to you. Remember what happens when you hear the word seven?"

It was the voice from her dream.

"Seven," he said again. "Would you like me to touch you again?"

Diana knew she had to blot out his voice, but she stood there unable to move. Some of the naked people on the floor stopped their orgy and stared, but it was only for a moment because then they went back to feasting orally on the person next to them in the ring.

"Seven," Luca said once more. "Come, join us and you will be satisfied, totally fulfilled. Safe and secure in our sex magick ritual."

Then Diana wasn't sure what was reality and what was fiction, because Luca came down from the platform and moved toward her, then gently took her hand and guided her into the center of the circle. A man and a woman moved apart just as they passed through the human ring of nakedness, and once they were in the center of the circle, Luca stared into Diana's eyes while he held both of her hands.

Still immobilized by the words he had just uttered, Diana could hear him yet she couldn't move. "This is not about sex, it's about magick," Luca said, with a deep, raspy voice. "You are about to have the most pleasurable sex you've ever had, because I will show you its magick."

As he spoke, he undid the buttons of her shirt, then deftly removed it from her body. In an instant, he removed the knife from the back pocket of her jeans, then unbuttoned her pants. "Remember, you are here for a reason because you were summoned by the *Malandanti*, and now we will prepare you for being our talisman. Are you ready to be naked in front of the group?"

Without hesitation, Diana nodded, then bit her lip.

"Seven ... seven ... seven," Luca chanted. "You want to be naked, don't you?"

Without thinking, Diana nodded. With those three words, Diana couldn't say no, and when he held her hand tight while she stepped out of her jeans, she stood clad only in her ivory lace bra and panties. "You are doing very well, and so is the *Malandanti.*" Luca's voice intensified, and the ring of naked people that had been watching her slip out of her clothes went back to their orgy. "This is not about an orgy. It's about spirituality, meaning and a cause. You just now stepped into a prolonged sederunt, and the *Malandanti* will keep in time with you and me. Everyone will know when the time is right."

Luca grinned as his eyes scanned her body. Standing in her lingerie, Diana didn't even cover her body with her hands. Instead she waited for his next word, his next touch, his next instruction.

"Now, after I take off your bra and panties, I want you to lower yourself down to the floor. Will you come down to the floor with me?" Luca asked.

Diana nodded, then stood there like a stick figure as Luca expertly unhooked her bra and let it fall to the floor, then put his fingers underneath the fabric of her panties and slid them down to her ankles. Taking her hand, he helped her step out of her lacy panties, then he held her hand and raised it out from her body as if he was proud of her nudity.

"Are you alright?" he asked. Smiling at her naked body, he quickly opened his cloak and threw back the fabric so that his robe slid to the floor and he too stood there naked. Diana, opening her eyes wide, looked down at his erection and immediately felt the desire to have it inside her. Not knowing why her body wasn't functioning to run away or why her mind couldn't think straight, she glanced at the ring of naked people that surrounded them and realized they were all in various states of ecstasy. She was awake, yet she felt unconscious. Feeling paralyzed, Diana had no control over her body or her mind. She wanted to flee, yet her thoughts wavered with desire. Her body responded with lustful craving, which made it even more complicated because then she was forced to stay. Confused, it didn't matter what she thought because her body wouldn't move.

"Do you remember the sound of seven?" he asked, positioning her on the floor, then fondling her breasts as if they'd been making love together for years.

Diana nodded. Perplexed by her inability to function, when he touched her she moved along with his touch as if she were responding to it. Just as the naked circle of people around them having oral sex were joined together in a ring, she moved and twisted, then writhed like those around her. Caught up in the erotic sensation of him pinching her nipples, when Luca moved his hand to her pussy, she let him fondle her there because she wanted him to do it.

"You can close your eyes if you like," he said. "Just remember the sound of my voice and the touch of my hands when you climax."

Just like the others around them, Luca slid down and put his head between her legs, then flicked his tongue inside her. He moved his head as he drank her juices and hummed, making his lips vibrate on her pussy, while Diana, propped up on her elbows, groaned with pleasure. When he continued, Diana felt herself slip into an ecstasy that she'd never felt before. She came without even trying. Afterward, he licked her until she felt weak, unable to move, yet she kept responding to his touch. Diana moaned.

With the sound of her moan, Luca stopped, then poked his head up from between her legs. "Did I hurt you?" he asked, his brow furrowed with concern.

Diana shook her head, still troubled by her inability to run or fight. It was just like the dream, except this time she was more conscious, even though she still couldn't move. Although she couldn't control herself, she stayed spread-eagle on the stone floor as if she were enjoying it. She watched as Luca came to her, kissing every part of her body, then climbed on top of her. Kissing her breasts, he slid his hard cock into her pussy without warning, and to Diana's surprise, she was ready, especially when he kept saying the word seven whenever he moved. On top, Luca gently started rocking inside her, and to Diana's horror, she moved with him, moaning at the feeling of pure pleasure. Everyone in the cave moved in harmony, and the excited, breathless wailing throughout the cavern intensified until Diana almost screamed.

Holding her buttocks with his hands, Luca pushed his cock in harder, and Diana instantly felt a spot inside that she never felt before, never even knew existed, and cried out with pleasure. It was a spot she had heard about, yet never experienced. And once Luca hit that G-spot inside her, which was way up inside and toward the front, he kept on poking it with his cock until Diana couldn't do anything but climax.

Luca pumped harder, then started to climax too. He kept it inside of her until the end and finally rolled off. Totally satisfied, Diana stared at the ring of naked people around her, then realized the entire group was escalating toward climaxing too. Frantically working on each other, they started to orgasm at exactly the same time. The ring of naked people started moving in on her as they climaxed. Men, holding their hard cocks that were about to explode, looked as if they were about to spurt their juices directly on Diana, and women, cupping their hands to carry the fluids, moved closer and Diana screamed.

After she touched the only thing she wore, the Moon Cross at the base of her neck, Diana immediately woke up from her hypnotic state, and felt her body move, then knew it was her only chance. Maybe it was the backdrop of the gurgling well in the cavern that sounded exactly like the one on her wedding day in the forest or maybe it was the jolt the Moon Cross gave her when she touched it, but something inside her flipped a switch and she had to escape the madness. In an instant, she jumped up, hurtled over the naked ring of orgasmic bliss and fled out of the cave. Since the ring of naked people were carrying and spurting their juices, Diana clearly had the advantage and easily passed through. But Luca was another story, because he came up from behind.

Initially, she thought she would be able to outrun him, but his endurance was far greater than hers. The tunnel ahead curved and narrowed, making her wonder if this passageway hadn't been excavated all the way through to an opening. She jumped over a fallen rock and picked up speed after Luca groaned and tumbled to the ground. Seizing the moment, she bolted into the tunnel to her left that didn't have the torches to light the way.

When she reached the dimly lit labyrinth of tunnels, she realized these tunnels were more complicated than the others, with each leading outward as if she were in the hub of a wheel. She hesitated, not knowing what to do. They all looked the same. She finally chose one, then realized it kept shrinking into something smaller and smaller until there was no tunnel at all. Knowing she couldn't turn back, Diana darted down another tunnel with vents above to light the way in hopes that it didn't also wind up being a dead end.

This one seemed wide enough at first, but after jogging down the twisted path, the sides became narrower and narrower with each step she took. Finally, the earthen ceiling overhead dipped down, making her bend over as she ran, and the sound of Luca behind her made her almost fall to her knees.

The carved-out ceiling became lower and lower until she was finally forced to the ground on all fours. She clawed her way forward until her knees ached from the roughness. Behind her, Luca grabbed at her heel, but she kicked him away. He grabbed again, then held her ankle tight until she collapsed onto her stomach. The tunnel had opened a bit wider and the ceiling had expanded, so Diana kicked to get away from his grip. She fought harder when she realized a bluish violet light had formed at the end of the tunnel.

"No," she yelled. "Let me go."

"But you are going to get hurt in there," Luca called out, holding onto her ankle so that she couldn't move forward anymore. Then he grabbed her leg with his other hand and started climbing it like a rope. Once he reached her knee, Diana kicked his face with her free leg, then catapulted forward to wriggle out of his grasp and claw her way to the violet flame.

"That's the wrong way," he yelled. "Let me help you."

Dirt rained down on her face, then sprinkled until it turned into an avalanche of moldy soil caving in on her. The tunnel then collapsed, and she screamed from the heavy debris that fell upon her body. Although she could no longer see the violet light at the end of the tunnel, she desperately tried digging her way out from underneath the rubble, but the tunnel had disappeared.

Diana had nowhere to go. Panicked, she realized she was trapped. Screams of terror howled behind her, and she realized Luca was being buried alive too. Horrified, she listened until his screams were stifled by falling debris and the avalanche snuffed out all sound of life from his lungs. She looked around and realized she was enclosed in a bubble of dirt. Closing her eyes, she yelled for help again and again until she realized no one could hear her or save her from being buried alive in these subterranean depths. Gasping for air, she knew her death would be slower than Luca's because she could breathe in the small pocket of earth that surrounded her.

She screamed once more, and dirt sprinkled down on her lips. Then darkness came to usurp her mind, and she became one of the layers buried within the murky depths of the *Sotterranea.*

Once Diana realized she was outside her body, she remembered what it felt like to die. Because she had done it before, she slipped into it immediately. Zapping out of her body didn't rile her as much this time, because she accepted it. She even accepted the violet flame when it approached her.

What she wasn't ready for was the violet light shifting into colors that in turn transformed into shapes, then scenes—scenes that displayed a panoramic view of her entire life just like a movie. The scenes portrayed every detail and made her feel as if it were actually happening again. Even though each event was emotionally charged, it appeared without incrimination, retribution or judgment. But all the scenes had the common thread of capturing past events that summed up what happened while she lived.

The scene of her parents dying in the plane crash made her feel the same loss and overwhelming guilt; the face of her husband after they catapulted off the road made her want him back in her arms again and the feeling of life inside her as the baby kicked made her grieve for the baby she never held. Finally, the scene of her being burned at the stake as a *Strega* flashed in her mind, and she saw the heinous faces of those who lit the fire. Hearing the heart wrenching screams as her baby boy reached out to her made her cry, while her husband's last good-bye made her mourn.

Just then, she understood. We are all the same, no matter what religion, no matter what faith or belief. In death, we are all alike. Her entire life meant something far greater than she could comprehend. It was something that illuminated the very purpose of her being—the meaning of her existence. But what it was, she didn't know.

As she watched herself melt into the flames that consumed her for being a *Strega*, the scene blended into a crimson pulse, then formed an opalescent-blue flame. Intense rays blended together to embrace her, and she basked in the warmth of its glow.

The vibrating sphere of violet light slowed its movement, then transferred the thought, *Did you learn how to love?*

Diana, worried whether she had indeed learned to love, realized the light wasn't trying to make her feel guilty or scramble to answer a question from some ungodly test.

As in if response, it transferred the thought, *If humans can learn to love, then they evolve to a far greater level in death. Only then can they transcend this realm with choice, either to higher dimensions or back to earth for the lesson. Only then can they prevent being a lost soul or repeating painful lifetimes. Humans cannot end their torment until they learn the vital lesson of humanity—we are the same no matter what belief we hold, country we come from or religion we follow. Those who harbor hatred and create warring over these differences are destroying the Life Force, as well as their very own soul, because love, even in the face of evil, strengthens the soul with light.*

The soul is light? Diana wondered.

Again, it responded without speaking the words. *Humans carry this light with them, and it can be revealed with a trained eye. Beings on earth have the ability to see it, but most have forgotten how. The ancients used it as their guiding light, and the Watchers taught them how to use it.*

Are you God? From the beginning she'd wondered, and now she had to know.

The name God has been misinterpreted by humankind, especially in this millennium. People of God do not war about religion, culture or beliefs because there are no differences.

"Who are you then? Jesus?" she asked, but since she had no physical form, Diana wasn't sure whether she had spoken or not. She was outside her body, yet under the earth with the light.

It responded through thought, *I am the Life Force, which is the aura that is within and around every being on planet earth—it is also the fabric of our universe. When used as it was meant to be, this aura can help beings transcend pain and even death just as Jesus once did. When beings understand this Life Force, they know the secret—that we are all connected through this grid. If you study the universe or quantum physics, you will begin to understand the principles and laws that govern this force. The light of Jesus and the Essenes was far greater than most can conceive. Light Beings cross the threshold from life to death effortlessly. They are like angels, although some still walk upon the earth as guardians. You see, my child, Light Beings live for the love of humanity.*

Instantly, Diana knew what to do. She would love again. Now she could get beyond the emotional scars and barriers she'd created from the loss of her mother and father, husband and unborn baby. Feeling transformed, she would learn the lesson of love. With that thought, she immediately zapped back into her body. Desperate fingers clawed at her feet, but this time she didn't fight to get away.

Chapter Twenty-Seven
Luca

Roma Sotterranea

February 27, 2004
4:30 a.m.

Luca knew he was dying as he felt his body crushed by the stones from above, below and around. The entire tunnel enclosed him, and now he couldn't move. Like his ancestors before him, the pain he felt made him call out, yet there was no place to go and no one to hear. Diana most certainly was dead, and it felt as if soon he would breathe no more. The air, thinner now, had vanished. His lungs collapsed along with his bones, crushed from the weight of the earth above.

Feeling his ethereal form leave his body, Luca knew he died. Crossing over the veil was much like experiencing the odic force for the first time; you knew it was there, but you couldn't see it—unless you used the innate, intuitive power within, that is. Such latent powers were hidden deep within everyone's soul, but most people never even knew they existed because they only knew the physical realm of life. In the spirit realm, Luca frowned when he saw his physical body buried inside the earth, then noticed Diana in front of his dead body and wondered if she would come out alive. In spirit form, deep within the folds of the earth, he could see she didn't have much farther to go until she reached the surface. Luca tried to move her with his ethereal hands, but they passed right through her body and didn't even awaken her. Trying with all his power, Luca then rose above the surface and looked down at the sunken rubble in the *Pincio* Gardens. He wanted to save her because then maybe she would lead the *Malandanti* in fighting the war. But no sooner did he have that thought than the *Malandanti* appeared in spirit form next to his etheric body. Without words, they transferred the thought that they too had been crushed by the ground collapsing in the *Villa de Marco.* Luca and Diana set off a series of cave-ins throughout the network of tunnels beneath the *Pincio* Gardens, so Luca's entire *boschetto* had died, then crossed over through the astral realm.

Saddened by the realization that there was no one left to stop the coming of the Second Inquisition, Luca decided to make the ultimate sacrifice and descend into the underground as a tortured soul. But just as he was about to dissolve his misty form into the earth, a spirit appeared. She spoke in words that could not be sensed by mere mortals; they could be heard only if one were attuned to the other dimensions.

"You must not grieve anymore," the beautiful spirit said, floating next to him above the garden.

"Who are you?" Luca asked, enthralled by her presence because she glowed from within and illuminated the area around her with a vibrant, clear white light.

"I am Aradia, the *Holy Strega*," she said. "I've come to tell you, there is no need to fight anymore because there is no war except that which is inside yourself, my loved one."

"You're *La Bella Pellegrina?*" Luca's misty form quivered from her words. "The Beautiful Pilgrim. Is it true that you wrote down the original teachings in the nine scrolls of Aradia, only to have it taken away by the Roman Catholic Church?" he asked.

"That is in the past, my beloved," she said. "And now we must make way for the future. Your thoughts about the *Gospel* being wrong are correct—the religion does not poison, nor do our people swear at the Goddess of All Witches if they are wronged. Your instincts were right. Those words are from the mouths of those who died during the Inquisition, and they had no choice but to lie, so do not blame them. The volumes produced using the corrupt records of the Inquisition are merely published words by people who perpetuate false beliefs. Leland did not mean to do wrong. But the *Gospel* was produced after the Inquisition, and it changed the teachings forever. However, that is on the earthly plane. In this dimension we know what is true because the ancients are with us."

Feeling lost, Luca came to her side in spirit. "But what am I to do?" he asked.

"Follow me to the outer realms of existence. There is much to do," she said, floating upward. "We cannot change what is hidden from us, nor that which has been recorded out of false beliefs. All we can do is go on without fear or pain. Now you can release the anger and sorrow for your ancestors, because soon you will commune with them in spirit."

Luca drifted upward with the *Holy Strega,* then took one last look below. Tess, with a man Luca had never seen before, rushed to the scene, then began digging furiously exactly were Luca's vapors had risen from the earth. As he dissipated into the heavens above, Luca watched them desperately pulling rocks out of the sunken hole, then prayed they would reach Diana in time.

CHAPTER TWENTY-EIGHT

VINCENT

Pincio Gardens

February 27, 2004
4:50 a.m.

"She's gone, isn't she?" Vincent asked, knowing the answer even before he asked the question.

"Vinny," said Tess as she pushed Diana's chest, which had Vincent's long jacket draped over it, while giving her CPR. "She's been dead too long." Tess shook her head, yet still kept pushing. She was pumping Diana's chest with the sole of her hand, then breathing into her mouth, pumping, then breathing.

Vincent was ready to take over the instant Tess got too tired. They'd been taking turns every five minutes, and now he knew he would continue until he brought Diana back. He wasn't going to let her die. But then again, he had no idea how long she'd been dead when they found her.

Moments ago, just as they left the *Castello,* a purple-blue funnel of light had illuminated a sunken pit in the grounds nearby. The bizarre violet light curved down into the pit as if it were a spot-light through the ominous clouds above. Then Vincent saw Diana's sickly hand sticking out of the ground, while the rest of her body was buried below. Vincent and Tess immediately unearthed her, while frantically trying to bring her back. From the first moment they unearthed her, she had no pulse, and Vincent worried about brain damage from lack of oxygen.

Now, after all they'd been through, Vincent finally realized what he'd been missing. Tonight, he discovered Diana was the only woman he could ever love. He had lusted after women, but with Diana he'd been faced with his match. She was a woman who made a man think twice about what he was doing with his life, especially when you lost her through death.

He still remembered the look on her face when she first met him—it was one of pure anger—out and out hostility. That was the kind of woman who made a man want to know why.

"Vinny," Tess said, looking up and stopping the resuscitation. "She's not going to make it. The ambulance should be here by now. I have no clue why they haven't come. We can't keep doing this forever. We have to let her go."

Vincent pushed Tess aside, not wanting to waste a minute even though she had only stopped for a few seconds. He pushed with the heel of his hand and breathed into Diana's mouth while Tess paced. Vincent watched Diana's face as he worked on bringing her back. He looked at her stony features in the pall of death and made a promise that he would never leave her side. He would never stop loving her if she would just survive.

When she didn't respond, Vincent felt hopelessness spread through his veins, yet he kept trying to resuscitate her. Knowing Diana was dead, he did something he hadn't done since he was a kid—he prayed. Like the blessing he gave Raven when he touched her head under that strange blanket, it just came out of him, and he talked to something he hadn't talked to for a long, long time. He decided to make one request, one attempt to communicate with a higher power.

I'll never stop believing. Just don't let her die, Vincent swore.

As if Diana could hear his vow, she moved, but her eyes remained shut. Vincent took her pulse and felt a beat, while Tess fell to her knees.

"Oh my God, Di!" Tess screamed, brushing the tears away. "You're alive."

"Diana, wake up." Once he was certain her lungs worked, Vincent kissed her cheek, but she didn't move.

Tess kept screaming, but Diana still wouldn't open her eyes. Sirens wailed in the background, just as Tess started crying. Vincent rushed into the street to make sure the emergency vehicle saw them, then tried to help as much as he could. But the rest of the night became a blur, because Vincent kept reminding himself that Diana was alive, and there was a reason for it. After calling out to the powers beyond, he had been answered. Along with that cry for help came a message—a message that there was something out there in the universe he studied. And that something responded when he communicated with it.

Before the doctor examined Diana, Vincent was certain she'd make it. Even when the doctor said she was of sound mind and body although still in a coma, Vincent still believed. After that, something shifted inside Vincent. His entire life changed because he could think about only one woman.

After several days in the hospital, Vincent pulled up his chair and whispered in Diana's ear, "No matter what happens, I love you forever."

Still unconscious, she didn't move.

Vincent kissed her cheek and eased back into his chair. He'd been in vigil since the day she arrived. He rubbed his chin and doubted his convictions for a moment, then reminded himself once again of the miracle. It was a miracle that happened by communicating with something he wasn't even sure existed—until now.

PART FIVE
THE RETURN

In the book Folklore by the Fireside: Text and Context of the Tuscan Veglia," author Alessandro Falassi relates the Italian custom known as the veglia (pronounced vay-yah). The word "veglia" is roughly translatable as "wake" and is similar to the Latin word vigilia, meaning to stay awake during the usual hours of sleep (a vigil).

Falassi describes the scene in which Italian peasants once returned from the fields at sunset and gathered before the fireplace. Here, they would first tell fairy tales to the youngest children that contained various messages and morals intended to merge the child into the Tuscan community as he or she grew up. Next, the older children were told stories of their family members and ancestors, in order to establish a sense of who they were and who they had been. Lastly, they spoke of their religious beliefs and customs in order to preserve their traditions. It is because of the traditions like the veglia that so much of hereditary Italian Witchcraft has survived and been passed on.

Raven Grimassi
Italian Witchcraft

CHAPTER TWENTY-NINE

DIANA

Le Vecchia Religione

Time Warp
May 18, 2004
New Moon

"I do not know anything about your beliefs, traditions or way of life." As she addressed Raven's *boschetto* assembled in the backroom of the *Le Vecchia Religione*, Diana used her hands to express herself as she spoke. "So, I don't know what to do."

She scanned the faces in the crowd, then realized they awaited her every word. Rather than be offended by her presence, they were totally accepting of her. After only asking one of them to meet, they all came. No one stayed home or dissented.

"I honor your faith, as well as all religions," Diana continued. "We are here because of Raven. And, for reasons I cannot explain, she willed this place to me." Instead of being alarmed or threatened, the *boschetto* seemed to welcome the notion, because some of the group even smiled as if they already knew.

The woman Diana had spoken to on the phone, known as Angelina, stepped forward. "But what of the *Malandanti?*" she asked.

"They died in the *Villa de Marco* when the walls crumbled and set off a chain reaction that collapsed the labyrinth of tunnels beneath the *Castello del Pincio*. Luca told me about the *Villa de Marco* in the *Roma Sotterranea* while I was comatose, just before I woke up." Diana hesitated to let them absorb this information.

"What did he say?" Angelina asked.

"He didn't talk, he just transferred his thoughts," she answered. "He was with Aradia, *La Bella Pellegrina*—both Luca and the *Malandanti* are with her now."

With those words, the *boschetto* excitedly talked all at once, but when Diana finally spoke, they were silent again. "Luca tried to save me before the tunnel collapsed, but I didn't listen. My heart goes out to those who lost their lives in the rubble. No one survived, except me." She shook her head from the strange sound of those familiar words.

After a moment of silence during which several prayers were whispered, Angelina spoke once again. "But will you be our *Sacerdotessa* like Raven wanted?"

Surprised the entire *boschetto* knew of Raven's plan, Diana wanted them to make the decision. "Surely one of you can." Diana looked into the eyes of the concerned faces throughout the room, not knowing what else to say, but Raven's last words echoed in her mind, *No one else can do this, except you.*

A commotion in the back of the room made everyone turn and the man she once knew as the Honorable Benandanti entered. With a painting tucked under his arm, he headed straight toward Diana. After he propped it against a ledge on the wall, Diana realized it was her work—the piece Luca bought.

The justice of the peace didn't speak right away, so Diana figured he would address the group in Italian, but then he turned to her and spoke fluent English.

"But what of this?" he asked.

"You speak English?" Diana, alarmed by the tactics of the handsome justice, thought he should feel obligated to tell the truth. "And you're a *Stregone?*" she asked.

"I'm Giovanni," he said, smiling and offering his hand. "Forgive me for hiding that I speak your language at your Rite of Marriage, but Antonio didn't want me to because he hadn't told you about our ways. He thought if I talked with you, then you would want to know more, and I most surely would have told you more. But Antonio wanted to tell you about our ways in his own time, that is certain. Your painting speaks to *Strega* on many levels. How can you paint this without knowing our ways?"

"Where did you get this painting?"

"In the *Sotterranea*," he answered.

The *boschetto* whispered, yet when Diana spoke they were quiet. "How did you enter the underground when the entrance collapsed under the *Castello?*"

Giovanni flashed a mischievous smile before he answered. "There are still many ways, one being through your cellar," he said. "I had to know whether our sacred *Sotterranea* was destroyed. But the *Grotto* and even the *Cripta dei Morti* remain unscathed."

"We must bury Luca in the *Cripta dei Morti*, because that's what he wanted," someone shouted.

Then the *boschetto* cheered.

"The web of tunnels beneath *Pincio* Gardens, the hidden entry in the Gardens, and the *Villa de Marco* were destroyed." The handsome justice bowed his head as if paying respect for the loss, then continued. "The authorities didn't discover the underground there, because there's no trace of the entry in the Gardens anymore since the earth collapsed where the elevator opened into the underground, while the structure that houses the elevator remains unscathed. Although the tunnels beneath *Pincio* Gardens and the *Castello* have been demolished, our other sacred sites are still there. So now there are only two portals to access our sacred *Sotterranea*—one through the opening in the cellar of the *Villa di Spagna* and the other through the manhole on *viale Trinità dei Monti*."

Diana frowned. "You call the *Sotterranea* sacred?"

He nodded.

"How did you get inside the *Villa?*" she asked.

Giovanni looked down. "Forgive me, I was there just this morning. Tess welcomed me because she knows you are with us and we take care of you here. She awaits your return."

Diana shook her head, ignoring his last comment. "How do you know about Luca's *Sotterranea?*"

"It used to be our place of worship long ago, but Janus took over those sites along with the *Malandanti*. We used to practice in the tunnels with Antonio, but we were driven out by Luca because the New Ways in the *Sotterranea* did not align with our ways. We honor the Arician Tradition, which means we follow the ancient beliefs and practices of our people who once flourished in the Arician groves of the Alban hills of Italy."

"Antonio was part of this *boschetto?*"

Giovanni nodded. "Both your husband and his sister, Raven Slade DeMarco, belonged to this *boschetto.*"

"Raven was Antonio's sister?" Diana bit her lip, then sat down to catch her breath. "Why didn't Raven tell me?" she moaned.

"She was an illegitimate sister, fathered by one of the Grigori brothers here in *Roma.* And since Raven was conceived while her mother was married to Janus, Janus disowned Raven as well as his wife," Giovanni explained. "That's why Raven grew up in Aspen, but when Antonio's mother died giving birth to Luca, Raven left for *Roma.* That's probably why Raven didn't tell you—because she considered her heritage a sacred secret. She loved her mother as well as her father, the Grigori."

"Speaking of secrets, why is there erotica at the *Villa?*" Diana asked, wanting to know the answers to all her questions now.

Without hesitation, Angelina answered. "Long ago, Luca lived in the *Villa di Spagna.* That's why it's filled with sex magick tools. But Antonio made Luca leave because he wanted to take back what was meant to be his through inheritance. Janus willed the *Villa* to his oldest son, Antonio, not to Luca."

Feeling awkward about having to ask something personal, Diana forced herself to ask the next question nevertheless. "Did Antonio do sex magick?"

Angelina quickly responded. "No, he didn't do sex magick the way Luca did, if that's what you mean. Antonio just couldn't find it in his heart to get rid of the sex tools Luca left at the *Villa*—it was all he had of his brother, because Antonio never saw him after they parted ways. But Antonio loved his brother. Sex magick is not something Antonio did in our *boschetto* if that's what you mean. We don't use sex magick—in fact, no *Strega* uses sex magick that I know of. It's an American practice."

"I'll give you a key that opens the gate from the Spanish Steps, and it also opens the garden door to the *Villa.* If someone will move an obelisk out of the way you can open the gate into the courtyard," Diana offered, searching through her bag to find the key. "This key opens the garden door, which is a private entrance that leads into the basement of the *Villa*." Diana scanned the eyes of the *boschetto* before she continued. "But please, don't ask me to be your *Sacerdotessa*, because I am not as knowledgeable as you."

Angelina stepped forward again, clearly upset. "Raven prepared us for this, and you are wrong about not being able to help us. We want to teach you, because we are supposed to—"

"What do you mean by *supposed?*" Diana asked.

"There's a reason why all this happened," she said. "You were supposed to see Antonio in your past life as a *Strega* when you died because that wisdom forced you to not only open your mind, but to stand up for what you believe in."

"How do you know this?" Diana rubbed her temples with her fingertips as she tried to understand how Angelina could know or even how Raven could have known such things.

"We have ways," she said. "Please, just be with us as we make the transition without Raven. Then you can leave us if you so desire."

Diana nodded, thinking that it felt good to be here, to be with these people, although she didn't know why. Maybe because it felt like she was exonerating what had been done to her in another lifetime, but she couldn't be sure. Or maybe it was because she felt closer to Antonio and Raven now that she was with their *boschetto*. Scanning the nameless faces of the crowd staring at her, Diana realized these people wanted her here. They believed in her, even though they didn't know her at all. Raven must have told them about the future, or the painting must mean more than Diana could conceive, because now they were enthralled by it. Several people gazed at it, as if mesmerized by the symbols Diana thought were original designs conjured up from her creative mind. But instead, they were ancient designs that meant something significant to the *Strega*.

Diana took a deep breath, then spoke. "I'll try to do what I can, but you'll have to help me."

A cheer resounded through the shop, and the *boschetto* ceremoniously mingled among each other while Diana wondered what she had just done. One thing she was sure of—she could learn from them. She could learn the things her husband had wanted to share with her during their marriage. Once she learned the Old Ways again, she could recall the life she had once loved with her beloved ones, yet in which she had been burned at the stake for using that ancient wisdom.

When Diana left the shop, she knew she did the right thing. But with Vincent and Tess, she didn't know what was right. When she awoke from her coma and left the hospital, she told both of them to stay away. Even though Vincent adamantly refused, she forced him to go. And she was relieved once he left. She didn't want to interfere with Tess and her relationship with him, so she'd been staying at Raven's flat above *Le Vecchia Religione*. Not knowing when they would leave so that she could return to the *Villa*, she was thankful for the safe haven with Raven's *boschetto*.

She walked all the way to *di Spagna*, then climbed the Spanish Steps. Breaking a sweat, she finally stopped for a moment to catch her breath. Once she opened the doors of the *Trinità dei Monti*, she slowed down and honored the silence in this sacred church. As she touched the Holy Water to her forehead, she shuddered and recalled the cursed talisman that had been cleansed from the basins months ago, though now it seemed like an eternity.

The church was deserted, and she was thankful to be alone. Diana collapsed on the wooden pew, then heard someone enter the church. Footfalls approached, then stopped at her pew. She looked up at Vincent, then he sat down next to her. Diana fought the impulse to leave when he slid next to her in the pew.

"*Buonasera*," Vincent whispered.

"We have nothing to say," she said. "Please go."

"Let me explain," he said, taking her hand and raising it to his lips. "You must know why."

"I don't want to know anything of the sort." Diana yanked her hand away from his grasp and clenched both of her hands together as if in prayer. "Why must you provoke me?"

"I no understand this word *provoke*."

Diana laughed at his broken English, and his sultry blue eyes merged with hers for a moment. "You know what I mean," she said, averting her eyes.

"It meant nothing with Tess. I don't know why I did—"

"It means nothing, yet you are sexually involved with her. Please leave."

"But you don't understand. It's not what you think. We didn't have sex, we were just playing around." Vincent stopped for a moment, then continued. "I've changed. It happened when you died."

"I'm with child—Luca's child."

Vincent touched her cheek just as he had done in the hospital. She remembered even though she'd been unconscious at the time. Not sure how she could know this while being unconscious, Diana was certain she was right because she had felt his touch then, and now she remembered it.

"When did you discover this?" Vincent asked.

"Luca would be pleased that the legacy continues. It's a little *Stregone.*" Diana fought the urge to cry.

"He had powers, but not enough power to change a newborn baby's journey in a particular lifetime. Someone may try to manifest their beliefs onto an unborn baby, but it is impossible to change the evolution of the soul."

Diana faltered. This man, with so few words, said things that made perfect sense and made her want to know more. "But how do you know Luca cannot change my baby's destiny?"

"Souls, including destiny, cannot be changed by a person on earth. Souls can only evolve though many lifetimes of experience or in other realms of higher dimensions. But destiny is determined by the imprint of the soul."

The words of the light came back to her, and she bit her lip as she recalled something very similar that she learned when she was dead.

Vincent slid off the pew onto the kneeler, then on bended knee, took her hand. "When you died, I found out how much I love you."

"What are you doing?" Diana tried to keep her voice down even though no one else was in the church. "How can you do that to Tess? Out of respect for her if nothing else, don't do this."

"Please hear me out," he said. "We were experimenting, just having some fun. We've never loved each other that way, as friends yes, but not as lovers. You are the only one I care about. We are

315

meant to be together—it is the destiny of our souls. Before you died, I didn't realize I was *supposed* to be with you."

There it was again—that word, *supposed*—as if it were destiny or a certain belief system regarding the way things should turn out or what they were to become. That word kept changing her life.

"Tess wants you back too. We can't go on without you." Looking up at her, still on bended knee, Vincent kissed the back of her hand. "I can never love anyone but you—only you."

Diana stared at him, remembering the words she uttered to Antonio the night he died, *My one and only love.*

"Only you," Vincent said, turning her hand over and kissing her palm. "When you died, I felt love for the first time. And that feeling has no limits because it's connected with something more," he added.

"More than what?"

"More than us—a force that's greater than what we've ever known before. And that force responds to thoughts filled with emotion and meaning." He paused for a moment, then kissed her hand once more. "A presence. You saw it when you died, didn't you? You communicated with it, right? I heard you speak of it when you were comatose. Almost losing you made me commit to honoring this Life Force forever—and the force between us that is love."

Words of the light flooded into her memory, and she fought back the tears. "What makes you think—"

"Love is everything." Vincent searched her eyes, still kneeling, still holding her hand. "You said it to me, but I didn't listen back then. We have a choice, and I chose love. Will you marry me?"

Diana stared at this man who had remained on constant vigil at her bedside the entire time she was in the hospital. While she was comatose, she heard everything Vincent said, and he spoke volumes during that time.

"The baby isn't yours." Diana watched for a negative reaction, but he smiled.

"I accept your child without hesitation, because this life is part of you. That means I love the life inside you already. I love everything about you, Diana. One last time, will you marry me?"

Diana slid off the pew onto her knees so that her eyes were level with his. "How can you be so sure?" She felt her heart quicken as she remembered the one question the omnipresent light asked.

Vincent took her into his arms. "From now to eternity, it's only you." From the tone of his voice, it was more than just words. "Will you marry me?"

She moved into his embrace, then felt his lips devour hers. After they'd kissed, long and hard, Diana whispered one word in his ear, "Yes."

Wanting him now more than ever, Diana realized she had finally learned how to love again.

Glossary

Arician Tradition A witchcraft sect based on the ancient beliefs and practices that once thrived in the Arician groves in the Alban hills of Italy. In 1998, Raven Grimassi established the Arician Tradition, which is a modernized version of the teachings; however, the beliefs and practices are based upon the original intent of the *La Bella Pellegrina* (The Beautiful Pilgrim).

Boschetto Coven of witches.

Castello del Pincio Castle or mansion located in the *Pincio* Gardens of Rome.

Cripta dei Morti Crypt of the Dead.

Goddess of All Witches Diana, Goddess of All Witches in Italy; known as the Goddess of the Moon.

Grigori Watchers or Light Beings. Guardians of the portals between the other dimensions. Known by the *Strega* as the Old Ones.

Grotto A small cave or cavern.

Holy Strega Endearing term used to describe the teachings of a legendary holy woman, Aradia, in fourteenth-century Italy. Famous for her natural healing powers and knowledge about herbal potions, she was known as The Beautiful Pilgrim, *La Bella Pellegrina,* who helped the poor and healed the sick. According to oral tradition, she documented the Old Ways in the *Scrolls of Aradia.* Also known as the daughter of Diana, the Goddess of All Witches, Aradia traveled the countryside teaching the Old Religion. When confronted by the church, she rebuked them for hypocrisy and was arrested for heresy, then was charged with treason against the kingdom because she wanted to free the peasants from servitude. After her arrest, the scrolls disappeared, which made her teachings even more legendary.

La Vecchia Religione Old Religion or the Old Ways.

Maddalena The *Strega* who provided the manuscript with the "doctrines of Italian witchcraft" to Charles Leland. Leland, folklorist and scholar, subsequently wrote the book *Aradia: Gospel of the Witches* in 1899. However, the source material for this book was delivered to Leland by Maddalena after ten years of published works that portrayed witches as good; whereas, this material from Maddalena outlined some negative aspects, which had never before appeared in the teachings. The differences in this manuscript may be an indirect result of the Inquisition. Undoubtedly, erroneous confessions were "extracted" from the *Strega*, who were tortured and executed during the Inquisition, and because inquisitors thoroughly documented "confessions," that record results in a corrupt view of the teachings for a healer, witch or *Strega*. Regardless, Leland's source material couldn't possibly originate from the nine *Scrolls of Aradia*, and because the scrolls vanished after Aradia's arrest, one must question whether Maddalena supplied accurate information or used documentation directly from, and therefore tainted by, the violent procedures of the Inquisition.

Magick Ancient spelling for *magic;* the ability to cause change and movement through shifting awareness in the conscious mind.

Malandanti "Evil Witches" who fought ritual battles in ages past. The *Malandanti* warred against the rich feudal lords and the church, which many times resulted in harm to the peasants.

Malleus Maleficarum Known as the Witch Hammer, this book instructed inquisitors and judges about how to identify witches and how to extract confessions through torture. Part one outlined how the "Devil and his witches perpetuate evil" on men and animals; part two explained the *maleficia,* or "evil" acts of witches and outlined spells and bewitchments; and part three recorded the legal procedures for inquisitors and judges to use when interrogating and sentencing the accused. These legal procedures included torture.

The papal edict executed by Pope Alexander IV for the prosecution of witches as heretics made the book second only to the Bible in sales until John Bunyan's *Pilgrim's Progress* was published in 1678. The use of the *Malleus Maleficarum,* written and published by two Dominican inquisitors in 1486, led to the extreme torture and violent deaths of innocent people for more than 200 years.

Malocchio The "evil eye" or the "overlook."

Old Religion Old Ways.

Old Ways Pre-Christian religion in Europe; an ancient fertility sect that worshipped the God and Goddess of Nature; the daily practice and awareness of people who live in harmony with the earth and the universe.

Piazza A public square in an Italian town or city.

Roma Sotterranea Underground Rome.

Sacerdote High Priest, or a male who leads the coven.

Sacerdotessa High Priestess, or a female who leads the coven.

Semjaza A Watcher who instructs in the ancient art of herbs.

Skyclad Naked.

Strega Female witch.

Stregheria The religion of witches in Italy.

Stregone Male witch.

Tana Star Goddess; the universe, companion of Tanus.

Tanus Star God; the universe, companion of Tana.

Time Warp A shift in time; when the clock is turned backward or forward and time is distorted. In the other realms, time is not sequential or a continuum, it is a frequency that is determined by the universe and recorded by the 13 Moon Calendar.

Villa de Marco Ancient *Villa* located beneath the *Castello del Pincio* in underground Rome.

Villa di Spagna *Villa* located next to the *Piazza di Spagna* in Rome.

Watchers Known as the guardians of the entrances and exits to the other dimensions. Light Beings and keepers of the ancient wisdom, as well as the guardians of the arts. In the mystery teachings, the Watchers once lived on the earth and are connected to Atlantis, Lemuria and ancient Egypt. Christian mythology associates Watchers with fallen angels, but the *Strega* know them as the *Grigori* or the Old Ones.

Although Coco does not consider the
Simultaneous Dimension Series religious,
some readers may consider the series spiritual.
Regardless of anyone's interpretation or opinion
about the messages in her work, Coco honors all
religions and believes there is no right or
wrong path. All paths lead to the same source,
especially after the physical body dies.

Coco Tralla

Tralla Productions

Unveil the Invisible and Discover the Magick

www.sevenbooks.com